WEST LAFAYETTE PUBLIC

SO-BEU-566

3 1951 00339 8432

LEAVING HOME

FIC   Janeway
JAN   Elizabeth.
        Leaving home

7/09

West Lafayette Public Library   DEMCO

West Lafayette, Indiana

LEAVING HOME

by Elizabeth Janeway

With a new Preface by the author
and an Afterword by Rachel M. Brownstein

West Lafayette Public Library
West Lafayette, Indiana

THE FEMINIST PRESS
at The City University of New York
New York

Leaving Home © 1953 by Elizabeth Janeway
Preface © 1987 by Elizabeth Janeway
Afterword © 1987 by The Feminist Press
at The City University of New York
All rights reserved. Published 1987
Printed in the United States of America
90 89 88 87 1 2 3 4 5

Library of Congress Cataloging-in-Publication Data

Janeway, Elizabeth.
  Leaving home.

  I. Title
PS3519.A72L4   1987   813'.52   87-13551
ISBN 0-935312-73-0

7/09 Gift

Cover art: Raphael Soyer. *Office Girls.* 1936. Oil on canvas.
        Collection of Whitney Museum of American Art.
        By permission.

PREFACE

THOUGH IT WAS WRITTEN IN THE FIFTIES, *Leaving Home* is indeed a novel about the thirties. Twenty years of history, including a war that changed this country internally and reshaped its foreign obligations and ambitions as well, supplies a perspective on the past. I hope that I profited from this longer view and that it did not lead me into anachronisms. For one thing, since I grew up and left home in the thirties myself, I remembered and remember the decade very well. Moreover, my decision to place the story in the earlier period was deliberate. It didn't just happen.

The choice was a while in coming. I was still uncertain about the date of the novel even while I was thinking out its opening scenes. Perhaps I should say that I can never plan a work of fiction to its end. I have always started with a character or two caught in a fix of some kind. It may be large or small, but working to solve it sets the plot in motion and permits the people involved to flesh out into human beings whose actions and ambitions will direct the "story line." Of course these folk must incorporate the theme and purpose of the book. They will dance, the author will choreograph as they do, and when they make mistakes and misinterpret the purpose of the exercise, we all have to go back and rewrite, redance, rethink.

Leaving Home is an exact title. This book is about young people growing up and growing out of a family setting, about the modes of separation each employed and, of course, about the family they are leaving behind. Perhaps it may seem today that families of the thirties and the fifties were alike in their "values" so that breaking away would have been the same. No doubt at all, they were more alike than either is to the family of the eighties; but the world into which Nina and Kermit and Marion moved was its own time, moving to its own tune.

One obvious difference was the economic climate: the thirties were an era of depression and overseas trouble, still distant however. The fifties were comfortable in economic terms but uncertain as to the new status in the world of the United States. Winning a great war brought a surge of patriotic optimism but also a sense of unresolved responsibility. Growing up in the fifties meant coming to adulthood in the age of the bomb. The cold war and McCarthyism were demanding new definitions of patriotism; to me, they seemed to decouple the simple connection between faith in one's country and humane morality. There were also shifts in class relations taking place: union power was making blue-collar work more stable and better paid than it had ever been. The GI Bill removed the old class status from a college education. Both the changes in the world that I liked and those I didn't raised questions.

Even so I wasn't sure which period to tackle, and so I turned to magic. "Muse," said I, "tell me the name of the character who opens my book, the older sister, walking home from the subway to a comfortable house in Thither Brooklyn, thinking about her job and her future, about life at home and life in the great desert of the world around. Once she is named I shall know where in time she belongs." "Her name is Nina," said the Muse courteously. So I knew the book was to be laid in the thirties. Do not ask me how I knew it, that's what magic is for.

Nina is in no way autobiographical. I have never written anything that is and never intend to. Psychoanalysis, not magic, might explain why I feel this way so strongly, but I myself am not terribly interested in knowing. In any case, my interests have always reached out from myself to the context of life, past or present. I want to know why things happen as they do in the world we live in, why we accept the rules and the myths and the prescriptions for proper behavior that shape our acts, our dreams, and our sins. The wind that blows off the landscape of reality is the medium in which we human creatures move. It directs us and hinders us, and though we are different among ourselves, we feel the same urgent zeitgeist.

My taste for seeing people in a landscape, responsive to pressures of social givens and temporal shifts, doesn't mean that I admire novels (and the thirties were full of them) that turn individuals into allegorical figures. The "socialist realism" of that period descended too easily into the cartoon plot, familiar from Soviet films, which we summed up as "Boy meets girl meets tractor." That all was quickly forgotten and of course the challenging radical art of the time was free from such banality; but there was a small bloc of opinion which felt that any serious piece of fiction ought to include a strike scene. A person who wanted to write fiction was naturally aware of the injunctions. By the fifties it had vanished, though other trends toward allegory did reappear in later years.

They need not detain us now. The time-machine had set me down in the thirties with my young people, due to leave home and move on: Nina, her younger sister Marion, and of course Kermit. His name is really more of a clue to the era than is Nina's, for it is that of Theodore Roosevelt's second son and it establishes the Bishop family as Progressive Republicans, aware of social responsibility and of the Manifest (Imperial) Destiny of America. Kermit deeply resented this placement. Indeed, he didn't welcome any label that he had not chosen himself. In particular, this name contributed to his rebellion against mainstream values, which he regarded as "middle-class morality," limited and self-deceiving. A later heroine of mine (Diana, in *The Third Choice*) firmly changed her own name, on much the same grounds. Kermit simply swore to wipe out the unwelcome contamination of bourgeois ideals and redefine his name in his own terms.

Kermit, in fact, meant to take his own path to power and as much money as was useful in the same spirit as that of any upwardly mobile son of a "ghetto." Tricky but not pigheaded, unable to ignore depression, class, and war, Kermit saw the world in terms of the opportunities its events and its structures offered him. To set up a small-time bootlegging business at college, make some money, and get out before he was caught was very much his style. Life taught him to be more circumspect, and he was never unconscious of the emotions and motives of others. His main problem was that his own emotions were, at times, more than he could deal with.

I meant once to write a sequel to *Leaving Home*. Kermit would, of course, have got himself caught in a dilemma in which head and heart pulled him crosswise and his only success would have had to become a sort of failure. Nina, whose life in *Leaving Home* becomes that of the "perfect wife and mother" whose tales she knew so well from the woman's magazine she had edited, would have changed too. Her approach to outer reality differed from Kermit's, in that she stepped into the offered role as a means of understanding it. But though she might play it to the hilt she was always aware, in the back of her head, that it was a role, one to which she could be committed while, at the same time, rather skeptical. Kermit and Nina, confronted by reality, could reach for a shield of irony.

Marion was more open and less protected. There's a sort of endangered female species, I think, to whom life happens. Marion responded intuitively to its demands but she was never sure of controlling herself or the relationships in which she found herself. Loving, generous, far from stupid, Marion dithers her way toward a happy ending. In that sequel, if I had written it, I know that her happiness would have self-destructed. Nina disliked risk and did her best to control the life around her. Kermit enjoyed danger but assumed that he could estimate its extent. Marion took risks without knowing it.

"Leaving home" implies that the leavers must divest themselves of some, at any rate, of the ideas and the conduct that prevails there. The older generation, remaining behind, always seems static, and so they are presented here: iconic, representing the past, typifying what has to be left, whether or not one admires or condemns it. Kermit left more than willingly, Nina minimized her departure by seeming to carry forward the traditional female role, and Marion's risky luck supplied a satisfying rite of passage, which she almost didn't take advantage of. The sequel I didn't write would have tested them all again with rather different results.

Why didn't I write it? Partly because I already knew a little too much about the Bishops and what could be expected of them. My novels have all been open ended, so that no future can be easily divined; and this time, another segment would have had to limit these characters more than I wanted to, or so it seemed to me at the time. In fact, my next novel *The Third Choice* (whose heroine objected to her name), collapses a longer story into one book.

Diana leaves home, marries well and, bored stiff, makes a mistake that even Marion might have refused to make; she lives to trace out the consequences in the compromises and the unchangeable error that follow. So perhaps it is an underground sequel.

A final note: what is autobiographical about the young Bishops is not any detail of their lives, simply the physical setting of Thither Brooklyn in the thirties. I grew up in one section, went to school in another, and on to Barnard College on Upper Broadway in Manhattan. Several old frame houses of my extended family and of friends merged into the Bishops' home, and of course I was a veteran subway commuter even before the year that I spent writing advertising copy for the basement store of Abraham and Straus when family resources simply would not stretch enough to keep me in college.

That apprentice year was an invaluable part of my education. I found new friends and acquaintances who came out of a rich diversity of backgrounds. It was quite intoxicating for me, raised within a relatively limited group of people. Because my mother was rather deaf, and consequently shy with strangers, her intimates were confined to family and old friends and though the context of my life had of course broadened at school and even more at Barnard, commuting students didn't have much chance to socialize with their peers outside of classes. My job landed me among people from all sorts of settings. I remember especially a proto-yuppie Southern Gentleman whose views of the world were distressing, but who danced like a dream, and a close colleague from the nearby (but to me unknown) world of Jewish life in Brooklyn. Here were people who really cared about ideas and argued about them with passion and humor. Under the continuing shadow of the depression and the growing shadow of despotism in Europe, we watched the clouds overhead but still managed to laugh together. Thinking back on those years, I am able to hope that even the changes that have shaken the world since the days when Nina and Kermit and Marion left home won't prevent this story of their emigration from speaking to those who came of age in other times and other places.

Elizabeth Janeway
May 1987

LEAVING HOME

I. NINA

*O*N THE LAST DAY OF SEPTEMBER IN 1933, UP A tree-lined street in furthest Brooklyn, Nina Bishop was walking home from the subway. Home was a big old Gothic monstrosity of a house set in a half-acre plot of ground. It had been built in the 1880s, when this part of Brooklyn was the country. Nina's Uncle Van had shot squirrels here when he was a boy, and ten or twelve years ago Nina herself, as a little girl, had picked daisies in fields that were just becoming building lots. Now the city had caught up, but Nina thought sometimes that neither the house nor her family realized it. They were anachronisms, still comfortably off in 1933, living within the protection of their privet hedges and Uncle Van's solid income, in an oasis in the middle of the upper middle class.

Nina at twenty-one—a year out of Vassar, pleasant-looking, with a job on a magazine and a young man in love with her—knew she was one of the lucky ones, and it made her very uneasy. The world she grew up in had been flattened under a storm except, it seemed to her, for the little bit exactly where she had grown up. From the hedges and sheltering trees of her home she looked out on a desert. There was no reason she could see why she and her brother and sister, her widowed mother and Uncle Van, were not all out there in the desert too. More than money had blown away in the storm, the rules of living had blown away as well. But neither Nina's mother nor her uncle seemed to know this. They took the freakish chance that had saved Henry Van Deusen's accountancy firm from destruction as part of the ordered working of the universe; and how terribly vulnerable, Nina thought, this made them all! There was the desert all about them, and no one to tell them how to go about living there.

In the desert, thought Nina, vaguely aware that she was turning the corner two blocks from home, in the desert you lived in the present. You grabbed. But grabbed what? If she grabbed now, she would grab Stuart Fanning—and did she want him? She had known him all her life; he was one of the lucky ones too, his father being a highly respected Federal judge. How eminently suitable it would be if she married Stuart, how in keeping with the old rules that she did not trust. How safe! Part of me is a coward, thought Nina, part of me wants to be safe. But another part of her longed perversely for the desert—for in the desert there were to be encountered Real Life and Experience. Nina had two great-aunts who shared a Victorian bungalow just three and a half blocks up to the right, Aunt Dora and Aunt Flora Van Deusen, little dried-up kernels of old ladies who had lived safe inside their shells all their lives, cherished and indulged and gossipy, and who someday soon now must come to die; and Nina could not imagine how they would manage it. It would not only be the biggest thing that had ever happened to them, it would be so grotesquely different from all the care and caution and chirruping little decisions which had served them for seventy-odd years! Aunt Dora and Aunt Flora had once frightened Nina badly, trying to be kind to her when she was five and had never seen them before. They were still portents in her mind of what would happen to you if nothing ever happened to you at all.

Something, thought Nina, stalking up the street from sun into shade and out again, clutching the bundles she carried, ignoring the shoe that rubbed her heel, something must happen soon! A door must open somewhere into some room and a young man most come in who would be—would be——

"Good evening, Nina," said a voice. "Isn't this heat dreadful? You'd think it was August!"

Transfixed on the pavement, bounced back to Bay Ridge, Nina searched for the speaker. Oh Lord, it was Mrs. Willis, rocking and fanning on her front porch. Mrs. Willis had taught Nina in Sunday school one year and she could, as Mrs. Bishop had put it, talk the hind leg off a donkey. Nina started walking again in self-protection. "It's awful," she said tersely.

"How was it in New York?" asked Mrs. Willis, to whom Brooklyn was still a separate city, quite distinct from Manhattan. "Must have been ninety, I should think. It was eighty-five right here at three o'clock, even with the breeze off the bay. It's dropped to seventy-nine now."

"And only sixty-seven shopping days till Christmas," said Nina. "I can't stop, Mrs. Willis, I'll never be able to start again if I do."

"What?" said Mrs. Willis, nonplussed. "Well! I'm sure I don't want to detain you, Nina. I daresay you have better things to do than chat with an old lady."

The trouble with being rude to Mrs. Willis, thought Nina, is that it doesn't stop her talking—she goes right on, only more unpleasantly. "No indeed, Mrs. Willis, I haven't. but I *am* hot and tired and the subway was terrible."

"All right dear, I quite understand. I know you young people nowadays have to think of yourselves."

Old biddy! thought Nina viciously. As if you ever thought of anyone else! The parcels she was carrying—a manila envelope full of work from the magazine, a box with a new blouse she had bought on her lunch hour, her purse, a newspaper—started to slip and she hitched them up furiously.

"Remember me to your mother," Mrs. Willis called.

"Thank you, I will," and Nina made a face now that she was safely past. Trust Mrs. Willis to tell you the temperature or the humidity or the inches of rainfall or the number of fatal accidents in Brooklyn last month and make you feel hotter or colder or wetter or more unlucky than ever before! Nina walked on in a cloud of self-pity, hot, dirty, crumpled and indignant. Childe Roland to the Dark Tower came, she thought, and blew the horn and the door opened and out came Mrs. Willis with a fan in her hand and said, Goodness, it's taken you a long time to get here. And served him right. Romance! And who will open a door for me, who will come in? Stuart Fanning.

But here was home, here was the 1880 house in the shade of its trees, waiting for her. Sixteen years ago her mother had brought the children here, herself and Kermit, Marion yet unborn, her father dead in New Mexico. Nina could remember none of it. The word house had always, would always, connote brown shingles, two cupolas, a small iron picket fence along the ridgepole, eaves writhing with fretwork and a stained-glass window which illuminated the stairs with tutti-frutti light. "General Grant's body may lie on Riverside Drive," Kermit was wont to say, "but his spirit is entombed with us, in the house of the seventeen gables." Nina, however, was used to it and never noticed any more.

The steps to the porch sagged slightly. Three rockers and a deck chair stood there, with a large tuberous begonia in a jar on an iron stand. A swing hung from hooks in the porch ceiling and varied in height from the floor as the ropes that supported it stretched in the wet or shrank in dry weather. The vestibule had a floor of hexagonal tiles and a door mat with a torn corner. Some little boys had ripped it last Halloween. The inner door stood open on to the cool cave of the hall, but the screen door was unaccountably hooked.

Oh no! thought Nina. The last straw. Her bundles began to slide again. "Help!" she called. "Someone come let me in! Help! Marion! Cora!" But no one came, neither her sister nor Cora, the cook; the house slumbered undisturbed, as if the Sleeping Beauty herself lay at its heart. "Damnation!" said Nina, and kicked the door.

"Temper, temper!" said her young sister appearing at the end of the hall. "What you said! I don't know if I should let you in."

"Oh stop it! I'm in no mood for adolescent comedy."

"Or any other kind," said Marion, unhooking the door. "I'm sorry. *Hasn't* it been hot!"

"Please! I've just had Mrs. Willis on the temperature. Don't favor me with any more weather reports."

"Oh what a pill is old Mrs. Willis. Do you remember when Kermit made that up and sang it at her? Let me take your things. What's in the box? Oh, you've got more manuscripts to read! Aren't you getting important!"

"They're the dregs. Mr. Daniels reads everything that's remotely printable. I only get the ones where the sentences don't parse and the author can't remember the color of the heroine's hair from one page to the next. In the box is a beautiful yellow blouse to go with my gray suit which Cora will undoubtedly shrink the first time it goes in the wash."

"Alas, no, she won't," said Marion. "Cora is no longer with us."

"Oh no! You don't mean it!" Nina collapsed on the chair by the telephone.

"Oh yes I do. Really, it's sad. I don't know why I should sound so flip. She got a telegram this morning saying her aunt in South Carolina had died——"

"So of course Mother packed her off to the funeral on the first train, and I haven't got any clean clothes!"

"Well really," said Marion, "if *that* isn't temper, temper! I think you're being very class-conscious or something."

"I'm being thoroughly utterly selfishly exasperated," said Nina, "and I know it. Of course I'm sorry for Cora, it's just I haven't got that far yet. Right now I'm sorry for me. When's Cora coming back?"

"I don't think she is. The aunt left her a farm."

"Good heavens!"

"I know," said Marion, "I felt the same way. We've been entertaining an heiress unawares. Why doesn't someone leave *me* a farm, do you suppose, full of darling little pink pigs and ducks and a brindled cow?"

"The government would make you plow them under."

"Well," said Marion, "*I* shan't try to cheer you up any more. Just sit there and be as stinky as you please! I shan't——"

"I'm sorry, darling——"

"——be sorry for you at all with your clean clothes and your new blouse and your no sympathy for people! I shan't——"

"Marion! Stop! I'm sorry, I'm sorry!"

"——feel proud because I have a sister who's an editor on a magazine, oh no, I shall tell people, she's not really my sister, *one* of us was *adopted,* that's what I shall say, because we certainly could not be blood relations and feel so different about every——"

"Girls!" Mrs. Bishop stood in the doorway leading to the kitchen. "What's going on here? Marion, what are you shouting about?"

"Pigs," said Nina.

"Nina, have you been teasing your little sister again?"

"Mother, will you please not talk to me as if I were eleven?"

"I talk to you the way you act," said Mrs. Bishop with little grammar but sufficient clarity. "Marion, go wash your face. You're a big silly to let your sister upset you. Nina, I should think you would have better things to think about than teasing a fifteen-year-old girl."

"I wasn't teasing——"

"Very well. See that you don't." Mrs. Bishop retired to the kitchen and Nina and Marion looked at each other warily, and burst out laughing.

"Nina," said Marion, "have you been teasing your little sister again?"

"Go wash your face. You look like one of your own little piggies. Oink, oink, oink. Hurry up, I want to snatch a bath before Kermit gets home, he can stay in the tub for an hour at a time without straining himself in the least."

Marion dashed up to the bathroom—it was the only one in the house except for a lavatory and shower sacred to Uncle Van—and Nina went out to the kitchen to appease her mother, who never lost her temper except when the children quarreled. Mrs. Bishop was sitting by the kitchen table shelling peas. Nina kissed the top of her head. "I'm sorry, Mum," she said. "We weren't *really* fighting. Why don't you leave those and let me do them when I've had a bath?"

"My goodness, no, it's so restful. I enjoy it."

"Marion says Cora's gone for good."

"Yes, I suppose so. Isn't it nice for her!"

"Dandy. But a little hard on you. Have you called the agency for a new girl?"

"Nina, you know, I think I won't. In these hard times it doesn't seem right to spend the money. Your Uncle Van is so good——"

"Oh Mummy!"

"Yes, dear, but I can't help but think it's a waste. Why, sometimes I feel so useless I'm ashamed! Goodness, it's so easy to run a house nowadays with cans and the new frozen things and a vacuum cleaner, I don't see why I can't do it. Millions of women do it all the time."

14

"Angel, millions of women have had millions of years of practice."

"You can't have practice unless you start sometime."

"They started as resilient young brides and practiced on resilient young husbands, not on three cranky children and a patient but particular brother."

"Darling, you sound as if I were quite incapable of learning anything. I may not have done a *great deal* of cooking, but I know how things ought to taste, and I'm sure it's easy enough to get them to come out that way."

"Famous last words," said Nina. "Well, I suppose it's no use arguing with you."

"Not in the least," said Mrs. Bishop jauntily. "Run up and have your bath, dear, and when you come down you can make a pitcher of iced tea. Oh, and you might ask Marion to set the table."

"Goody, goody, goody, we'll all pitch in and co-operate. I don't suppose Cora ironed any clothes before she departed weeping, did she?"

"No," said Mrs. Bishop, ignoring her daughter's crossness, "but I did. Your clean underwear's on your bed."

"Oh Mummy, you shouldn't have! Ironing in this heat! *Why* did you? Can't you see no one wants you to be a martyr?"

"I see," said Mrs. Bishop, "that nothing seems to satisfy you! Why do you pick on people so, Nina? First it's Marion and now it's me! I assure you I had *no idea* that I was being martyred by doing a little ironing. As a matter of fact I had a very pleasant afternoon. I turned the radio up so I could hear it out here, and made myself some lemonade, and sat on that high stool and ironed *very comfortably* for an hour or two. Now stop fussing, Nina, and run upstairs and clean up. And please try to come down in a better temper."

"Oh damnation!" cried Nina, and left, banging the door behind her, but since it was a swinging door it did not bang. She raged into the bathroom, turned on the taps, collected some neatly pressed clothes from her bedroom and returned to collapse into a cool bath. Where, in a very short time, she was feeling ashamed of herself. I do, I do, I do pick on people, she thought in an agony of self-recrimination. I'm as mean as a prickly pear. What on earth can I do about it? Oh dear, how nice it would be if Stuart were someone else and

I *longed* to marry him! Out into the world, out into the real, but safe, safe, because of the togetherness. How nice I could be to everyone if I were only happy! Dear Dorothy Dix, she thought, beginning to laugh at herself, I am a young girl aged twenty-one with a bad temper. What can I do to develop a sweeter disposition? Signed, Nina.

Dear Nina, Trying as it may be to be a young girl aged twenty-one, it is the duty of every woman to rise above her disadvantages and make the best of things. Try concentrating on the good qualities of those about you instead of on their faults. Soon you will find the world a more sunshiny spot. Signed, Dorothy Dix.

But Dear Miss Dix, it is the good qualities of those about me which I seem to find most irritating. My mother is good, my uncle is patient, my little sister is sweet, my—well, let's call him my boy friend—he's dependable and kind, and it is just these virtues which are the very most exasperat——

A thunderous knock on the door interrupted her and her brother's voice cried, "Come on out, Toots! Your time's up!" Nina, who had been lazily soaping her left foot, jumped, slid and got the hair at the back of her neck wet.

"Go away!" she screamed with wholehearted fury. "Damn it to hell!"

"Damn it to hell yourself and get going," Kermit replied. "I'm just as hot and dirty as you are, or more so."

"You idiot, you made me jump so I slipped and got my hair simply soaked, and it isn't as if it were naturally curly, like your little ringlets!"

"You should wear it straight and look distinctive. Come on. I've just had an hour and a quarter on that stinking subway all the way down from Columbia."

"Why didn't you work a little harder at Yale and hang on to your scholarship there?"

There was a pause during which Nina finished soaping and took one last luxurious wallow. Kermit's voice, silky with anger, said, "Nina, I think you made an unkind remark. I hate to believe it. Did you, Nina? I hope for your sake you say no."

"I made the unkindest I could think of." And *that* will fix Dorothy Dix and her sunshiny spots, she thought, pulling out the stopper. She stood up, stretching. In the wavy light through the ground-glass window she looked like a river nymph in her watery home. She stretched again, watching herself in the mirror, admiring the way her ribs flowed up, her back rose fluidly, from her narrow waist. Pleasant to have a figure and clothes that fitted it after those horrible waistless sacks of the twenties. Graduating from high school in 1928, she had worn a flowered chiffon horror with a bertha collar and a flounced skirt that reached her knees, falling from the sash that swathed her hips. But by her junior year at Vassar clothes were romantic, she had danced in net and lace that swept the floor——

"Have you fallen down the drain? Shall I break the door in?"

"Gracious, Kermit dear, you overestimate your own strength, don't you think?" Nina pulled on her robe and stopped to pick up the dirty clothes she had taken off. "I shan't stop to wash the tub if it's that urgent." She opened the door.

Her brother's face was white. He took her arm and pulled it behind her. The soiled clothes she was carrying fell to the floor. "Take it back," he said.

"Take what back?" said Nina through her teeth. "Of course you're stronger than a *girl*. Of course you can twist my arm if you want to!"

Apparently he wanted to. "Damn you," Nina whispered. "That hurts! Kermit, stop it!" She kicked back, aiming for his shin, but her mule flew off across the hall. Kermit continued to drag her arm upward.

The telephone exploded in the downstairs hall.

"Let me go," said Nina.

"It's not for you."

In the downstairs hall Marion picked up the phone. "Hello?" she said. "Oh, hi. Sure, just a minute." Kermit and Nina, straining together in whatever ritual demanded this infliction and acceptance of pain, heard her put down the receiver and come to the foot of the stairs. "Nina!" she called.

"Ah!" said Kermit, gave his sister's arm one last twist, pulling her around toward him, and let her go. He opened the bathroom door and went in.

Nina leaned against the wall, surveying her scattered clothes on the floor before her. Dear Dorothy Dix, I also have a brother who has no virtues at all. He doesn't irritate me, he scares me to death.

"Nina, oh Nee—na!" cried Marion.

"Here I am, chick," said Nina, not moving. "Who is it?"

"It's Stu. He wants you."

"All right. I'm coming. Tell him to hang on for a minute." She picked up her clothes, dropped them in her bedroom and started downstairs, rubbing her shoulder. At the moment Stuart's devotion and solidity and kindness seemed most attractive. Marion was deep in conversation with him, but relinquished the receiver as Nina appeared, saying, "He wants you to go down on the Island for dinner."

"Thank you, I'd be enchanted," said Nina into the phone. "I take it the car is running again?"

"It was the distributor points. I had 'em ground, and it was all she needed."

"Perhaps that's what *I* need. What *are* distributor points?"

"Well," said Stuart, "they're——"

"Stuart! You wouldn't *really* tell me!"

"No? I thought you wanted to know. I'll be over in half an hour. Okay?"

"Yes, fine."

Nina went out to the kitchen. The distributor points made a faintly uneasy spot in her mind. Had Stuart been teasing? He surely couldn't have intended seriously to describe them; but Stuart *teasing* her was a surprising conception. For a moment her picture of him blurred, she almost admitted she was puzzled. Nonsense! she thought. Stuart is Stuart! "Mum," she said, "I'm going out for dinner. Stuart just called. Can you manage all right with Marion to help?"

Her mother did not turn. "Yes, of course. Have a good time."

Nina forgot Stuart. Mrs. Bishop had now an air of being weary of her task, of going through it mechanically, very different from the gay if rather unsure challenge with which she had been meeting it earlier. What's happened? Nina thought. *I* didn't do that to her, goodness knows she handled me very neatly! Oh Lord, I suppose it was Kermit! She looked hopelessly at her mother's back. Kermit was the one who could upset her, and Nina and Marion had always known it. Of course she held herself to a rigid standard of fairness among the children, of course she would refuse things to Kermit, refuse them firmly and finally. But when she did, she suffered agonies. What's Kermit up to? Nina wanted to ask her now. Has he been after you? What about? But it would be no use. Mrs. Bishop would *never* complain to one child about another. And anyway, thought Nina in sudden rebellion, I'm tired of thinking about this family! I resign! I *won't* worry about another soul! She turned and went upstairs. In the bathroom Kermit was whistling, as if he hadn't a care in the world.

At ten-thirty that evening Stuart put his arm around Nina and kissed her, and she said "Ouch!" and pushed him away.

"What's the matter?" he asked, letting her go.

Nina was annoyed at herself. She didn't want to take her confusion and distress out on Stuart! I've quarreled with enough people today, she thought, now I just want to relax and be lazy. "It's all right," she said. "It's nothing, really. I seem to have strained my shoulder somehow, it's sore just there in back where your hand was."

"Sorry, baby," said Stuart amiably. "Is that better?"

"Mhm, fine." She turned a little, settled herself against his chest. They were parked at the end of a dirt road looking out on Great South Bay. A faint wind rustled the beach grass around them and the track of the moon shone clean and cold on the water. How empty and old and cold it is, thought Nina, the night must have looked like this a million years ago, moon on water. Why do people call this romantic? It's frightening. Even the space in the sky around the moon is empty, nothing can come near her. Her radiance poisons the stars.

"Pretty night," said Stuart. He kissed the top of her head and then turned her face up to his. When he let her lips go he said, "Marry me, Nina, will you?"

Nina sat up and leaned away from him toward the window, the moon and the sea. Stuart waited. But it was as if she waited with him, waited for something inside to answer for her. And nothing

19

West Lafayette Public Library

West Lafayette Indiana

spoke. In the bright night the crickets and katydids shrilled, filling the stillness, but the stillness was there around them, containing them just the same. Get married? The words chirped like the crickets, the silence echoed in her ears.

Outside the oasis lay the desert. Outside her life lay the great world. Even if the desert were to bloom again, what did she know of the great world? The narrow little, comfortable little experience that trailed behind her and lay like such a thin thread across the years could tell her nothing at all of what might lie ahead. In the great world anything was possible—surges of emotion, devastation, irremediable blunders, greed, poetry and all kinds of passion. She was a stranger there, ignorant and unreal, casting no shadow. Yet could you live if you did not live there, where everything happened? Love, love should take you there, thought Nina, trembling. Love should be the gate through which you would pass to find the world not frightening, but splendid. There should be trumpet calls! You should ache to run through the gate, clutching love in your hand like a talisman.

Stuart loved her. She had cheated by letting him. And cheated no one worse than herself. For if she did not love him, she was alone, she had no talisman. The world could overwhelm her.

"Hmm?" said Stuart. "I asked you a question." In spite of the length of her silence his voice was untroubled, unresentful.

Nothing had answered for her, so she had to answer for herself. "And what would we live on? Love?" She could not tell him about her emotions, and took refuge, therefore, in the practical.

Stuart was invincibly amiable. "You've got a job," he said, "and in June I'll have a beautiful law degree, worth ten bucks a week in any man's law firm. Also, Papa would make a contribution."

Nina felt as if she were being tracked down by a large placid resolute elephant. "I don't want to be kept by your father!"

"You wouldn't be, my little breadwinner. It would only be me, and I am anyway."

"No, Stuart, it wouldn't be—I don't want to get married like that! I don't want to belong to the Judge!"

"Now baby, be fair. He's not so bad. He wouldn't stick his nose in."

That's what you think, Nina said to herself. How in the name of heaven, she wondered, did Stuart manage to live so cheerfully with his father? Not so bad! He's awful! Nina wanted to shout, and his opinions are worse—pompous, stuffy, rigid! The only time Nina had ever felt any sympathy for Communism, which was enjoying a certain vogue in the colleges, had been when a revolutionary classmate had attacked the American judiciary in terms which had irresistibly brought Judge Fanning before Nina's eyes. If I had to live with him, she thought, I would absolutely throw bombs. But she could hardly say this to Stuart. She said instead, "Stu darling, I don't know—that I ought to get married. Right now."

"Ought to, right now? Why not?"

So she had, after all, let herself in for trying to explain her emotions! "I don't feel like getting married. Aren't we all right the way we are?"

"No," said Stuart, "we're not. I'm not."

"Oh Stu, don't be mad, dear, but I feel—somehow—as if there ought to be more. More to it."

"More what?" asked Stuart, frankly puzzled. "More to what?"

"Life," said Nina hopelessly. "Marriage. Now ask me what I mean."

"Well I surely don't know without asking. Do you mean you aren't in love with me?"

Here it is, here it is, thought Nina. Why couldn't I leave it alone? He wants me to tell him, yes or no. And neither one is true. Yes isn't true; but neither is no. For she wanted, she willed passionately, in this moment, to love Stuart. In a sense—in a way that made her uneasy—Stuart lived in that real world that frightened her so. At least for Stuart, there seemed to be no dreadful difference between emotions and events. What he wanted to do, he did, and nothing so far had conspired to stop him. Was this because his wants were so limited and his circumstances so lucky that no matter how rigid the bounds of the possibilities open to him he would stay within them? Or did he know the secret, know it instinctively if inarticulately? Was Stuart's normality not complacence, but really all one needed to control the dragons that dwelt in the desert? Dared she trust it, dared she love him? Things would be so easy if she loved Stuart, she would never have to go home and pick on Marion and nag her mother and be tormented by Kermit if she loved Stuart—and she might love him, she might quite easily if only she could achieve that mysterious relaxing act of faith that would allow her to resign herself to his command. To say—I don't love you—was not true, not finally true. And it was to condemn herself to be alone in this ancient bright night, in the desert. "No, I don't mean that," she said.

Stuart found this unconvincing and unsatisfactory. "Then what do you mean?" he asked.

"I don't know," said Nina, "I truly don't know." She turned to look at him, to search behind his familiar features for the stranger with the secret who might move her, who could make it all plain. Stuart saw that she was shaking, her teeth were chattering.

"Why, you're freezing," he said, and put his arm around her, drew her gently close to him and rubbed her back to warm her.

Oh Lord, thought Nina, nuzzling into his shirt, what would I do without him! He's so good! "Dear Stuart, dear Stuart," she said, "I do love you, I do."

"All right, baby," he said, "all right. I believe you." He rubbed her, he warmed her, the warmth of his body was like a steady fire; and no affection (she knew it, she knew it!) could stop him from going on to what he said next—"But you don't want to marry me."

"I didn't say that, Stu!" She spoke quickly. "I said, not right now!"

He held her away from him, looking down into her face. What does he see, she thought, how much can he know? "And you don't know why," said Stuart broodingly.

Nina, looking up at him, felt herself grow cold with fright. He might, she saw suddenly, know a great deal. She had been treating Stuart as if he were stupid; it occurred to her now that she had been quite wrong. Stuart was inarticulate—but he was not stupid. How could he get through Columbia Law School if he were stupid? she asked herself—and not just squeak through either! But far beyond this obvious fact, she found that she really knew herself, in a personal way, that Stuart was not stupid. *Situations* obeyed Stuart—his actions turned out right. It was only his words that were clumsy, not what he did and not, Nina guessed, what he perceived. Yes, he might truly know the secret: the secret, that is, might be what Stuart knew. I'm the fool, thought Nina, not Stuart. She spoke quickly, desperately, and in what she meant to be a kind of apology: "Stuart, perhaps I'm just having the vapors. Perhaps you ought to rape me."

Stuart sat perfectly still and blinked at her. Oh Lord, she thought, maybe I've shocked him terribly! Her lips parted, she tried to think of something to say. But he spoke first.

"Now?" he said.

Nina slid back along the seat away from him, unaware of what she was doing until she felt the door handle in her back. She reached behind her for it, got ready to turn it and run. Stuart was making some strange kind of noise—she supposed it was from sexual excitement. She pressed on the door handle.

He was laughing. He laughed uncontrollably. It was a great shock to her. She sat and stared through the windshield and thought that, in spite of its being a Victorian thing to say, men were coarse. He was laughing at her because she had offered herself to him. Well—if it hadn't sounded that way, it was still what she had meant. And he was howling.

"I don't think it's so funny," said Nina coldly.

Stuart sobered slowly. "You're right," he said, "it's not. But if I hadn't laughed, I'd have knocked your block off." He started the motor, gave it a moment to warm up—for his car was eleven years old and required delicate handling—and backed out onto the road. Long Island, astonished by the moon, was silent about them and in silence they rode through the ragged suburbs back to the city.

"Good night," said Nina when Stuart stopped the car in front of her house.

"Good night," said Stuart politely.

Nina looked at him doubtfully. She had been trying to tell herself that she felt offended, but she knew that what she really felt was frustrated confusion. She had done something silly, but she didn't know what. On the other hand, her pride wouldn't let her ask. She waited a moment, hoping that Stuart would kiss her good night to signify that whatever it was she had done was forgiven and to be passed over in silence.

He didn't say anything and he didn't kiss her either.

"Good night," said Nina again, and got out of the car.

"I'll call you," said Stuart, and drove away.

Up the path silvered by the moon, into the black shadow of the porch, Nina walked. As she came into the darkness she shivered again, though the night was warm. How sweet the garden smelled! The nicotiana and stocks were blooming still. What was it? thought Nina, breathing in their scent. What did I do? She laid her hand on her breast, her heart pumped against it; but her flesh could tell her only that she had been stupid, it could not explain to her how. A kind of despair came down upon her. All day she had been stupid—clumsy, angry, at cross-purposes with life.

On the dark porch she sank down in one of the rocking chairs and sat looking at the maples and elms along the street, at the magnolias and dogwoods in the yard, of which Uncle Van was so proud. It should quiet her, she thought, to look at their beauty. She ought to be able to move into their world and out of her own. But not tonight. A sense of failure oppressed her. Over her hung the weight of the years ahead of her, a great slow wheel waiting to turn. I can't live like this, she thought, doing everything wrong. Mother and Marion and Stuart can be happy. Even Kermit knows something I don't, wants something, gets somewhere. But I do everything wrong! Aunt Flora and Aunt Dora floated through her mind, the little old ladies who had never done anything at all. I must get through, somehow, she cried to herself, get through this barrier between me and life, to where what happens is real and I feel it and understand it! Why can't I let go and just *be*? Why can't I learn how?

For a long time she sat in the darkness, looking out into the silvery night, trying to carry her loneliness with her into the community of beauty and falling back constantly into being merely alone, tired, and shivering a little in her isolated flesh. Two blocks away a trolley went by and behind her, in the harbor, a ship called long and low. Nina got up and went through the dark house to put her trouble to bed.

Sleep was sweet, dreams were kind. She waked easily next morning to a new day, Kermit whistling down the hall, Uncle Van's shower running. She opened one eye to see that the sun was shining and the time was five minutes to seven, and curled herself back into a drowsy ball, thinking that if it were cool enough she would wear her gray suit and the new yellow blouse. And if not, her dark green linen—was clean—— She dozed and somewhere much further away than the turn of the stairs where it stood the grandfather's clock cleared its throat and said, "Bong! Bong! Bong! Bong! Bong! A—hem-m-m Bong! Bong!" Kermit's whistle went back down the hall, he banged her door as he passed and called, "Get up, sister mine! The bathroom's all yours!"

The door opened and Marion crept in, her eyes tight-shut and her arms full of clothes. She dropped the clothes on the Boston rocker by the window and came over and got into bed with Nina. She put her arms affectionately around her sister's neck and said, "How can Kermit be so cheerful in the morning?"

"Perhaps he's sold his soul to the devil."

"What would the devil do with it?"

"Just what Kermit would do, I should think."

There was a long sleepy silence. Out of it Marion, apparently slumbering, said, "No Cora."

"Oh damnation! Pardon my language."

"Mother's getting breakfast. Corn-meal mush."

"Go on, you're teasing. You know it's my unfavorite food."

"I'm not teasing. Uncle Van likes it."

"He can't like it!"

"He said so last night when she asked him."

"That's just his manners. Oh dear, why does he have such nice manners!"

"I love Uncle Van."

"I love him too, but I wish——"

"But I love him the way he is, and you want him different."

"I want everything different, one way or another," said Nina wryly. "Change the world. Re-wolt! You have nothing to lose but your chains."

"What's that?"

"The Communist Manifesto."

"Do you know any Communists?"

"I did at Vassar. Maggy Holden was a Communist."

"Was she nice?"

"She was awful. But give her credit, she'd have been awful whether she was a Communist or an International Psycho-Intuitive."

"You aren't a Communist, are you?"

"No, I'm an International Psycho-Intuitive."

"Will I like Vassar?"

"You like everything."

"That's right, I do. But Nina, I *love* you." Marion hugged her sister. "Don't get married, not right now."

"But I thought you adored Stu," said Nina in surprise.

"Well, it's not me that's marrying him."

"How true. Oh Lord, look at the time. Come on, you'll be late for school. Marion, how much do you weigh? You're all horrid puppy-fat. Go on, get up, get up——"

"No, Nina, no, Nina, don't tickle! No!" But Nina chased her down the hall to the bathroom, where they amicably brushed their teeth together.

Uncle Van was sitting alone at the round mahogany dining table, reading the *Herald Tribune*. He lowered it as the girls came in and said, "Good morning, dears. Go see if you can help your mother."

Nina kissed him on his bald spot and Marion stopped to pick up the empty orange-juice glass in front of him and take it out to the kitchen. There Mrs. Bishop, in a pink apron, was muttering softly to herself as she stirred some concoction which was plopping gently over the flame. Kermit was holding a coffeepot and contemplating a line of cups.

"Oh Nina, this wants to stick!" said Mrs. Bishop.

"Sweetie, it ought to be in a double boiler."

"Oh of course! Oh Nina, thank goodness! Here, you stir and I'll——"

"Just take it off the flame for a minute, Mummy. Here, this will do. I'll run a little water in and it will boil in no time. You go drink your juice and amuse Uncle Van. Kermit, leave my coffee till later. Take in that dish of jam, though. Marion, put some toast on, and then bring me my juice and I'll drink it here." Mrs. Bishop took off her apron and retired, murmuring, "Poor Van, all alone." Kermit followed. Marion scurried out and in and out again. Nina stood by the stove, looking out into the garden—the kitchen and dining room shared the rear of the house—where Uncle Van's dahlias and asters bloomed like mad. On the arbor over the back porch grapes were ripening. Spider webs on the grass were shiny with dew. The odor of mignonette and mint hung on the morning air. Uncle Van was a gardener at once passionate and meticulous, and the half-acre lot on which the ugly old house stood gave him just the scope he needed and enjoyed most. His garden flamed all summer long, and even in winter his thoughts were busy as moles, creeping about the beds in a constant act of creation.

Uncle Van is married to the garden, thought Nina. Of course he plays the fiddle too, that's his mistress. Do you suppose his partners know? Uncle Van's two partners, who each came to dinner once a year, always impressed Nina as having been mummified sometime back in the era of Dickens and Balzac. They had affected her with a profound disinterest in the American business economy. How was it that Uncle Van had remained human? Perhaps it was Mother, thought Nina; and not just because she was dependent on him. I don't think she *feels* dependent, she takes that for granted. She feels grateful. Imagine being able to feel grateful for sixteen years without even trying! She didn't just hand him a ready-made family, she made us *all* a family, together.

Nina came to with a start and stirred the mush. Unappetizing stuff! She blew on a spoonful and tasted it. Not enough salt. What would happen if I put molasses in? she thought; and then at once, Well, well! Nina, the little homemaker. I sound like the woman's page in the paper about how Mrs. Huey Long met her fate at a cake contest. How I won the contest and the Governor, a tested recipe. "Marion! Come help me carry this in. Have you buttered the toast?"

"Yes ma'am, but Uncle Van wants more coffee, can you bring the percolator? No you can't. I'll come back."

Somehow they all assembled at the table. The sun winked in on the silver. Uncle Van was still reading the *Herald Tribune,* but he was reading it aloud now, Walter Lippmann on world conditions, very gloomy. Mrs. Bishop exclaimed gently at intervals. It was going to be hot again. Marion ate steadily through her mush. Kermit was making private faces, working something out as he drank his coffee.

Suddenly Nina was overwhelmed with affection for them all. For a moment the tension within her relaxed and she was happy and at home. Even Kermit had his own special value, because he was part of her and of this. The big, grotesque house—seven bedrooms and one bath—the wainscoted walls of this room with the willowware on the plate rail around the top of the walls—the red brocaded furniture in the parlor which was used two or three times a year—all this, her family, her house, were fiercely close to her. Here they would forgive her for being stupid. No matter how they might quarrel, Marion would crawl into bed with her the next morning, her mother would hand her the spoon to stir the mush, Kermit, even Kermit, if he twisted her arm one evening would wake her cheerfully the next day. How, even setting aside last night (and she did not want to remember it or puzzle about it), how could she ever hope in the never-never land of marriage to Stuart to build another family in another house which, thirty years from now, would be as warm and vital and —and *filling* as this one? It didn't seem probable, hardly reasonable. When you thought of all you had to do, the years of meals, the miles of marketing——

I'll leave it to Marion, she thought. She can't help but do it. And I'll be a career girl. I'll be the maiden aunt who buys all the best presents and takes the children to matinees. And before the specters of Aunt Flora and Aunt Dora could appear, the clock on the stairs cleared its throat and began on eight o'clock. "Bong! Bong!——"

"Oh me, I must fly," said Nina. "Kermit, aren't you late?"

"Not me. First class is a ten o'clock today."

Uncle Van looked at his watch. "Clock's a minute fast. Nina, I'll be ready in eight minutes. Will that suit you?"

"Absolutely. I'll go powder my face, knowing perfectly well it will wear off before I get to the office, but wot the hell, wot the hell."

"Nina, I wish you wouldn't swear," said her mother.

"That's not swearing, it's a quotation," said Nina. "From mehitabel. Mummy, may I have a cat if I name her mehitabel?"

"Why, dear, I don't know—I didn't know you wanted a cat."

"Neither did I, till just now. But I'd like a nice big mother cat and four kittens. Vicarious maternity."

"Oh Nina, not a girl cat! Not again!"

"Four kittens at a time, you mean," said Kermit. "Four kittens in April in the linen closet. Four kittens in August someplace in the farther reaches of the garage where it's still the carriage house and nobody can find them. Four kittens in December in the coalbin, saved from the fiery furnace by the merest chance——"

"I know, I know," said Nina. "But I need a cat."

"Perhaps Mr. Daniels would like one at the office," Marion offered helpfully. "A literary sort of cat."

"Darling, what have you been reading!" said Nina. "Christopher Morley? This isn't a literary sort of magazine, you know. Well. To quote Mummy, we'll see. Good-by, all."

The subway, empty in the far reaches of Bay Ridge where Nina and Mr. Van Deusen got on, was jammed by the time they reached Manhattan. Uncle Van got off in the lower stretches of the island and Nina went on alone, reading her longitudinally folded *Times,* to the more cultural Thirties. She and Mr. Daniels, representing the fiction department of *Godey's Lady's Book,* shared a corner office. On the whole Nina found this pleasantly chummy and a relief to her spells of loneliness, but it left her exposed to his conversation. Mr. Daniels, a tweedy man, regarded himself as a Wise and Interested Human Being. He believed that the proper study of mankind was man, and that nothing human was alien to him. Nina was afraid that little of her life, at any rate, was alien to him any more, and she could have shut her eyes and drawn an architectural plan of his house in Bronxville though she had contrived never to see it. She knew what marks his children got in school and had shopped for Mrs. Daniels' Christmas and birthday presents. She had started originally as Mr. Daniels' secretary, but in the course of the past year they had both decided that her shorthand was better not put to the test, and she was now officially assistant fiction editor. She had got the job in the bleak year of 1932 because one of Uncle Van's business friends controlled a considerable block of shares in the publishing company, but her rise in status was due to her own efforts; and though her salary had not increased, her self-confidence had. She now wrote Mr. Daniels' letters for him from scratch instead of from scratches in her notebook, and read unsolicited manuscripts. Mr.

Daniels took care of the phone conversations and the writers with agents. Of course when he had to talk to another editor or anyone else who rated as secretary, it was Nina who made the call and handled the "My man's ready, put your man on" situation. She was capable of getting even an Eastern story editor for a film company on the line first, and Mr. Daniels was grateful to her.

This morning she took off her hat, opened the windows wide, uncovered her typewriter and started dusting about. Mr. Daniels had obviously missed the eight-thirteen, which was the train he liked to think he took, and would be arriving by the eight thirty-seven. The mail was waiting. There were, Nina saw with horror, seventeen unsolicited manuscripts (besides a clutter of eleven at home that she hadn't looked at). She picked up the first, discovered that it was in dialect, shuddered and put it down. The second was forty-three pages long and described on the cover sheet as a novella. Good heavens, she thought, they've sent us *Story's* mail. I knew we never should have printed that thing about the deaf boy in the Ozarks. Despondently she put her dust rag away and sat down to read.

Kermit was wedged into a seat on the subway, reading a book on the Ewe-speaking tribes of Northern Rhodesia. Anthropology was divided down the middle by the authorities at Columbia between Science and Sociology. Several courses counted toward the scientific requirement for a degree quite as much as equivalent points in biochemistry or astrophysics, and Kermit was taking one and picking up, incidentally, a number of odd bits of information about various segments of the human race. The Rhodesian tribes, however, appeared to be rather dull or to have found an unimaginative chronicler. Of course not all anthropologists could be Malinowski or Ruth Benedict, but Rhodesia could certainly have been better represented. Kermit found himself increasingly diverted from the Ewe speakers by the girl who swung on a strap just in front of him.

Not an attractive girl at all. But still, a girl. Her hair, which was shoulder-length, needed washing and she was pudgy through the middle. Given any choice, Kermit would not have looked at her twice. On her own plane she was almost as dull and second-rate as the Ewe speakers seemed to be. And intellectually, Kermit did not want to look at her, he wanted to finish his reading assignment for he had decided to become, for this year at any rate, a brilliant student. In this he did not overestimate himself. All the chameleon roles that Kermit essayed were merely fittings for the cutting-edge of his personality. Brilliance was not only possible for him: it was necessary. But still, distractingly, the girl bumped and shook and vibrated in front of him, and for the life of him Kermit could not help thinking about her body, and other more attractive bodies in pleasant contrast to hers—— He swore at her, to himself, for a damned nuisance.

The train slowed and shook, coming into Pacific Street. Kermit put down his book and twisted to look over his shoulder at the platform. Mobbed. Why so many people this late? Why couldn't they get to their damn offices by nine o'clock? The rush hour should be over. He felt cheated. The crowd surged in as the doors opened and the succubus before him was now jammed securely against his knees. She grunted indignantly as someone shoved her. This is insane, thought Kermit. Why should I have to sit here and be grunted at? I'd be better off in Rhodesia. Probably cooler, too. Last year in New Haven——

But no. He *would not* think about the scholarship he had lost and Uncle Van's refusal to make up the difference in his tuition. Yet in spite of himself, the words went through his head. "I'm sorry, Kermit, I won't cheat your sisters for your sake. I cannot feel that after your failure to justify our hopes——"

No, don't think about it, Kermit told himself. The old bugger! Commuting to Columbia, that was a hell of a way to get a degree! "I warn you, Uncle Van, this will jeopardize my whole future."

"I'm afraid I don't see that, Kermit. Columbia's academic standing is——"

"But who goes there? Who commutes? A lot of——"

"And I might further point out that I have not found even the entire absence of a college degree to be an insuperable obstacle for a man who is determined to get ahead." No use. Watch it now, Kermit, no use losing your temper. When he starts to be a self-made man, you're licked. Give up. Give up. Take Columbia. Yes, that's all right, take Columbia, sure. A hell of a lot of choice I have.

And his mother, with a quick smile at Nina, saying, "After all, dear, Stuart Fanning is commuting to Columbia too. I'm sure the Judge wouldn't let him go to a school that was not the best."

"But that's the Law School, Mother! Everybody knows the Law School's good. Stuart graduated from Harvard before he——"

"It's the same place, isn't it? I must say, if it's good enough for Judge Fanning it ought to be good enough for——" Yes, even his mother was against him. She doesn't trust me, he thought. Even Mother. Four hundred dollars, that's all I needed to make up for losing the scholarship, and she wouldn't ask Van for it, she was against me. She thought more of Van's money than of me. That's what they all think of, that's how they judge, in that mean little, tight little world! Money, just money!

Money! thought Kermit himself, suddenly. What am I going to do? What am I going to do! I've got to get hold of——

Stop it! he told himself. You're in a panic, you fool, you can't think straight when you're in a panic. Slow down. Take it easy. You'll get it someplace, you'll think of something!

The train lurched. The girl in front of him lost her hold on her strap and fell against him. He got her newspaper in his face and most of herself in his lap.

"Excuse me for not offering you my seat earlier," said Kermit between his teeth.

"Huh?"

"Or perhaps I should have spoken in Ewe?"

"Smart guy, huh! I dint ast to land in your lap! Some gentleman, I'll say. Keep your seat." She got herself to her feet. One of her heels ground into Kermit's toe and she glared at him.

Oh Lord, oh Lord, oh Lord, he thought, sitting and sweating and hating her. Hating people made him feel weak, the emotion came out of him like sweat and ran off his body, taking some of his substance with it, leaving him more vulnerable than before. Hate, love, all emotions were like wounds. He wanted to walk inviolate, unmoved, untouched in a cool armor of indifference: an ambition which many of us have cherished at the age of eighteen and a half. But Kermit held this ideal of passionless superiority with a passionate intensity and a conscious determination that few who aspire to it have shared. I won't be like other people! I won't be weak. I am different, I am different, Kermit thought, striving to calm himself.

The train shot out of the tunnel into the sunlight on Manhattan Bridge, its rumble changed its note, the air freshened a little. The momentary freedom pierced him with a knowledge of his captivity, his puppetship. Stuffed in the belly of the train, he rode to Manhattan like a prisoner, not the indifferent conqueror he longed to be. How could he ever get free? He was undergoing an apprenticeship in servitude. A pang of terror shot through him. These daily slave journeys, the role of bright and obedient student he was acting, surely they would end by tying him into his fate with strengthening cords of habit never to be broken.

"And wild for to hold, though I seem tame," he whispered to himself, his eyes widening, fixing themselves on the waist of the girl in front of him. "Wild for to hold, wild!" The wildness was there, he could feel it within him, shivering, precious, subject to no law. But how to preserve it, to preserve his secret treasure, his cruelty and passion! It was fluid, it came and went, it could sink down and leave him all laughter and happy astonishment. But it never went far. If it did, if he lost it, there could be no pleasure. This was himself and he was not going to be tamed. No one need think she could tame him—not even by forcing him to the average indulgence of hating and suffering in this admirable approximation of hell, an overcrowded subway train.

He relaxed suddenly. He had risen above it, he was free of his hate. Speculatively his eyes ranged over the body of the girl in front of him. Not even if she were thinned down could she hope to be made sensually attractive, her very bones were thick and ungainly. And yet if one embraced her it would be a whole civilization embraced, all of urban petit bourgeoisie, all trolley riders, dwellers in two-family houses, all filing clerks who left high school in their second year, all Coney Island and half of Brooklyn. It would be, in a sense, a gesture of patriotism to the borough where he and his family dwelt as near anachronisms. He grinned at the idea. A gesture, after all, more amusing to think of than to make.

The train, back in its mole hole, stopped at Canal Street. For a moment, as people got off, the crowd thinned. Kermit got up. "I'm

33

sorry if you thought I was rude," he said, and smiled at the girl. "Sit down, won't you?"

She stared at him in amazed suspicion, but plopped hastily into the seat before it could vanish. She was struggling, he was sure, with the desire to say something unpleasant, the inability to think of what it might be, and the very real handicap of wondering whether he was not just acting like a traditional gentleman. He stood above her, smiling gently down at her puzzled brown eyes, her doughy face. Reluctantly she smiled back and said, "Well, thanks." As plainly as if he were Daniel reading his *Mene, mene,* he could see other words forming in her brains: Gee, he's kind of cute. She wriggled in her seat and he could see her getting excited, making a story in her mind about her adventures with this cute boy to tell cronies. Opening his book, bending his golden head, he returned to the Ewe, his mouth curved in a grave smile. Once he thought he might give himself the pleasure of pinching her hard as she got up to get off, but no. She was the kind that would open her smeared mouth and scream. The girls to pinch were the quiet ones who disliked embarrassment. Nina, now. Would she scream? Well, she might. There was no telling about Nina. She was, in the last instance, irritable, and you couldn't tell about irritable people.

Nina! He looked up as if someone had called his name. Of course! Nina was the answer to his problem! A wave of thanksgiving shook him, he almost burst out laughing. See now, he thought, that's what I get for not giving in! It's my reward for my Boy Scout good deed! When I didn't think of it right away it's obvious I wouldn't have thought of it by myself. The girl he had given his seat to was looking at him, he saw, and he smiled at her reassuringly. Had she not, after all, given him the sign? Roundabout she had led him to Nina and the way. Yes, he thought, yes.

At Times Square he stopped in a phone booth, called his sister and told her he was going to come by to see her that afternoon.

Nina, puzzled by Kermit's call, grew progressively uneasier through the day. She was not helped by Mr. Daniels, who did not understand why the prospect of a visit from her brother should disturb her.

34

"It's not just a visit, it's a visitation," said Nina.

"He's probably just in some schoolboy scrape," said Mr. Daniels.

"Just!" She shuddered. Any scrape of Kermit's that he needed her help to get out of would not be mere.

"You're not very sympathetic to him, Nina," said Mr. Daniels judiciously.

"No, I'm not."

"I thought all your family was very close."

"Positively stuffy."

"You're a cynic, my dear. That's a sign of immaturity, if you'll forgive my saying so. I think you'll find as you grow older—I hope you will, anyway—that most people are worthy of your trust."

"And there's so much good in the worst of us, etc."

"Well, isn't there?"

"Kermit, like Huey Long, is *sui generis*. You know,"—Nina made a desperate effort to change the subject—"I seem to be haunted by Huey Long. I find myself thinking about him at the oddest times, like getting breakfast this morning. Do you think there's something behind it? If he's going to haunt, I mean, why pick on me? Why not Roosevelt?"

"He probably does haunt Roosevelt. He's a dangerous man, Nina. Long, I mean. Not that I'd want to swear Roosevelt wasn't. I voted for Hoover, myself. Who did—— Oh, you weren't twenty-one till last May, were you? What do you mean, getting breakfast? Did Cora quit?"

Good God, thought Nina, why couldn't I have a strong silent boss who appreciates reticence? Well at least I'll never need to be psychoanalyzed, I've already told all to Mr. Daniels. "Yes, she quit," she said, and was spared further details by the telephone, which announced that Mr. Palmer, the executive editor, was ready to see Mr. Daniels.

"He wants to upgrade our fiction," said Mr. Daniels sadly.

"And I," said Nina cynically, "am Marie of Rumania." Her attitude seemed to hearten Mr. Daniels this time, for he patted her on the shoulder as he went out.

Between three and four o'clock Nina, waiting for Kermit, was no good to anyone. Mr. Daniels, returning from his conference with his philosophy a little strained, at last sent her out to the washroom for a cigarette. She came back to find Mr. Daniels looking rather more strained than before and Kermit waiting for her.

"Can you come out for half an hour?" said Kermit, getting up. "I'll buy you a soda."

"Run along," said Mr. Daniels, nodding emphatically.

They went out to the elevator and rode down. Kermit was whistling softly.

"You seem very sunny," said Nina.

"Pretty good, thanks."

"We'll go in here." Nina turned into the drugstore-lunchroom on the corner.

They found a table. "What'll you have?" said Kermit.

"Coffee frosted."

"Black and white," he nodded at the waitress, who went off scribbling on her pad. "Nina, you have some money, don't you?" he went on in the same tone.

"You mean for the sodas?" said Nina weakly.

"Well, no. I meant rather a larger sum than that. In the bank, for instance."

But Nina just looked at him.

"Come now, darling," he said, "you're not a stingy girl. It just so happens that I need some money."

"What for?"

"I hoped you were going to say how much. Wouldn't you rather say that?"

Nina waited.

"Well," said Kermit reluctantly, "I'm afraid I've got in with kind of a bad crowd. Almost a gang, you might say. They're—ah—well, they're kidnapers. They're thinking of holding me for ransom."

"Can't you be serious?" said Nina violently.

"I can, of course. But I thought it would be easier all around if I weren't. I need some money very badly."

"And?"

"And what?"

"I won't give it to you without knowing what for. Not that I

36

have much, as a matter of fact. I blew two hundred dollars on my vacation. What do you want it for, Kermit?"

Kermit waited while the waitress put their drinks in front of them. Then he said, "I think you'd really rather not know. There won't be a repetition, if that's what you're worried about." He sucked at his soda.

Nina watched him, fascinated. His golden hair fitted his head like a cap. His eyes were shielded by lashes half an inch long. His face was a precise and perfect mask. I suppose I've never seen anyone more beautiful than Kermit, she thought. "Is it a girl?" she asked.

Kermit did not look up.

"Is it for—for a doctor?" asked Nina.

"I won't tell you," said Kermit, and smiled at her.

But Nina's face shook him. "Don't be so goddamn nosy!" he said. "You should see yourself. You look like a Grant Wood D.A.R. smelling sin and lusting to hear about it. Isn't it enough if I tell you I need help and I can't get it anywhere else?"

"What's her name?" said Nina stubbornly.

"I won't—— Oh hell. Antonia. Tony, for short. Yes, I need a doctor. Now I hope you're pleased!"

"But you aren't nineteen yet," said Nina.

"Dear Nina! My virgin sister. You're a little naïve, darling. Do you think you need an initiation ceremony? This is New York, not Northern Rhodesia."

"How much do you need?" asked Nina mechanically.

"How much have you got? To be quite frank."

Nina opened her purse and took out her bankbook. She saw with surprise that her hand was shaking.

"It's tough on you, isn't it?" said Kermit unexpectedly. "I really don't like it much myself, you know. But we can't both sit here and shake."

"I have a hundred and twenty-two dollars."

"I'll take the hundred. And thank you very much."

"I'll get it tomorrow at lunch. Do you want to meet me somewhere?"

"That's a good idea. Where?"

"Why—I don't know—— Let me think——"

"How about the Algonquin?"

"All right. One o'clock?"

"Sure."

Nina put the bankbook back and found that her eyes were full of tears. She blew her nose.

"For Christ's sake," said Kermit. "I didn't know my fall would mean that much to you."

"Shut up," said Nina. "I hope you *have* got enough to pay for the sodas because I'm going back to the office." She stood up.

"You didn't drink your frosted."

"You may have it."

"Thank you, I will. Give my love to Mr. Daniels."

She went out, moving by instinct and habit. On the way up to the office she concentrated on thinking about Mr. Daniels. What lie was she going to tell him when he asked what Kermit had wanted? She worked up a good passion against Mr. Daniels' nosiness, but no lie. Mr. Daniels, however, looked at her and didn't say a word. Goodness, Nina thought, I must look ready for the grave if he's being tactful; but she didn't have enough energy to try to dissimulate the shock that Kermit had given her.

"Go on home, Nina," said Mr. Daniels. "It's half-past four."

"Well—all right. Thanks. Funny how you feel the heat sometimes. It's in my head, kind of."

"Yes," said Mr. Daniels, obviously not daring to say another word lest he be unable to repress a flood of questions. How he must be suffering, thought Nina, he really is very kind! She smiled wanly at Mr. Daniels and went out, to begin her journey home on the great contra-beat of the daily migration.

But it was not Kermit she thought about, joggling home on the Sea Beach Express. All the Kermit-part of her mind was bruised and numb. She couldn't let him down, he had to have the money; but the action was really a reflex, quite automatic. And if the gift helped Kermit out of his "scrape," did it not also protect Nina from discovering the reality of Kermit's trouble? Did it not keep it out there in the desert at a decent distance—a distance too great to be penetrated by seduced maidens, who would now *not* come to shriek and tear their hair in Uncle Van's living room? The distance was precious. Kermit's trouble did not bear thinking about, and Nina did not think about it.

Instead, helplessly, she remembered Stuart's laughter. Always, she realized now (for the past year, that is, which had come to seem "always") marriage to Stuart had existed in the back of her mind as her ace in the hole. Well, she had grown accustomed to think, if this doesn't happen or I don't like that, I can always marry Stuart. Stuart had represented tedium and security, a kind of insurance. And she had not wanted to take it. She had told herself again and again that there must be something else, something more—a bright danger that left you breathless and weak in the knees while you asked yourself, Is this the one? Is this the very one? And then, at once, you would know, and knowing, be unable to escape, be bowled along like a stone in a freshet.

The antithesis of this enchantment, the embodiment of familiar solidity, had been Stuart; until he had laughed. And now—sitting in the subway eighteen hours later, she blushed all over. It was certainly not *enchantment* she had found. Things had got much, much worse. It had always seemed possible, she realized shamedly, to marry Stuart without loving him. That, at any rate, was over. She could not do such a thing now. For now, between herself and Stuart, there stretched the tension of emotion. Only, alas, it was the wrong emotion.

Not love, not passion, not romance. But perhaps, she thought, afraid to relinquish the security he represented, perhaps I shall *never* find those things, never be hurled into love. Why should I think I must have it? Plenty of people don't have it, don't even expect it. Why should I always have counted on looking up someday as the door opened to find the one?

I suppose, she thought, and the thought seemed strange, that it was Mother who taught me to believe that. Because she must have had it, you can tell. He's still alive for her somewhere. She says his name in her sleep. They were only married seven years, too, before he went down that mine—— Oh Lord, please Lord, don't let me think about it, it still can frighten me worse than anything, being crushed to death in the dark! And I can't remember him at all, or just that he had black hair—— And boots! Yes! He wore cowboy boots with high heels!

The memory burst inside her head like a star shell. In the center was herself, small, on the floor, in bright sunlight. Her finger traced the cutout designs on the boot. Up from this center, supporting her, ran her father's leg in a tight black trouser. What else? What else? she asked herself. But everything else blurred out into dimness. It was her father, though, no one else. Pride and security came to her through the contact of her body with the warm rigidity of his leg. Why, how wonderful, she thought, how wonderful! Stuart and Kermit were ghosts, remote in the remote future. Nina was transported back to the mining country of the Southwest, to a past time as solid and complete as the one possession she had from those years before Brooklyn, her big lump of turquoise matrix.

Where is that turquoise? she thought. Where is it? Is it in my top drawer? Is it in the little toy bureau? It used to be wrapped in cotton wool, in a white cardboard box that said Tiffany, but the box broke finally, I think. Oh goodness, where is it? She fretted until the train reached her station, and then ran upstairs to the air and hurried home to search.

Tonight the door was open and as soon as she was in the hall, before the door slammed behind her, Nina called, "Mother!"

There was a scurrying at the back of the house as Nina went down the hall and her mother met her in the dining room with a dish towel in her hand. "What is it?" she said. "What's wrong?"

"Nothing's wrong," said Nina, and at the moment it was true. "Where's my turquoise?"

"Your turquoise?" Mrs. Bishop sat down on one of the dining-room chairs and looked up at her daughter.

"Yes, you know. My lump of turquoise from New Mexico. Is it——"

"Nina, why are you home so early?"

"Home? Oh. Yes I am, aren't I? It was too hot to work. Mr. Daniels chased me out. Mum, where's the turquoise?"

"Nina, are you telling me the truth? You don't have to keep anything from me, you know. I'll understand. Are you *positive* you haven't lost your job?"

40

Nina dropped to the floor beside her mother's chair and hugged her. "Mummy," she said, "I swear I haven't lost my job. I just——"

"But you're all excited, dear. And after all—the turquoise—I don't suppose you've thought of it in five years."

Nina sat back on her heels and looked up at her mother's face. Then she reached up and brushed a smudge of flour off Mrs. Bishop's cheek. "Something happened on the way home in the subway," she began, but hesitated. Did her mother know she couldn't remember her father? It would make her so unhappy! But after all, that was the point, wasn't it? Now she had remembered. "Tell me," she went on, "did Daddy wear boots, cowboy boots, black ones with yellow cutouts?"

"Good heavens!" said Mrs. Bishop. "Yes, darling, he had a perfectly beautiful pair from Tuscon, handmade, of course. He wore them all the time. Not the same ones, I mean, but—— Yes, he did. You remembered?"

"I remembered. Just now in the subway. I remembered sitting on the floor, leaning against him and running my finger around the patterns. And I remembered what it felt like to be near him."

"Yes." Mrs. Bishop paused, welcoming memory. "He used to take you everywhere. He called you Two-bits, do you remember that?"

Nina nodded slowly. She didn't think she remembered, but she couldn't be sure that there was no memory hidden away somewhere within her that reverberated at the touch of her mother's words.

"That was because he always said you were so little he could put you in his pocket and take you anyplace. The year you were four, when you grew so, he teased you and said you were getting past pocket size and how could he take you around without a wheelbarrow?"

"I don't remember that."

"No, of course not."

"But I know about the boots. And I thought if I had the turquoise—I don't know. As if I might remember more?"

"I'll get it."

"Can't I? Tell me where."

"I'll get it." Her mother smiled and went out.

Nina rested her cheek against the chair where Mrs. Bishop had been seated and waited. She felt a quiet peace and happiness, and wondered idly whether her mother, who lived in these memories so much, was rewarded by knowing such peace constantly. It must be almost worth it, she thought, to have your happiness all behind you, if you can live in its memory like Mother. She tried to imagine herself, grown old, in another house on a late afternoon, waiting for activity to return and take her into its sphere——

Her mother came back, the lump of turquoise filling her palm. It was as big as a duck's egg. Nina took it and turned it over curiously in her hand. Cool and mysterious, it brought her no immediate reward. It was there, she tried to tell herself, when everything happened. There must be some way of getting back there, I was there, it happened to me—— But the only thing that occurred to her was an irrelevance. "There were opals, too, weren't there?" she said. "In a little brown leather box?"

"Yes, dear. I'm keeping them for Marion. It's her birthstone. Uncle Van put them in the vault. Would you like to see them? I'll ask him to bring them home. Oh Nina!"

"What, darling?"

"Let's have one put in a ring for her! Could we do it in time for her birthday? If not, for the toe of her Christmas stocking."

"Oh yes! Oh Mummy, that's a wonderful idea!"

"Van shall bring them home as soon as he can, and we'll decide which one, and see about a setting. Think of your remembering that, Nina."

"I wish I hadn't forgotten everything else."

"You were so little." Her mother's fingers stroked her hair. "Kermit doesn't remember anything, of course. And Marion wasn't even born until afterwards."

"I don't know how you managed, Mum."

"I don't know myself, dear. Except that I knew I had to manage for you children. If you have to do something, you do it. Van came out to me right away, he dropped everything. He'd begun to do very well by then, after the struggle he'd had when your grandfather died, when he'd had to leave college—— He's so good, Nina! But I know you know that. And then—later, of course—I was so blessedly thankful to have you three children."

Her mother's words jarred Nina. So blessedly thankful, she thought. She is, yes, but for how long? Because surely Kermit will do something—something awful—— Why does he have to be like that? Oh, how can life be so cruel to her after all she's had to bear? Why must we *all* be lost in a "world we never made"? And always struggling to make another, living each of us in a dream and stumbling over reality and seeing our hopes break up all around us! What is Kermit going to do to her?

And why only Kermit? Marion and I too. What am *I* going to do to her? God knows it can't be what she expects, even though I don't know what it is she expects. I suppose she expects Stuart—— And even if I could marry Stuart, it wouldn't be the *way* she expects it. She sat quietly, pleating her fingers into her mother's skirt.

Whether Mrs. Bishop was expert at general family telepathy or had simply arrived at the same place by another route (substituting her daughter's future for her own past), she now said gently, "I wish you'd get married, Nina dear." She spoke timidly, anxious not to intrude but testing this moment of intimacy to see if it would bear the weight of the present.

Nina shook her head slowly.

"Stuart is a dear boy."

"I don't want to marry a dear boy."

Her mother sighed. "You're very young, of course. Younger than I was at your age."

Nina was shocked. "Oh Mother! I'm as old as the hills compared to you! Right now! You're the baby!"

"I don't think so, dear. I'm old-fashioned, perhaps, but that's just a matter of custom. Can there be a new fashion in women?"

Nina moved restlessly. "I should think that's just what there was. We're independent now. We work. We look after ourselves." But she thought then of Kermit's girl, Tony-for-short. She hadn't looked after herself very well. Suddenly she was riven with hate and fury. How dare he do it? To Tony, to her, to her mother! How like Kermit, to be just that irresponsible and leave them to pick up the pieces!

"It's not life," said her mother, "being independent. You won't want it long. You'll find out."

"I'll feel differently when I'm married," said Nina almost contemptuously.

"Well, you will." Her mother's tone was mild. But the moment of closeness was over. They were back on different sides of the generations now; and though her mother would still counsel, still try to teach, it was across the barrier of the years, and all her wisdom would turn into trash; into clichés or lies or irrelevancies. She tilted Nina's chin up and said lightly, "Did you quarrel with Stuart last night?"

"I never quarrel with Stuart," said Nina, masking sudden anger in her eyes, smiling tightly. "No one could."

"Yes, he's patient. He is so good! Too good, perhaps."

"Too good for your impatient daughter?"

"Well, dear, I sometimes think——"

"That he is?"

"No, not that. Never. But I wish you knew more of the world."

Nina's mouth opened in real astonishment. "*I* knew more!"

"You're very young, dear," said her mother again, "and romantic. Life doesn't always turn out the way you expect, you know! You mustn't think—you mustn't count on controlling it. I'm afraid you may get a knock or two before you learn to compromise." But Nina just gaped at her, as it came home to her that her mother was trying to tell her what she had been afraid to tell her mother: that our expectations are worthless, that all things change. Mrs. Bishop went on, "In some ways Kermit is older than you."

"Kermit!"

"Yes, Kermit. They say girls grow up faster than boys, but it isn't true of you and Kermit."

Now Nina was really shocked, shocked down to the pit of her stomach. Was it conceivable that Kermit had told their mother about the girl, had asked her for money? Did her mother, could her mother know all about it already? Was she accepting so calmly what had revolted Nina herself? Oh no, she thought, oh no, it's too terrible, it can't be true! She was very shaken.

"You won't grow up till you marry," continued Mrs. Bishop calmly, "but Kermit is grown up in some ways now."

"Not every way," said Nina, almost choking.

"No, not every way. I hope he won't get into trouble because of it. He's so good-looking that girls will chase him, of course. But he's not ready for that yet." Nina drew a long shaky breath. Then she doesn't know, she thought. She felt as if she had escaped from some unknown but unspeakable horror. "I'm not really thinking about girls," Mrs. Bishop pursued her subject, "though I have been afraid sometimes that he might—oh, it's awful to say—get trapped into the wrong kind of marriage. But I don't think so. Kermit is very fastidious." Oh Mother, Mother, thought Nina; but she was recovering herself, her world was nowhere so nearly cracked across as she had thought. "I don't suppose he'll marry for a long time. And then he'll marry someone special. I wasn't thinking of physical maturity so much as I was of—well—self-knowledge. I feel Kermit is impatient of us sometimes because he knows so well what he is, what he wants."

"Certainly what he wants," said Nina. She got to her feet. Her mother's misinterpretation of Kermit, now that she was sure it *was* misinterpretation, was beginning to grate on her. It was at once heartbreaking and bitterly ludicrous.

"You mean he's selfish," said Mrs. Bishop, and shut her eyes for for a moment. She looked suddenly old and worn. But when she opened her eyes, she smiled at Nina with a momentary glint of deviltry. "Well, sometimes that's a help, you know. Sometimes it's a good thing to be selfish." She sobered then and took Nina's hand. "Promise me something, though, Nina."

"What?" asked Nina warily.

"Promise you won't let him be selfish to you. I think you sometimes think I love Kermit best, that I'd sacrifice you and Marion to him. No, I know you don't *really* think that, Nina, but all children are a little jealous of each other, growing up, of course they are, it's natural. Well now, I want you to promise me that you won't do yourself what you suspect me of trying to do. That you won't sacrifice yourself for Kermit in any way at all." Mrs. Bishop stopped at this point and searched her daughter's face, but Nina was so surprised that her expression carried only this emotion and Mrs. Bishop had no suspicion that her lecture was too late. Satisfied, she said, "He has some schoolboy idea of making money, now. I suppose he's still smarting a little over not getting back to Yale and he wants to show off his independence. He has a chance to go in with another boy at Columbia, selling sweaters and jackets, and things like that, and he wants some money to begin. I told him it was just a swindle, Nina, I told him right out—How can you expect to get anywhere starting with only a hundred and fifty dollars? It's absurd on the face of it, even I can see that. Whether the other boy is in it or not, I don't know, of course, and don't expect to. But I did warn him.

"But Nina, you know the way he is when he makes up his mind! And particularly about money. Do you remember the chickens he raised? How he pestered me? And how furious the neighbors were, chickens in our backyard? And then they all died anyway—— But he wouldn't give up, I thought he'd break his heart. Nina, I won't have him starting something like that again. Now you promise me on your word of honor that if Kermit asks you for money you won't give it to him. Promise me!"

Nina reached one hand behind her and crossed her fingers. "I promise," she said. She had not had the faintest idea she was going to do this, and when she realized she had used the ancient protection to liars familiar to every child, she gave a hysterical little giggle. How long since she'd promised something with her fingers crossed? Since she was eleven? But Mrs. Bishop relaxed and was satisfied.

Then the screen door banged and Marion's voice called out, swollen with triumph, "Mummy! Oh Mummy! Guess what!" She appeared radiant in the doorway, and Nina and Mrs. Bishop, happy to jettison their own scene, gave her their fullest attention. "I'm a cheerleader!" said Marion.

"Why dearie, how nice," said Mrs. Bishop, and Nina hugged her sister and assured her that she had a great future before her.

"We were there all afternoon," said Marion blissfully, sinking down into a chair and ready to detail the entire story. "There were twenty-seven girls to start, and they eliminated eight right away. But that left eighteen——"

"Nineteen," said Nina.

"Did it? I suppose so. Well, nineteen. So we stood up in line and——"

"Goodness me, *look* at the time! Come out in the kitchen, chick, and finish telling me there."

Marion trailed after her mother, and Nina stood by herself in the dining room. She could hear the icebox door open and close, her mother interrupt the steady flow of Marion's story to ask her something, without diverting it in the least. The egg beater whirled. Water boiled on the stove. Nina picked up her turquoise and weighed it in her hand. I was there then, she whispered to it. I am here now. She tried to imagine, to remember, to hold in her head somehow, the long bridge of minutes, of seconds, from that time to this. Impossible. The years lay behind her in darkness with occasional patches of sunlight falling across them, like a dark hall with high windows facing south, full of old furniture, lumber of the past. If you went back you would stumble over it, bark your shins. And yet—if that was real, was true, so was this. This moment, right now, when the egg beater whined and Marion's story was coming to its breathless end, when the saved-daylight still lay solid outside the windows, this very afternoon was of the same stuff as those past years which were imprisoned in the turquoise. It is all one, thought Nina, and between herself and life felt the barrier dissolve. This is enchanted too. It is alive. Everything is always, because it is all one.

And nothing is lost.

"Nina, are you there?" called her mother. "Set the table, will you, dear?" Obediently Nina picked up the centerpiece—Uncle Van's button chrysanthemums—moved it to the sideboard and got out the tablecloth and pad. But as she put them on, as she returned the flowers to their place and began to set the silver out, she remembered that Uncle Van and Kermit would be home soon. The peace she had achieved began to seep away and desolation grew about her. How can I bear it, she thought, how can I bear it? Time was hurrying now, roughly, as she listened for the next slam of the door, and the world no longer was one. Kermit had opened the door to shame and cruelty and unhappiness and Nina had no armor to wear against them.

It was easy enough to retire to her room to read manuscripts that evening, and thus to avoid Kermit after dinner, but there was no avoiding lunch the next day. It seemed to Nina that even her trip to the bank was difficult. Mr. Daniels, innocently enough, kept her later than she had expected. There was a line ahead of her at the window when she got to the bank, and a kind of unholy urgency mixed itself up with her shame and disgust at the whole affair. She wanted to cry and stamp and scream with frustration as she waited. When she got to the Algonquin at last she couldn't see Kermit and she thought for a moment that he hadn't come at all. She almost exploded with fury then; but Kermit came, at that moment, out of a telephone booth and she hung onto her temper. When they were seated in the dining room, though, at a table against the wall, she could wait no longer. She took the bills she had for him out of her pocketbook and gave them to him at once. "Here," was all she said, and she wiped her hands on her napkin after passing him the money.

Kermit lifted his eyebrows at the gesture, said "Thanks," and put the bills away.

"Don't lose it," Nina couldn't help herself from adding bitterly.

"Don't worry, I won't."

Then they sat in silence. Nina was raging closer and closer to telling him that she had promised their mother not to give him money; to thanking him for taking less from her than he had asked Mrs. Bishop for. *But of course he found out how much I had first. He just asked for the nearest round sum!* She was in a fury but she sat and bit her lip and didn't speak.

"Have you read any good books lately?" asked Kermit politely into the silence.

"How can I read any good books if I'm going to be an assistant editor of *Godey's Lady's Book?*" said Nina snappishly. "Do you want to break down all my standards?"

"All right, all right," said Kermit. "Sorry I spoke. I thought you liked it there."

Nina looked at the menu and then ordered salad and coffee. Kermit decided on a rather more substantial meal and ordered in a man-of-the-world fashion which required a good deal of consultation with the waiter, while Nina fretted. When he finished he said, "Who's here today? Anyone famous?"

"I suppose so. There usually is. You can't see the round table from here, though."

"Shall I go and pry? Ask Woollcott for an autograph?"

"Really, Kermit!"

"He'd adore it, I should think. I could creep up and sort of purr at him in his own highly imitable fashion. No?"

"I doubt if he'd be amused."

"Maybe not, but I would. However."

"Where did you meet this girl?" Nina burst out at him. She was furious with herself at once, and clenched her hands in her lap.

"Well, well. I wondered when we were going to come to it." Kermit leaned forward and, looking into her face, reached for her clenched hands and covered them with one of his own. "Look, Nina," he said. But she wouldn't look, she stared straight in front of her. He didn't seem to mind, but said in a surprisingly gentle tone, "Get this through your head, darling. I'm not going to tell you one little thing about it. You bought no confidences with your money. You bought nothing, in fact, not even my gratitude."

"I'm sure of that!" said Nina under her breath.

"Because gratitude can't be bought," said Kermit, and his voice hardened a little. "It can only be given freely. At the moment I am extremely grateful to you. I'm also prepared to make allowances for your reactions to discovering that your little brother is (a), wicked, and (b), more experienced than you. You lead a sheltered life and this is a shock to you."

"A sheltered life!" said Nina.

"Good God, yes. At home there's the little feathered nest you haven't thought of venturing from. At the office Mr. Daniels bumbles at you like someone written by J. B. Priestly. And in between times good old Stuart kisses you reverently and asks you to marry him, which I assume you'll do—in a year or two when you both get itchier."

"Kermit!"

"What do you know about life and living? You go around this city as if it were Wenatchee, Washington. You're all swathed up like a mummy in beautiful girlish dreams. You not only don't understand what goes on around you, you can't even see it going on.

This place is a jungle, New York. When the sun falls just right you can see the tigers in the depths, you can smell them and hear them if you listen right—and know what to listen for. And if you're smart they'll come and lick your hand. But you walk through it all like—like Little Red Riding Hood!"

"You're smart, I suppose. This was a very smart thing just now!"

"There you have me. I have to admit it. I made a very stupid mistake. But don't think I'll ever do it again."

Nina laughed harshly. "Never again! You sound like a drunkard saying he'll never touch another drop of whiskey."

"And you sound like his nagging wife," said Kermit as the waiter brought his soup. He started to eat unhurriedly, and there was silence until Nina, beside him, suddenly sniffled and reached in her pocketbook for her handkerchief.

"Why Neen," said Kermit, "you're crying!"

"Don't call me that!" Nina blew her nose vehemently. "Damn it, haven't I got enough to bear!"

"I'm sorry, Neen. I was too tough on you."

"Please, Kermit, don't!" She took a deep breath and struggled to compose herself. A blonde girl across the room was watching them. "Don't make me bawl in front of that snoopy blonde over there."

"Where?" said Kermit. "Hmm—not bad. *I'll* scare her off!" And leaning forward, he made a horrible face at her.

The blonde, in utter astonishment, touched her escort's arm and pointed, but by the time he had found out whom she meant, Kermit was once more eating his soup with quiet relish.

Nina sniffled and giggled at once. "What are they doing now?" asked Kermit.

"She's saying, 'He did, he did!' He isn't so sure."

"That's fortunate. Is he big?"

"Pretty big. Stupid though. You could lick him."

"Or I could simply claim to have St. Vitus' dance. Can you see how close they are to being through? If they're on coffee I don't mind but I won't sit here and twitch for an hour if they're just beginning.'

"About medium, I should say. Yes, he's cutting something now Chicken, from the way he's sawing. She's mad at him."

"Shall I wink at her?"

"Don't you dare!"

"Later, maybe." And quickly he winked at the blonde girl, who took so deep a breath that her breasts burst open the top button of her suit jacket—and then looked hastily down at her plate and began to eat, chatting meanwhile in a fetching way with a good deal of gesticulation. Nina, a little puzzled, looked from her to Kermit, but her brother quickly offered her a cigarette and succeeded in distracting her.

All in all, she thought, walking back to the magazine and Mr. Daniels, it had been an unsatisfactory lunch. Kermit, in trouble, had turned to her. She had helped him. Surely in return for that she should have been able to do her duty, to talk to him quietly and maturely of irresponsibility and—not immorality, perhaps, she was too modern to use the word—but of what he owed to other people with whom he involved himself. Suppose she had not helped him? Suppose it had all come out at home? She pictured her mother in hysterics, Uncle Van white with disgust, Kermit silent and shamefaced, forced to face up to what he had done and submit to being rescued by that older generation which would not hesitate to talk of immorality. Surely her hundred dollars which had bought Kermit's salvation (bought? Yes. That was just what it had done. In spite of Kermit, bought was the word), surely it should have given her the right to scare him, to turn him from the course he had taken. Kermit's defenses should have been broken down!

But instead, it was she who had been on the verge of tears. It was her defenses that were inadequate. It was Kermit who had lectured her. "Oh, he's impossible!" she muttered to herself, waiting to cross a street, and a man waiting beside her turned and stared. Nina blushed up to her hair. And now this, now this! she thought. He had set her to talking to herself in the street, made her a figure of fun, called her naïve, likened her to a nagging wife! Her mother's words of yesterday came back, too—"You're young, romantic, I wish you knew more of the world." All because she had protected each from the other, averted that terrible scene of desolate anger and hurt when Kermit would have had to confess! She was hot with their injustice, wrenched with their ingratitude and misunderstanding.

Kermit had been wrong, wrong, wrong. Her mother had been unsympathetic, imperceptive. Certainly she had not wanted to bring Kermit to confession, her mother to hysterics, Uncle Van to disgust. But someone should appreciate what she had done! Someone should thank her! She should be more than Nina: A Convenience, Nina: A Buffer, to be lectured from both sides! She turned into her office building, rode up in the elevator in tight-lipped rage and snapped at Mr. Daniels unpardonably all afternoon.

When she got home there was still no cook and, in addition, her mother had sliced her thumb almost to the bone and was attempting to get dinner literally singlehanded.

"I have no sympathy with you at all," said Nina.

"Don't scold, dear," said Mrs. Bishop, "it was an accident."

"Well, I didn't think you did it on purpose. But you shouldn't have to have such accidents! You should——"

"I know, I should get a cook. All right, I'll call Mrs. Hilliard Monday. It's no use calling tomorrow, it's Saturday."

"Why? Do all potential cooks go away for the week end?"

"You know perfectly well what I mean, dear. They *don't* go to agencies on Saturday."

"They can't *like* being unemployed! I should think——"

"Nina, I'm older than you. I have hired cooks for nearly thirty years. I shall hire one on Monday. Now I don't want to hear any more about it. Go and read the paper. Or something." Mrs. Bishop pushed the hair out of her eyes with the back of her hand and looked distracted and a little harassed.

Oh dear, thought Nina, I'm nagging her again. Why do we have to wrangle over *everything*? But she could no more have stopped her next words, the continuation of the wrangle, than she could have held back the tide. "Nonsense! You go read the paper yourself. I'll do this." And she picked up a paring knife.

"I won't have you working all day and coming home to get dinner! You do quite enough as it is. I can manage perfectly well, and Marion will help me as soon as she gets home. If you and Kermit would do the dishes—— Oh no, Kermit won't be home. Well, perhaps Marion——"

"Where is she, anyway? Leading cheers again?" Nina changed the subject half unwillingly, still angry, still wanting to quarrel with someone.

"No, I think it's basketball today. Or is it the Debating Club?" Mrs. Bishop co-operated gladly.

"I don't know. Her activities are beyond me."

"I used to worry about sending her to a public high school instead of to Packer. But you know, Nina, I think she enjoys this."

"She certainly needs the scope, if you ask me. Cribbed, cabined and confined is what she would have been at—— I'll get the phone. You leave the rest of the potatoes now till I get back." She went out to the hall and picked up the receiver.

"Do you want to go up to Janey's and sail tomorrow?" asked Stuart's voice.

"Hello," said Nina.

"Hello. How about it?"

Well, how about it? Nina asked herself. Here it is again, all the same. Whatever it was that happened is over, and we can go right on. Dependable Stuart is back—and how about it? While she thought this she was saying, "Well—we haven't any cook and Mother cut her hand and I have a raft of manuscripts to read still——"

"Bring the manuscripts along and be one less mouth to feed."

Nina was silent. What difference does it make whether I go or stay? she asked herself desolately. Who cares? Does Stuart really care at all? Or am I just a habit for him—am I dependable Nina? Does he understand in the least what I think and how I feel? Oh, perhaps he cares about what he thinks is me—but how can he know, how can he care about what I really am, how I really feel? He laughed at me! She wanted to hate him, but instead she felt ready to cry.

"Come on," said Stuart. "You know you like sailing. And this is our last chance. They're going to put the boat up next week." Janey was Stuart's married sister who lived in Cos Cob. Nina had stayed there for sailing week ends half a dozen times this past summer.

Yes, it's the end of something, even if just the summer, thought Nina, but suppose it is? Why do I have to go and celebrate it? Janey certainly doesn't care whether I come or not, I'm just something to keep Stuart happy as far as she's concerned. "I don't think I'd better go," she said abruptly. In her present mood, she felt it would be much better and nobler to stay home and cook for the family than to do something she liked. I don't want to enjoy myself, she thought willfully, more determined to be martyred than her mother ever had been. Yet as soon as she had spoken, she regretted it. She felt lost and left out.

But Stuart gave her scope for neither martyrdom nor regret. "Oh don't be a dope," he said equably. "You come along. I want you. Go ask your mother."

"Ask my mother! How old do you think I am? Ask my mother! Or do you think you're talking to Marion?"

"I'm talking to the one with the bad temper," said Stuart pleasantly. "Go ask her if she needs you. Go on, baby. I want you to come."

"I don't——"

"Go on now."

"Stuart, I'm not going to come!"

Someone was coming up the walk, whistling.

"Sure you are," said Stuart.

Oh Lord, thought Nina, Kermit! I don't want to see him! She had quite forgotten, for the moment, that he wasn't coming home for dinner. "All right," she said hastily. "I'll come. I'm sorry," she added halfheartedly.

Marion opened the door and came in. Nina's irritation fixed on the new target. She covered the mouthpiece of the phone and said, "Go on out and help Mother! Where have you been!"

"I stayed late to——" Marion began, blinking in surprise.

"She's cut her hand badly. I don't know why you can't come home when people expect you!"

"Oh poor Mums!" cried Marion, and fled out to the kitchen, with no more thought of defending herself.

Nina came back to hearing Stuart telling her that she was a good girl, but she only half listened, for she was angry at herself for changing her mind. It was the kind of weakness she deplored. He wanted to come for her right away, but she told him she would not be ready till eight. When he agreed amicably, it made her still angrier. She hung up the phone and sat thinking first that she would like to throw something at an etching of Notre Dame which hung on the stairs, and then that she would like to cry. But basically, neither activity seemed sufficient to relieve her feelings and besides, having thought of them, she could not do them. She felt coerced and frustrated. She wanted really neither to go with Stuart nor to stay home; but to be transported in some fashion to another world—only there was no other world, she could not even imagine one in which she would be happy.

She got up and went sullenly out to the kitchen, finding some relief in feeling guilty over leaving her mother. But even this failed, for Mrs. Bishop was frankily delighted to have her go, Marion swore she would do the cooking and washing up and dragoon Kermit into helping. And when Uncle Van came home, he produced tickets for the theater Saturday night and informed Mrs. Bishop she was going out to dinner with him first.

"Nina," said Marion as the three women were serving up dinner, "you look as if you wanted to go out in the garden and eat worms."

"I do," said Nina, "I do, I do, I do!" She sat down on a kitchen chair and cried, "Oh what's the matter with me! I wish I knew!"

"Why dearie," said Mrs. Bishop, patting her on the shoulder. "There's nothing the matter with you, except perhaps that you're in love."

"I'm not!" shouted Nina, springing to her feet, and this time she did throw something, but fortunately it was only the order pad. "I'm not," she said again, disgustedly. But in spite of herself she felt better.

At seven-thirty Stuart appeared, took Nina's dish towel away from her and sent her up to pack. He and Marion sang duets in the kitchen and Nina, throwing things into an overnight case, thought with returning irritation how good he was. He didn't even have to try; it was as natural to him as breathing. Everyone—and Nina too— had only to look at him to think what a wonderful husband he would make. He was kind, thoughtful, patient, reasonably intelligent, quite good-looking in a tall, slab-sided sort of way, with a square solid dependable face. He had followed his father into the law without the least hesitation, apparently experiencing no adolescent revolt, and without attempting to assert his right to choose another profession. He did, in fact, like the law and had done very well at Columbia, though he was not one of the brilliant top three or four boys. But since he was one of the top fifteen or twenty, since he was the son of Judge Fanning, and since—to be fair—he had the kind of balance and maturity of mind which can sometimes make brilliance look foolish, he had a secure and certain career before him. In June, after graduation, he would go as clerk to one of the important law shops. In ten years he would be a junior partner, there or somewhere else. In twenty years his name might very well be in the firm. In thirty years he might be a judge himself.

And all the time, thought Nina, he will be happy! This is just what he wants to do! Not, she was sure, that it was a bad career for Stuart; but she could not understand how he could plan it all—accept others' planning, really—and then go ahead and do it without worrying about what he was missing! To be brought up to be a lawyer and then to go and *be* a lawyer, without ever rebelling, or lusting after strange gods of other pursuits, this seemed to Nina so strange as to be almost inhuman. And yet Stuart was human—kind, thoughtful, patient, reasonably intelligent—in spite of this queer quality of acceptance of his life. Of natural acceptance, of cheerful equanimity. Nothing within Stuart would spring out at the wrong moment to make jest of his professors, to speak rudely to a prospective employer or important client, to tangle his feet.

And I, thought Nina, can be his wife and help his career, be charming to senior partners and dutiful to their wives and never, never, say anything mean or rude or unkind! And how should she manage that?

She sat down on the bed and switched off the lamp. The light from the hall lay across the floor. The half-country smells of this garden-rich part of the city came in at the open window. She stared at the future she had been conjuring up for herself. Stuart's wife, Stuart's helpmeet. She would always be proper—and how should she manage that? There would be healthy children to raise, a house in the suburbs (a cut above Mr. Daniels') with a modern kitchen and a living room out of *House Beautiful*. Everything she imagined looked like photographs she had already seen. Ersatz, she thought. Strictly ersatz. And her heart swelled up within her, beating as if it wanted to suffocate her before it released itself and her to this artificial prison, this reasonable facsimile of life, which her vengeful imagination pictured as marriage to Stuart.

Be quiet, she told herself. What is the other choice, if I don't marry him? But this was really frightening. Everything grew fluid and wavered. Years of listening to Mr. Daniels. Of riding the subway. Of going to parties as if she were going on a border foray, always an eye open for the right young man, the bright young man, the man who would laugh at her jokes and know what she was talking about, the wary, neurotic young man who would take her to bed but not to church and leave her to clench her fists and cry at torch songs. One of the denizens of the desert, the natural fauna of Kermit's jungle—except that he would be stupider and less successful than Kermit because he would not realize it was a jungle. He would expect laws and would be puzzled when there were none. He would want terribly to be understood and approved of, he would expect to be comforted by Nina. Send the tigers away, he would ask her. Then, when she could not, he would hate her and hurt her, calling her ungrateful, striking out at her for being woman, more than man, less than mother——

"Nina!" called Stuart.

Nina heaved herself up off the bed, turned on the light and blinked down at her suitcase. Toothbrush, cold cream, she had almost forgotten both. She added handkerchiefs, brushed her hair quickly and dropped the brush in, and shut the bag. She walked out to the stairs feeling curiously numb, as if this were some very important occasion. She had been of two minds about Stuart for over a year now, and she tried to tell herself that it was absurd for her to feel as if his voice had interrupted her at, and at the same time brought her to, a point of decision. Yet she felt this numbness, the kind that precedes stage fright.

Coming down the stairs, she looked searchingly at the top of Stuart's head. He was struggling into an old trench coat to which he was deeply attached—it would be almost worth marrying him, she thought, to be able to make him get a new coat and give that one to the Bureau of Charity. This is Stuart, she said to herself, pausing at

the turn and watching him, trying to imagine that she had never
seen him before, trying to deduce what a stranger would know of
him and she never, the shape of Stuart in the world. He was a little
clumsy—not really awkward, but with none of Kermit's easy economy of movement. He used more power than he needed, thrusting
his fist down the sleeve of his coat. Was there, then, something a
little heavy-handed, something a little brutal, under Stuart's good
nature? Thinking this, she remembered again his coarse incomprehensible mirth, and felt suddenly cold up the spine. Could it be that
she didn't know Stuart at all?

He turned then and saw her, and came over to the foot of the
stairs. Nina was conscious of a desire to retreat, she felt as if danger
waited with Stuart in the hall below, and for a moment she faltered.
Then she said sternly to herself, This is very neurotic behavior!
Kermit must have upset me; and she went firmly downstairs,
greeted Stuart with a friendly and rather smacking kiss, and went
into the living room to say good-by.

"When will you be home?" asked Mrs. Bishop.

"Sunday. But don't expect me for a meal. If we come down in the
afternoon we'll get a bite somewhere when we get back. If the
weather's good we won't be home till evening."

"Give my love to Janey Fanning—Janey Cushman, I mean."

"She wants you and Uncle Van to come up. She keeps asking me."

"Well, we will someday." Mrs. Bishop sounded comfortably in
possession of a future in which everything was possible, capacious
enough to hold all the activities anyone might suggest.

"Come on, Nina," said Stuart. "Good night, Mrs. Bishop, Mr. Van
Deusen. So long, Marion."

"Take good care of my little girl!" said Mrs. Bishop in an extra
rush of maternity.

"Mother!" cried Nina, shocked.

"I will," said Stuart. Nina glared at him, and they went out.

Stuart put Nina's bag in the luggage compartment—his car was
pre-rumble-seat—and came around to get in. Nina, sitting and biting
her lip in irritation and indecision, saw a figure come up the street
toward them. Under the street lamp it became Kermit. He walked
wearily, hunched forward, his schoolbooks under one arm pulling

his shoulders uneven. He didn't look up until he came opposite them, and then he jumped a bit as the car gave a hysterical little scream and cough and began to shake to the rhythm of the motor. He peered over at them and Stuart said, "Hi there." He was not fond of Kermit and there was no warmth in his voice.

"Hullo?" said Kermit, came over to the car and stuck his head in. "Oh—hello, Stuart, I should have recognized your magic carpet by ear. Hello, Neen. You off somewhere?"

"Cos Cob for the week end."

"Oh? Have fun."

To Stuart his tone sounded neutral, but Nina found herself provoked into answering indignantly, "We're staying with Stuart's sister."

"Naturally," said Kermit. His eyes were darting around the inside of the car as if he were looking for the bait in a trap. Yet he leaned on the door, apparently reluctant to go. He can't want to come along, can he? thought Nina.

Before she knew what she was doing she said, "Do you want to come?"

The measure of Stuart's consternation was that the engine choked and died as his foot fell off the gas pedal. He said nothing, but in the astonished silence he didn't need to.

"That sounds delightful," said Kermit. "I'd love to."

Nina swallowed and said, "Of course we'll be sailing all week end, and I don't know how much room——"

"Oh don't worry about me," said Kermit cheerfully. "I'm always glad to join in the fun and games. Don't take up much room, either. Yes, I'd love to come. It's a shame I've got a date tomorrow and can't."

Stuart stepped on the starter again. The motor was ruffled now, however, and coughed and spat indignantly.

"It was awfully kind of you to ask me," said Kermit. "I certainly appreciate it. Perhaps I might manage it another time."

"We won't be sailing any more after this," said Nina nervously.

"Well, sailing, hiking, any good sport, I like them all. Or just stimulating conversation beside the roaring fire while the storm howls outside. It's a fine way to spend a week end." The engine settled down to its business, Stuart shifted gears, Kermit stood back and said, "So long, have a good time." He sounded, Nina thought, both tired and lonely. It was, she knew, absurd to have compunctions about Kermit. Pity provoked him to heights of outrageous behavior beyond even *his* normal capacity. But she found herself repeating that most futile wish in the world—If only he were different!

"You know," she said, "I think he almost wanted to come!"

Stuart grunted.

"Don't be angry," said Nina, hardly believing her ears. Stuart angry! "He really had no intention of coming at all."

"I'm not angry," said Stuart, very vexed. Nina was really astounded. Stuart, who never lost his temper, had lost it. "Only it was a damn-fool thing to do."

"Then I'm a damn fool."

Stuart ignored this. "Suppose he had come?"

"He was just teasing. He had no intention——"

"I know, I know, I heard you. But you weren't so sure yourself, there, for a while. You sounded scared. Suppose he *had* had the intention? You didn't know——"

"He just looked so lonesome," said Nina meekly. Stuart's anger awed her, it was so unfamiliar.

"Lonesome!"

"And tired!"

"Tired!"

"All right!" A second ago Nina had been meek. Now her anger came up like a geyser. "Suppose he had come! Would that have been so awful? He's funny and amusing and my brother and I don't see why he shouldn't come! Suppose he had?"

Stuart folded his lips and was resolutely silent. The car turned onto the boulevard that would take them downtown and to Manhattan.

"He can get along with people," said Nina. "You don't like him, and so you won't believe it, but lots of people like Kermit very much! You have this prejudice and you don't see——"

"He's a stinker!" said Stuart, pressed beyond human endurance. "You know you don't like him yourself."

"No I don't! I mean I don't know it! I find Kermit very— very——"

"Oh shut up!" shouted Stuart. Then he clamped his lips shut and wouldn't say another word, appalled at how he had lost his temper. Nina shook herself and retired to her corner to sulk. Brooklyn rolled by, the traffic lights changed, held them up, released them, and neither spoke.

How childish, how childish, Nina was thinking. How can two grown people behave like this! Stuart's anger was upsetting. It did not simply provoke her on. She wanted to end the situation. She wriggled in her corner and tried to think of something to say, but it was difficult to think of something which would at once appease Stuart and leave her, Nina, in the right—— Everything that occurred to her began with an apology, and she was not going to apologize!

They reached the bridge to Manhattan and the car panted up onto the top drive. The wind came down the river with a real autumn chill to it. Kermit's jungle drew closer, waiting to receive them, the honeycomb city with its tall flasks of light. It will be winter soon, thought Nina, and found herself desolate. I hate the cold, I hate it, she thought; ice on the gritty pavements, the wind off the bay when I come home at night in the darkness, it will be dark then. Oh why, why isn't there a place for me, a warm rich place, far away from the cold!

> *Oh love, how utterly am I bereaved*
> *By Time, who sucks the honey of our days,*
> *Sets sickle to our Aprils, and betrays*
> *To killing winter all the sun achieved!*
> *Our parted spirits are perplexed and grieved——**

Only, she went on thinking, I have no love to be saying that to, no one bound up with me, woven into me as Elinor Wylie must have had—or was she imagining too? I have never been in love, never, never! Stuart is nothing, a pillar, a statue. Where is the living man? The enchanter? But in all the great city to which they now descended, there was no one.

"Would you like a cigarette?" asked Stuart abruptly.

"Thank you," said Nina coldly, "I have some of my own." They rode on.

*Reprinted from *Collected Poems of Elinor Wylie* by permission of Alfred A. Knopf, Inc. Copyright, 1929, 1932 by Alfred A. Knopf, Inc.

They got to Janey Cushman's after ten o'clock, and Nina had a highball, talked to Janey about slip covers and listened to her on the subject of children, smiled at Howard Cushman and went to bed without exchanging a word with Stuart. But she woke up Saturday morning ashamed of herself, resolved to be kind and affectionate all day—in fact, from then on. Perhaps everyone who had told her that she was a young romantic fool had been right. Why should she not try mere pleasant settled affection? She lay in bed attempting to hypnotize herself into behaving properly by the application of Dr. Coué's methods, which had made a deep impression on her as a child. "Every day in every way I will be nicer to Stuart," she muttered to herself. The house was still. A little breeze off the Manus River wafted a scent of tidal flats and salt mud into the room. The sun made up its mind and came up briskly. "I will be nicer to Stuart," whispered Nina, screwing up her face in concentration.

The doorknob turned, the door creaked. Nina opened her eyes, her magic formulae silenced on her lips. Arthur Francis Cushman, aged six and a half, hung on the doorknob and said tentatively, "Hullo."

Nina turned on her side. "Hello, Arthur."

"I have a turtle," said Arthur.

"How nice!"

"Would you like to see it?"

"Very much. When I——"

"Here," said Arthur kindly, and put a turtle about three inches long on Nina's bed.

Nina's shriek was really very small, and her leap merely carried her out onto the floor. When Janey and Stuart appeared together, she was on her knees apologizing to Arthur and helping him look under the bed for the turtle, who had been quite as surprised as Nina at the turn of events.

"I'm terribly sorry," said Nina, "it was just that I wasn't expecting it. There he is, Arthur. Have you got an aquarium for him? I'm sure he wants to rest and be quiet."

"Young man," said his mother, "that turtle's going right outside now. You know what I said."

"No!" said Arthur. "You can't take him!" He put the turtle in his pocket and kept his hand on it.

"Look," said Stuart, kneeling down too. "He'll be happier outside. He doesn't like it in your pocket."

"Yes he does," said Arthur.

"Turtles don't."

"This one does. He likes me."

"It isn't healthy for him. He needs fresh air."

"No he doesn't. He's an amphibian."

At this evidence of erudition on the part of her young, Janey Cushman softened. "Well, go take him somewhere else," she said. "Give him a swim in your washbasin. Anyway, you shouldn't wake up Nina at only seven o'clock."

"I'm sorry, Nina," said Arthur, and went away.

"So say we all," said Janey. "Of course I'm besotted about him, but he shouldn't do that. Well—can you sleep again? Or do you want to have breakfast and start early? With any kind of a wind, we might get over to Cold Spring or Lloyds Neck and picnic there."

"Frankly, I'd rather stay up. Somehow that bed doesn't seem quite the same, though I know it was a very small turtle and quite tame. Don't tell Howard. Arthur didn't mean to scare me. I knew as soon as I screeched that I didn't need to, and tried to stop. But it's awfully hard to do it. Have you ever tried to stop in the middle of a scream?"

"I can't say I have. Don't you think it would be a good idea to get Arthur a puppy? Howard says he isn't old enough, but good heavens, wouldn't you rather have a puppy than a turtle in bed with you?"

"Well, to tell you the truth——"

"She'd rather have neither," said Stuart sternly to his sister. "Arthur's spoiled and you know it. All right, we're all up, let's have breakfast, old girl. Can we fix it ourselves? We'll be a lot quicker than Nellie, the beautiful Mother's Helper."

"She's looking after the baby now, anyway. But I'll——"

"I'll be right down to help," said Nina. "Au revoir." There's one thing to be said for children with turtles, she thought, splashing cold water on her face. They do wake you up thoroughly. Besides, she discovered later, Arthur had been sufficiently abashed to put up only a token resistance when his elders went sailing and left him behind with his baby sister and Nellie. He howled once, his mother paused to look distracted, her husband took her by the arm and walked her firmly off, and Arthur was left to search for another turtle.

It was a beautiful day. The Cushmans' boat, *Amalie,* was a twenty-four-foot sloop, too small for anything but day-sailing, but solid and broad enough in the beam to wallow safely across the Sound. On this sparkling morning, she did more than wallow, she almost flew. Nina lay out forward on the windward side, snuggled against the low roof of the cabin. The voice of the water and the wind surrounded her, shielded her, from the voices of her friends back in the cockpit. The sun, in its last access of strength, was hot on her back, her arm, her cheek. The deck smelled of paint and brass polish and salt water. Long Island, just a smudge on the horizon when they started, was now definitely a line of dunes.

This is the rate of speed at which people ought to travel, thought Nina idly. This, and oxcart. Oh, horseback maybe, for emergencies. Nobody needs to go faster than that. Why should they? What news could possibly be important enough to be spread faster than drums and smoke signals can carry it? What reason can make people want to go faster than this, live on top of each other, spend their lives crowded together in offices to put out nonsense like *Godey's?* Nothing sensible. Nothing but making money, and what a lot of idiocy that is! She felt estranged, oppressed, by the whole modern world, by the generation of men who had striven so madly to make money and ended by throwing twenty millions of their fellow citizens out of work and into apathy and despair. Even the methods that the New Deal was using to try to remedy the situation seemed elaborate and insane fantasies to Nina. Why shouldn't people who needed food just go and take food? Why shouldn't the acreage being plowed under yield its abundance to the poor and all Marion's little pigs live to be bacon? Any woman could see that men were just making trouble for themselves—trying to patch up the world with their eyes still shut, muttering about Profits and Assets and Property Values and all the other sterile gods of her Uncle Van's hierarchy of heaven. For goodness' sake, she thought—but thought lazily, for the sun was warm and soothing—for goodness' sake, why don't they forget about all that nonsense and just do things simply and sensibly, see that

64

people get fed? All the apparatus of living, she thought, that's what I hate. It gets in the way so. It's such a waste of time.

Now, if Stuart had a boat like this and a little house that we had built together with our own hands and maybe a little help from our neighbors on one of those points back there, if he fished and I raised a vegetable garden—well now, that's a sensible way to live, and so much to do we'd never worry about romance. Why didn't we stop back there a hundred or more years ago? She sighed, trying to nestle closer to simplicity, to the golden age, by rubbing her cheek on the deck. Don't forget, said her intelligence acidly, that you would bear approximately thirteen children without benefit of anesthetic, if civilization had stopped back there; and if half of them lived to grow up, you'd be lucky. Yes, I know, said Nina's emotions to her mind, I know. I'd have been very uncomfortable and possibly dead, but this way I'm not anything, not anything at all. All my bright talk, all my fine activity, doesn't mean a thing. I could drop out of the world and what would happen? A girl who needed it more would get my job, my family would be sorry, and that's absolutely all the difference it would make. Here I am, with all this time and education invested in me, and all the ideas marching around in my brain—and every single bit of me is useless! Just think, for instance, of all the meals that I'll eat, for the rest of my life. Think of that mountain of food, tons of food, piled up and waiting, that I'll have to eat my way through just to keep my body going while it gets older and older and less able and less attractive, until someday it lies down and dies, poor thing. Why, it makes you sick to think of it! Food! Ugh!

"Coming about, Nina!" called Howard Cushman, and Nina, startled, raised her head and then ducked quickly as the boom swung over. Her reverie had been disturbed, and she lay now in the shadow of the sail, while the new tilt of the deck was unfamiliar. She slid back to the cockpit and to human companionship and spent the rest of the day remembering her vows of the morning and striving to be kind and affectionate. She was as successful as one usually is in such efforts.

Coming home was much more exciting—and uncomfortable— than the morning's sail. The wind had freshened and swung into the northwest and the *Amalie* groaned her way back across the Sound in a series of long tacks. The sun lost its heat and dropped fast, and the dusk caught them still offshore. They beat into harbor at last, cold and wet and hungry, got the sails down and made all fast in a kind of sullen confusion of wet lashings, recalcitrant fastenings and broken fingernails. Nina's hands were so cold that they felt like independent creatures. She watched them trying to untie a knot which they couldn't manage, and she could not help them at all, no thunderbolt from her brain could stop their fumbling. Driving back to the house, she huddled against Stuart, in the back of the Cushmans' car, for sheer physical warmth, though she knew that their quarrel was not over. In spite of all her efforts at sweetness and light, she had not actually intended that it should be over. She had simply desired to impress everyone with the charm of her character, while abating not one jot of her hurt dignity. Only it was too cold and she was too tired to maintain her distance! Common sense, her better nature, or both were having their way with her.

"There's a dance at the club," said Janey, lighting the fire in the living room while Howard got out ice for a cocktail. "Do you want to go? It's the last of the season."

"Murder, no," said Nina, huddling over the flame long before any heat could come from it. "Anyway, I didn't bring a long dress. But you go, Janey. All of you go. I'll get into bed and read my unspeakable manuscripts. Incidentally, if you want to let Nellie go to the movies, I can give the baby her ten o'clock bottle."

"She doesn't get a ten o'clock bottle any more," said Janey smugly, "not for two weeks. But do come, Nina. You can wear something of mine."

Nina, letting Janey's wardrobe run through her head, refused again. "All I want is the fire and bed," she said. "Just to be warm again! Besides, I'm tired. I'd probably fall over in the middle of the floor if I tried to dance."

"Nonsense," said Howard, handing her a glass, "this will fix you up. Tell her to come, Stuart. You know—last dance, and everything. It'll be good. Everyone will be there."

"She doesn't have to go if she doesn't want to," said Stuart calmly. "What's this? A manhattan?"

"Sure it is," said Howard defensively. "That's real bonded rye, Louis says. Now that repeal's coming, you can get better stuff."

Stuart grunted. "Not from Louis."

"It tastes fine to me," said Nina hastily. "What do you suppose all the bootleggers will do now? Why, there'll be another million unemployed."

"But Nina," said Janey, "I sort of thought we'd *eat* at the club, getting back late like this and all. I—I really don't have much in the house for dinner—if you don't want to come. Why don't you come over for a while, anyway, and then if you——"

"That's all right, Janey, now, never mind," said Stuart. "There are other places to eat than the club. Do you want to find a dog-wagon, Nina? Or if you feel like going up to Dorlon's we can get a shore dinner."

Nina opened her mouth to say, impatiently, that all she wanted was a sandwich which she could fix for herself; but she realized that Stuart's affectionate responsibility and Janey's ingrained notion of hospitality would combine to keep her from doing any such thing. If she kept on trying to be no trouble at all she would make a real nuisance of herself. "The dog-wagon sounds fine, Stu," she said. "Wait till I get warm, and I'll change into a skirt and we'll go."

Janey was still protesting when Nina and Stuart started off in his ancient car for the Post Road and a dog-wagon. Autumn had come all at once, the wind had an edge to it. Usually Nina loved the fall. It always felt like the real beginning of the year. But her mind kept turning now to the desolate months of winter and cold that lay ahead. Her mood of uselessness and fatality came back and, riding beside silent Stuart, she felt herself, her hopes, her intentions, sink into a swamp of insignificance and futility.

Stuart turned off the road and stopped by a diner. "This look all right, baby?" he asked her.

"I suppose so," Nina said. Then before she knew she was going to do it, she heard her voice go on, "No, it looks awful, it looks terrible, but everything's terrible, so what does it matter? Oh I'm unhappy, I'm so unhappy! What am I going to do? What am I ever going to do?"

By this time Stuart was rocking her in his arms and asking, "What

is it? What is it? What's the trouble, baby? For God's sake tell me!
What's the matter?"

"I don't know, I don't know," sobbed Nina. "Just the human
situation, I guess. We're all in cages, aren't we? In solitary cells?
What am I going to do?"

"But I'm here," said Stuart, "I'm right here. And I love you." He
tried to kiss her, but her lips were cold and slack and her eyes
stared over his shoulder at the ugly little roadhouse with its neon
sign, at the gasoline pumps in front of the service station across the
road. She felt as if she were lost in a wilderness of ugliness and
nastiness. The desert had come into the oasis after her. Everything
was sullenly hostile or reluctantly indifferent to her, so that nothing
would answer to her touch—all knives would cut her, all bulky barri-
cades would move, after infinite labor, to her gross and mortal in-
jury. In this gray and dusty country Stuart's words of comfort
flapped about her head like crows and ravens. She ignored him, she
concentrated on her journey into limbo. The wind blew, she
shivered.

Stuart, by now, was distressed but not frightened. Emotions,
troubles of that kind, did not upset him. He was sympathetic, not
callous at all; but his own internal stability was so secure that he was
untouched by the fear of experiencing, himself, the desolation
which he pitied. If the times were out of joint, Stuart did not aspire
to set them right. He knew that they had been dislocated before and
that people had got along and patched things up and gone on with
their business, and this he could and would do, in his turn. Stuart did
not draw back from suffering, for it was not a disease which he
feared to catch. He had never, in fact, been infected with it, it might
well be that he was immune. He was therefore much, much kinder
than would have been anyone who had wandered with Nina
through her lonesome hell. Her unhappiness was something with
which he must, and could, deal. Something had upset her, no doubt,
but he knew that she was temperamental and sensitive, and the last
thing he wanted was to make her go back over whatever had disturbed her and tell him about it. Stuart had no opinion of psychoanalysis and soul-searching, he thought such things morbid. Something had upset Nina, but it had upset her in a very general, almost

an abstract way. The things she was saying about human loneliness were things Stuart had heard and read before. People felt that way from time to time, he knew, and when they did, you couldn't argue with them. He had learned that in his sophomore year at Harvard, when a friend of his had first threatened to hang himself, then made the swmming team and turned into an entirely different person. You just had to get them over their feelings, and when they stopped being unhappy and frightened, they would stop crying out about the agonizing loneliness of the human situation. Nina was saying nothing about any specific problem which could be taken up by itself and dealt with; so that action was not called for, but only comfort.

Except that Stuart, with the crying girl in his arms, began to think that perhaps one specific form of action would be the best—perhaps the only—way to comfort Nina. She needs to be made love to, thought Stuart seriously. She's all jangled up about that, poor kid. She wouldn't have said that the other night if she wasn't all mixed up about it. I guess I shouldn't have got mad at her. She wouldn't talk that way if she knew what she was talking about. Only where can I take her? He cursed the chilly air and the homeless state which civilization imposes upon the young. The autumn fields, the autumn beaches, were inhospitable; and back at Janey's was Arthur Francis Cushman, turtle fancier, his little sister and nurse. Nina was quieting in his arms and he felt that if he did not do something, decide something at once, she would fall back into apathy and depression. He wanted to reach her now, when she needed him.

At that moment the idea came to him as it does to the denizens of comic strips. He felt as if an electric light bulb had been turned on over his head. He released Nina and said, "You don't want to go in that diner, but you don't want to starve either. I'll go in and get some sandwiches and coffee and we'll take them somewhere and eat them."

"All right," said Nina indifferently. She felt cold and lonesome— more lonesome—without Stuart's arms around her, her head rolled limply on the back of the seat. "Can you lend me a handkerchief?" Stuart produced one. "Where could we go to eat?" she said. "I can't go in anyplace with my face like this."

"How about taking the stuff down to the boat?" Stuart spoke very carefully, and his tone was consequently so wooden and unemotional that, after he had gone, Nina became suspicious of it. What does he want to go down to the boat for? she thought. He has something up his sleeve! But preventing her from jumping to the obvious and correct conclusion was Stuart's laughter of the earlier night and her bitter hurt over it. It seemed to her that he had rejected her then almost contemptuously. So she would not think about—about what she had suggested and he had laughed at. She would avoid the whole subject. Sex! People thought too much about it! It was a shibboleth, a cliché, everything had to be tied up to sex nowadays, which was surely just as narrow-minded as Puritanism had been in the other direction! And Nina indignantly thought about sex herself in this condemnatory way until she grew warm and stopped shivering; until the sight of Stuart coming out of the diner with two paper bags made her feel rather queer.

He climbed in beside her silently. She took the bags. They drove down toward the water. Nina felt as if she ought to say something to prove that no suspicion, no idea of sex, had entered her head; but she could not think of a remark that would convey this clearly, and only this. As they stopped by the dock she said instead, "How can we get inside, though? Isn't the cabin locked?"

"I locked it," said Stuart simply, "and forgot to give Howard the key. Can you get into the dinghy all right with the food? Don't drop the sandwiches! I've got the oars." He dropped into the dinghy after her and started to row out to where the *Amalie* swung at her mooring, looking over his shoulder as he sculled so that his head was turned away from Nina. It was late in the season, too cold for parties on any of the yachts. Everyone who sailed was at the dance and the boats were deserted. What a funny thing for me to be doing! thought Nina, looking at Stuart's profile.

When they reached the *Amalie,* Stuart pulled the oars into the dinghy, climbed aboard, and helped Nina up. She stood in the autumn air, hugging the coffee containers to her breast for warmth. Stuart made the dinghy fast, moving silently in his sneakers, before the keys jangled in his hand and he was unlocking the door to the cabin. "All right," he said, and Nina ducked past him down into the

70

dark. She found the table forward and put the packages on it. Stuart was doing something behind her, groping around. She heard a cupboard open. It suddenly became a matter of the utmost importance whether he was going to light the lamp. She waited in the dark. He came closer to her. He had her in his arms and said into her ear, "Take off your dress."

Nina could find nothing better to say than, "I'll be cold."

"No you won't," said Stuart.

Later Nina tried to identify the exact moment when she fell in love with Stuart. But it was very difficult to do. At the time it came to her as a message from the past. She was remembering something. She was remembering being in love with Stuart before. She felt as if a curtain had been rolled back, pulled back, and light and warmth flooded into her world. She could see, she could see so much further! She could see a world of beauty and order and joy! But I've been here, she thought, I've been here before! I've loved Stuart before this!

A mounting wave of memory swung her back ten years, back to where she had been eleven and he fourteen. For months she had dogged his footsteps, invaded by an emotion so huge and solid that it had been accepted as fact by everyone, leaving no room for embarrassment. Nina was beyond embarrassment, she had simply gone everywhere that Stuart went if it was in any way possible. Stuart, not being given to embarrassment, had been kind to her, and as long as Stuart was kind, his contemporaries had put up with her and even contrived to make her usful. When they played football they let her referee. When they played baseball she had been a permanent outfielder for both teams. When Stuart went somewhere without her, she rode her bicycle up and down in front of his house until he returned. Once she had attempted to impress him by riding "no hands." When she had seen him coming up the block, returning from some activity where even the ingenuity and persistence of monomania had not contrived to make her welcome, she had let go of the handle bars and ridden toward him, beaming. Unfortunately the wheel had turned and she had ridden right up the curb and fallen off into the gutter. Stuart had picked her up and taken her in to be patched up with gauze and iodine. "Well, Nina, you're quite a tomboy," Mrs. Fanning had said on this occasion, and Nina had hated her for a long time afterward. Why, I've been in love with Stuart for ten years, just like a nice old married couple, thought Nina. Lying in the darkness on the bunk in the *Amalie's* cabin, surrounded by a faint odor of kerosene, she began to laugh.

"Oh my darling," said Stuart, "are you happy?"

"Yes," said Nina. "I've never been so happy in my life. I'll never be unhappy again."

"Do you love me?"

"Why, I've loved you forever." Then they were silent, because that was naturally all that Stuart needed to know, and for Nina, who had moved into Stuart's world, it was also enough, then. The moments streamed slowly by, while Nina lay in glory. The *Amalie* swung at her mooring, little waves lapped at her hull. Nina heard them dreamily, they were like the waves of sleep that lapped at her content. And all the time, she thought, this was waiting for me! Her whole life was irradiated now, Stuart and love cast a golden glow back over everything. The path she had followed had had this for its goal, and was thus itself enchanted. I have a new life, thought Nina. Stuart took the old one away and gave me this instead. It looks the same from the outside, but it isn't.

"Do you remember?" she said at last (how wonderful to talk in the dark, to be sure of an answer!), "the time when I fell off my bicycle in the gutter in front of your house?"

"You were always falling off your bike," said Stuart, unperturbed by the introduction of this peculiar subject. "Can you ride yet?"

"Nonsense, of course I can. This time was important, though."

"Was it?"

"Yes. I remember it. Stuart!"

"Uh-huh?"

"Why did you laugh at me the other night? You must remember that!"

"Well—see, the way you said it—it was foolish. I wasn't going to rape you! I love you! Why should you have to be raped? I wasn't going to hurt you or force you or frighten you! And I didn't think you should think that way. It was a hell of a thing to call it! What do you think I am? I love you."

"And I sounded as if I was frightened and expected to be hurt."

"Yes, and as if—as if I'd turned into somebody else, a stranger. As if loving you that way would be different from the way I do love you. As if it was just an act, an event, and I was just a guy, and maybe it would be good medicine if you got it over with."

"Oh."

"It made me mad. Afterwards I thought, well, hell, you were a little frightened and you didn't know what you were talking about, you didn't mean it that way. But then I thought—— Hell, then I thought, Rape her, by God, she can damn well ask for it before I'll—— Well, you see what I mean. I'm sorry, baby, that wasn't very polite."

"I'll forgive you," said Nina, the new Nina. "Especially since you changed your mind."

"Are you glad I changed my mind?"

"Do you have to know everything?"

"Mmhm."

"I'm glad. Oh Stuart, oh Stu, I'm glad."

"Well, so am I," said Stuart comfortably.

After a while Nina said, "Listen, it's raining. Oh my! The next voice you hear will be that of my stomach announcing it's hungry."

"You want a sandwich?" Stuart got up and groped around in the dark. They ate the sandwiches they had brought, huddled on the edge of the bunk together and giggling. The coffee was ice-cold, they dropped the containers overboard. Then they rowed back through the rain and Nina, lifting her head, thought that even the air was new and that the rain fell with the quality of mercy, dropping on her face like a blessing.

It seemed strange to be coming back to the house, but Janey and Howard were not home yet, Arthur and his pets slept, everything was still. Stuart walked her upstairs with his arm around her waist and kissed her good night at her door. She took a bath, looking at her body with wonder as she washed it, and then fell dreamlessly asleep.

It rained the next day. Nina woke at first light and heard it happily, for its gentle monotony seemed to tie last night's joyful content to this morning. Not that she was awake enough to remember everything, but only that something wonderful had happened, a promise had come true. In the rain. It was raining still. Far off a church bell called for early mass through the rainy air, crying across the miles to Nina's ears, True! It's true, true! She curled herself tighter beneath the covers and slept, smiling, while the rain came down.

Even when she woke the day was like a dream. It did not seem to her that she had changed (though she would have admitted that that was the rational way to put it), but that she was the same and the world was different. It was a world in which she was much freer than she had been in the old one. She did not have to think before she spoke and she could act much more spontaneously. It was like— well, it was like what the astronomers said about living on the moon. The force of gravity was so much less that you could jump eighteen feet without even trying. Nina felt just like that, so light, so free, nothing was difficult.

It was a very quiet day, but there was one queer thing about it— its time was not uniform. The minutes and hours speeded up and slowed down in the strangest way. When Nina came downstairs (hurrying, hurrying, and yet reluctant too), when she came down about ten she thought first there was no one around at all, and then she heard Stuart's voice in the living room. He said, "Bang! Bang, bang!"

Nina stopped in the doorway. Stuart was in an armchair, his nephew sat on his lap, they were reading the funnies together. "Take that," said Stuart solemnly, and Arthur echoed, "Bang, bang!" Then Stuart looked up.

And time slowed down until it almost stopped. She was drowning in his eyes. She was melting inside. She put her hand on the door-frame to steady herself, she was sure she would have fallen without it.

"Hello," said Stuart. "Did you sleep?"

"Hello." It was almost impossible to form the word. She concentrated. The world grew up again around her, her dizziness receded. "Yes, I slept like a top."

"Coffee's on the stove," said Stuart. "Orange juice in the ice box.

Nellie's at church, I'm the nursery maid. Janey and Howard haven't been heard from. Must have been quite a party. If you'll wait till we finish Dick Tracy I'll fry you some eggs."

"Nonsense, I'll fry them!" The dizziness was gone, she was up at the moon again, light as a cork on the surface of time. She felt like dancing, she was sure she could cross the living room in a grand jeté of incredible elevation. Out in the kitchen, in a laughing dream, she actually had a skillet out and on the stove before it occurred to her that she didn't want fried eggs in the least. She put juice, coffee and a bun on a tray and carried it into the living room.

"That all you want?" said Stuart. "Arthur eats more than that, don't you, Tonto? *You'll* never grow up."

"She'll grow down!" said Arthur, and was stricken with enormous mirth.

"I'm finished," said Nina. "I don't want me to grow any more. I want everything just the way it is now."

Stuart's eyes found hers, she felt herself quake. "Oh," he said, "we might take a few little changes, get married, maybe."

"Are you going to marry Nina?" Arthur asked, pausing in his laughter.

"If she can catch me."

"She'd better eat more then. Else she'll grow down!" He burst out again, this was a wonderful joke.

"Hush," said Stuart, "you'll wake up your poor overhung mother. Now listen. Here's the posse, see, and here's the bad guys, and here's Tonto sneaking up. Now when he fires twice the Lone Ranger'll hear him and then——" He went on with the interminable legend and Nina sipped her coffee and watched him across the edge of the cup and dodged his eyes and felt like a cat with a saucer of cream. And it rained and rained and rained.

They started home about five o'clock, from an afternoon when Nina dozed over her manuscripts, Stuart and Howard wrangled about football and Janey tried to get them to play bridge. No one except Howard played bridge very much and Howard did not want to play with Janey, he played austerely on the club car of the commuters' train and that was all the bridge he desired. Nina's new mood of loving-kindness broke down at Janey. She was perfectly happy to join the men's silent conspiracy to frustrate Janey's plans. I don't belong to Janey's world, I belong to Stuart's, she felt smugly; I will never never become a wife who wants to play bridge when her husband doesn't. Stuart and I are one person and will always want the same thing. Janey was reduced to playing dominoes with Arthur, and so distractedly that Arthur won every game and crowed in incessant triumph. This at last got on even Stuart's nerves and he stood up and said they were leaving.

"But don't you want supper?" said Janey indignantly. "And it's pouring rain. You know the roof of that awful car leaks. You'll get soaked."

"It isn't going to stop raining. I'd just as soon get soaked now and get it over with. Come on, Nina. Are you packed?"

"Just about." Nina sat up. "I'll put these manuscripts in and bring my bag down."

"I'll come up and get it," Stuart said.

"I bet Nina would rather stay for supper than starve and soak," said Janey.

"We'd better go now," said Nina without even looking at Stuart.

"Hmm," said Janey viciously. "*You're* docile enough all of a sudden. What's happened?"

"I'm always docile," said Nina lightly, and it was true, for her "always" began with last night, now, and was projected into the future. The past had nothing to do with it. She went upstairs. Stuart followed her and in her room took her in his arms.

"Oh Nina," he said into her hair. "You're all right, you're really all right, you love me?"

"I love you," said Nina. They clung together, hearing the rain against the window in the beginning of dusk.

"Oh Nina," said Stuart.

"Have you got everything?" Janey called up the stairs greedily, and then they could hear her feet on the treads. "Nina, I'm going to give you an umbrella, you can hold it over you in the car——"

"Oh my God!" said Stuart. "Will you for God's sake stop fussing? We aren't going to melt!"

"Yes but——" Janey began.

"Nina doesn't want an umbrella!" Stuart met Janey in the doorway, glaring in absolute fury. Janey looked from one to the other of them.

"Oh very well," she said, and leaned against the doorjamb, humming. Stuart thrust his hands in his pockets and stood immobile. Nina threw odds and ends hastily into her suitcase and closed it as quickly as she could. Stuart took it and they started downstairs. Janey vanished for a moment and then they heard her behind them. "I'm just putting your toothbrushes in Stuart's kit," she called. "Here it is." She clattered down after them, smiling in triumph.

"Thanks," said Stuart sullenly.

"Thank you so much, Janey," said Nina hastily. "I had a lovely time."

"I'm so glad," said Janey. "You must come again soon."

Howard's and Arthur's farewells were warmer, but they pushed their way through them and got out to the car, which was indeed wet. Stuart produced an old Army blanket from the back and spread it over the seat, first brushing a puddle or two off onto the floor. At that moment Howard appeared and said, "Here—in case you need them. So long." He handed Stuart some sailing slickers.

"Well——" said Stuart doubtfully. He put a sou'wester on and handed another to Nina, who began to laugh incontinently.

"We look—like—'Elsie Darling'—or someone out of O'Neill's one-act plays," she gasped. But she bundled her slicker on and climbed in, and Stuart, after a moment, grunted and followed suit. The car was sullen about starting. "She doesn't like to work on the Sabbath," said Nina.

"Or any other time," said Stuart, but he got it going at last and they rolled out of the drive and set off for home. The rain streamed down the windshield and dribbled through the roof and the peculiar odor of inhabited slickers pervaded the atmosphere. Nina leaned against Stuart's shoulder and, out of a full heart, sang all the way home.

"Are you hungry?" he asked her once, tenderly. "I'll take you to the Ritz, if you want."

"We'd make a deep impression," said Nina. "Mr. and Mrs. Stuart Fanning of Brooklyn and Fulton Fish Market——"

"This is so sudden," said Stuart, and stopped the car. Nina's sou'wester fell off as he kissed her, a leak dripped on her forehead, and several cars honked indignantly as they passed.

"Oh Stu——" Nina breathed finally.

"Ah, God," said Stuart, and thrust her away. "Got to take you home."

They stopped for hamburgers and beer when they got to Brooklyn and drew up before Nina's house about nine o'clock. Nina sat looking at the lighted windows and strangeness grew slowly all about her.

"Don't come in," she said abruptly.

"Okay," said Stuart after a minute.

She felt his surprise. "I wouldn't—— I don't—— Janey knew something just by looking at us. I don't want everyone to see——"

He pulled her to him. "I don't give a damn what they see. They'll know soon enough because we're going to get married." He kissed her. "Next week." He kissed her again, though her lips fought to argue with him.

"Oh Stu, we can't——"

"Yes we can. Now you run on in. Oh, I'll put your bag on the porch and take Howard's slicker." He climbed out, got the suitcase and opened her door on the rain. "Now shut up," he said, though she hadn't spoken again, took her arm, walked her up to the house and kissed her quickly. "I'll call you tomorrow," he said, took her raincoat and went off, the light from the windows gleaming on his wet shoulders as he went unhurriedly, without turning, down the path to the car.

He's gone! thought Nina, and her whole body ached with loneliness. She stood struck dumb with pain as Stuart drove off. It was physical, she could feel it all down her, the sensation of separation. But he's mine, he's mine now! she thought, and joy bubbled up in her heart. Torn by the two emotions, she was ready to cry for a moment. Then, slowly, as if awakening, she returned to herself on the familiar porch, before the familiar door, everything as it always was —except, except for the new world, the new body, the new self that Stuart had given her. Taking a deep breath, she found her key, unlocked the door and went in.

The chandelier in the hall cast a circle of light on the floor. The parlor was dark, but light from the living room spilled out in the hall. Across from it, behind the shut door of Uncle Van's den, came a cough and the scrape of a bow on strings, and then notes poured off Uncle Van's violin like syrup from a spoon in a thin sweet thread. Nina shut the door softly behind her and stood still. Next week, Stuart had said. Soon, at any rate, she would go. It seemed to her that the house where she stood had suddenly become fragile, vulnerable, as if when she shut the door behind her for the last time she could shatter it to pieces by too sharp a closing. The stairway would tilt, lean, crash sideward down into the hall. The chandelier would come down with a smash and bounce brazenly, crazily, on the floor already sagging for its descent onto the coalbin and the hot-air furnace. The people, reduced to shadows, would crumple like paper dolls. Only a heap of rubble and a house-size puff of dust would remain of all Nina's former life.

How precious it seemed in that moment! How the presage of its ruin invested the past with the aura of security! The ghosts of a hundred thousand cookies wafted from the oven. Nina and Marion knelt tightening skates in an infinite series of separate events. Christmas trees bloomed and faded in the parlor as the years ran by like a movie gone crazy, a crescendo of gardens threw their sweetness into the air, and through it, sustaining it by an effortless magic, Uncle Van's fiddle cried and soared, weaving the spell which raised the house, hollowed it, roofed it over into a dwelling place for his sister and her children. Oh Mother, oh Uncle Van—— Nina stood, choked, on the threshold, hearing her mother say, "You'll feel differently when you're married." But I feel differently now! thought Nina at the moment of parting. The dear past, the dear care and all the love that formed her would be left behind and in their center would be an intaglio-wound, the space where Nina had been. She could not return to that niche which she had left behind but she wanted somehow to embrace it, to heal and soothe——

Uncle Van's fiddle ceased, the rain beat on the porch roof, her mother's voice spoke indistinguishably from the living room. Unable to bear the pain of her departure alone, Nina moved like an arrow from a bow straight to the wound she must make. Like a sleepwalker, she went silently down the hall and into the living room. Kermit was curled uncomfortably on the uncomfortable sofa, frowning at a textbook. Marion was muttering over algebra at the living-room table, but Nina went straight to her mother, who sat between the two with a lapful of socks.

All the voices spoke in welcome, saying something about the rain and her trip, even Kermit said "Hi."

But Nina knelt by her mother's chair and said, "Mummy, I'm going to be married to Stuart. Right away——" Her voice faltered. "He says right away," and she looked up longingly into her mother's face.

Mrs. Bishop sat quite still. What emotions struggled behind her eyes? I would give anything, thought Nina, in a thunderclap of passion, to pass into her mind and tell her—and know—and tell her—— But the struggle was over at once. Mrs. Bishop took Nina's face between her hands and, as Marion cried "Nina!" in excitement and exultation, as Kermit's book fell with a bang to the floor, she said, "Oh darling!" She gathered Nina's head to her breast and said, "Oh I'm so glad for you!" and Nina began to laugh and cry, knowing she was hysterical and not caring.

But Marion was upon her like a whirlwind, kneeling beside her, laughing and kissing her. "Children! Children!" cried Mrs. Bishop, "Stop, stop, you're beside yourselves! Nina, do behave!"

Then Uncle Van's voice said from the doorway, "What's all this?"

Nina turned to tell him, trying to catch her breath, but before she could speak, Kermit said in a voice as thin and cutting as a steel wire, "Nina has just announced her engagement," and Nina's eyes stopped on his face. Why, he hates me! she thought. No, not hate—— He's jealous. He could kill me for jealousy! The moment of communion that she had ached for with her mother hung now between Kermit and herself. Kermit's passion entered into her, her knowledge of it into Kermit. She could see him acknowledging it. It could neither increase nor decrease what he felt, since he felt it inescapably with every inch of himself, but it changed it slightly, as a dye may be set by a chemical. So now you know, said Kermit's eyes. Now you know. And Nina accepted the knowledge, accepted his judgment. Now I know, she knew. But she did not know what she knew.

"Why, Nina, my dear!" said Uncle Van, coming in, crossing in front of Kermit. "My best love and heartiest good wishes! Am I right in assuming that your fiancé is Stuart Fanning?"

Nina couldn't speak but she nodded violently as her eyes brimmed over again.

"Then I'm sure you'll be happy," said Uncle Van, and gave her a clean handkerchief.

"Oh Nina," cried Marion blissfully, "what does it feel like to be engaged? How do you feel?"

"Dizzy," said Nina. "Oh Mummy, I shouldn't have told you like this! I wouldn't let Stuart come in because I wanted to keep it a secret. He'll think I'm crazy. I didn't mean to tell. It was just——" She looked up at her mother, trying to explain her need for reassurance, her need to reassure, which had produced this bombshell. For it seemed like a bombshell of news, to Nina. "I just wanted you to know," she finished weakly.

"Bless you, my child," said Kermit behind her. "If the marriage settlements are in order you have my consent." He was leaning against the end of the sofa and he had himself much more under control, but he wouldn't look at Nina. "How about a toast, Uncle Van?"

"Just the thing," said Uncle Van. "Now that December will see the end of the Noble Experiment, we can drink up our medicinal supply. Marion, get some glasses, my dear. That medium size, for an old-fashioned cocktail. Bring a lemon and a sharp knife. It's not the most appropriate drink, Nina, but we'll be able to have champagne for your wedding, at any rate."

"I thought Stuart wanted to be married right away," said Kermit in a curiously neutral tone. Nina looked at him suspiciously. It's as plain as the nose on my face, she thought, that he's going to make trouble if he can—if he can do it without letting on that he means to, to the "grownups." She remembered this mood well.

But Uncle Van was gently superb. "I don't blame Stuart," he said. "I quite agree that Nina is worth a little impatience. But if she agrees not to run away, perhaps we can persuade him to wait a month or two."

"Oh Nina," said Mrs. Bishop, "a Christmas wedding would be lovely! That is, if he won't wait till June. What do you think?"

"*I* won't wait till June," said Nina, and blushed up to her hair. Kermit, not looking at her, said "Hear, hear," and went to take some of the glasses Marion brought in. Uncle Van went back into the den and returned in a moment carrying tenderly an unopened bottle of pre-war bourbon.

"What about ice?" said Kermit, and went for some.

"Not too much, not too much," called Uncle Van. "You want to be able to taste this liquor, it's twenty-five years old." And so with a bustle the drinks got made by Uncle Van, with Kermit and Marion as his attendants. But Nina sat on the floor with her hand in her mother's and did not move, except to stroke gently the blue-veined hand that held hers, where the gold wedding ring was a little too large.

"To Nina!" said Kermit as he took the last glass.

"To Nina," they all echoed, and drank.

Nina looked down at the glass in her hand and said, "I can't drink that. I'll give you another toast." She looked up at her mother and said, "To Daddy. I wish——"

"Ah, Nina," said Mrs. Bishop, and was silent, looking over her daughter's head before she was able to smile and say, "Yes, to your father." They drank again in silence and then Mrs. Bishop said, "Now—to Uncle Van."

"Uncle Van!"

"There's one gentleman who's been forgotten, however," said Uncle Van, laughing. "I shall drink to Stuart."

But Kermit put down his glass and said, "I'm afraid I was a little too hearty before, I haven't anything left to drink. Stuart'll just have to take my eternal congratulations without a toast. Nina, I hate to say it, but I have to read eight more pages of Pascal's exceptionally irritating *pensées,* so will you excuse me, please?" He grinned, picked up his book and went out. There was a queer little silence after he had gone.

Then Mrs. Bishop leaned back in her chair, put down her glass and picked up the sock she had been darning when Nina burst in. "Nina," she said, "if you were married just after Christmas—say, in the first week of January—we could still catch people home from college. Or even between Christmas and New Year's. I must talk to Dr. Graves about the church. Of course you wouldn't get much of a honeymoon, but you can't expect to do that anyway, if you don't wait till June. It's too bad Stuart hasn't graduated."

"He'll have quite a year!" said Uncle Van, laughing. "I wouldn't want to add getting married to my last term of law school. Still—being engaged might be worse."

"Why Uncle Van!" said Nina.

"Now Nina, now Nina, I was just thinking of all those parties and what-do-you-call-'ems—showers—receptions and so on! If you waited till June he'd be going through that while he took his final examinations. Christmas is better, Christmas is better. Where do you think you'll live? With the Judge?"

"Now Van, they haven't had a chance to think!" said Mrs. Bishop. "And here sit the old folks planning everything for them. Nina, though, one thing—don't, for goodness' sake, have too big a wedding! It's so vulgar! I thought Margery Houghton's was just awful! Twelve bridesmaids! A ringbearer! The church decked out as if—as if—they were having a bazaar! I *never* saw such a show. And Margery in the middle of it all as white as an egg, and just as much expression, too!"

"Some eggs are brown," said Marion.

"Well Margery wasn't," said her mother. "Now six bridesmaids in pretty pastels—or darker shades, actually, at this time of year—— That lovely tawny orange-rose you find in talisman roses, and just the roses in the church—— You can use plenty of them without having it seem ornate—just simple and rich—— And the music! Nina, if you let them play 'The Voice That Breathed o'er Eden,' I shall disown you! Or 'Oh Promise Me.'"

But Nina was laughing so hard she couldn't answer.

"Don't plan anything," gasped Marion. "Let the young people do it all!"

"Well!" said Mrs. Bishop in mock umbrage. "Of course if you don't want my opinion——"

"Oh Mummy, Mummy, we do, we do! After all, you're the only one who's been through it!" Marion laughed again and pirouetted.

"Marion," said her mother, "that liquor—I don't know——"

But Marion went on irrepressibly, "And I shall be maid of honor! Oh wait till the girls hear this!"

"Well, now," said Mrs. Bishop, "Janey Fanning will expect——"

"Oh Lord, Janey," said Nina, and got up from the floor to stretch while her mother went into the details of Janey's claims, of wedding invitations, of possible places to hold the reception——

"The garden would be pretty in June," said Uncle Van wistfully.

"I'll be married in June," Marion promised him, and Mrs. Bishop, rocking, sewing, plunged on to wedding gowns.

Lying awake later, Nina thought, How funny! How absurd! How funny! What a fuss! But if it makes Mummy happy—— And then the memory of Stuart's lips pressed hers, his voice said in her ear, "Right away," and she turned restlessly in her bed. Stuart, Stuart, and she had meant to do everything just as he wished it! But he couldn't mind waiting just till Christmas. After all, they were in love —and she gave herself up to the thought of that love, rocked in its swaying embrace as the *Amalie* had rocked last night in the rain, the waves lapping at the hull. Stuart, Stuart! she thought, like an incantation, sliding into sleep. On the way she met Kermit's eyes, cold as stone in his set face. No, no, she thought—Stuart, Stuart! And at last slept.

Of course Stuart agreed to wait until Christmas. He looked at Nina in a kind of dogged desperation when she talked to him, but they did not even—really—fight about it. Stuart said, "I don't see the point of it. Why should we wait?"

Nina answered, "Oh darling, you know I don't want to. But it would make them all so unhappy!"

"Why? If we're going to do it anyway? They aren't unhappy about that. What's the difference between next week and after Christmas?"

Nina giggled. "I'll tell you one reason. If we did it next week, every single soul we know would be sure I was going to have a baby."

"I wish you were," said Stuart. But a law school student on an allowance from his father could hardly imitate Young Lochinvar.

And though Nina shivered with a sense of betrayal, she told herself that the betrayal was not only sensible, but necessary. Marriage was a ceremony, and therefore it was public. Their families could not be left out of it. Only from time to time, as the weeks passed and Nina began to feel more and more like a golden calf, did she think with occasional longing of an elopement. But the news of her engagement, and the clipping, with her picture, from the Brooklyn *Eagle,* had rustled away among her relatives near and far like wind in a field of corn. Cousin Nettie Dawson from Perkasie sent the traditional Van Deusen recipe for wedding cake ("Take the yolks of twenty-four eggs," it began); Aunt Dora's gift to Nina was a complete parure—earrings, necklace and bracelets—of garnets that had been presented to Nina's grandmother on her wedding day by Chauncey Depew. Janey Cushman, in one grim rush of the battlements, made good her right to be matron of honor and Marion was reduced to bridesmaid and studied Janey, when they met, with an unflattering gleam in her eye.

Mr. Daniels, of course, was beside himself. When Nina told him about it, sometime around the middle of October, he slapped the desk and said, "I knew it! I knew it! I never get a good secretary but she gets married!"

"I think that's a very selfish remark," said Nina coldly. "You can hardly expect me to devote my life to you. That's for Mrs. Daniels. Anyway, I'm not a secretary, I'm——"

"We'll leave Mrs. Daniels out of this, Nina. She has nothing to do with the case, which is the job you're paid to do for me. But I must say, it's odd, when you think of the suffragettes and how they struggled, that so many women still prefer marriage to a career. A man doesn't feel that way."

"A man doesn't bear children."

Mr. Daniels looked at her for a moment with an expression of wild surmise. "You're not——"

"No I'm not!" said Nina. "And I'm not quitting either—or at least I wasn't until that last remark of yours. Now——"

"I'm sorry, I'm sorry," said Mr. Daniels hastily, wiping his brow. "I didn't mean—— These things are natural, after all—— I'm as broad-minded as the next man, I hope——"

"Or broader," Nina muttered.

"But I understand, of course. Stuart doesn't graduate till June, does he? Where are you going to live? His father's a widower, isn't he? Are you going to live there? Have you considered the problems of——"

"Mr. Daniels!" cried Nina. "I told you about it because I want to take an extra hour at lunch and meet my mother at Tiffany's to see about the invitations. If I answer all those questions now I won't get there till it's time to close. Please!"

"Tiffany's, hey?" said Mr. Daniels. Nina could see her social standing rise a notch, while Mr. Daniels', she had to admit, sank slightly because he did not take Tiffany's for granted. "Well, well, run along then. Don't stand here chattering. And take your time. I guess I'll have to learn to get on by myself while you run out to market or leave early to get supper."

"I shan't leave early. But thank you. I'm sorry if I was rude."

Mr. Daniels waved his hand, forgiving her. Nina picked up her pocketbook and took her coat, getting ready to run before he could ask her anything more. His eyes followed her reflectively. "When did——" he began.

"I'll be back by three," said Nina, and left. She had a sudden vision of Mr. Daniels' eyes when she returned from her brief honeymoon. Perhaps it would be as well to quit, after all.

Over the months of that fall, Kermit's reaction to Nina's marriage turned out to be one of withdrawal. He stood apart from all the excitement, polite to his mother and sisters but refusing to take part in the family discussions of the wedding, of Nina's trousseau, of the little apartment on Brooklyn Heights which Nina found. He stayed late at Columbia (working in the library, he told them), and when he was home he studied alone in his room. One Sunday morning when Uncle Van had been questioning him gently about his work —he had done very well on his mid-term exams and Uncle Van was attempting to convey his gratitude and approbation—Kermit told his family that he had decided to go into the State Department and become a career diplomat. This ambition distressed Uncle Van a trifle, for he had hoped, though not very confidently, that Kermit might wish to go into his firm; and besides, he could not regard government service under a Democratic administration as being quite as sound a career as if the Republicans had been in office. Marion was thrilled, however, for the Foreign Service seemed a most romantic pursuit to her.

Mrs. Bishop said, "You will have to work very hard at your languages, then."

"I am working hard," Kermit said.

"Yes, dear, I know," his mother replied.

When did you decide this? Nina wanted to ask her brother, but she did not. For looking across the table at him, she knew he was talking nonsense and that he did not believe in a Foreign Service career at all. You're lying, Kermit, she thought. Kermit, feeling her gaze, looked up at her then. His expression was stiff, and carefully unreadable, but from behind his eyes his cold anger looked out once again. Touch me if you dare, his eyes said. Intrude on me at your peril. Nina did not dare, she looked down at her plate and began to butter a piece of toast. Is it that girl, is he seeing her again? she wondered, but she had no idea at all whether she was right or wrong. She glanced at her mother and wondered briefly whether Mrs. Bishop did not herself have doubts about Kermit's intentions. But Stuart was coming for her and getting ready for him drove Kermit from her mind.

Whatever Mrs. Bishop may have thought at the time of Kermit's announcement, she apparently decided to accept it. "He's settling down," she said to Nina one evening later in the week when they were alone. But some residual uneasiness made her sigh.

"Mhm," said Nina, who was reading manuscripts on the sofa. "What's that for?"

"What's what for? Nina, how many slips do you own?"

"Three old, four new. I have a lot. That sigh. Don't you—want him to settle down?"

"I didn't sigh! Of course I'm delighted."

"You did sigh."

"No I didn't," said Mrs. Bishop positively. But her needle hesitated in the monogram she was putting on a pillowcase. Had she sighed? Why should Kermit's application to his work upset her? The uneasiness stirred beneath the surface of her mind. Mrs. Bishop, not given to introspection, was disturbed by her concern with her own thoughts. She felt as if she were sitting in a mental draft. Nina had put down her manuscript and was looking at her. Mrs. Bishop's mind plunged toward a neutral subject. Slips—gowns—how many nightgowns—she was ready to begin.

But Nina said, "Mother."

"Yes, dear."

"Kermit——" Nina stopped. She could not say to her mother, Kermit is lying. Don't trust him. Don't love him too much. She hung speechless, poised on the edge of the unpleasant. "Kermit is—is different," she compromised.

Mrs. Bishop sewed on. After a minute she said, "Yes, I know."

"Other people's rules don't always apply, for Kermit."

"I know." Mrs. Bishop ducked her head suddenly. Why—why—should her eyes have filled with tears? She was angry with Nina! Why must the young people, she thought unhappily, be so uncompromising? You don't understand Kermit, she wanted to tell Nina. Why shouldn't he be different? Why should you be allowed to judge him harshly just because you are happy? Perhaps if he were happy too, if your happiness were not always flaunted before him, things would be easier for him. But she could not say this because she would have cried if she had begun.

Nina sighed now and rubbed her eyes. Why should it be so hard —impossible, really—to talk to the older generation? Why should frankness always result in hurt feelings? Her mother was a dear, Uncle Van was sweet, but none of the business of life could ever be discussed with them. Surely she and Stuart would never become like that! And yet, she knew perfectly well that she could not discuss Kermit with Stuart any more than she could with her mother. And what would happen when she had left home and Kermit was in direct contact with—and opposition to, of course—the older generation? You could not, obviously, refuse to get married because your brother had a difficult temperament, but—but—you could see trouble ahead. Nina felt sick at the prospect. What Nina and her mother both knew about Kermit—and could not say—was that his passion to be passionless, his violent drive for self-control, was desperately needed and could never be entirely successful. Kermit was vulnerable and he hated his vulnerability. They knew it, they had both suffered when Kermit's fear of being hurt had turned a devastating, remorseless fury loose on the world about him, most devastating, of course, to those closest to him. Mrs. Bishop understood this and forgave him. Nina understood it and had resolved never to forgive him again. Both had been hurt too much to talk about it directly.

"Are you tired, dear?" asked Mrs. Bishop in her normal tone.

"I'm disgusted," said Nina, picking up her chore again. "Why in the name of heaven do so many people want to write? If they have unsatisfied creative urges why don't they try making quilts? Or painting china? Or tatting?"

"Tatting's so ugly," said her mother. "Cousin Nettie Dawson used to paint china. Perhaps she still does. Perhaps she'll send you a service for a wedding present."

"Oh God," said Nina.

"Now, Nina, she was really quite talented. I know Dora has a tea set she did, with pansies on it. It's charming."

"If you like that kind of thing, I'm sure it's just what you like."

"I assure you, my dear, that Picasso will be just as dated someday. There, that's four cases done. If you'd waited till June I could have done a whole dozen, but as it is, you'll have to get along with six, and I honestly don't know about the sheets. What time is it? Shouldn't Marion be home? Would you like a glass of milk?"

"It's quarter past ten, I don't know where Marion went, no thank you."

"I believe they're decorating the gym for a dance."

"Well, Marion will be there till the last strip of crepe paper goes up." Nina yawned agonizedly and dropped the manuscript she had been reading to the floor.

"You're tired," said Mrs. Bishop. "I do wish you'd quit working."

"I'm afraid I wouldn't be able to support Stuart in the style to which he is accustomed, if I did."

"No, I suppose not. It doesn't really seem like getting married though. Still, I'm glad you're not going to live with the Judge. *There's* tatting for you! All those doilies, finger bowls all the time—he's a very distinguished man, of course, but oh my! How he fusses if dinner is late!"

"I wonder where Stuart got his beautiful nature. I was never very fond of his mother."

"No, I wasn't either. But I admired her. She had great character. Spartan, I suppose you'd say."

"Spartan? With doilies?"

"Oh that has nothing to do with it, except that if they were there they had to be just right. If she decided that was the style they were to live in, they lived in it to the last fraction of an inch. Stuart's nature probably came from his nurse. Old Annie. She was devoted to him. I *think* her name was Annie. Don't they say now that what-you-may-call-it—environment—is the important thing? Well, Annie was Stuart's environment. If it was Annie."

"Then why did Janey turn out such a—such a—flibbertigibbet?"

"Well now, dear, perhaps she had another nurse. I don't know, I'm sure. I was in the West then. I think the Judge is pleased, though."

"With Janey?"

"No, silly, with you. All the flat silver *looks* as if he were pleased. I must say I'm much happier to be left with the linens." Mrs. Bishop picked up another pillowcase and began measuring to see where the monogram should go.

"Mummy, you'll sew your eyes out if you don't stop!"

"I'll never get to the sheets if I *do* stop." She murmured figures to herself, and consulted a creased scrap of paper. Nina lay and considered her. Was that how she would look when she was forty-eight? Her heart warmed slowly. It will be all right if I do, she thought.

Mrs. Bishop lifted her head. A door had opened.

"Marion?" said Nina.

"No, it's Van. That's the study door, foolish, not the front door. Van dear, come and have some crackers and milk with us. I was just going to get some." She bundled her work up onto the table and stepped out into the hall as Uncle Van came in. "Oh Kermit, Kermit!" she called upstairs. "Crackers and milk, dear?" But Kermit said he was still working and could not stop.

Next week was Thanksgiving. Nina alternated between being totally calm and placidly happy over the prospect of being married in a month, and an unsettling feeling that the whole idea was a figment of her imagination, that the month would never pass, that time's flow had slowed down and caught Stuart and herself in this congealing month of waiting that would never be over. Forever they would reach out hands to each other across the weeks between them, as Vergil's unhappy dead had reached helplessly toward Aeneas across the Styx. Frightened, she would grow impatient and greedy, trying to rush time on——

Judge Fanning insisted that all of Stuart's prospective in-laws must dine at his house. Mrs. Bishop had explained that Thanksgiving always meant Aunt Dora and Aunt Flora Van Deusen, and the Judge firmly invited them too. In addition there had been a descent of three young Dawsons from the Perkasie connection who had telephoned on Wednesday and been made welcome.

The day was bright, the sun deceptively warm. For once the parlor was opened and used. It was understood that in Judge Fanning's position he could serve no liquor until Prohibition had ended officially. But it was understood equally well that Aunt Flora and Aunt Dora would not regard Thanksgiving as Thanksgiving, or themselves as properly welcomed to the family gathering, without a libation to the lares and penates being offered in the form of a glass of rather sweet sherry. At one o'clock, therefore, forty-five minutes before they were expected at the Fannings', Nina's family gathered on the red brocaded sofas and chairs. There was a decanter of sherry for the aunts and cocktails for the rest. There were imported biscuits, hard as nuts and much drier, thin toast and a terrine of pâté de foie that Nina had brought home from Charles'. The young Dawsons had brought a dozen enormous yellow chrysanthemums, and Uncle Van eyed them morosely for he always resented bought flowers.

The room was stuffy. Mrs. Bishop had lit the gas log to make sure the aunts would be comfortable, though it was probably not the added warmth that they liked, but the faint smell of gas reminiscent of their youth. Nina sat on the edge of a horsehair side chair, feeling impatient and knowing it was absurd to feel so, for the only thing she could expect to happen would be the slow promenade of the company to the Fanning house three blocks away. Stuart would be there of course, but embedded in his family like a fly in amber, just as she was in her own. The young Dawsons called her Cousin Nina, and that was just what she felt like.

"Nina," said her mother, "the sherry, dear. Aunt Flora's glass is empty."

"Gracious," said Aunt Flora, "I don't know—do you think I should? I can feel it in my elbows, you know, when I've had enough!"

"Oh, but these glasses are tiny."

Kermit stood up abruptly and went to take a glass from the female young Dawson, Cousin Clara, who wanted to be known as Claire. "Another?" he asked.

His mother's eye flickered at him. "Have we time——" she began gently.

"Plenty. Nina?"

"Thanks. You need more ice, though. I'll come out to the kitchen and help you make another shakerful." If she had sat still another minute, Nina thought as she followed Kermit, she would have screamed. Whatever their quarrels, there was still between Kermit and herself an instinctive knowledge of how the other felt. They had shared enough boredom in their childhood to know very well how to engineer a joint escape. Now Kermit poured out the dregs of the last cocktail and began measuring whiskey into the shaker, while Nina ran water over an ice tray at the sink. She splashed her new yellow velveteen dress, and said "Damn."

"Damn indeed," said Kermit.

"Oh it's not so bad. Really."

"It's hell. Don't be so pleasant. Look, I'll make an extra for you and me. You won't get anything to drink at the Judge's."

"I know."

"Why in hell," said Kermit in the same accommodating and co-operative tone, dropping lumps of ice carefully into the shaker, "did you have to pick such a bastard for your father-in-law? Pompous fool."

"He was hardly my first concern. Anyway——"

"Don't say he isn't a pompous fool. He is. Imagine thinking he'd lose judicial dignity if he served a glass of wine in his own home, in the bosom of his family-to-be! He's an idiot."

Nina said nothing.

"I think *you're* being a damned fool, too."

Nina continued to say nothing.

"You're marrying Stuart," said Kermit, "because you're scared not to. You're insane."

"I am in love with Stuart," said Nina.

"If you really think that you're a fool. A bigger fool, though it hardly seems possible, than your papa-in-law, or even your intended."

Nina pressed her lips together and watched Kermit's hands mixing the drink. He swung the shaker hard, took the kitchen tumbler from over the sink, poured himself a cocktail and sipped it. "This is a lousy drink."

"You made it."

"I mean in principle. There's no excuse for a manhattan."

"The Dawsons like it."

"There is no excuse for the Dawsons. Do you realize that, married to Stuart, you must expect to have children like the Dawsons? Claire-Clara. Harry. And Ben Junior."

"As long as I don't have one like you." But she had to turn away from him. He had made her eyes suddenly brim with tears. She went to the sink and began refilling the ice tray.

"Weeping into the ice?" said Kermit. "Here. Dry your eyes on a dish towel and have another drink before we go inside."

"No."

"No charity from your hated sibling? Go on. It'll do you good." He poured another two inches into the tumbler and gave it to her. Nina took the glass and drank in order to swallow the lump in her throat.

"Kermit," she said rapidly, "I don't hate you. Why do you hate me so? Why do you say the worst possible things to me? They're not true. You don't really mean them. Stuart isn't——"

"Stuart is a very stupid fellow," said Kermit somberly.

"But he isn't! He's different from you so——"

"That he is."

"——so you don't see it, but he's anything but stupid! He's intuitive, he's sensitive, really he is. You just——"

"Good God!" said Kermit. He sounded really shocked that Nina should believe this.

93

Nina felt herself go cold. How could she have said that about Stuart to Kermit? It was her own private secret, Stuart's sure knowledge of her, his quiet unconscious command of their relationship. She had meant never to betray it to a soul, for Stuart would have hated so for anyone to know the inside of their feeling for each other. And now she had blurted it out to Kermit! She tried momentarily to tell herself that it did not matter, since Kermit did not believe her. But that was no good. Whether Kermit believed her or not, he now knew the way she felt, he knew the geography and landscape of her connection with Stuart, and no knowledge about that connection was safe with Kermit. I *am* insane, she thought. I must never trust him for an instant, never!

"Come on," she said. "We've got to go back."

"Why?" asked Kermit bitterly. "But I suppose you want to get going so you can see this Captain of your Soul." He took the shaker, and she followed him, quaking inwardly.

Dinner at the Judge's was no improvement on the earlier gathering. The meal itself was massive. The turkey must have weighed thirty pounds. The Judge stood up to carve, his silver hair gleaming in the light from the chandelier (though it was the middle of the day, the Fannings' enormous dining room was hedged in by shrubs and nearly as dark as the bottom of a well), his pince-nez perched flightily on the bridge of his distinguished nose. The Judge looked *extremely* distinguished; people were always seeing in him a resemblance to statesmen and great jurists of the past, but seldom to the same one. Arthur Francis Cushman, allowed at his grandfather's table for dinner for the first time, was too overawed to speak, or even to eat, and the young Dawsons were distinctly incoherent. Even Marion and Uncle Van, who shared an ability to chat on any occasion, were rather silent, and dinner went on and on through the afternoon like a ritual Juggernaut that no one had really desired to invoke, but that no one, either, could stop.

Coffee was served in the living room at half-past three, and Nina felt as stuffed as a bolster. The day was crisping toward dusk, and the last sunlight glinted outside like a last opportunity to save a lost promise. Oh lonesome, lonesome! thought Nina. Will this long month never be over? Will I spend my whole youth here, waiting for Stuart? And she looked agonizedly across the room to him, where he sat solidly between Aunt Dora and Cousin Claire. He met her eye and then looked over her head to the onyx and ormolu clock which ticked away on the mantelpiece under a glass bell. But he made no move, only went on listening to Claire describing a tennis tournament at the Perkasie Country Club. He would move in good time, Nina knew, when the daimons of family hospitality had been appeased; but she wanted to go now, out into the crinkly chill gold of late afternoon.

Kermit, who had been standing with an elbow on the mantel, said, "Claire. Have you seen Shore Road, and the view of the Narrows? You really should. Why don't we walk a bit? Before the sun goes."

"Oh that would be lovely!" said Claire, who showed no sign of ever having said no to anything male in her life.

"Can you move, Nina? Or have you foundered?"

"How delicately you put it," said Nina, getting up. "I can move, thank you. Stuart——"

But Stuart was looking at his father. The Judge's eyebrows had risen into barbs of surprise and indignation at this unmannerly exodus from his hospitality. He only said, however, "Ah, youth. Is it aspiration, Van Deusen, or merely restlessness?"

"Well," said Uncle Van pleasantly, "I've often thought digestion undergoes some remarkable change around age twenty-five. Before that a hearty meal is just a preliminary to a baseball game or an hour's swim. Afterwards, you become very content to sit and sip coffee."

"And enjoy a cigar—if the ladies don't mind?" The Judge looked around with an air of ingratiating command. "Stuart, would you bring the humidor from my desk?"

As Stuart went out, Nina felt a shock of rebellion. She wanted desperately to pick up the silver ash tray next to her and throw it at the Judge.

"Fresh air or a smoke-filled room, is that it, sir?" asked Kermit. "It seems to me youth has the best of it, hygienically speaking."

This time the Judge looked at him as if, thought Nina, Kermit were about to be sentenced. The silence waited for the opening words, "Prisoner at the bar——" and the Judge seemed anxious to pronounce them. Since he could not, the silence went on waiting, for the Judge must be equally unwilling and unable to say anything else.

"Now, children," said Mrs. Bishop fondly, and twinkled flirtatiously at the Judge as she did so. "They are restless, of course. It's one of the joys of growing older to know that when you're happy where you are you aren't missing something somewhere else. Run along, all of you, and walk up to Fort Hamilton and back. I'm sure it will do you good. Janey Fanning Cushman, you look to me as if you'd enjoy a rubber of bridge. I know I would, particularly if I can cut the Judge for partner. Do you remember that little slam in spades, Judge? Doubled *and* redoubled, wasn't it?"

"Now, Elizabeth," said the Judge, "you're a flatterer. Doubled only, and it was just luck the clubs broke as they did. Have we two tables?" He looked around with a calculating eye, and Nina's heart sank as she foresaw Stuart's being sucked in to make a fourth.

But one of the young Dawsons, Ben Junior, it was, who was practicing law in Perkasie, offered eagerly to play. I hope his game is better than his conversation, thought Nina, or he won't cut much ice with the Judge.

Stuart returned with the cigars and he and Ben Junior got the tables set up. Aunt Dora fluttered when it was made clear that they were to play contract, not auction, and Aunt Flora said coldly that Dora should perhaps have stuck to whist. Aunt Dora retorted that she had been whist champion of the Ladies' Thursday Club for three years, and Aunt Flora replied, "That's what I meant." The Judge looked alarmed, but Aunt Dora was safely settled at the other table, and so, alas, were Ben Junior and Janey Cushman. Uncle Van joined them and the Judge settled down with Aunt Flora, who was a kind of idiot savant about bridge—no one knew how she managed to win since she herself said she could neither add nor subtract, but win she did—along with Mrs. Bishop and Howard Cushman.

Nina waited impatiently on the edge of the dark hall. Kermit, with some badinage, was helping Claire into her coat, and Harry Dawson was attempting to join in. Time passes, time passes, thought Nina, and Stuart lit his father's cigar. At last he grinned at her, said good-by, and came out to the hall. She let him help her on with her coat and they followed the other three out.

Kermit, Claire and Harry set a swift pace down the block and laughter blew back from them like scraps of confetti. Nina and Stuart walked in silence. Nina felt anger within her no more digested than her dinner. But it was unformulated, there was no settled point upon which she wished to begin an attack on Stuart. He seemed content merely to walk and say nothing. This can't be right, thought Nina in despair. If there's something wrong between us, we should be able to talk it out. But she could hardly start by saying, Your father is a stinker!

They came out on Shore Road and paused. Before them, below them, the Narrows glittered in the sun. At anchor off Quarantine lay a huge liner, and Kermit was showing her off to Claire as if she were his personal property. Stuart listened for a moment, his shoulders hunched, and then said abruptly, "Come on," and started walking.

"How the animals do order one about!" said Nina, raising her eyebrows.

Stuart turned and looked at her. "We came out to walk," he said. "Let's do it."

I'm going to be angry, thought Nina, the way sailing, once or twice, she had known she was going to be sick. I don't want to be— I won't! But after the smooth weeks of happiness and peace with Stuart, anger was dragging her down like undertow.

"I came out for air," she said levelly. "I like it here."

Stuart looked over her head consideringly at the other group and Nina knew, with a chill of fear, that she had tried to start a quarrel in front of Kermit and the young Dawsons. Swiftly she took Stuart's arm and turned to walk with him away from Kermit, who was now doing a travelogue in the manner of Burton Holmes, while Claire giggled.

After half a block Stuart said, "You're mad at the Judge. Kermit——"

"Oh shut up, shut up!" cried Nina, and could have bitten off her tongue. What am I doing? she thought. Why am I like this?

"All right," said Stuart, and they walked in silence again. The sun slowly withdrew back of Staten Island, the light clotted and thickened, the wind blew colder. Time was slowing down again, slowly dying of cold around her. Nina felt as if she were walking through a thickening, freezing stream—alone, all alone. She felt her eyes fill with tears. I won't cry, I won't cry, she thought wildly, and began reciting the seven times table to herself as a distraction.

"You'll just have to learn to manage the Judge," said Stuart mildly. "Your mother's wonderful at it."

At this Nina sobbed aloud.

"There, there," said Stuart, and put an arm around her. "Have you got a handkerchief?"

"Oh don't be so reasonable and kind!" cried Nina. "It's your fault! Why didn't you come when I wanted you to? You went and you lit his cigar!"

"Well——" said Stuart, nonplussed. "I lit your Uncle Van's too."

"What's this?" asked Kermit, coming up behind them, arm in arm with Claire. "A slight case of pre-marital hysterics?"

"Oh damn you, Kermit!" cried Nina. "I could kill you!"

Kermit at once dropped to his knees on the sidewalk and pulled his scarf off. "I offer you my throat," he said. "It is a far, far better thing I do now than I have ever——"

"Get up!" said Stuart, while Claire and Harry stared with their mouths open.

"Why?" said Kermit. "So you can knock me down?"

"Oh Kermit, please!" cried Nina.

"Well, call off your fiancé, then. I don't like St. Bernards."

"You damned little faggot!" said Stuart, driven in his rage to a confusion of categories that he knew was not true.

Claire screamed with pleasurable shock. Kermit came up off the sidewalk and hit Stuart on the mouth. Stuart swung. Kermit ducked and hit him again.

"Here, here," said Harry, advancing bravely into the thicket of blows, got Stuart's right in his midriff and drew back gasping.

"Stop it, stop it!" Nina shrieked furiously. "You idiots, you—stop it!"

At this point Stuart, who weighed fifty pounds more, knocked Kermit down and a car came cruising past. Faces peered curiously out and Nina felt herself grow sick with horror. She looked from Kermit on the sidewalk, blinking, to Stuart standing and staring at the bloody hand with which he had wiped his mouth.

"Apologize. Both of you," she said fiercely. "You ought to be *ashamed* of yourselves. I'm *ashamed* of you. Apologize."

"I'm sorry," said Stuart gruffly, still looking at his hand.

"Kermit," said Nina, waiting. I sound just like Janey scolding Arthur, she thought.

"Like hell," said Kermit. He sat up and then got shakily to his feet. Harry put out a hand to steady him and Kermit said, swaying, "Apologize to that bastard? Like hell!"

"Look here," said Stuart, "I didn't mean——"

Kermit swung at him again. But Harry caught his arm and he could only stand glaring in Harry's grip.

"I didn't mean what I said," said Stuart.

"You're a bastard," said Kermit, who seemed to have found a formula he liked. After a minute he shrugged out of Harry's grasp, turned, and walked unsteadily away from them. About fifty feet away he stopped and, leaning on a low wall, was sick over it into somebody's front garden.

"Oh God!" said Nina.

"You," said Stuart. "Harry. You walk the girls around the block." He pulled out a handkerchief, wiped his mouth and set off after Kermit.

"Come along, Cousin Nina," said Harry.

"No, I——" Nina began pulling back, watching Stuart reach Kermit and take his arm. Kermit tried to pull it away and then stood still while Stuart talked to him.

"Come along. Really. Much better. They'll settle it better without us. Can't interfere in these things without making more trouble." He rubbed himself thoughtfully where Stuart's fist had caught him.

"I'm so sorry!" Nina cried, walking fast now. "I don't know what to say! I'm so——"

"Now you mustn't feel that way, Cousin Nina."

"No indeed," cried Claire. "It happens all the time. Why, at the Country Club dance Labor Day, in Perkasie, three boys got into the most awful tangle. I declare, I don't know what gets into them. This first one, Bob Hallam, he kept cutting in, see, and Don—he's the one I'd come with—he——" And Claire babbled on while Nina walked with her head down in a state of shock.

Harry dutifully walked them around the block. At the corner Stuart stood waiting for them, patting his bleeding lip. "It's all right," he said. "He went home. He's not mad any more." At this Nina, who had been looking at him anxiously, dropped her eyes. If Stuart could seriously believe Kermit "wasn't mad any more" he must be slightly touched himself. Or else he was lying to her. In neither case could she learn anything from him. He felt her eyes leave him and said, "I'm sorry, Nina."

"It's all right," said Nina politely.

He looked at her helplessly, but Nina was too irritated at his insensitivity to meet his eyes, and the four of them might have stood there indefinitely if Harry Dawson had not said, "You know what I think would be a good idea? If we all went someplace and had a drink. Is there somewhere we can go?"

"That's one hell of a good idea," said Stuart. He rubbed his forehead for a moment and added, "I know. I've got a bottle in my locker at the Schermerhorn Club. Won't be a soul there today, either. Come on. We can pick up a cab on Ridge Boulevard or Third Avenue." They all trailed off after him in the dusk. As Nina walked, she kept seeing Kermit's figure as he must have gone off, as if it walked ahead of her through the darkening streets in a darkening cloud of shame and anger.

She didn't see him at all the next day. Everyone was in a short temper. Mrs. Bishop felt the young people should have come back to the Fannings'. Marion was hurt because they had gone off without her, leaving her to play nursemaid to Arthur Cushman. Uncle Van's stomach had kept him awake all night. With Marion and Kermit free for the long week end, Nina was annoyed at having to go to the office. She and Uncle Van rode to Manhattan feeling like slave labor.

Stuart called up around noon to ask Nina how she was. "I'm well, thank you," she said.

"That's good." He waited. When she did not ask how he was, he volunteered, "You can tell your kid brother I look like hell. The Judge thinks I was in a barroom brawl and has been acting like God Almighty to a black beetle. How—how does he look?"

"I don't know. He wasn't down when I left."

"Oh. Listen, Nina. I want to tell you, I was wrong. I didn't mean that, what I said. He isn't queer and I shouldn't have called him that. It's just—he does the goddamnedest things! I tried to tell him I didn't blame him for fighting, I would have too, I know it was my fault. Do you see what I mean? I mean, he's—queer—the way he isn't like most other people, but not the way I said. And I shouldn't have said it, it's just I got the two things mixed up in my mind. It was a hell of a thing to say, and I apologize. I told him that, but I don't know—if he heard me. I don't want to bring it all up again, but I thought maybe, if there was a chance, you could tell him again, I apologize. Because I do."

Nina said, after a minute in which she knew that Stuart's embarrassment was as deep as her own, "It was an awful thing to say." Mr. Daniels was taking a long week end too, so she could talk freely.

"I know it," said Stuart.

"He isn't, Stuart, he isn't really. He—I know about girls of his."

"I know he isn't," said Stuart again. "But when you're mad you get stupid. And when you're stupid you think any kind of difference is the same difference, if you see what I mean."

Nina sat silent. She had, she knew, to forgive Stuart. No one else in the world, she thought, could have seen so clearly what he had done and why he had done it, or apologized so thoroughly as Stuart had! It proved everything she knew about him, everything she had told Kermit about his perception.

. And in spite of this—how hard it was to forgive him! Once, she remembered, though she did not remember when, she had seen a kind of brutality in Stuart. What he had done was brutal. He had offered Kermit the ultimate insult; Kermit, who would never forget and never forgive. Kermit, who felt all emotions like wounds, had been stripped naked of his armor of indifference, had suffered humiliation, the meanest of emotions, in the worst possible way. Had Kermit, she wondered, suffered that particular humiliation before? Had other stupidity done what Stuart suggested, mixed up Kermit's difference from other people with the usual difference, expressed it in the dirty usual words? Suddenly she saw that girl, Tony-for-short, as Kermit's defense, the only possible defense he could make.

"Stuart," she said, "who can I trust not to be stupid if I can't trust you?"

"Oh honey," said Stuart, "listen, I'm apologizing to you too. Don't you know that? It's this goddamn being engaged. It's got me in a kink."

"Oh Stu!" cried Nina, and shame flooded her. "That's my fault," she said, and knew it was true. In transit from Kermit to Stuart, from the old childhood loyalty to the new, she put an intolerable strain on both of them. And yesterday she had made things worse. She had given Kermit chapter and verse on her love for Stuart, she had offered him no choice but to see she was really moving away from him. Then she had nagged and plagued Stuart for what he couldn't help. Even impossible Claire had known it was her fault—had Claire not, at once, started telling about how men fought over *her?*

"Now honey, now baby," said Stuart's voice, roughened with love and the need to comfort her, "don't say that, no it isn't! Just say you know I'm sorry——"

"Oh Stuart, I do. I'll tell him if I can, but I don't think I can."

"Well—I'll tell him again if I can. When he sees me he'll know I didn't get off for nothing, anyway. Do you mind going to the dance tomorrow with a character who's got a black eye?"

"I'd go with you anywhere, any time," she said firmly. Forgiveness had come spontaneously, without any trouble at all. "You probably look very distinguished with your black eye."

"That's good," said Stuart in quite another tone. Then he repeated, "How are you? How are you, baby?"

"Really all right. Really."

"Good. Look. I—better not come over tonight. I'll see you tomorrow. When?"

"Oh lordy, there's luncheon—and a tea—— Well, I'll be ready for the dance around nine. All right?"

"All right. But it's a long time."

"Yes," said Nina.

"We should have eloped."

"Yes."

"Next time you do as I say. Hear?"

"I hear. I will. Oh Stu—I love you."

"Well, keep it up now. 'By."

She hung up and leaned back in her chair and stretched. At once she realized that her head was aching, that she was tired. But in spite of discovering her physical discomfort, she felt much better than before. She had taken Stuart's side, not Kermit's, but that was where she belonged.

Her mother had an eye out for her when she got home that night and pounced immediately. "What happened to Kermit, Nina?" she asked, glancing conspiratorially around the empty living room.

Nina looked back at her helplessly, but there seemed absolutely no lie she could tell that would stick. When her mother saw Stuart's battered face tomorrow, she would know anyway. "He and Stuart had a fight," she said.

Mrs. Bishop sat down in a chair. Nina knelt beside her and caught her hand, but her mother shook her head emphatically as Nina started to speak, and she waited. "I thought so," said Mrs. Bishop after a minute. "What about?"

"About nothing," said Nina very seriously indeed. "About nonsense. They called each other—names, and then Kermit hit Stuart and—in a little while Stuart knocked him down. He's so much bigger, you know," she interpolated apologetically. "Harry tried to stop them and got hit himself——"

"In front of the Dawsons!" said Mrs. Bishop. "Oh, how could they! It will be all over Perkasie."

At this Nina laughed, a little shrilly. "Wouldn't you rather it was all over Perkasie than all over Bay Ridge? I would."

"I'd rather it wasn't all over anywhere." Mrs. Bishop was sitting with her eyes closed and she looked very tired. Then both of them heard the front door shut and Mrs. Bishop's eyes opened and she and Nina waited, looking at each other and thinking, Kermit, is it Kermit? What shall we do about him if it is? But Marion's whistle sounded in the front hall then and life ran along again, the rocks in the river had not yet been reached.

Kermit managed to stay out of everyone's way that night, but the next day being Saturday, he had to appear sometime. About ten o'clock in the morning he came down for breakfast. The first of the wedding presents were beginning to arrive and Nina, Marion and Mrs. Bishop were in the dining room contemplating a cut-glass pitcher and a set of cocktail glasses with horses on them. Kermit came in and said "Good morning." His place for breakfast was still set.

"Good morning, dear," said Mrs. Bishop calmly.

Marion said, "Look, Nina's loot is beginning to come."

Kermit glanced at the glassware and said, "She'll have to do better than that."

Nina looked at him then. His face was pale and there were dark patches under his eyes and one dark bruised-looking place on his cheekbone, but otherwise he was unmarked. Nina drew a breath of relief. Then his eyes flicked at her like a lash. He didn't speak. He didn't have to. Apologies at once became absurd. He won't forgive me, thought Nina. Just even for being there, he won't forgive me. But for marrying Stuart——

She looked across the table, out the window. Well? So? Suppose he doesn't? What do I care? I am on Stuart's side, I belong there. I'll be married, I'll have another life, Kermit won't matter in the least. But she knew it wasn't true. She had failed somehow. It was failure to leave Kermit behind her, hurt and furious, pushed toward irresponsibility by frustration. She had wanted everyone to be happy, everyone to love her—— Not only she and Stuart should "live happily ever after" when they married. Everyone around, Nina had felt, should be touched by the radiation of their happiness and good fortune. But it seemed as if her happiness poisoned Kermit. She stole a look at him.

He looked calmly past her and, pitying him, furious with him, she knew his control was admirable, she must admire and respect him. He said, "Is that a pitcher or a cut-glass chamber pot? Where do you suppose someone found it? I'm wrong, though. It's not anything you could find. It must be something they *had*. Who's it from?"

"Cousin Emma Dawson Cassidy," said Marion. "Who in the dickens is she?"

"Shh," said Kermit. "Don't speak of her. She married a papist."

"Now, Kermit," said his mother. "She's *my* second cousin and *your* second cousin once removed. She must be Harry's and Claire's aunt, and Ben Junior—well, a cousin of some kind, I guess. It's true, she did marry a Roman Catholic, but I'm sure he's a fine man, and she's never regretted it. He does quite well as a contractor, I believe, but of course they have six children—or is it seven?"

"Eight," said Kermit, eating grapefruit.

"No, no! Nothing like eight."

"Seven's like eight," said Marion.

"And I suppose she couldn't afford to send more," continued Mrs. Bishop. "It's very kind of her to have sent anything. I'm sure I don't know whether she's got any children married or not!"

"At any rate," said Kermit, "they aren't married to the scions of distinguished jurists, or you would have heard about it."

Nina got up decisively and left the room. She would respect him, but she could not stay to be devastated. Out in the hall, however, she stopped, not knowing where to go, feeling time heavy on her hands. Dorothy Blair was giving a luncheon at one—a shower, it would turn out to be, Nina supposed—where ten or twelve of the girls she had grown up with would meet and tell her how lucky she was to be getting married. Mrs. Merriweather was having a tea at five. And the dance tonight at the club—it was a lot of things to do. I'd better figure out what I'm going to wear, and if I have to change between lunch and tea, Nina thought, and started up to her room, depressed by the practicality of her thought.

But on the stairs she stopped. For halfway up the steps Kermit's anger was only a pool of thunder at her feet. Now she could look across it and see beyond it. Stuart's love for her stood up like a great rock, gilded by sunlight. I am going there, she thought, that is my home. Suddenly nothing mattered any more, not time's slow tread, not Kermit's thunderous eyes, nothing but the rock of love. Nina sat down on the stairs and leaned her head against the balustrade. Her knees were weak with love and desire and the overweening knowledge of joy. She sat there for twenty minutes, transported to a future of fulfillment.

Then Marion came out of the dining room and started upstairs, whistling. She saw Nina and stopped short. "What are you doing?" she said.

"Being happy," said Nina.

Marion sat down and put her arms around her sister. "Be happy for me too," she said.

"No," said Nina, "you must be happy for yourself." But she was lost in her dream and could not turn to see whether or not this advice made an impression on her sister.

By Christmas the house was in a turmoil. Christmas had always been a tumultuous festival in Nina's family. There had always been showers of presents, and the decorations on the tree, the wreaths in the windows were always there as true expressions of the joy and laughter within. This year was the apogee of Christmases. Nina's wedding presents were stacked up like dams and reefs and shoals in the parlor. She was to be married on December twenty-eighth and the reception would be at the Schermerhorn Club. Nina and her mother worked frantically on plans and arrangements, but they were not plans for a real event in the real world, where people came to parties in unpleasant moods, said spiteful and calculating things to one another and went home slightly drunk to Kermit's jungle. Nina was living in a fairy tale and everything was a little enchanted. When she thought of her wedding dress hanging upstairs under a protective sheet in the guest-room closet, it seemed to her to glow in the dark. When she and Marion wrote thank-you notes to-gether—their handwriting was sufficiently alike for Marion to write in Nina's name—they went into spells of choking laughter over the form letters they had devised. There was one for cocktail shakers, of which Nina had now received eight in celebration of the passing prohibition, one for candy dishes, one for table linens, one for vases and bric-a-brac.

Marion's present was a Persian kitten named Ivan because, in her opinion, all Persian cats looked Russian from behind, as if they were wearing baggy trousers and tight boots. "Besides," she said, "when he's wicked you can call him Ivan the Terrible."

"But he'll never be wicked," cried Nina, hugging him in a passion of delight, while the kitten chewed angrily at the ribbon around his neck.

Christmas Eve the Fannings and the Cushmans came to dinner.

The Cushmans had come down from Cos Cob for Christmas and the wedding to the Judge's big house, and Mrs. Bishop insisted that Arthur come to dinner too, though Janey evidently felt that dining out would upset her son's schedule. Prohibition having finally died the death, everyone had cocktails together comfortably. Marion insisted on using one glass each from Nina's numerous cocktail-glass presents and by piecing out with family glassware achieved serving everyone in a different kind of glass. Arthur had the prettiest of all, containing ginger ale and a cherry and laughed until his mother was afraid he was going to get hiccoughs. Since she had given Nina one set of glasses and a shaker, she was not too highly amused by the whole idea, anyway. Under the influence of Christmas, Uncle Van's liquor and Mrs. Bishop's graceful attention, even the Judge unbent and told some lengthy legal stories which, Nina thought, were funnier than anyone had any right to expect.

Only Kermit was not there. He had gone out in the afternoon. Upon being reminded of the dinner party as he was leaving, he replied, "I know." His knowledge had kept him from home until past seven o'clock, when dinner was scenting the air with promise and Mrs. Bishop had glanced several times at the clock. Just after seven Nina went out to the kitchen to get some more potato chips. As she passed through the hall the phone rang.

"Hello," she said.

"Is—Kermit there?" said the voice at the other end, a girl's voice, curiously rough.

"I'm sorry," said Nina. "He isn't."

"No," said the voice derisively. "Of course. He wouldn't be."

"I'm sorry," said Nina again, surprised. "But he really isn't. I expect him any minute, though. Can I give him——"

"Yes. Tell him Tony called. Tell him to call me." She hung up.

Nina put the phone down slowly. Tony. Tony-for-short. Who had been in trouble and made trouble and needed a hundred dollars and now called up to make trouble again. Tony, Kermit's defense. What hostages had he given for his pride? Nina shivered. Her fairy-tale world was ripped to shreds. Inside the living room everyone laughed as the Judge finished a story.

The front door opened and Kermit came in.

"Hello," he said. "It's snowing."

"You just missed a phone call," said Nina.

"Yes?" Kermit took off his coat and opened the door of the hall closet.

"It was Tony. She'd like you to call her back."

Kermit stood still with his back to Nina. Then he hung up his coat, shut the door, and said, "Thank you." Ivan the Terrible, dressed up in a red bow for Christmas, leaped out at Kermit's shoe-laces from under the chair by the telephone. Kermit picked him up and walked past Nina into the living room, petting the kitten. After a minute Nina followed him with the potato chips.

When Nina was frightened she was given to retreating into generalizations, into trying to relate the disagreeable situation about her to some eternal and impersonal natural law. So she thought, as she passed the bowl of potato chips around, This will be a really good opportunity for me to find out how selfish I am. Everyone is having a happy time. But I'm not happy—I'm scared. Now how much can I forget I'm scared, and how happy can I be even while I remember it, so that no one will know and the party will go on being wonderful? "Kermit says it's snowing," she announced. "Isn't that heavenly? We'll have a white Christmas."

"Oh, glorious!" cried Marion, and then Caroline, the new cook, came out of the kitchen and said dinner was ready.

It was a terrific dinner. Mrs. Bishop had decided against turkey, since she could not possibly have one bigger than the Judge's Thanksgiving offering, and neither she nor Caroline had been willing to face up to a suckling pig. So there were two plump geese with fruit stuffing that steamed and smelled heavenly, and sweet potatoes baked and pinched open and sprinkled with nutmeg, and fresh peas and spiced crab apples and green salad that Nina had mixed because Caroline never got the lettuce dry enough, and Caroline's yeast rolls and a fig pudding to finish off with burning in brandy and so light it nearly flew off the plate. Uncle Van provided a light red wine and everybody ate until they were scarlet in the face and talked with their mouths full, including Arthur Francis Cushman, who couldn't finish his pudding and finally got into his mother's lap and fell happily asleep. And the wine or the atmosphere had mellowed Janey so that she did not tell Arthur he was being rude, but kissed the top of his head and picked up her coffee cup with her left hand so that she would not disturb him.

Then the Judge made a speech. "Ladies and gentlemen," he began, brushing cigar ash off his vest and rising while Marion looked surprised and Kermit incredulous, "on this propitious—this most propitious occasion, I want to seize the opportunity—yes, seize time by the forelock—not to make a speech—no, not that. Don't be afraid of that, dear friends. But merely to express the happiness, the satisfaction, the joy of Christmastide that I feel welling up within me. As we all do. As all of us here, seated around this laden board, feel."

"Hear, hear," said Uncle Van, and Nina felt a wave of measureless gratitude to him, for being willing to participate in the Judge's exhibition.

"Yes indeed," said the Judge. "Our thanks first of all to the charming hostess who has brought us together tonight to enjoy this feast. Although her graciousness and charm could make of the simplest repast a feast indeed."

"Hooray!" cried Nina firmly, loyally. "A toast to Mum!" Everybody laughed and drank, and Kermit cried, "Answer, answer!"

But the Judge wasn't through. Inexorably he rolled out felicitations and congratulations to the bride and groom. The company waited, fingering glasses, ready to drink again, while the Judge told them that he was not losing a son but gaining a daughter. "And so," he declaimed, climbing to his peroration, "it is with gratitude as well as affection that I present my daughter-to-be with a Christmas gift——"

"Not now!" cried Marion. "Presents later!"

"Sh-h-h!" hissed Mrs. Bishop, Nina and Uncle Van together. Marion subsided.

The Judge had blinked in surprise for a moment, but when Nina's face and Mrs. Bishop's were again turned to his with fixed attention, he continued, "—a gift that will, I hope, remind her through the many, many years to come of this first Christmas which we shared. Nina, my dear." And the Judge took a leather box out of his breast pocket and passed it to Nina.

"The emeralds!" said Janey, and Arthur jerked awake in his mother's lap.

It was the emeralds. Necklace and earrings glittered like green fire in the candlelight. Janey's eyes were exactly as green with jealousy.

"Nina!" said Marion, and got up to come around the table and lean over Nina's shoulder.

"Oh Judge," said Nina, "you shouldn't! It's—they're too—it's too much." She sounded, she knew, both insincere and unconvincing. But she meant every word. She didn't want the Judge's emeralds, Stuart's mother's emeralds. They were ludicrously out of place in the life she saw herself leading, and they put a load of gratitude upon her soul that, she felt, she could never, never repay to the Judge; because she did not like the Judge in the least, and she did not want to be grateful to him. Besides, Janey was glaring at her with absolute hate.

"Janey," said Nina. "Janey should have——"

"Put them on, put them on!" boomed the Judge.

"My goodness, Nina!" cried Mrs. Bishop as Nina lifted an earring from the box. "Are those catches tight?"

"Good God." This was Uncle Van, reverently. "*Are they insured?*"

"Here." Stuart took the necklace. "I'll fasten it for you." Nina swung her hair forward and Stuart fumbled with the diamond clasp. There was a little space of tension and silence in which Janey Fanning's nostrils could be seen to move as she breathed.

Kermit broke it, in a soft, a nostalgic tone. " 'God bless us, one and all,' said Tiny Tim." Marion laughed, Arthur joined in shrilly because he was frightened, and Mrs. Bishop gathered the company up and transported it to the parlor, where the Christmas tree stood knee-deep in a tide of bright packages; but only after Nina had dutifully kissed her father-in-law, and Arthur had spilled his mother's coffee and been slapped for it.

"Let's have presents first and carols later, this year," said Mrs. Bishop in the parlor.

"Oh *no*, Mother! Carols first, like always!" cried Marion. "And the lights out, except for the ones on the tree."

"I'm afraid Arthur might drift right off to the Land of Nod again if he had to wait for his presents in the dark," said Mrs. Bishop, who felt that the atmosphere needed a bit of sweetening before the Christmas spirit could be properly celebrated in song. "Marion, will you and Kermit pass them out?"

"Me too, me too," cried Arthur.

"Now, Arthur," said Janey ominously.

"He can take my place," said Kermit, and sat down just behind Nina and Stuart, who were settled appropriately on the small and slippery sofa which was known as the love seat. "Those are really spectacular, Nina," he said affably. "Will you have your picture taken in them? If I had a snapshot of you wearing them to flash every now and then, I have a feeling it would do a lot for my credit rating. 'That's my sister,' I could say. 'Look what there is in the family to hock.'"

"Marion," said Mrs. Bishop commandingly, "this is for the Judge. And this—oh, that's for poor Aunt Flora. She and Dora both have the grippe. I'm so sorry they can't be here tonight, but they were afraid of coming out and then getting worse and missing the wedding, and of course that would never do. Marion, just put everything for Dora and Flora over on that table, and we'll go over with them tomorrow morning. After church. Shall we see you in church, Judge? Who's that for, Arthur dearie? For me? Why, goodness gracious! What can it be? And such beautiful paper! Janey! From you! Why, it's too pretty to open."

Arthur gurgled with laughter at this absurd idea, and the evening was back on its track again, rocking along as if no emeralds swung from Nina's ears or circled her throat. Tie racks, handkerchiefs, bed jackets, soap, cigars and perfume were unwrapped, and Arthur, having received a pair of roller skates, sat in the middle of the floor putting them on and ignoring everything else. Ivan, the kitten, leaped about through the crumpled paper wrappings and ribbon like one possessed until a real demoniac frenzy sent him halfway up the Christmas tree, at which point he had to be removed to the kitchen, where Caroline had a plate of goose scraps for him. The Judge gave Stuart a check to complete the furnishing of the apartment, he gave Janey and Howard a check, for which Janey embraced him and Howard pumped his hand, and he gave Arthur two shares of General Motors stock. If it had not been for the emeralds, indeed, it would have seemed doubtful that the Judge knew one could give an object as a present, not a piece of paper with writing on it. The rest of the Bishops received books from the Judge (more paper with writing on it, quite suitable and less expensive than checks). Uncle Van's was Lloyd George's *Memoirs,* Mrs. Bishop's the new *Jalna* novel, Marion's an excellent dictionary and Kermit's a copy of *Anthony Adverse,* for which he thanked the Judge impressively.

Marion gave Nina a cookbook and Stuart a pair of socks she had knitted herself. "Most people have one foot a little larger than the other," she said as he opened the box. "I hope you do."

Nina had got Stuart some gold cuff links engraved with his monogram. She had spent every lunch hour for an entire week in October at the jeweler's, hanging over the counter deciding which set she liked best and which style of monogram to have put on. She had no idea what Stuart had got for her and was nonplussed when Marion plumped a big square white box into her lap. She could feel Kermit behind her, watching, and Janey's eyes glued to her earrings, and she wished she had her mother's or Marion's ability to exclaim and apostrophize while her fingers fumbled at the wrapping. Even Uncle Van put down the pipe rack he had been admiring and looked. Suppose, thought Nina, growing cold, it is something perfectly awful. She remembered Stuart's ancient battered trench coat and the fact that she had once or twice looked at his ties and wondered if he were color-blind. I love him, she told herself staunchly, and the clasp of the necklace caught in her hair and pulled, and she thought, I can't go through anything like the emeralds again. She took the top off the box and was confronted with a mass of wadded tissue paper. When this was removed, it was apparent that Stuart had given her a bowl.

She lifted it out, her mouth drooping a little with surprise and uncertainty. It was fairly large, a dull blue green, and decorated about the sides with a looped and interwoven design of gold wire sunk in the deep crackled glaze. "Why, it's——" Nina's voice paused, and then grew certain. "It's the Persian bowl that was in Bellamy's window. It's—it's perfectly beautiful! How did you ever know I wanted it?"

"Mr. Bellamy said you stopped and looked at it every time you went by."

"Who's Mr. Bellamy?" said the Judge, who was looking at the bowl with a good deal of astonishment.

"He runs a kind of antique store on Fulton Street, near the apartment. Stuart and I were in there about a month ago asking about a cherry-wood desk he had. And it's perfectly true. I saw the bowl then and after that I stopped and stared at it every time I passed. Why, Stuart, I—I didn't know myself I wanted it so much! It's beautiful. It's perfectly beautiful."

"Just think," said Marion. "Now you have a Persian bowl and a Persian kitten to match. Isn't that lucky?"

"I wonder just what you'll use it for," said Janey. "It's an odd color for fruit or flowers and it's too big for salad——"

"I'll use it to look at," said Nina firmly. "Just think of all the things I have that are beautiful and useless. It makes me feel so rich! There's the bowl and the kitten and——"

"And the emeralds," said Kermit gently.

"Hrm!" said the Judge.

"Well those," Mrs. Bishop interposed hastily, "are hardly in the same class. Though I am sure the bowl is very valuable too. It's an amazing piece, Stuart. I don't know when I've seen anything so handsome. Bellamy's, you say. I think I know where it is. I wonder if he'd have any covers for my Rose Canton soup cups. I must go in and look next week. Goodness me, what a lot of beautiful things. What a Christmas! It seems almost wrong with the world in such a sad state, Roosevelt and Hitler and unemployment and everything, to have so much. But then, we shouldn't be ashamed of being happy. That would be wrong too. Well—it looks to me as if it were time for carols. Van dear, your violin? Kermit, would you turn off the lights?"

"In a second," said Kermit. "I too have a surprise for Nina." He stood up and dropped an envelope in Nina's lap and went over to the light switch. Just before he snapped it, Nina pulled out the flap of the envelope and saw what was inside.

"What is it, Nina? What is it, Nina?" said Marion.

In the darkness Nina's voice sounded odd in her own ears. "It's —it's some money," she said.

"Why, Kermit!" said Mrs. Bishop. "Have you—did you save it?"

"I did not steal it," said Kermit gently.

"Well I think that's very intelligent," said Janey. "Now you can buy yourself something practical that everyone's forgotten to give you."

"Yes," said Nina. Where did he get it? she thought, and heard Tony's voice on the telephone again. Could it have come from her? How was it possible? And if not, from where? From where? Contemplating possibilities, Nina knew that she had absolutely no way of evaluating them. Kermit might have obtained anywhere, anyhow, the hundred dollars with which he had repaid her loan. She would never know how, or where, it had come from.

"Silent night," began Uncle Van's violin. The lights on the Christmas tree glistened on the looping tinsel, the silver spheres and the star on the topmost branch. "Holy night," sang Kermit's voice from the corner, pure-toned and true as a bell. Then everyone joined in.

II. KERMIT

*N*INA WAS MARRIED AT THE END OF DECEMBER 1933, and nothing was the same after that. Kermit was realistic enough to know the name of his disability. He had, he presumed, a fixation on his elder sister. Undoubtedly, in psychoanalysts' files, there were ten thousand case histories to duplicate his story. Ten thousand other people had felt this betrayal and been pierced to the heart by the ease with which the beloved competitor and conspirator had turned traitor. They all shared the humiliation of knowing that the gangrenous wounds of love must be hidden, that the cry of treason can be raised only against those who betray some large institution like a nation, or some idea like democracy, not against those who commit the immediate simple act of betraying the one who loves them. Murder is a crime, while mass killing is war and justified. But the law of treason functions in reverse, and the victim of individual betrayal has no recourse. Fools, of course, would pour out their stories, weeping and choking with indignation and shame, to the ears of the analyst, paid to listen, who would attempt in the name of hygiene to cure them of what they felt. Kermit smiled coldly at himself when he occasionally experienced the need for indulging in such absurdities. The magic purge was for the simple-minded who wanted only to feel better in order to be at home and cozy in life; for people who expected to be happy and believed they were cheated if they were not. Kermit did not expect to be happy. He had long regarded it as an irrelevance.

Even so, there were times when his hatred of Nina rose up in his throat like vomit and he longed, how he longed, to pour the whole story out. He saved himself from this by picturing the uneasiness with which the listener—always some stranger—would regard him, drawing away from him, frightened and embarrassed. It was neither an interesting nor a convincing tale he had to tell, and he knew it. So he gritted his teeth and swallowed his hate and his fury and told no one that he knew what passion and frenzy were.

He spent the spring of 1934 commuting to Columbia and working hard, though with occasional lapses, when he would sit unhearing through lectures and leave assignments undone. Never too long, however. He always made them up in time, and he stood well with his professors. It is possible that his reputation as a serious-minded, hard-working young man stood him in good stead in the late spring, when a scandal broke over the college; but it is a good deal more likely that Kermit's involvement in it was never suspected at all.

Briefly, Kermit had been bootlegging liquor. Or rather, he had organized and financed the scheme on a moderately large basis. An imaginative zoology student had long since discovered that it was possible to extract alcohol from the zo. laboratory. He had kept it, however, merely for his personal use, or sold a small surplus. Kermit stumbled on this opportunity early in his career at the university, through being offered a drink of alcohol and grapefruit juice at a small party for sophomore transfers given by the zoologist's fraternity, which was looking for members with a B average. Kermit saw at once the dangers and the potentialities of the idea and proceeded to reorganize it. Alcohol, first of all, was never to be sold as alcohol, recognizable as such and capable of betraying its source. After an experiment or two, it was cut with water, covered with apricot flavoring and dispensed as apricot brandy. Secondly, it was not on sale casually, every now and then. It was to be had from eight to ten every Friday evening, but from eight to ten only. And the market place was never the same, but moved weekly. Kermit invested in the apricot flavoring and the pint bottles, he had keys made to assist the zoology student in his extractive work, and he once advanced ten dollars to cover a small bribe to a janitor who had laid hands on an assistant to the zoology student at the door of the laboratory—fortunately before he had taken possession of that week's ration of alcohol. Kermit had quite an argument about that ten dollars. The zoology student, whose name was Vincent, wanted to give the janitor twenty dollars and it took all of Kermit's logic and authority to make him see that giving the janitor too much was as fatal as giving him nothing.

"If you give him twenty dollars," Kermit kept saying, "he'll know something's up and he'll lie in wait. Ten dollars is enough to cover up a one-time shot. As it is, we'll have to quit using the east door for a while. How else can you get in?"

"But we only have a key for——"

"You'll get all the keys you need. How else can you get in?" Although he kept the key to the laboratory himself, between raids, since he did not trust Vincent to stay away, he took great care not to go near the place himself. Nor did he take any part in the actual sale of goods. Salesmen were recruited from steady customers—for the use of their rooms on a Friday night, they got a quart of the product free.

Oddly enough, it was not Nina's hundred dollars that had set Kermit up in business. That had actually gone to Tony. It was the first hundred dollars which had been intended for Tony that Kermit invested in his liquor-distributing plan. This he had scraped up by himself, selling an old suit of his own, a slide rule that Uncle Van had misplaced some time before and some books; adding his meager savings and borrowing the rest. When opportunity knocked, however, in the person of Vincent the zoology student, Kermit had not hesitated to put this sum to work, particularly since he suffered recurrent doubts over the reality of Tony's condition or his own responsibility for it. When Tony had learned, however, that a hundred dollars had actually existed and then gone elsewhere, she became inconsolable and extraordinarily convincing, and Kermit had therefore been pressed into borrowing from Nina. Of course, if Tony had only been willing to wait a little, the liquor distributorship would have produced enough to take care of her, but she insisted she could not wait. By Christmas, Kermit was in comfortable financial shape and able to give himself the pleasure of returning Nina's money.

When December saw the end of Prohibition, Kermit considered abandoning the business. Still, the supply of whiskey and gin was not yet large, the young ladies who went to Columbia dances had grown used to apricot brandy and, as the expense was small, the price of the product could be kept competitive. Kermit, however, foresaw the end of this phase of his business activity and was content to let the demand slowly dry up and the production decline. Not so, however, Vincent the zoology student, who advocated an aggressive selling policy. Kermit would not agree. Vincent had come upon him in one of his spring moods of acute lassitude and he sat and looked at the arguing Vincent without saying a word in reply.

"All right," said Vincent at last, "if you don't want to do it any more, I know people who will. How about that?"

Without a word Kermit took out the key to the laboratory and tossed it over. Then he picked up his books and left.

Two weeks later Vincent, a pre-med student, and an aspirant tackle to the football varsity were caught in possession of two gallons of alcohol and fifty pint bottles waiting for apricot brandy. They were all three expelled. Kermit wanted to ask Vincent if he had given the janitor twenty dollars, but decided against any provocative act. Instead, when Vincent came to him, he took him downtown, bought him some lunch and a ticket to Pawtucket, Rhode Island, where Vincent's uncle operated a high-class dog and cat hospital, and put him on the train. Vincent later took a course in veterinary medicine at a state university, and set up in business in Providence. When he came to New York he invariably called Kermit up.

Kermit turned up with two As and three Bs as marks for that term and Uncle Van was inordinately pleased and arranged a summer job for Kermit with a brokerage house that had a large number of foreign clients. "You can practice your diplomacy on them, my boy," he said, and chuckled.

"Thanks very much," said Kermit consideringly, but he took the job and rode to Wall Street with his uncle through the hot summer mornings when the gardens of thither Brooklyn smelled like the country and the locusts in the maple trees sang warningly of the solid blaze of noon to come, and the asphalt of Lower Manhattan melted and caught at the slipper heels of unwary typists and clerks, and the sea-smell and the voices of ships came in the high office windows on bright afternoons. Kermit was punctual, sober and intelligent and Uncle Van's broker friend was impressed with him as a promising young man.

In August, rather suddenly, Kermit announced that he was going to quit and go to Maine to visit a friend. The broker was surprised and Uncle Van a trifle chagrined; but Kermit had certainly worked hard and no one could deny that he was entitled to three weeks of loafing before classes began again.

"I wish you'd mentioned it in June, however," said Uncle Van.

"I didn't know it in June," said Kermit reasonably. "Mercer wrote me just now."

"Mercer?" asked his mother. The three of them were sitting on the porch after supper in the cool dusk. Marion was away being a junior counselor in New Hampshire. "Is that your friend, dear? I don't believe I know him."

"Mercer Davies," said Kermit.

"And where in Maine——"

"Davies?" said Uncle Van. "Mercer Davies? Is that the son of——"

"Yes it is," said Kermit. "At least I presume you're thinking of the Superior Biscuit Company."

"I know the company," said Uncle Van.

"Then you certainly know if they're responsible enough for me to visit."

"Now, dear," said Mrs. Bishop automatically. "No one meant to question your friends, of course. Still, it's nice to know——"

"That I won't have to make my own bed? It doesn't seem likely."

"Where—where is their home?"

"The summer place is at Northeast Harbor. Otherwise, Lake Forest and Aiken."

"Oh. Well—that's lovely. Goodness, though, Kermit, your clothes! Have you got what you need? Do they dress for dinner, dear? Van, hadn't he better go to Brooks tomorrow?"

"Why, yes—yes he had. The boy can't go off without being presentable. Get what you need, Kermit. I guess we can afford it."

"Thanks," said Kermit. He had banked over five hundred dollars from his money-making ventures, licit and illicit, but this did not seem the time to mention it. He did, however, spend his own money for the best tennis racket Feron had to sell and for a hand-woven raw-silk bathrobe that cost eighty-five dollars. It was not that he would have hesitated to stick Uncle Van for the price, but that, while a presentable wardrobe was a necessity, these two things were peculiarly his own. They were spectacular in a quiet way and he wanted to pay for them himself, not to owe them to Uncle Van's kindness. To own something that was, of its kind, the best that money could buy had a very special significance for Kermit. He also obtained a copy of *Ulysses,* which was still not published in America, as a gift to Mercer, who found, in six hours, every single dirty word in the book. Thus equipped, he packed his presentable wardrobe, kissed his mother good-by and boarded the Bar Harbor Express. He never came back home to live.

Nina was horrified when her mother told her about it. She sat on the porch and gaped. It was a warm Saturday afternoon in September. Stuart and Marion were picking crab apples—that is, Stuart was up the tree shaking it and Marion was collecting the fruit underneath—and Uncle Van was tying his heavy-headed dahlias to stakes.

"When—did this happen?" said Nina at last.

"He wrote me last week," said her mother.

"But you didn't say anything——"

"I wanted to wait—to wait till I'd written him again and got an answer back. I didn't believe—— Kermit's always been impulsive, but this—— And then I thought the Davies might put *their* foot down. But it seems that's the way Mercer's always lived. He has an apartment near the university and goes to classes and——"

"And Kermit's going to move in."

"I haven't told Van yet. I couldn't. I just said—he'd asked to stay on another week. I——"

"Have you seen this Mercer?"

"No."

Nina looked at her mother.

"He's very rich," Mrs. Bishop said helplessly. "I don't mean," she added after a minute, "that that makes it a good thing. But it makes it uncontrollable. I don't know what to do, Nina. I can't think of anything to do."

"He isn't of age," said Nina, and then burst into sudden hysterical laughter. " I was just thinking—of the Judge," she gasped. "If we went to court to get a restraining order or whatever—— I'm sorry. I guess I'm upset."

"It's all right," said Mrs. Bishop stoically. "I'm upset too. I don't think he's had his tuition money yet," she added suddenly. "I don't know. If we didn't give it to him——" She sat silently rocking in the sun and shut her eyes, and Nina saw that their lashes were wet with tears. The sun showed cruelly every line in her mother's face and the flesh that, tired, was sagging away from the bone. Mrs. Bishop's lips quivered and she wiped her eyelids and went on, "No, I couldn't do that, Nina. Whatever he's done. I couldn't do that."

"He must have made enough to pay it himself, anyway," said Nina.

"I don't know," said Mrs. Bishop. "He doesn't—he didn't tell me anything. He hasn't had his allowance while he was working, but Van gave him a hundred dollars before he went to Maine."

"Does he want his allowance to go on once he's moved out?"

"I don't know," said Mrs. Bishop. "He didn't say."

"What about the rent on the apartment? Would he let Mercer pay all that? And food? And clothes? How does he expect to pay for his clothes?"

"I don't know."

Nina looked at her mother in helpless exasperation. "Do you want Stuart to talk to him?" she said.

"No, dear. Van will talk to him," said Mrs. Bishop, and Nina felt gently reproved for having flaunted her husband in her mother's face. "I just thought we might think of something——" Some way to reach him gently and without force and talking-tos, she meant, something the women could do. Nina moved uneasily, half proud, half contemptuous of herself for sitting with her mother rocking in the sun and being a woman. You'll feel differently when you're married! Oh dear, how true it was! A year ago she would have been up the crab-apple tree with Stuart, or pelting Marion with the worm-eaten windfalls they could not use. She would have been Nina first, woman second; and not saddled with this problem of arranging and rearranging emotions—Kermit's, Van's, her mother's, her own.

Not that I'm any good to Mother, she thought angrily. I don't want to work out a compromise that will bring Kermit home. I'd order him home and punish him when he got here! I'd—I'd—like to beat him! And if he didn't come (and she had to admit that Kermit would be unlikely to be frightened home), then I'd let him go and say, Good riddance! In her own mind she was through with Kermit. After Kermit's dreadful fight with Stuart, she had abdicated her responsibility to him. She had her life with Stuart to build and all her emotions centered in it. There were the things which were particularly hers, like the apartment, and the girl who came in mornings to do the breakfast dishes and make the bed and clean, and shopping for food and dish towels and furniture polish. There was her participation in what was Stuart's, his career at Jones, Cooper and Germaine, the Wall Street law firm he had joined after graduation from law school. And there was all that belonged to both of them, which was love and the interrelation and adjustment of marriage. To have to worry about Kermit was an exasperation. She could not feel that the problems he created had any right to intrude upon her preoccupation with herself and Stuart, and she resented their doing so. She had pleased everyone, including herself, by her marriage (well, everyone but Kermit—which was another count against him), and she felt that in the light of this achievement she should be let off coping with the leftover problems of her youth, with Kermit and Kermit's adventures.

"I went wrong somewhere with Kermit," said her mother suddenly. "I tried—how I tried!—not to spoil him. If his father had lived——"

Nina sat in appalled silence. She wanted desperately not to hear her mother's self-questioning.

"He resents Van," her mother said. "I think sometimes he resents me for having given him a father who didn't live. I tried so hard, Nina, to—give him enough freedom. I didn't expect to understand all that a boy needs. I've always tried to be reasonable and not to demand too much from him. There's nothing worse than the only son of a widow who's been raised to be his mother's pet. I've always leaned over backwards trying not to let myself become dependent on

Kermit, and now I see I was wrong. But I don't know why or how. If I could just know——"

"Oh Mother," said Nina, "it's just Kermit—it's the way he is. You mustn't think it was your fault. He's just—irresponsible!"

"But I brought him up. I must have made him irresponsible." She fell silent, rocking in the sun, feeling back along the years of the children's youth, the years that had been so precious to her, so good, that had seemed to justify her femininity. But somewhere in those years she had failed, failed with Kermit, the son her husband had entrusted to her. How had they come about, Kermit's emotions and his fear of emotion, his need to dominate, and his rages? Oh, they were never, never intended! The pain in her breast grew as she faced the knowledge that she had not done what she had thought she was doing with Kermit and that nothing, therefore, was what it seemed. She too experienced betrayal.

But I must bear this! she thought. All the years of protecting the children, of minimizing any hurt they had caused her, of excusing them and loving them, came to her aid. I must not worry Nina this way, Mrs. Bishop told herself. No doubt I am exaggerating what Kermit wants to do. It's nothing but self-indulgence to let myself worry so. Perhaps it is all for the best, perhaps what Kermit really needs, what will make him the fine man he can be, is independence. I must try to believe that. Since there's no help. "Well, perhaps it will come out all right," she said. "Kermit's nearly twenty. I mustn't make a mountain out of a molehill, must I? After all, Nina, you had four years away at Vassar and Kermit had only the year at Yale. I can understand that he might want to be on his own."

"I shouldn't call living off Mercer Davies being on his own," said Nina.

"Well," said her mother, "I suppose he just didn't think about that part of it."

Then Marion came up with a bushel basket half full of crab apples and said, "Look, Mum, at all we got! Caroline will be jellying for days!"

Uncle Van, it turned out, was less disturbed about Kermit than Mrs. Bishop had expected. Uncle Van, who had not finished his sophomore year at college because his father's business had been badly hit by the 1893 panic, put more value on contacts than he was willing to admit out loud. Mercer Davies was definitely a contact and Uncle Van was actually rather surprised that Kermit had become his friend. It showed you could not tell about the boy: Uncle Van would have expected him to prefer arty and bohemian companions who could not be asked to dinner. Whereas the only question with Mercer Davies was whether he could be persuaded to ride the subway to Brooklyn's hinterland in order to dine with the Bishop-Van Deusen family. But Mercer Davies had a car ("I should have thought of that," Uncle Van said to himself) and was delighted to drive out to Bay Ridge, dine en famille and take Kermit back with his suitcases, his books, the Feron tennis racket and a cabinet photograph of his mother and sisters.

This was two days after Kermit came home from Maine. On that occasion Kermit had ridden the subway and walked, with his bag, the blocks home. The suitcase, full of dirty clothes, tugged at his arm and he said to himself savagely, over and over, This is the last time. This is the last time. But although he knew that, although he was certain of his escape, something within him could not really believe that it was true, that his boyhood was over, that the walls of his Gothic Victorian prison house could not again close about him. Only now was he realizing, with shock on shock of rage, how he had hated it—hated Brooklyn, hated the house, hated the warm food-smelling dusty bourgeoisness of his youth. His mother's gentle but slightly inept housekeeping, the ugly bulbous furniture, Uncle Van's air of probity and business morality, the hideous lamps and vases and china and glass—all of this lived with, unquestioned, allowed to distort emotion and stultify longing—all this he hated and longed to destroy. He turned into the path between the privet hedges and walked slowly up to the house, feeling like a revenant from another world, so completely had his fury burned away all connection with this past life. It hadn't been life, he believed. It had been false. His place was somewhere else. The winds from some other climate had nourished him, blowing across the deserts of Brooklyn and the middle class.

Then he went up the stoop and opened the door and his mother came out in the hall. I feel nothing, he told himself, put down his suitcase and went and kissed her cheek.

"Oh Kermit," she said, and put her arms around him.

No, he thought, I feel nothing, enduring her embrace. After a second she let him go and stood away from him, laughing shakily.

"You look tired, dear," she said. "I thought you'd have more of a tan."

"It got too cold for swimming," said Kermit.

"Of course. Well. You'll want a bath, I suppose, after that long trip. Go on up, dear. If you'll just dump all your dirty clothes on a chair I'll be up for them later."

That evening he had his talk with Uncle Van. It was wearing. At the end of it, Kermit was to have an allowance of sixty dollars a month and it was understood—at least by Uncle Van—that he was to get himself a job for Saturdays. His mother was distressed over this because she wanted him to come home week ends. Uncle Van was distressed because he wanted to get Kermit a job and Kermit refused, saying he would get something through the university.

"But there must be other young men who need those jobs more," Uncle Van protested.

"They all get FERA," said Kermit. "There's research I can do for one of the professors—he doesn't want just anyone."

In the end Uncle Van had to agree because he couldn't do anything else. Kermit unpacked and repacked while his mother fussed over his clothes because she couldn't let herself fuss over him, and finally Mercer arrived for dinner, the God from the machine.

Nina and Stuart had come out to dinner too, which put Kermit in a cold fury. Nina tried to charm Mercer and Stuart sat silently through dinner, observing everything from a distance and with calm. Marion wore a new dress, and lipstick, and Kermit saw with some surprise that she was going to be pretty—prettier than Nina. Mercer saw it too; and he also seemed quite ready to be charmed by Nina, who had a number of stories to tell about her bouts with housewifery.

"You must be quite an asset to the magazine these days," said Kermit. "You can really give them the woman's point of view."

"I try," said Nina, flashing him a murderous glance. "Mr. Daniels asked me if I could knit, the other day. That's my boss," she explained to Mercer.

"You mean you really have a job?" asked Mercer.

"Yes indeed. I'm the pillar of *Godey's Lady's Book.*"

"No kidding!" He gaped at her. "Do you write the things that go into it?"

"Well, no. I just straighten out the spelling and the punctuation and figure out what the artists' pictures are supposed to illustrate and write captions and——"

"Hey, will you do that for me on a term paper or two? Straighten out the spelling, I mean? I'm always getting into trouble on it."

"I'd be delighted."

"That's a deal, now. Don't forget it."

Marion broke out into laughter. "Don't let her tease you, Mr. Davies! She can't spell either."

"Can't she? You mean she's trying to kid me? How about you, now—Marion, isn't it? Just call me Mercer. How about you? Will you take over my spelling?"

"Well—what would I get for it?"

"Marion!" said her mother.

"Why—I don't know—— Guess you're a little young for perfume, isn't she, Mrs. Bishop? But how about going to the Yale game? Would you let her, Mrs. Bishop? Say, would you all come too?"

"Why, that might be very nice, Mr. Davies—Mercer. We'll have to see——"

"Oh Mother, *please!*" cried Marion.

"I'd drive you all up," said Mercer ardently, beaming at the Bishops. He seemed enchanted with them, and Kermit watched him trying to persuade Mrs. Bishop to come with him to New Haven in cold disdain. What an ape! Kermit said to himself, resenting Mercer's capacity to be pleased with people and things. It stemmed from Mercer's money. *He'd* never had to pick and choose the one best thing because he could only afford one. He could buy whatever he wanted, he didn't need judgment or taste to get the right thing because he got everything. What an ape, thought Kermit again, for Mercer's pleasure in the Bishops made Kermit feel profoundly insecure. To want to be liked, to work to be liked by Kermit's family seemed to Kermit to be akin to imbecility. No, worse. He'd always assumed Mercer was an imbecile. It smacked of recklessness, of irresponsibility, of large-hearted foolish generosity. Kermit liked none of these things. Becoming Mercer's friend was too easy. How could you depend on the friendship of a friendly man?

"You know, I never had much of a family," said Mercer to Mrs. Bishop later, in the living room. "This is wonderful. Gee—you'll kind of have to adopt me, Mrs. Bishop. I'll be around a lot."

"I'm sure we'll be happy to have you," said Mrs. Bishop comfortably, while Kermit glared at his friend. "You'll have to come out with Kermit often."

"You bet I will. You'll be sick of the sight of me, probably."

"No, indeed we won't." Mrs. Bishop was canny enough not to add that if Mercer brought Kermit home, he would always be welcome. Though relieved at this young man's pleasure in her son's family, she did not put a great deal of stock in it. It was, she saw clearly, a weapon she could use to hold onto Kermit only if she used it carefully and undemandingly. She did not make friends easily, she was really as single of purpose as Kermit, save that her devotion was not to herself alone, but to her family. As far as Mercer went, she could see him only dimly as a poor little rich boy to be sorry for. He was first and always the intruder who was stealing her son. What difference did it make whether the thief was a pleasant person or not? He was a thief.

So Mercer completed his thievery with a number of artless speeches about his unhappy childhood and how he would be back often to become part of the Bishop family. Then, still talking, inviting himself to Nina's and Stuart's for dinner, reminding Marion that she had a date for the Yale game, he removed Kermit and his possessions and the house became very still. Mrs. Bishop, who had been sewing, stopped and leaned back in her chair with her eyes shut.

Uncle Van cleared his throat and said that Mercer seemed like a nice young man.

"Yes," said Mrs. Bishop.

"I thought," said Marion, "that he was going to say you weren't losing a son but gaining another. Like Nina and the Judge."

"*You* certainly fell for him," rejoined Nina.

"I fell for the Yale game. Oh holy crumb! Wait till I tell the girls."

"You aren't going to that game alone, young lady," said Mrs. Bishop, reviving for a moment. It did not last. She picked up her sewing, looked at it and put it down again.

"Now, Elizabeth," said Uncle Van, "you mustn't worry."

"I know it," said Mrs. Bishop. "I don't."

This was so palpably a lie that no one could think of anything to say except Stuart, who had been pursuing his own line of thought. "I think he's all right," said Stuart.

"Do you, Stuart?" Mrs. Bishop caught at this pronouncement almost greedily.

"Yeah. He isn't—he won't——" Stuart paused, fighting for words. To Nina he could say later that there was no faintest whiff of anything abnormal about Mercer or Kermit's relation to him. But, of course, he could not suggest this now. There was, however, something else he was trying laboriously to say. "He won't get Kermit spoiled. He likes things. He liked everybody. See what I mean?"

"He means Mercer isn't finicky and fantastical, the way a rich boy might be because he's had so much," Nina interpreted, and Stuart nodded, relieved. If she saw that much perhaps he would not have to say the other thing.

"Yes, I see that," said Mrs. Bishop. She smiled at her son-in-law. "You're a comfort, Stuart."

"Well," said Stuart seriously, "I'm fond of you."

"I know you are." She took off her glasses and smoothed her forehead between her eyes where the little wrinkles went up and down and wished futilely that Kermit had some of Stuart's balance and kindness. She knew it was futile, but it was the only thing she could wish, since she could not wish to love Kermit less.

"Let's have a rubber of bridge," said Uncle Van abruptly.

"I want to play with Stuart," said Marion.

"You'll play with your Cicero," said Nina. "Don't you want to get to Vassar?"

"Pooh to you! And pooh to Vassar too. I'm going to live home and go to Barnard."

"Well, Barnard's no snap. You go on and straighten out your subjunctives and your ablatives."

"That's right, dear," said Mrs. Bishop. "If you get through early you can take my hand."

So Marion went off into the corner and groaned over the sins of Catiline and his fellow travelers while the rest of them played bridge, and Nina and Uncle Van beat Stuart and Mrs. Bishop roundly.

Meanwhile Mercer was telling Kermit that he didn't know how lucky he was.

"Lucky to be getting out," said Kermit bitterly.

"You wouldn't be feeling that way," Mercer told him, "if your mother'd always liked horses better than you. God, how I hate horses. They know it, too. They bite me whenever they can. Can't even give one of the bastards a lump of sugar without having it bite me in the hand. No, but she's swell, your mother. I wish she was mine. I like your sisters too. That little one's going to be quite a piece. Not that Nina isn't. How long's she been married?"

"Since last December."

Mercer sighed. "Guess it's too soon to try anything there. I'll have to stick to Marion."

"Damn it," said Kermit, "she's just a kid! You can't——"

Mercer roared. "Got you there, boy. Thought you didn't give a damn about any of them. Sure, I know she's a kid. She's a sweet kid. I was ribbing you, boy. You don't think I'd touch your sister!" He was really shocked.

"Well, don't talk about her either," Kermit muttered, feeling like a fool.

"Gee, I'm sorry. Honest, I liked them all a lot. It's a wonderful family. Wonderful. I wish I had something like that behind me."

"As long as it's behind me I can stand it too."

"Yeah, I suppose so. You're nearly twenty, you don't want them sitting on you, asking where you've been. I suppose they all do. Hey, what's this idea of yours about making some dough with the apartment?"

It was a simple idea, really. Dormitory residents at the university frequently felt the need of a place to repair with a young lady. Last year, Kermit told Mercer, he had heard of a large shabby apartment on a cross street near Riverside Drive where a young man who had five dollars and a need for a place of rendezvous could rent a room for the night. Well, they had an apartment to start with. It wasn't as large as the other, but if they tried the system and it worked, they could certainly make enough to take care of the rent of a larger apartment——

At this point Mercer objected that he had a number of possessions he valued and he didn't want drunks breaking them and being sick on the rug.

"Why should we let drunks in?" said Kermit coldly. "We can choose who we want. I don't want drunks. They make trouble."

"Yeah—I don't know," said Mercer. He moved his shoulders uneasily. "I don't want them in the apartment anyway. I don't like it."

Kermit sat silent beside him as they drove uptown. He was furious. Mercer! The rich boy! He could kill him.

Mercer glanced at him, disturbed by getting no answer. "Look," he said. "I don't say it isn't a good idea. But——"

"But you won't do it."

"Not in my apartment." He was getting stubborn.

Kermit sat, revolving in his mind where he would go if he told Mercer to stop the car and let him out. He had three dollars in his pocket, Uncle Van's check for sixty dollars for his first month's allowance and three hundred and eighty-seven dollars and sixty cents in the bank.

Mercer said, "Look, what I mean is why don't we rent another apartment to start with and just use it for that?"

It was a measure of how shaken Kermit had been that when he could speak he made an objection. "Where would we get furniture?"

"Buy it," said Mercer promptly, and then remembered that money was important to Kermit, he didn't have it the way Mercer had it, and this was not just a lark to him. "I'll do that. You had the idea, I buy the furniture. That's fair, isn't it? Hey, it'll be fun. I know some pictures we could put up——" He leaned forward across the wheel, laughing.

"We'll have to get a woman to clean," said Kermit slowly.

"Hell, Mattie will do that. The cleaning woman I have now."

"No. We should have somebody who doesn't know you. And we'd better rent a place under a different name——"

"Hey!" Mercer exclaimed again. "That's smart as hell. Who'll we be? Nicholas Murray Butler and Dean Hawkes? Laurel and Hardy? Gallagher and——"

"We'll be Mr. John Smith, you dope. And don't try to give the guy a check for the rent with your name signed to it."

"Okay, okay. What do you think I am, fathead, a fathead?" In case Kermit might say yes, he hurried on. "Where'll we look?"

"I'll look," said Kermit. "I know what we want. About eight rooms."

"Judas Priest!" Mercer was awe-struck by the magnitude of the operation. "Eight rooms at five bucks a night is——"

"We won't rent them all every night. Mostly week ends. We could have a special week-end rate. Twenty dollars for just a room. Fifty— no, say seventy-five if someone wanted the whole apartment——"

"Judas!" said Mercer again. "You ain't kiddin', boy. There's dough in this."

There was a profit, when the enterprise got under way, of around three hundred dollars a month. Kermit bought himself one good suit and banked the rest of his money until after Christmas, which he passed at home. During the holidays he pleased his uncle very much by suggesting that they lunch with the broker for whom he had worked during the summer, and after that he started investing, though of course through a different brokerage house. His work fell off a bit when his aircraft holdings took a tumble, but he got out without being hurt and bought in again at the low. By the end of the year he had pulled his marks back up to a B average, and had almost two thousand dollars in the market. He sublet the apartment for the vacation to the family of a professor from Bowling Green who was spending his fifth summer at Columbia looking for a Ph.D.

Mercer wanted Kermit to come to Northeast Harbor with him, and Uncle Van was hopeful that his nephew would return to the job he had had the year before. Kermit did neither. One of his teachers had a brother-in-law with a great deal of money and a son who was a high-grade moron. Kermit went to Europe with the family—their name was Morrison—as the boy's tutor. Before he left, he sold the market and put his money in Republic Steel four and a halfs.

And he went home for ten days. Mercer was hurt because Kermit didn't want to come to Maine—"It's too damn cold," Kermit kept saying. At last he brought Mercer home to Brooklyn for a couple of nights. In spite of his sincere admiration for the Bishops, this was only the fourth time Mercer had been there.

Mrs. Bishop greeted them both cheerfully, but her eyes looked at Kermit's face as if she were trying to see through the flesh to the bone, through the skull to the slanting alien mind that lay within. What has happened to the baby I nursed, to the little boy who liked stories only if they had no wolves or bears in them? she seemed to be saying. Where is Kermit? But this was Kermit—at least there was no Kermit other than this.

"You boys have both lost weight," she said, addressing them collectively so that she would not seem to be worrying about her son. "I suppose it's those examinations. Were they very bad?"

"They were awful, Mrs. Bishop," said Mercer, reveling in sympathy. "Golly, that medieval history! 'Give seven reasons for the growth of towns in the twelfth century'—and I always have to count on my fingers to get the centuries right. You know the twelfth isn't the twelve-hundreds at all. It's the thirteens—— No, it's the elevens. Why the—why do they *do* that to you?"

"It is silly, isn't it? Goodness—seven reasons for the growth of towns—— I suppose people just decided they liked to have neighbors, don't you?"

"That's a lot more sensible than what we were supposed to say! I wish I'd thought of that." Commiserating with himself, showering admiration on everyone near him, he was taken upstairs and shown his room. Before he left, Mrs. Bishop was willing to pity him aloud for being affection-starved, but in her heart she could feel nothing but enormous irritation. Whenever she wanted to sit down quietly with Kermit—he reading, herself sewing—and hint around through his life with little irrelevant questions that might receive revealing answers, whenever she thought she saw a clue to Kermit, there would be Mercer, as cheerful and clumsy and inflated with harmless egotism as a puppy, getting in her way. She drew a long breath of thankfulness when he finally left, having prolonged his stay three days.

And then Kermit announced that he was going to Southampton for the week end. "The Morrisons want me to get acquainted with Chuck before we sail," he explained.

"Oh Kermit, no!" his mother was betrayed into saying.

"It's a shame, but I'm afraid it's part of the job. After all, I'm going to see Europe first-class and on a salary. I guess I'd better do what they want. I'll be back Monday, and we don't leave till Wednesday, you know."

But his mother for once was speechless. Kermit looked at her, attempting to suppress both the guilt and the anger with which he was smitten by the sight of her face; trying to think only, since he did not approve of emotions, This is what it's like for her, what it's like for a mother. It's interesting, I must be interested in this and remember. Before he left, standing in the living room—she did not go to the door with him—he said, "Don't be hard on me, Mum."

"Hard on you! Hard on *you!*" cried Mrs. Bishop's poor heart, before she could stop the accusing words.

"Yes. I have to do things my way. I'm trying to do my best. I don't think I'll have to take any money from Van next year."

"But Van—but your uncle *wants* to help——"

"I want to be where I don't need help. Anybody's."

"Everyone needs help, Kermit. One way or another."

But Kermit did not believe her. He went out in the hall and picked up his suitcase and left. Later, he remembered those years as insanely full of suitcase carrying, as if he were always leaving, never arriving at a destination where he could settle. Today the idea of the subway was maddening and at the corner of the first boulevard he hailed a taxi and climbed in, saying, "Penn Station," knowing he was squandering money, money which was so important, but knowing also that money *had* to be squandered sometimes. In a kind of half-superstitious way Kermit believed that you must not be too careful of your money, you must not be afraid of spending it once in a while, or you would risk losing it. You had to show it, occasionally, who was master, by throwing a little over your left shoulder, as it were, to the grinning Fates who waited there.

Whether the Morrisons were the masters of their money Kermit was not sure. Mrs. Morrison seemed to have organized her life on the fundamental principle that spending was the most important possible female activity. She had, of course, hedged this principle about with certain rules and restrictions. Her husband was wealthy, even in 1935. But he did not have one of the world's great fortunes, the kind that no insanity could touch. Mrs. Morrison had to reckon with a definite limit to her income. She had more money than Mercer did, but she also had a great many more desires, and thus, unlike Kermit's first rich friend, she had to make choices. She had to have taste. She could not excel (and she wanted badly to excel) by quantity, so she had to know about quality. The house in Southampton was charming, and so was she.

Kermit regarded her warily, but he could feel her charm. It was not merely that he was very young. All his life he was to admire anyone who did a job well, no matter what the job was. The life of the Morrison family, including this tour (which was deliberately undertaken in the grand tradition, with children and tutors and nurses and maids), was superbly organized. Chuck, of course, was a difficulty; but his little sisters were pretty and pert and well brought up.

Mr. Morrison looked like a Captain of Industry—as indeed he was. When, years later, a whiskey company ran a series of advertisements hawking Men of Distinction, it occurred to Kermit that they were attempting to approximate Mr. Morrison. Not that Mr. Morrison would have sat for a photographer from an advertising agency. Even during the war to come, when he was a dollar-a-year man in Washington, he was difficult about the publicity which many people felt was so vital to the morale of the Home Front. As it was, he was brusque with the ship-news reporters who saw the Morrison family off.

"By God," he said to Kermit afterward, mopping his forehead, "a man can't have any privacy any more. A simple pleasure trip with my family—and they have to cross-examine me about international cartels! How can a cartel not be international nowadays, tell me that? Not that I think it's a healthy trend. But the way things stand today" (this was one of his favorite phrases), "you can't do business without some kind of understanding. No one's going to compete himself out of business, and if the government doesn't know that, the government's an ass. Isn't that what Dickens said? You can't beat Dickens! The government's an ass."

"I think he said the law," said Kermit.

"Same thing," said Mr. Morrison. "Well, close enough. Law's an ass, government's an ass—— Government of the asses, by the asses, for the asses. And if you're not an ass yourself, you've got to look out, young man. Remember that. If you're not an ass yourself, you're out of step with our great modern civilization of asinine idiocy, and you'd better be careful."

"I try to be," said Kermit.

"Good, good," said Mr. Morrison, but he shot a quick glance at Kermit as if to say, So you think you're not an ass, do you? And Kermit blushed.

At this slightly awkward moment Mrs. Morrison appeared, as she had a talent for doing, to dispel all awkwardness. "Nannie's getting the girls settled," she said happily in her clear lovely voice. "Chuck and I want to see the last of New York. Kermit, I suppose you do too, since you've never sailed before. It's exciting, isn't it? Come over to the rail. Aren't the tugs absurd? I love them. Oh my, this beautiful city! I adore it—from this distance."

"Why don't you buy a houseboat and anchor off here?" said Kermit. "Or even a place on Staten Island?"

"Oh Kermit, that's a charming idea. Do you hear that, Charles? I should adore to live on Staten Island! And we could send you across to Manhattan in the morning on a natty little launch. Wouldn't that be amusing, Charles?"

"It might also be a trifle chilly in January," said Mr. Morrison.

Mrs. Morrison laughed like a tinkling of bells. "But it never would *be* January," she said. "Not in my world. Not when I get it made and live on Staten Island. It would always be June, like this."

"Yes. Well," said Mr. Morrison, "since you haven't finished your world yet and we're still in this one, I'm afraid I have to get off a cable." He nodded and walked off with a leisurely owner's pace. Kermit watched New York recede and was amused by Mrs. Morrison until it became time for him to take Chuck below for "settling"—he supposed the word was as appropriate to his task as to Nannie's. Within him, however, stirred the determination to prove to Mr. Morrison that he too could live in the real world of business and pressures so unremitting that within fifteen minutes of sailing on a pleasure trip with one's family one had to dispatch cables.

His job with Chuck, he came to see fairly soon, was more or less hopeless. Into the little Morrison girls, Lucia and Anne, had gone all their parents' drive and intelligence. Chuck was a throwback to some remote agricultural ancestor, some stubborn master of land and oxen. Tutoring Chuck in Latin and mathematics was the undertaking of some terrible fairy-tale task, climbing the glassy mountain, spinning gold out of straw. Before they got past the first declension in the grammar review that Kermit instituted, he realized that Chuck's reasoning powers were tenuous and decided to fall back on memory work and drilling. Unfortunately, Chuck did not particularly want to remember anything. Somewhere back in the elementary grades his desire for knowledge had been fully sated. He *did* like animals very much—Kermit discovered this in probing for some interest which he could enlist to aid him, and wished briefly that he knew as much about horses as Mercer Davies' mother. He attempted to set algebra problems in animal terms—the speed of greyhounds, how many bushels of oats a race horse ate—but since he knew nothing about the potential speeds or appetites of such creatures he got his data wrong and Chuck shook with laughter. However, he kept stubbornly on, scratching away at the monolith of Chuck's psyche with his feeble instruments of instruction for two hours every morning and as often as possible in the afternoon.

When they landed in England they went straight to London for as much of the season as was left. The Morrisons had many English friends and Kermit met quite a few. He did not, of course, attend the dinners and parties to which Mr. and Mrs. Morrison went alone, but when Chuck was included in an invitation Mrs. Morrison saw to it that Kermit was too, and occasionally when Mr. Morrison was engaged in an afternoon or evening of transatlantic telephoning she employed him as an escort. Kermit had some clothes made in Savile Row so as to be, as his uncle would have said, presentable. He had expected to be excited by London, though he would have hated to admit it, but when he got there he found that it made him feel provincial. Mrs. Morrison's friends all had absurd nicknames which, Kermit felt, were rather like the appellations Tom Sawyer and his cronies had assumed in forming their secret society. There was definitely a secret-society feeling about the group and Kermit determined at once that to be completely an outsider was more dignified than to attempt to join it and become a hanger-on. He was therefore unusually, gravely silent. This, and his good looks, intrigued Mrs. Morrison's friends.

He had accompanied her to the theater one night, Mr. Morrison having elected to spend the evening with the telephone and a stack of half-yearly company reports. Afterward they met six or eight of the secret society at a club, where a great deal of incomprehensible chat took place. Kermit rather suspected that Helena Morrison did not follow all the allusions any better than he did, but she smiled and laughed her lovely laugh and used the right adjectives at the right time. One of the English girls, Lady Something-or-other, who was called Poppy, attached herself to Kermit and spent an hour or two murmuring confidences which he could barely hear, with her arm tucked through his. Kermit was deeply embarrassed. He did not want to hold Poppy's hand and have her play with his fingers in private, let alone in the middle of a shrieking night club. He was no more attracted to her than he would have been to an Afghan hound bitch, whom in fact she rather resembled. She seemed to him to belong to another species, he could feel no connection with her at all. He was alienated, he was lost, he was homesick. If only someone would walk in the door, someone from the real world!—his mother, or Marion, or Mercer—and say, "Oh there you are, Kermit!" he might have wept with relief.

When, finally, Mrs. Morrison made up her mind to leave, Kermit was sunk fathoms deep in silence, faced with the totally unfamiliar experience of wondering whether he was right to be where he was. Perhaps he had taken a wrong turn! Perhaps his long struggle to escape had all been a grotesque mistake and he had been engaged for years in desperately attempting to break into prison. He felt very lonely and strangely unsure of himself. Were his standards false? But by what standards did one judge one's standards? I am Kermit, I am Kermit, he tried to tell himself, but did not receive therefrom the usual comfort of self-immersion, self-loss in self.

At the hotel they discovered that Mr. Morrison had gone to bed, leaving the parlor of the large suite the Morrisons had engaged for themselves and their entourage scattered with cigar ash and littered with crumpled papers covered with figures. Mrs. Morrison made a face at the mess, and stirred a paper or two with her toe before she sank down on the sofa and leaned back.

"I'm tired," she said. "Really it's absurd," but she did not explain what. "Ring for a boy, will you, Kermit? I want a glass of milk."

Kermit did as he was told and then stood uncertainly in the center of the room. It would be rude to leave Mrs. Morrison before she dismissed him, and yet he was, for once, profoundly disinterested in the life of wealth, luxury and power which she represented. He wanted to get away from her, bemused by the problems that loneliness, strangeness and insecurity had set for him. He needed to know as never before, whether power equated with pleasure; whether to dominate events meant to enjoy them.

But Mrs. Morrison said, "I want to talk to you, Kermit."

He was startled. He looked at her stretched out on the couch and his skin prickled with a sense of danger. Warily he retreated into his defenses which (he did not even take time to think) had magically risen again around him.

"Sit down," said Mrs. Morrison. "Oh, don't be scared." She laughed. "It's nothing, really. But why—why are you so difficult? And diffident? You shouldn't be, you know. Everyone likes you and is interested in you. You're quite an arresting young man, actually. But why—as Toto says, why behave like a noble savage?"

Kermit blinked once. "I'm sorry if I've been rude," he said.

"Oh for God's sake, don't be stuffy!" Mrs. Morrison ran her fingers through her dark hair and stretched her lovely white arms above her head. "I didn't say you'd been rude. I didn't even say you'd been unaccommodating, which is a better word, because you haven't been really in any way I can put my finger on. But why don't—why don't you *mix* more?"

"Well," said Kermit cautiously, "I suppose I feel I don't want to intrude or presume——"

She sat up furiously. "Have I made you feel like an intruder? Has anyone hinted that you're not welcome? How dare you say such a thing!" Kermit stared at her in amazement. She sank back against the cushions and said, "Oh it's absurd! Why should I lose my temper? It isn't worth it. But it makes me angry to see the opportunities you have and to see you sitting there like a parochial little idiot, refusing to take them. I can't stand people who don't take advantage of their opportunities! Do you want Poppy? You can have her perfectly well. Oh I know she's obvious, but that's just because she's shy. You made her very, very unhappy tonight. Or do you want Nonie? You could cut Toto out in a minute."

"But I don't," said Kermit, reduced to honesty. "I don't want either of them."

"Now why not? You see what I mean. You're provincial, parochial, scared, middle-class!" cried Mrs. Morrison. At this moment there was a knock on the door. "Oh, it's my milk," she said. "Go let him in."

Kermit opened the door and the waiter brought in the milk. Neither Kermit nor Mrs. Morrison spoke until the door closed again behind the man, but Mrs. Morrison's emotion vibrated in the room. Can she possibly mean, thought Kermit, that she—that I—— He looked at her stretched out on the couch. She was very expensively beautiful.

The waiter left and Kermit walked over to the window and looked out at the London night. Was it hostile, or merely neutral?

"I take it then," said Mrs. Morrison, "that you don't like my friends."

"Not particularly."

"Now that's rude!"

"You asked me."

There was a pause while she looked at the back of his head. He continued to gaze out the window. Nothing told him that he had reached a fork in the road, a place of choice. He was conscious only of anger. I will not give in, he thought. I will not give in to her.

"You're very young," said Mrs. Morrison in a voice that combined contempt with a cautious promise.

Kermit felt the hairs on his neck prickle and rise and he was transported by a clap of fury greater than any he had experienced since his tantrum days. He left the window and went to her. She sat up to meet him, looking incongruously startled. He took her bare shoulders in his hands and said, "Yes I am, aren't I?" and kissed her as hard and as viciously as he could, hoping that he was hurting her.

Then he let her go and sat, panting and trembling a little, looking at her to see what she was going to do next.

For a moment she didn't know. She put her hand to her mouth, and her eyes were round above it, simulating surprise, while she too waited. But Kermit had satisfied much of his emotion in that brutal kiss, while it had only stimulated her. He waited longer.

She was going to seduce him. Her eyes changed and she said, "Oh Kermit! You mustn't hurt me, you know."

On a great surge of triumph, Kermit laughed. Dear God! he thought. Women!

"Shhh," said Mrs. Morrison. Kermit reached up and turned off the lamp by the couch.

The next day felt very odd. He couldn't stop thinking about her, but there was nothing warm in his thoughts. His lust, yearning toward Helena Morrison, invested her not with an affectionate aura, but with one of cold contempt. He wanted to be rude to her, to treat her with mulish arrogance. The morning hours with Chuck were real torture, and it was then that he more or less decided to give up any attempt to teach Chuck anything and regard himself simply as bear-leader. He could guess that other people employed by the Morrisons had had to come to that decision too, for Chuck accepted Kermit's closing of the textbooks with relief. His acceptance, in fact, made Kermit a little sick. Partly it was his defeat in the struggle with Chuck's stupidity, partly it was the Puritan ambition within him, partly it was because he was tired, but when he let Chuck lean back and begin to tell him music-hall jokes, Kermit knew he was disgusted with himself, and it was then that he came closer to losing his temper than in any of the time he had been trying really to teach Chuck.

Mrs. Morrison was lunching out. As Kermit emerged from his capitulation to Chuck she was standing before a mirror, adjusting her hat. "Oh Kermit," she said. "How are you, dear? This is a horrible hat, I should never have bought it I thought at the time I was wrong, and then I thought—— No, it's a perfect luncheon hat for London, and so it is, but my God, I don't have to *wear* perfect luncheon hats, do I, I don't *live* here! Well—I suppose that's the best I can do. How are you today?"

Kermit met her eyes in the glass without saying anything.

Mrs. Morrison returned his gaze for a moment and then raised her eyebrows and said "Really!" She swung around to face him and took a deep breath; and just then Mr. Morrison came out of his bedroom, smoothing the back of his head with one hand and said, "Ah. All set?"

"Quite," said Mrs. Morrison, glaring at Kermit. She snapped her eyes away from his like turning off a light, went to her husband and attempted to straighten his tie.

"That's all right, that's all right," he said, retreating from her, for he had a real horror of being touched in public.

But she pursued him relentlessly, saying over her shoulder, "Kermit, Nannie's not well today. I want you to take the little girls off her hands this afternoon for a while, will you please? Go sight-seeing— the Abbey, the Tower—I don't know what they've seen and what they haven't. They'll tell you. There, dear, that's better," she finished to Mr. Morrison, who at once stretched his chin and jerked his tie back the way it had been. Mrs. Morrison picked up a pair of fawn doeskin gloves and began to put them on.

"I——" said Kermit, and saw that Mr. Morrison was watching him. He swallowed the rest of his sentence and finished expressionlessly, "Very well." Then he went to the door and opened it for Mrs. Morrison as a footman might. She walked past him without turning her head.

But as he shut the door he heard Mr. Morrison begin, "You had no right to ask the boy——" and he clicked the door smartly to.

As a matter of fact he had a fine time with the little girls. Lucia was eleven and Anne was nine, and they knew a great deal more about London than he did. Lucia had memorized most of Baedeker and Anne knew all the bus routes. "It's that idiotic school they send us to," Lucia explained. "I don't know why Mummy got it into her bean that we should be educated progressively. You don't learn to read or write until you want to, and believe me, Kermit, there are girls as old as I am who can't do either. And then they come and play phonograph records and you're supposed to get up and interpret them—— Well, I like dancing, I've thought very seriously about ballet, but interpreting a Chopin nocturne with no more idea of how to move your body and no training—it's the most *awful* waste of time. What is the sense of a school that doesn't teach you anything? It isn't as if we were going to be young forever, you know. I said to Anne two years ago, we just haven't got the time to waste. So we started our own program, Anne and I. At least they have books there, and they will answer questions—though a lot of them don't know much—and so we've been working on English and French history and geography this year since we knew we were coming abroad. We felt we'd better prepare ourselves. Isn't that so, Anne?"

"Nobody else would," said Anne.

"We appreciate your taking us out," Lucia continued. "We asked Mother often enough before if she wouldn't ask you, but she wouldn't. Nannie's no earthly use, you know. We have to pluck her off the wrong busses all the time. She never knows where she is, and of course she couldn't tell Christopher Wren from Christopher Robin. Well. Where shall we go today?"

"You know more than I do," said Kermit, "you choose. Or Anne."

Lucia struggled for a moment and then said, "Well. Anne?"

Anne picked Kew Gardens mainly (Lucia accused her) because it involved a long and complicated bus ride. It was a pleasantly warm afternoon—the English newspapers all said "Heat Wave!"—and Kermit found himself relaxing and enjoying himself and the little girls in a kind of gently euphoric trance. On the way back from Kew ("Very interesting," said Lucia, "but not my idea of a *garden*") he almost dozed off and had to be rescued by Anne as ignominiously as Nannie from riding past their stop.

"But this isn't where we should get off," he protested, standing on the pavement.

"It's very close," said Lucia soothingly. "And we would like to take you to tea before we go home. We needn't be back till half-past five. Anne says this is the best tea place. I like Rumpelmayer's myself, but it's her afternoon for picking."

"But——" said Kermit. "Mayn't I take *you* to tea? I mean, after all, the gentleman usually——"

"Another day," said Lucia rather grandly. "We have *quite* enough money with us, and we would like to very much." So Kermit was taken to tea and plied with cornucopias filled with cream and almond-paste tartlets and petits fours and all the things that grown-ups groan at the sight of, and ate almost as much as Anne, but not nearly as much as Lucia, who was a tall thin ethereal-looking child. Then they went home to face Mrs. Morrison.

She looked at them thoughtfully and asked them if they had had a nice time.

"Very nice, thank you," said Lucia.

"Anne?"

"Oh yes."

"And Kermit?"

"I enjoyed it very much." He smiled at the girls.

"Then you must go soon again. Run off now, dears. I must rest before dinner." But as Kermit went she called him back.

He stood in front of the chaise longue where she lay and waited.

"Understand me," she said, and her eyes were narrow. "If you annoy me, I'll have you sent home." He did not answer. "Do you hear me?"

"Naturally I hear you."

She waited. "And what do you say about it? Do you want to go?"

Kermit considered her. It would be easy to say that it was immaterial to him whether he went or stayed; but it would not be true. He thought of what such a return would be like—New York, defeat, and his family, all weltering in summer. "I'm sorry if I was rude," he said stiffly.

"You were very rude. I won't put up with it. Suppose you remember that."

Again Kermit couldn't speak, but this time Helena Morrison smiled suddenly. "All right," she said, and took his hand. "I'm not such a bitch, really, Kermit. You can remember that too."

"I'll try," said Kermit, and smiled slowly back.

Mrs. Morrison sighed and said, "I do have to rest, you know. Run along. I think we'll go to France next week. Do you drive, Kermit? You can see so much more that way. Charles is going to Sweden for two weeks; we'll be staying down in the château country. It would be nice if you could drive me about. And the children, of course. Lucia's bright, isn't she? You really enjoyed them?"

And Kermit saw that a doorknob was turning, Mr. Morrison was coming in to find his wife dutifully receiving a report from Chuck's tutor on an afternoon with the children.

So they went to France, to a storybook castle near the Loire, where swans swam in the moat and clipped yew hedges defined a famous garden. The air was honey-sweet and the horizons were blue and distant and Kermit, remembering his medieval history, wondered whether the young knights at Queen Eleanor's twelfth-century Courts of Love had had as bad a time as he did. For Mrs. Morrison turned into a witch. She was capricious and demanding, easily bored and, when bored, reckless. She ordered Kermit about, she used him as a chauffeur, left him in the car when she went calling on someone to whom she had a letter of introduction and then, coming back through soft dusk, wooed and nagged him into love-making. For hours in the afternoons she would lie on the terrace, before a view so lovely as to break the heart, with her eyes shut while Kermit read bad French novels aloud to her and she corrected his accent. Her graceful public personality disappeared, abandoned like a mask. What effort it must have cost her to build it up, he thought. How she must hate the charming woman she had made herself learn to be! Even her voice seemed to Kermit to grow strident, shattering peace whenever she called him. The children's nurse, who had been a friendly old thing, retreated into disapproval and dislike. Chuck's admiration for him vanished and Lucia and Anne looked at him with sorrowing pity. How much they knew of his situation he was unsure, but they must have seen their mother and other young men acting out some similar unpleasant charade before. He was caught like a bird in lime—everyone knew that much, at any rate. Waking in the mornings to the beautiful weather and the landscape like poetry, the church and the village below, the hills beyond, he would feel that he was waking into nightmare. Today, he would resolve, he would end it somehow; somehow he would defeat Mrs. Morrison's devouring rapacity, prevent her touch from freezing and blackening beauty. But he never did.

Then Mr. Morrison flew down from Sweden and she went to Paris to meet him and to shop. At once the atmosphere was transformed. Kermit felt as if he had been let out of jail. Shocked into hate of sophisticated maturity, since maturity was Mrs. Morrison, he fell back into the children's world, never wondering whether or not they would accept his return. Under Lucia's pitying leadership they did. Her determination dissipated Chuck's contempt and Anne's grief; and for ten days they lived in a holiday world, laughing at nothing, talking and talking, making jokes and telling stories until Anne, at meals, would choke on her milk and have to be pounded on the back. Kermit took them on long slow afternoon tours to the old sleepy villages round about where they inspected ruins and climbed church towers while Lucia, who had primed herself on the subject, detailed the history of the Angevin empire. Then they would stop at an inn for refreshment—the little girls drank wine and water or sweet sirops diluted to pale stained-glass colors—and entertainment. They found a place where a one-legged man who had been a sailor played the concertina and they went there three times. Then, coming home, the little girls would droop into a doze and Chuck would hum the concertina's songs and Kermit would feel the day gone not as pain and loss but as wealth stored up somewhere, in some bank, against deprivation to come.

Of course they all knew Mrs. Morrison was coming back, but happiness by its very nature blinds people to what its antithesis is like —one cannot remember distress in happiness, one can feel only a twinge, a compression at the heart, that is no more than a hint. So in this make-believe idyll, this childish fairy tale, Kermit and the little girls and Chuck rioted illicitly in happiness and, if they thought of Mrs. Morrison's return, crossed their fingers and hoped that she would come back cat-sleek and smooth from the Paris fashion showings, with Mr. Morrison behind her like a period piece of furniture, expressing stability.

She came back like a cat in a frenzy, lashing its tail and moaning of fury in its throat. She came back like bad weather, wiping out not only joy and well-being but the very memory of them. At nine o'clock one evening Lucia and Anne and Chuck and Kermit were in the salon playing a card game of extreme simplicity called "I Doubt It," it having been Chuck's turn to choose the entertainment. Outside in the courtyard they heard, between bursts of laughter, a car draw up and stop; and, momentarily silent, stared at each other, feeling the lid of Fate ready to slam down upon them.

Nannie, dozing in the corner over a dress she was embroidering for Anne, woke up at the stillness and said, "What is it?" And Lucia darted to the window and hung out.

"It is," she said, turning back, turning pale. "It's Mother come home," she said to Nannie.

"Bless me," Nannie cried, "and you two children still up after nine! Well, run down and kiss her and I'll pack you off. Is your father there too?"

"No—yes," said Lucia. "It's a taxi they've come in. He's paying the man. There's Jean for the bags."

"Well, run down now, like good children." The little girls went reluctantly to the door and Chuck followed. Kermit took Lucia's place by the window and looked down on Mr. Morrison's back as he entered the house. Mrs. Morrison had gone ahead. For a moment, before the taxi started up again, everything was still. Nannie was bundling her sewing up into a clean linen towel and Kermit, uneasy at the sight of the cards littered about the table where they had been playing, went over and began to put them away.

Mrs. Morrison came into the doorway. Against his will, Kermit's hands, straightening the cards, fumbled and stopped and he waited, looking at her. "Well, Kermit," she said, came into the room with her stride that was a little too long for her and sat down on the cream brocade sofa by the fireplace.

"How are you?" said Kermit automatically. "I hope Paris was fun."

"Do you?" said Mrs. Morrison. She took her hat off and leaned her head back. Lucia and Anne paused in the doorway uncertainly.

"Good night——" said Lucia.

"I'm just coming, my lambs," said Nannie. "It's fine to have you back, Mrs. Morrison. I hope——"

"I hope it won't upset your new routine," said Mrs. Morrison, "to see the children get to bed at something closer to a reasonable hour. It's half-past nine. They should have been asleep an hour ago." Her voice hung in the air for a moment, hoping for opposition.

But the little girls and Kermit were still, and Nannie only said, "Very well, madam," and went toward the door.

Mrs. Morrison watched the woman like a cat watching a mouse, as if Nannie walked not in the real world but only in the area of Mrs. Morrison's attention, a moving vulnerable target, and the only question whether or not to make it scream. But Mrs. Morrison only breathed a little harder, and Nannie crossed the room and took the little girls away.

Anne said, before she vanished, "Good night, Kermit."

"Good night," said Kermit, and Mrs. Morrison took another long breath.

"I'm glad," said Mrs. Morrison, "that you've been amusing yourself. It must have been delightful. Quite the Pied Piper of Hamelin you seem to be."

I should say now, thought Kermit, that the girls remind me of her, that I keep seeing her eyes when I look at Anne, that Lucia has her wit and charm—but he could not get the words out. His quick tongue, his pleasure in lying, seemed to have deserted him. The children must have corrupted me, he thought, happiness has corrupted me into honesty. And if I try to lie to her I won't believe it at all and then neither, of course, will she. And desperately he wondered what had happened to Mr. Morrison.

"We had—a very quiet time," he said. "Today we drove to Fontevrault——"

"And enjoyed yourself, I hope?"

"Yes, the old church is beautiful and Lucia——"

"Lucia!" Mrs. Morrison hissed her daughter's name. "The old church is beautiful! While I stumble about in the dark of a provincial railroad station twenty miles from home—exhausted, not a soul to meet me—all the luggage——"

Kermit stared at her, shocked. "I'm so sorry!" he began. "We had no idea you were coming——"

"Oh you didn't! I suppose the telegraph has broken down now."

"Did you wire? I never——"

"Did I wire! The hotel wired. You just didn't bother to notice a wire if it interfered with your delightful trips to old churches with Lucia——"

"Mrs. Morrison, I promise you that no wire——"

"Mrs. Morrison!" said Mrs. Morrison.

"Helena——" Kermit began again desperately.

"How dare you use my name!" she cried, glaring at him across the beautiful stately dignity of the room. Kermit felt himself grow cold and thought, She is crazy. What am I going to do? My God, my God! And Mr. Morrison came in the door with a slip of paper in his hand and sat down wearily.

He waved the paper absently and said, "Jean had it. He didn't bother to see it got to anyone who could deal with it. Hello, Kermit. This was a mess."

"I'm so sorry, sir," Kermit said. His tongue and jaw felt numb. "I feel awfully about this. I had no idea——"

"No," said Mr. Morrison, leaning back with his eyes closed, yawning. "Of course you didn't."

"Of course I would have come if——"

"But you should have had," Mr. Morrison went on. "You're paid a fair amount of money to use your intelligence and avoid trouble for Mrs. Morrison and myself. You ought to know that servants get slack if you let them. It would have been a simple enough rule to have Jean bring you any notes or wires immediately, and not to trust him to know the difference between what's important and what isn't."

"Sir," said Kermit, "I'm terribly sorry. I can only say that I didn't realize you expected me to be in charge of making arrangements."

"And who did you expect to be in charge?" said Mr. Morrison. "Nannie?"

"You're unfair," said Kermit slowly. "You never told me I was to give Jean orders. I was hired to tutor Chuck——" But he remembered what else he had been doing. He remembered Helena Morrison's embraces, and he could not go on defending himself. There was a long silence. Kermit stood with clenched fists, wishing himself away—anywhere else. Endure, he told himself, endure this. But his determination was only halfhearted. He did not want to endure this for any price at all.

"Very well," said Mr. Morrison finally. "You were hired to tutor Chuck. You are now unemployed."

Kermit took a deep breath. "Certainly," he said. "I'll leave at once."

Mrs. Morrison laughed and Kermit winced.

"No," said Mr. Morrison. "You'll leave in the morning when it's convenient to have you driven to the station."

"I——" Kermit began, wanting to say that he would be happy to walk, but he couldn't very well walk twenty miles. He was silent, looking at Mr. Morrison—measuring him.

Mrs. Morrison laughed again. "Isn't he angry!" she said. "Just as angry as I was when I got off the train into that *dirty* little station. Go to bed, Kermit. You've had a lesson that you ought to remember and I'm willing to forgive you. Tomorrow you can take me to see the *beautiful* church in wherever-it-is."

"Helena," said Mr. Morrison, "I just fired him."

"Don't be silly, dear," said Mrs. Morrison. "You can just hire him again. Who's going to look after Chuck if you fire Kermit?"

"I can wire Meredith in Paris to find someone——"

"I *will not* have some riffraff Meredith picks up on a moment's notice trailing about with us. Chuck likes Kermit, Kermit likes Chuck, he's a perfectly nice boy who's very fond of the children and if he was a little selfish and thoughtless, he's sorry now and he'll know better next time, won't you, Kermit?"

All I have to do is say Yes, thought Kermit, and everything will be fixed up. Mrs. Morrison, waiting for him to say it, smiled at him, her beautiful, gracious, social smile. All I have to do is say Yes. There will be a scandal if I don't. She will hate me forever, and Morrison can make trouble for me easily enough, inside college and out. All I have to do is say Yes. We'll be home in a month. I can stand it for a month. Chuck and the kids depend on me. There is only one sensible thing to do and that is to say Yes.

But he said instead, "Thank you, but I would prefer to leave." As soon as he had spoken, terror shook him. Mrs. Morrison's pride and Mr. Morrison's complacence lay about him in shards. What would they do to him now? He wanted to run.

They spoke together.

"No!" said Mrs. Morrison.

"Very well," said Mr. Morrison. His voice was heavier and it prevailed. "As I first told you, you will be driven to the station tomorrow morning. Good night."

Why, he is afraid too, Kermit thought. He is as terrified of a scene and of things being said as I am! "Good night," he replied, and went to the door. He could feel, behind him, passion and fury mounting inside Helena Morrison and the walk across the room while he waited for them to explode was the longest he had ever taken. He opened the door.

"You dirty little toady!" screamed Mrs. Morrison. "You nasty little hanger-on! Do you think you're too good——"

"Helena!" Mr. Morrison's voice was loud, furious and uncertain.

Kermit went through the door and shut it behind him. As it latched something hit it and fell to the floor with a shattering smash. By the sound, she had thrown a glass candlestick or a vase. He went along the hall to the stairs and up to his room, thinking, I wonder how much she costs him in breakage, ready to laugh hysterically at the feeble joke. In his room he fumbled frantically at the lock—he had never troubled to see if there was a key. There was. He locked the door and fell face down on the bed in the dark. Lying there, he said over and over, "I had to do it. I had to do it."

About half an hour later there was a knock on the door. Kermit didn't answer. A hand tried the door, found it locked and knocked again. "Yes?" Kermit said wearily.

But it was only Jean with his suitcases. Kermit let him in, learned that the car would be ready for him at eight in the morning, let him out and locked the door again. As he packed he began to feel worse and worse. By eleven o'clock he was moist with self-pity and righteous indignation. Why did this have to happen to him? Why couldn't she have left him alone? Why had he been such a fool as to lose his temper? He could have stood a month more! What was he going to do in New York until classes began? What would Mr. Morrison tell the professor who was his brother-in-law and had got Kermit the job? And then, one horrible shattering thought—*What about money?* Would they pay his passage home? They'd have to pay what they owed him, at any rate! Of course he had money in New York, he wasn't going to be stranded—but he had grown used to the casual attitude of the wealthy that money was simply about like air.

He felt his deprivation of it as if he was threatened with smothering.

At last his bags were packed. He sat back and rubbed his head. He was very tired. Was I a fool? he thought wearily. Should I have said I'd stay?

But some old pride rose up within him. I had to do it, he said again. Or become her possession. She was right, she made me a toady. She had every reason to think I wasn't too good to put up with anything. Probing, he felt down within himself for the wildness that had always been the deepest part of himself, the self that was most Kermit. Arrogantly it rose to meet his mind. Yes, it was there, still there. But he might have killed it tonight. She, that witch-woman, had tamed him, had all but gelded him, so that carelessly, not know- ing, he might have said Yes and killed it. He had wanted to do well, to get on, to show Nina—— What had Nina to do with this? He shook his head angrily at the way things got mixed up together be- cause he was tired. I mustn't want to do too well, he told himself. There is power as well as money, and money is useful to get power. Morrison has both and I can have both, but power must always come first. He felt suddenly much older, and bitterly ashamed of his stupidity. He had been a fool weeks ago when he kissed Helena Morrison, not tonight when he had said he would go. How could he not have seen what she was, the spider that ate her mate, the yawn- ing abyss of feminine hunger that enjoyed only the destruction of all male freedom, power and pride? Never, he vowed, never would he misread the signs and put himself again in the witch's power. At once, with this resolve he fell from his height of poetic exaggeration, rubbed his face wearily, undressed and got into bed. Exhausted, he slept.

He roused once when the handle of his door turned—turned once, twice, and rattled angrily as the lock held the door shut. Kermit rolled over and sighed, half awake. Outside the door someone waited a moment in silence, hand half raised to knock, and then, in a sud- den wave of fear and revulsion, moved away into the darkness, back down the corridor. Kermit slept on.

At breakfast Jean gave him an envelope which contained, he dis- covered, his full salary and the price of a tourist passage home. Look- ing at it, he had to bite his lip not to laugh in a sudden wave of angry pleasure. It was evident that Mr. Morrison wanted him to have nothing to complain of, and if this was so, Mr. Morrison was afraid of him and of what he might say! The idea gave him a mean satisfaction.

But as he got into the car in the courtyard a window was thrown up in the upstairs hall, and a head leaned out. It was Lucia, and in a moment Anne joined her. Somehow they had sensed something wrong.

"Kermit, Kermit!" Lucia called, while Anne stared wide-eyed.

Kermit waved at them, there was nothing else to do. "Good-by," he called, for there was nothing else to say. The bags were in the car, Jean was waiting, it was time to leave.

Lucia leaned out into the milky morning air and her white cotton nightgown fell off her bony little-girl's shoulder. "Kermit!" she cried. "Don't go!"

"I have to go," he said. "Good-by. Be good and enjoy yourselves."

But the girls looked after him appalled and Lucia's voice again cried out, "Don't go! Don't go!"

He had to wait four hours at the junction for a train to Paris. Jean deposited him and the bags at the station and left. It wasn't until he had driven off that Kermit realized he should have tipped him. He sat down on a bench and laughed. When he recovered, wiping his eyes, he felt better. Mrs. Morrison's witch-voice, Lucia's cry from the window had both vanished. He was delighted not to have tipped Jean. The small mean revenge exactly suited his mood. He felt miserly. He was determined never to be generous again, never to be greedy again. If no witches, then no abandoned princesses either, should appear in his future life. He took a third-class ticket, ate an inexpensive lunch at a cafe and rode to Paris in a mood of sober exhilaration. He was rid of Mrs. Morrison, he was loose in France with a month of freedom ahead of him. He was going to enjoy himself.

It was easy to do. There were plenty of other young Americans in Paris without much money, and Kermit found himself a group at once. There were four pretty girls attached to it, but he was wary of American women, not anxious to appropriate any one of them—and be appropriated by her. He supplemented their daytime companionship by picking up tarts at night, and the arrangement worked excellently for ten days. Then he met three young men who were planning a bicycle trip through the Ile de France, and joined up with them. This was frankly as riotous as the villages they stopped in would allow, but it was a kind of poetic riot. The weather was beautiful, the country was beautiful, the young men rode together in a mood of such complacent and innocent pleasure that everything seemed golden, everything said was witty, everything seen was touched with wonder. Kermit felt younger, gayer, freer than he had ever felt before. He wanted nothing from anyone. He let past and future go, and relaxed. It was impossible to decide what to write his family about the breakup with the Morrisons, since he didn't want to think about the Morrisons. So he didn't write at all. For the first time in his life he was irresponsible not only to others, but to himself as well.

Early in September he landed in New York. He had crossed with his three new friends, who lived in Denver, and had agreed not to go home at once, but to stay at a hotel with them for three or four days and show them about New York. He took them to the Algonquin as being at once atmospheric and inexpensive.

They were registering at the desk when Nina came out of the lobby and saw Kermit. She came over to the group, but Kermit was the last to know it. His friends stopped talking, Kermit heard the silence, turned and saw that his sister was standing next to him.

"Kermit," she said.

She looks awful, was his first thought, in shock. She was pale, there were circles under her eyes and, looking down, he saw that she was pregnant. He had a horrible vision of what his friends must be thinking of this ugly stranger, carrying her belly awkwardly, confronting him. His mind scrambled furiously.

"Nina darling!" he said, and heard guilt and uneasiness in his voice. "How have you been? I was just going to call home. We landed this morning. Oh—this is John Tierney and Mac Watts and Les Houston. This is my sister Nina. Mrs. Fanning. How's Stuart? How's——"

"Kermit," said Nina, "could I speak to you alone for a minute? Oh—— How do you do."

"Yes of course." He walked her back into the lobby. She moved heavily and slowly and sat down at once in the first chair she came to. "Will you have a drink?" Kermit asked.

She shook her head impatiently. "Where were you? We didn't know where to find you. The Morrisons——"

"I left. They were——"

"Why didn't you write?"

"I'm sorry. I just——"

"I thought I'd go mad. Mother—— Actually she was much better than I was. I've been half out of my mind. Don't ever ask me to forgive you, Kermit, because no matter how much I might want to, I couldn't. I couldn't do it."

"I have no intention of asking you to forgive me!" said Kermit furiously. "How dare you make such a scene! How dare you bother the Morrisons and go hunting about for me like a—like a——"

"Uncle Van had a stroke," said Nina. "He's dead. He died a week ago. We wanted to find you."

Kermit swayed forward over the table for a second and then sat back perfectly still. After a minute he reached out and rang the little bell on the table to call the waiter. "You'd better have a drink," he said.

"I can't." Nina indicated her belly. "It makes me sick as a dog."

"I have to have one." The waiter appeared. "A double scotch," said Kermit. The waiter went away. "I'll have to go tell them."

Nina didn't say anything.

"I was really going to call," Kermit said dully. "Shall I—are you going out to the house?"

"I wasn't. This is my first day back at work. But I can. Mr. Daniels is terrified of me because he thinks I'm going to calve in the office at any moment."

"When are you——"

"Not till November, but he doesn't believe it."

"I agree with him."

"You wait. This is nothing."

"Perhaps it's twins."

"It isn't. All women get like this. It just isn't fashionable to admit it."

"Do you mind?"

"What good would it do if I minded? No, I don't mind. Here's your drink."

Kermit picked up the scotch, tried to toss it off, choked and strangled. Nina unkindly burst into laughter. "I'm sorry," she gasped. "You just looked so—so confident and——" She broke down again. "And then you couldn't do it! I'm sorry, Kermit. It's not you —it's anybody looking so certain and——"

"All right, all right," Kermit managed to say between gulps of water. He finished the scotch. "I'll go get my bags and say I have to go."

His friends had gone up to their rooms. "I'm sorry," Kermit said abruptly when Mac let him in. "My uncle died last week. There was a mix-up about addresses—I never got the cable. He was—— My mother's a widow and lived with him—— He brought us up—— I'm awfully sorry, but I've got to get home."

"That's a shame, boy," Mac said, and all the nice young men told Kermit how sorry they were.

"I'll try to come over tomorrow," said Kermit. "I'll phone."

"Sure, sure, that'll be fine."

"They'll get you tickets for a show downstairs."

"That's all right, don't you worry. Phone if you can. Tell your sister we're awfully sorry. If there's anything we can do——"

"Thanks," said Kermit, took his bags, and left.

Going out to Brooklyn in a taxi (they went very slowly because the driver was fervently resolved not to shake Nina up), they hardly spoke at all. Once Nina said, "He left her an annuity. She'll be perfectly comfortable. And a policy or something to pay for Marion's college." Later she said, "Of course we have to sell the house."

Then the taxi stopped.

Kermit could feel the house looking at him from its staring windows as he paid the driver and lugged his bags up to the porch. The grass had been cut, but the flower beds, which Uncle Van had kept looking like brown velvet, were getting weedy. Nina unlocked the door. It jarred Kermit somehow to see her with a key when he didn't have one and would have had to ring like a stranger. He resented the edge of ownership that she had gained by accepting responsibility for her mother.

"Oh Mum!" she called. The house was silent about them. "Mumm—ee!" She waited, her hand on the newel post, looking upstairs. "Maybe she's asleep," she said to Kermit.

"Maybe she's out. Does she have to be a recluse all of a sudden?"

"Of course not." Nina leaned her head on her arms. "Ooh—I have to sit down for a minute." And she plumped into the chair by the telephone.

"I'll go and look," said Kermit, and started upstairs. Nina, looking after him, thought, at any rate he isn't a coward.

But Kermit, climbing through the light from the stained-glass window, was frightened. Dust and silence and emptiness. The doors in the upstairs hall were closed. His mother's room, Nina's room, Marion's, his own, Uncle Van's—there was no one there behind them. This was his childhood and there was no one there. He had renounced it. But now it had renounced him. The rooms were empty and hollow. Everyone had gone away. Afternoon sun possessed them in a long, long pause. I am Kermit, he thought, but he wasn't Kermit because Kermit was nothing. How lonesome a ghost must be, purged of the flesh of his past! He was alone in the house with Nina monstrously, alienly, committed to the flesh and future she carried. He was only a watcher, a thread of consciousness, standing at the top of the stairs with his hand on the bannister, unable to go up or down. Terrible life had left him, desire had died, he was lost. Mother, he ought to call, Mother! But he couldn't make a sound.

"Is she there?" asked Nina, below him.

Without answering he pushed himself away from the bannister and went to a door. Uncle Van's room. Why here? I don't want—— He opened the door. His mother sat in a rocking chair by the window looking over the garden. There was a basket at her feet and her lap was full of Van's socks and underwear, which she had been sorting. She was fast asleep.

As Kermit stood in the doorway her eyes opened. He couldn't meet them. With a strangled sob he crossed the room and dropped on his knees with his head in her lap. "Kermit!" she said. "Why, Kermit dear!" And her hand stroked his hair while he cried abjectly, agonizedly, into the clean wool-smelling socks in her lap.

About half an hour later Mrs. Bishop went downstairs to find

Nina stretched out on the sofa in the living room with her eyes shut. She promptly said, however, though she did not open her eyes, "I'm not asleep."

"Why don't you take a nap?" said her mother.

"I don't sleep through the night if I nap in the daytime. What did he say? Where was he?"

Mrs. Bishop was silent.

"I bet you didn't ask him!" cried Nina indignantly.

"Now, Nina, I don't know that it's anything you need worry about, dear."

"In other words, mind my own business? But Mummy, how do you know——"

"Know what?"

"Oh—everything. Anything. Whether he'll do it again. Or maybe I should say *when* he'll do it again. Mummy, you can't *trust* Kermit."

"Yes I can," said Mrs. Bishop.

"I don't know what you mean! Here he vanishes——"

"Nina, be quiet, dear! I mean I know what I can trust Kermit for and what I can't. I don't depend on him for what he can't do. I——"

"I'd like to know what it is he *can* do!"

"Nina, you're old enough not to have to use that tone of voice about your brother. You're grown up and married and expecting a child. You mustn't get so excited about Kermit."

"Good Lord!" Nina was speechless, glaring. It always happens, she thought, trying to control her temper. Kermit gets in a scrape and I get him out and then everyone tells me I'm unkind to him! "Where is he?" she said.

"Taking a bath."

"Oh my God! Isn't that typical? Well, I'd better go home. Have **you** got enough in the house for dinner, or shall I stop at Gristede's and have them send something?"

"Oh Nina, would you? Eight lamb chops and three pounds of peas, if you don't mind. That would be a help."

"The fatted calf," said Nina, struggled to her feet and departed.

Nevertheless, Nina *was* unkind to Kermit, who was having a very hard time. He was not used to indecision. He had always known where he was going. Now the Morrison affair and Uncle Van's death had combined to inspire him with doubts. Had he been tearing at top speed up a blind alley? Surely the kind of existence that his mother and Uncle Van had led and that Nina was obviously undertaking was totally meaningless? Surely power and wealth were adequate goals? Were at the very least goals—to differentiate their pursuers from the Ninas and the Stuarts who merely lived without even wondering why? These average folk, the purposeless meanderers, useless after they had ceased to bear children—Aunt Dora, Aunt Flora, the Perkasie cousins and ninety-nine per cent of the population—were they not absurd alongside Kermit and Mr. Morrison? To Kermit's disturbed horror, he found that he could no longer answer that question with a certain yes. For only the trivia of his mother's life served to preserve him from utter desolation. He woke up at night sweating from nightmares he could not remember. He lay awake agonizing, determining that he would quit college, live at home, get a job—an average middle-class job—be a model son and enjoy it! He wanted wildly to destroy the wildness within him, to wipe out that fatal difference which Stuart had once, years ago, seen and called by the wrong name. He wanted to be like Stuart.

All this lasted about a week. His mother put an end to it. She had put the house up for sale and a broker had gone over it. When he had left she sat down by Kermit, who had suffered the indignity of this inspection in austere silence, and said, "I think I'll move to the Heights."

Kermit took a deep breath. This was the time. "That would be more convenient for me."

His mother pursed her lips. "Do you mean you want to live with me?" she asked doubtfully. "Or just that it would be handier to visit?"

"I'm going to live with you," Kermit said grimly.

His mother rocked gently to and fro beside him. "Are you sure, dear?"

"Of course I'm sure."

"Well, that would be lovely. Only——"

"Don't you want me?"

"Don't jump down my throat, darling. It's just that—you're almost twenty-one. I want to settle, dear. I don't like moving about. Now an apartment for the three of us—you and Marion and me—will end up in four or five years with only me in it. We couldn't possibly get along with less than six rooms for the three of us, and even that means that only one of you could have company at the same time. Eight rooms would be more comfortable and more sensible. But what will I do with eight rooms four years from now? Now please don't think I don't want you. But I know you found it impractical to commute to Columbia. If you don't want to share with Mercer again, why not go into a dormitory? I can afford it, bless Van for that."

"What about Marion? Are you going to throw her out too?"

"She'll be going to college next year, Kermit. What I thought was, if I had four rooms in one of those new buildings on Columbia Heights or Hicks Street, I'd have an extra bedroom for you or Marion whenever you want it and——"

Kermit got up and left.

Mrs. Bishop looked after him. Her heart contracted. O God, she thought (she meant it reverently, she often asked God questions), am I wrong? Oh my darling, darling boy, how I would love to have you with me! And how could you stand it? You'd hate me in a month! O God, am I being a coward? Oh don't let him hate me now because I'm trying to keep him from hating me later! I couldn't stand feeling him hate me! Her mind told her that she was right to prevent the sacrifice that Kermit would so soon resent making, the sacrifice of Kermit as he was to the Kermit that he suddenly—she always—wanted him to be. The sacrifice that would not succeed. But her heart murmured that to refuse a gift of love was always wrong. All by herself, with no one to confide in, she wrung her hands. Van had given her so much! Each day she found something new that she had lost with him. But perhaps this was the worst loss—the illusion he had given her of knowing right from wrong.

There was, after all, nothing for Kermit to do but go back to school and get his degree. He managed to get into a dormitory, late though it was, and spent the winter in a room that looked out on a gray brick ventilation shaft. Marion, upon hearing about it, declared that it reminded her of the bit in *Alice in Wonderland* about the three little girls who lived at the bottom of a treacle-well and drew pictures of all manner of things that began with *M*. For this reason she gave him a photograph of herself. She had grown very pretty and the picture received much favorable comment from visitors to Kermit's room.

Mercer, of course, had been hurt when Kermit refused to move back into his apartment. Nor did Kermit go on with his extra-curricular money-making. He had been shocked into a state of retreat and withdrawal. "You're awfully different this year," Mercer told him one afternoon when Kermit hadn't been able to get rid of him. After his first spell of sulking, he had taken to following Kermit around again. "What do you want to work so hard at this crap for?" he asked.

"You never know when something might come in handy," Kermit said.

"I believe you want to make Phi Bete," Mercer said scornfully.

"Why not?"

"For Christ's sake! You can hire them for thirty bucks a week."

"That's fine—if you've got thirty bucks a week to pay them."

Mercer revolved this slowly in his mind. Then he said, "Why don't we go into business?"

"Doing what?"

"Anything you want. As long as it hasn't got anything to do with horses, or biscuits."

"I'll bear it in mind."

But Kermit didn't want to think about business. In past years he had regarded the university, his classes and normal collegiate activities as rather irritating distractions from his real interests. Now in his senior year he plunged into his work as if he were determined to experience what he had scorned before—being at college, being young, being not fully formed and finished. He became for a little while more normal, he succeeded in becoming more average, than he had ever been.

It was in October, when this mood was strong, that Kermit got a letter from Lucia Morrison.

Dear Kermit [it read], Anne and I felt awfully about your leaving. We did not enjoy ourselves after that. We have talked about it a good deal and wonder whether your kindness to us was not partly what made her so mad. We felt we should write and tell you that for us *it was worth it.* I don't mean of course that it was worth it for you, to get fired. But you gave Anne and me great pleasure and happiness. The unpleasantness *was not in vain.* This does not make up to you, we know. But we felt it would not be right for you not to know that we *care*—both ways, because of enjoying ourselves with you and not enjoying ourselves afterwards. And being so sorry.

Anne says this is not very clear, but it is difficult to make feelings clear, I find. At any rate, this is the way we feel, as closely as I can say it, so perhaps you will understand.

It would be delightful to see you sometime. During this month Anne and I can usually be found on fine Thursdays (after 3:30) at the Central Park Zoo. (We are doing some sketching.) I do not think Nannie would think it odd if you happened to be there some week. People *do* meet accidentally in New York, I am sure.

Anne says I should explain that we do not like to be dishonest but that it would be unkind to ask Nannie to lie for us. If a lie must be told, viz.: that you met us accidentally, it is only right that we should tell it ourselves.

I hope we shall soon meet again.

With kindest regards,
Lucia Morrison.

P.S. I feal the sam as Lucia, but she can spel beter.

Anne Morrison.

P.P.S. You see she is right!

L. M.

Having received this on a Monday when he got back to college from a week end in Brooklyn, Kermit had several days to think it over. His first impulse was to ignore it. He wanted to forget the whole Morrison episode in which he had played such an inadequate and sorry part. He remembered his vow—not to be generous, not to be greedy; no more witches, no more princesses. Lucia's emotion, to anyone who had sworn such a oath, was frightening: too pure, too clear. What adult, involved with his own dreary personality and ambitions, could meet Lucia on equal terms? "I won't go," Kermit decided.

He went, in the end, out of sentimentality. He knew it for what it was, and knew that it was not what Lucia wanted. But it was all he had to give her. What she had to give him he could not take. On no possible plane could his world and Lucia's intercept. But he couldn't stand thinking of her face as she left the park reluctantly when he had not appeared. He imagined her accepting his dereliction quietly, giving an ear to the voice of logical hope which would say that Kermit might appear the week after, accepting the burden which this would put upon her (and she would know it) of being disappointed again—he couldn't do it. He was going to do nothing for her (what could he do?), but he couldn't stand for her to find it out so irretrievably as by his failing her in *every* way. Anne too; whom one always thought of a little late, yet whose almost silent presence transformed Lucia from being merely an individual, a statistically negligible deviation from the norm of selfishness, into being a Voice, speaking for more than herself.

Thursday was gray and threatening rain. Kermit was not at all sure that the girls would have managed to get to the rendezvous. He came into the zoo from the south, past the pony ride and the camels and yak and the bison, glancing uneasily at benches, trying not to appear to be looking for someone and being, in consequence, enormously furtive. The zoo was quite empty. The balloons of the vendor at the corner strained desperately in the wind.

Then Kermit saw her. She was standing alone, watching the seals, not looking about at all, but in the very center of the zoo where no one could miss her. He was smitten suddenly with a degree of embarrassment. She looked so alone! He wanted to look about for Anne and Nannie, but felt that such a search might seem to indicate that he knew they would be there and that it would give Lucia away. He walked toward her slowly, trying to act normally and uncertain of what normal behavior would be. The wind blew Lucia's gray coat, the seals dived hypnotically before her. He reached the railing beside her and said, "Lucia! It is, isn't it? How nice to see you! Do you come here often?"

Lucia turned to him, her face was irradiated with happiness. "Kermit," she said, "you came!"

"Shh!" said Kermit. "Where are they? Where's Nannie?"

Lucia, with a gesture, brushed conspiracy aside. "Anne has the German measles. I came alone. Oh Kermit, how *nice* of you!"

"You mean you're all by yourself? Won't there be trouble?"

"I'm twelve," said Lucia. "I had a birthday last week." She smiled, a little painfully. "Now you should tell me that I've grown."

"No," said Kermit, "you look just the same." At his words her gaze sank into his and she blushed.

"I hope that's pleasant," she said heroically.

"Very," said Kermit, and squeezed her arm affectionately. Lucia stood a little straighter.

"Anne will be so happy to know that you came. She felt miserable not to be here, but there was the temperature and there was the rash—— Well. I wasn't even sure where to write. I simply hoped that writing to the college would be all right."

"It was fine. It was awfully nice of you to. I appreciated it very much."

Lucia, listening to the tone under the words, sighed. Then she turned her back on the seals and looked up at the sky. "It's going to rain," she said. "Perhaps I should go home."

"But I just came! You haven't told me anything. How is school? Is it any better?" Large drops suddenly descended upon them. "Quick!" Kermit said. "You'll get wet. Let's go somewhere and sit down and—and have tea." He took her arm and they ran together through the rain out to Fifth Avenue, where Kermit got a taxi. "I owe you a tea," he said, almost accusingly. "At Rumpelmayer's." Lucia smiled and the taxi drove down Fifth Avenue and across Fifty-ninth Street.

When they were settled at the restaurant and had ordered a large meal of hot chocolate and pastry, Lucia seemed more at ease. "We go to a new school now," she said. "It's much better. Of course, discipline has its disadvantages too. We have to skip things I would like to know about. But then, when I'm grown up, I can go back and find out about them."

"Is that what you're going to do when you're grown up?" Kermit grinned at her. Lucia looked puzzled. "I mean—aren't you going to be getting married and falling in and out of love?"

"I think you have the order wrong," said Lucia. "I'll try to get through falling *out* of love, at any rate, before I get married." She played with her napkin for a moment and then said, "Is that all there is to being grown up, Kermit? Falling in and out of love?"

"Don't you look forward to it? I thought all girls did."

"No," said Lucia, "I don't. It seems so—wasteful."

"I'm afraid you won't be able to stop it. At least, stop people from falling in love with you. You're going to be beautiful." Lucia turned her face to Kermit and he added involuntarily, "You're beautiful now."

At this moment the waiter began to put cups and plates and silver chocolate pots and cinnamon toast and éclairs on the table and Lucia's "Thank you" was almost smothered by his activity. She poured herself a cup of chocolate, put a spoonful of whipped cream in it and said, "Chuck is going to school in Arizona. They do a great deal of riding. He says he likes it." For the next half hour she talked almost as steadily as she ate. When she was finished she leaned back and sighed happily. "This has been *wonderful!* Poor Anne! I wish I could take her home something, but everything is so squashy. Besides, it would make her sick. She wouldn't mind, but they might want to know where it came from."

"Isn't there something else," said Kermit, "something not to eat, that we could send her?"

"Well——" Lucia looked at him thoughtfully. "There's something at Schwarz's—but it's quite expensive."

Kermit took out his wallet and counted his money. Then he looked at the check which the waiter produced. "How much?"

"Twelve dollars," said Lucia unhappily.

"All right."

"Oh!" cried Lucia, beaming. "It's a little coach-and-four—the coronation coach, I think. And the King and the Queen are in it! Oh Kermit, really?"

"Yes really. Come on."

They found the coronation coach on the second floor at Schwarz's and Kermit was as fascinated as Lucia. Even his sober undergraduate mood could not totally overcome his old arrogance about money, the feeling that once in a while it *must* be thrown away. He could think of no more pleasant method of throwing it away than to delight Lucia by being generous to Anne. If his funds had held out, he would have sent a regiment of horse to guard their majesties.

Lucia, having gloated, declared that the package must be delivered. "If I bring it," she said apologetically, "I'll have to explain—— It would be difficult."

"Yes, I see." Kermit considered. "Shall I put in a card saying 'From an unknown admirer'?"

"I'm afraid not. If you don't put in *any* card, Mother can think it's from a friend of hers or an aunt, or Father's secretary or something, and the card got lost. And of course I'll *tell* Anne."

"All right."

They went downstairs and out. The rain, which had stopped, was beginning again. Lucia looked wistfully at the sky.

"Had I better take you home?" Kermit asked.

"No. I'll take a bus. If I drove up in a taxi——" He was amused by her assumption that to be escorted meant inevitably to be taken home in a cab. Lucia's penetration of one's heart, even her generous concern over one's pocketbook, did not really take in the financial facts of life. She would always value emotions, truth and personal relationships above money. She had not found out, and might never, the unfortunate effect that money or its lack might have on personal relationships, emotions and truth.

They walked through the drizzle to a bus stop.

"Thank you," said Lucia. "I had a lovely time. Oh, I did."

"I hope you won't get scolded."

"I probably shall, but I shan't mind. I'll think about the tea. And the coach will be there to be looked at."

"Lucia," said Kermit, "I had a lovely time too."

"I'm so glad. There's my bus."

"Have you a dime?"

"Yes of course."

"Give Anne my love."

"I shall."

The bus stopped. "Lucia——" Kermit said, not knowing what to add.

Lucia smiled at him brilliantly and climbed aboard, and the bus drove off. Kermit turned down Fifth Avenue through the rain. After a while he began to laugh at himself. "I had a date with a girl," he imagined himself telling Mercer. "She's beautiful and rich, and exactly twelve years old." He heard Helena Morrison's voice saying, "Quite the Pied Piper of Hamelin." That bitch! he said to himself in an ecstasy of rage. That bitch! He tried to imagine her face when, six years from now, he married Lucia. She would be old, her hair would be dyed, her chin would have a sag——

But Lucia's face unfortunately came into the picture instead and Kermit knew that his fantasy was absurd. No one would marry Lucia for revenge on her mother. Lucia was beautiful and intelligent and good. The combination would be terrifying and obsessive. Lucia, in fact, would be the world's revenge on her mother and anyone who married her might very well end by being sorry for his mother-in-law. It won't be me! Kermit promised himself. Lucia would be too much for him, or for anyone else he could think of.

He turned off Fifth Avenue and went into a bar in a side street. Lucia had depleted his funds to a point where he could buy himself one drink and make a couple of phone calls. He considered his list of girls carefully and finally called one named Sue who lived nearby and worked as a model. She was home and her roommate had a date in twenty minutes. Kermit had his drink and set out for Sue's, who was a nice simple stupid ambitious girl. He did not hear from Lucia again.

Along about Thanksgiving, Nina had her baby. It was a boy and she named it John. As there were no Johns in her family or in Stuart's, this puzzled everyone. Nina confided to Marion that she had chosen the name just because it didn't belong to anyone in particular. "I don't want him to have to live up to someone—or *not* to live up to someone. John is almost as good as being anonymous. I mean, there's an infinite variety of Johns. He can be *anything*."

"What does the Judge say?" Marion asked.

"Well, Janey took care of *him* with Arthur, so I didn't have to name the baby for the Judge. And I told him I hated Juniors. I do, too. He doesn't worry about my side of the family, of course. Stuart thought it would be nice to name him for Uncle Van or for Father. He's so sweet. But he let me choose. I think he likes this."

Marion, who was sitting beside Nina's hospital bed, leaned forward and put her head against Nina's arm. "Was it bad having him?"

"Well yes, it was. But of course it doesn't last long. You aren't frightened of it, are you?"

"Yes."

"Oh that's silly. It's not worth being frightened of."

"I hate pain."

"Well, but you can't help it. Everybody gets pain one way or other."

"But this—to go out looking for it—to know it's coming and you're going to be torn apart——"

"Oh for heaven's sake! Do I look torn apart?"

"No. But——"

"I tell you it's nothing to worry about!" Nina's voice was exasperated, but she smoothed Marion's hair with her hand. Marion shivered suddenly. Then the nurse came in with two vases of flowers.

Early in January, Nina went back to work. This was barely economic since she paid a nurse almost as much as she made herself. Mrs. Bishop closed the big house in Bay Ridge and took an apartment for herself and Marion quite close to Nina. She relieved the nurse blissfully whenever she could, though she attempted to hide her delight, since the nurse was extremely scientific and let John howl heartily if it wasn't time for a feeding. "I suppose it's good for his lungs," Mrs. Bishop would say distractedly if she was within hearing.

"Yes of course," Nina would reply, firmly but not too convincedly. By late spring the whole thing got to be too much for her and she fired the nurse and quit her job. Mr. Daniels looked at her like a spaniel being left at the vet's when she told him. "I almost thought it might be kinder to shoot him," she declared. "I *never* saw such a face! As if I'd utterly betrayed him!" She picked up the baby and hugged him. "John, you wicked boy! Think what you've made me do to that poor man!"

Stuart, sitting across their living room with his legs stretched out in front of him, said, "What about this poor man? I had Miss Burp for breakfast and dinner for six months. I can't worry about Daniels."

Nina said, "Well, I know she was awful. I couldn't stand her. Only now I don't have any career. Do you mind?"

"Why don't you learn how to make slip covers and cook? Isn't that what women do?"

"Honestly, Stuart! I can cook!"

"You know what I mean—fancy. Hollandaise sauce and salad with bananas in it, and things."

"Do you like bananas in salad? You never said——"

"No I don't like them. But if you want something to do—— Come here and kiss me. All right, bring the baby. My lovely Nina. My darling girl. John and I are your career. Why don't you knit me a sweater? Why don't you find a house in the country for the summer?"

"My goodness! Can we afford it?"

"Yeah, I guess so. They're giving me a cut on the Blackman fee."

"Why, Stuart, how wonderful! Why, Stuart! Why that's magnificent! Goodness me! Hooray for your career, anyway!"

The house Nina rented was in Connecticut, near Westport. She had no particular desire to get this close to Stuart's sister Janey, but the commuting was better than from Jersey or Long Island. She got a big house cheap and most of the family wandered in and out for most of the summer. They were all there, even Judge Fanning, one week end in June for Kermit's twenty-first birthday. To the Judge's intense and fully disclosed surprise, Kermit had graduated cum laude from Columbia.

"That was *easy* for him," said Mercer, who had driven Kermit out and was as surprised as the Judge at the latter's astonishment. "Gee, his hardest job was getting *me* through. He had to——"

"Shut up," said Kermit pleasantly.

"Kermit *dear*," said Mrs. Bishop. "So rude! Mercer, I'm sure he's sorry."

"Oh that's all right." Mercer grinned.

"You keep your trap shut," said Kermit, finishing a Tom Collins, "and it will be. Come on. Let's go for a swim."

Mercer promptly downed his drink. "Anyone else want to come? Marion?"

"If Nina doesn't need me."

"Go along. Dinner's under control. I'm going to feed the baby in a minute. Be back in an hour, will you?"

Kermit, Marion and Mercer drove off to the beach and the rest of the party remained seated on the porch. Little Johnny was in his play pen at the far end, singing to himself and banging every now and then on the bottom of an old pot with a spoon. When he did, the Judge winced.

"I'm sorry about the noise," said Nina. "I tried taking it away from him and he roared *much* louder."

Stuart went over, picked up his son and went off with him under one arm. The baby made swimming motions. "He thinks he's flying," Nina explained.

"Elizabeth," said the Judge abruptly to Mrs. Bishop, "this proves I was right."

"I suppose so," said Mrs. Bishop unhappily. "I hope it won't be a shock to him."

"A sixty-thousand-dollar shock," said the Judge, "is something one can get over rather quickly."

"What's all this?" Nina asked.

"It's Kermit," Mrs. Bishop told her. "Van left him some money. It's—— Is it really that much, Judge?"

"As one of the trustees, my dear, I can assure you it is."

"But why—but what——" Nina gasped. "But Kermit doesn't know?"

"He's to get it tomorrow on his birthday," Mrs. Bishop said. "The Judge thought——"

"After that exhibition of irresponsibility last summer, and since your uncle left me with full discretionary powers—along with the trust company, of course—I persuaded your mother that Kermit should be left in ignorance of his inheritance until——"

"I wanted him to finish college," Mrs. Bishop said. "The Judge was afraid he might—well—just go off, you know. And spend it."

"Sixty—thousand dollars!" Nina sat staring.

"Now, my dear," the Judge said, "when my estate is settled you and Stuart will find you have no reason for envy. Ahem!"

"Envy!" Nina cried. "I'm not—envious! But Kermit will be furious! Mother, you know he will!"

"But darling, he did graduate, and cum laude too." Mrs. Bishop looked back and forth from Nina to the Judge. "He—he has settled down so nicely this year——"

"Well, if you ask me, he'll go right off now! Now he's graduated and there's nothing to hold him, and he's mad besides, because he *will* be. He'll simply be fit to be *tied* about this, having it kept from him and all! As if he were a child."

"Perhaps it will teach him to keep his family informed of his whereabouts instead of wandering off into the blue." Nina bowed her head, remembering that terrible week last August when they had not been able to find Kermit anywhere, when Uncle Van lay dying in bed in the heat, his breath rasping, his eyes fixed. "I will never forgive you," she had said to Kermit. But that had been anger. What the Judge had meted out had been punishment. Even in anger, Nina had not wanted that kind of cold justice for Kermit.

"When are you going to tell him?" she asked.

"Why, tomorrow, I suppose. That's his twenty-first birthday."

"Please, please tell him tonight, Judge! Tell him right off. I can't stand it, knowing and waiting. I don't see how you stood it, Mother!"

Mrs. Bishop said, "I had to stand it, Nina, once I'd given my word to the Judge."

"Well, I don't think it makes much difference, Nina," agreed the Judge. "I'll announce it tonight at dinner, if you want. I was going to do that tomorrow."

"Couldn't you—just take him aside and tell him quietly?"

The Judge looked at her as if she were mad. "My dear child, this is *good* news I have for your brother. You act as if he were going to be told—— Good heavens, I don't know—as if he'd *lost* sixty thousand dollars."

"But he'll be so mad," Nina said faintly. Then she got up and fled to the kitchen, where she heated the baby's bottle and fixed his Pablum and his applesauce in a distracted way. The maid was mashing potatoes and Nina could only mutter under her breath of her distress.

Stuart appeared in a few minutes with the baby. "The Judge thinks we ought to have some wine so everybody can toast Kermit."

"Oh my God!" said Nina. She took the baby from Stuart and held him out to the maid. "Margaret, go change the baby, please. I'll watch the roast. And feed him upstairs, will you? He gets so excited with a lot of people around. Yes, I'll baste the meat. What are we having to start, jellied soup? All right. Stuart, carry that plate up for her. She can't manage everything." The baby roared at the sight of the bottle, Stuart and Margaret went off and Nina collapsed by the kitchen table.

When Stuart came back she said, "Did you know about this?"

"No," said Stuart.

"I don't believe you," said Nina.

Stuart raised his eyebrows.

"Oh I'm sorry!" Nina cried. "I do believe you. It's just—I'm so mad!"

"Why don't you let Kermit fight his own battles?" said Stuart.

Nina looked at him with her mouth open.

"Why don't you let Kermit get mad if he wants to get mad? You don't have to get mad for him. Maybe he'll be delighted. Personally, if anyone handed me sixty thousand dollars, I wouldn't be mad."

Nina continued to stare.

"Let the Judge handle it," said Stuart. "It's his job, not yours. What's burning?" He took the potatoes off the stove and handed the pan to Nina. She began automatically to put them in a vegetable dish. "I'll make another drink," Stuart continued. "What about the wine?"

"There isn't any. I was going to get some tomorrow for his birthday dinner. The Judge'll just have to announce it over cocktails."

"It could wait till tomorrow," Stuart suggested.

Nina was silent.

"All right," said Stuart. "Will you be long?"

"As long as it takes her to feed Johnny." She put the potatoes in the warming oven and said, "Oh Stuart!"

He took her in his arms. "There, there. Have a good cry. What's it about?"

"It's about—Uncle Van, I guess. I loved him so!"

"There, there, we don't need any of his money. I'm——"

"Why does everybody think I want the money!" Nina almost screamed with exasperation. "I loved him! That's why I'm crying. He was so sweet! Sixty thousand dollars, and after Mother's annuity and Marion's college—— I had no idea! He never let on. He never took anything for himself! I *loved* him so, and I can never tell him now!"

Stuart kissed her. "Go wash your face," he said. "I can manage things here till Margaret's through. They'll be back from swimming soon. That's my good girl."

Nina stayed upstairs, bathing her swollen face with cold water, until she heard Mercer's car drive up. Then a fit of nervousness came over her. She stood in the middle of the room, unable to go down, uncertain whether the Judge would make his announcement without her. At last she went out in the hall and stood listening. Everything was quiet. Only the baby was singing to himself in the little room next door. She went in and he cooed at her and tried to pull himself up on the bars of his crib. Nina picked him up and hugged him. "You be a good boy, now," she whispered fiercely. "You be a good boy!" Then she went downstairs with Johnny in her arms.

"There you are," said Mrs. Bishop. "And there's my darling come to say good night." She held out her arms for the baby, but Nina did not see because she was watching Kermit, who was sitting on the floor leaning against a pillar. She sat down with the baby in her arms and Stuart gave her a drink.

"Kermit," said the Judge, "I have a piece of news for you. Good news."

Oh God, thought Nina; and Kermit looked at the Judge and blinked and then said, "Yes?" politely.

The Judge swallowed. Kermit's inability to say "sir" to him never failed to irritate him. Nonetheless, he announced firmly, "Tomorrow is your twenty-first birthday."

"Thank you," said Kermit. "That *is* good news."

Marion, who was combing her damp hair, giggled and said, "Don't be an idiot, Kermit."

The Judge ignored both remarks. "On that day you are regarded by the law as reaching your maturity. You may vote. You are no longer a minor. You may undertake legal responsibilities."

Kermit looked at him sharply but did not say anything.

"Specifically," the Judge said, "you may inherit property without the necessity of guardianship, or of trustees. You will therefore inherit—tomorrow, mind you, not tonight" (and he waved a finger in mock severity), "the balance of your uncle's estate which has not gone to insure your mother's comfort or been put aside for your sister's education. You are, to use a legal term, your uncle's residuary legatee. Do I make myself plain?"

"No," said Kermit. "How much do I get?"

Nina drew in her breath in a hiss and the Judge went red; but he had to answer. "Approximately sixty thousand dollars," he said.

Kermit sat absolutely silent, staring at him.

"Wow!" shouted Mercer.

Marion screamed, "Kermit!"

Kermit said to the Judge, "You've known this since he died, of course."

"Of course," said the Judge. "I am one of the trustees under his will. The other is the Centenary Trust Company, which has handled the investment of the money. It's all there."

Kermit's eyes traveled from the Judge to his mother's face and then to Nina's. Very briefly Nina shook her head. She didn't know whether he saw it or not, for he put his head down on his bent knee just then and stared at the floor.

"My golly!" said Mercer. "Sixty thousand dollars all your own! What are you going to do with it?" The fact that he would never, himself, be in charge of the Davies millions without trustees had been made clear to him long ago. Mercer could have accumulated sixty thousand dollars without too much trouble by living simply and saving most of his allowance for a few years, but such an idea had never occurred to him. It was not the amount, it was the fact that Kermit could do what he wanted with his inheritance, that made Mercer look at him in awe. "What are you going to do with it?" he repeated.

Kermit shook his bowed head. "First—first," he said, "I have to get used to having it."

"That's sensible," said the Judge. "You can leave it with the trust company while you think things over. It's well invested."

"It's undoubtedly invested horribly," said Kermit absently. "One third in government bonds, the rest in blue chips bought at a premium. If there's anything that pays more than four per cent in the portfolio, I'll eat it. No, I'll have to reinvest right away."

"You know more than the trust company?" said the Judge with heavy sarcasm.

Kermit didn't even answer.

Mrs. Bishop said, "Oh Kermit—don't you think you ought to leave it where it is?"

For the first time since the Judge's announcement Kermit moved, swinging himself across the floor to lean against her chair. He smiled up at her. "No, darling, I don't."

"You—you will be careful?"

"Do you think I'd take any chances on losing this? I'd as soon cut my throat. Why, this—this means that I'm free."

"Free!" The Judge looked his horror. "You mean you aren't going to work?"

Kermit laughed. His mother said indignantly, "Kermit has always worked very hard."

Kermit said, "Perhaps I'll become a judge. Nina, may I have another drink, on the strength of being well off?"

What Kermit did astonished everyone. He went to work in Washington in the Treasury Department. The first wave of Columbia professors who had formed Roosevelt's original Brain Trust had receded from its high tide of power, but Kermit's professor of economics (Mr. Morrison's brother-in-law) had a number of connections in the government. He had suggested to Kermit, before he graduated, that the Administration offered an interesting field for service. To Kermit, who was highly uninterested in service, it also offered opportunities for power that he would never come near in any other fashion. "The government's an ass," Mr. Morrison had told him firmly. Kermit did not dispute this judgment, but he had decided to make it *his* ass. Perhaps he could persuade the ass to bite Mr. Morrison. It was a pleasant thought.

The year Kermit went to Washington was the high tide of the

new Deal, the year that Roosevelt beat Landon and the first person said, "As Maine goes, so goes Vermont." Kermit had an obscure job in an office which he shared with three other ambitious young men who, even combined, were no match for him at all. He had a pleasant small house in Georgetown where he occasionally gave excellent parties. He had good clothes, and was asked about quite a bit in diplomatic society and plain society-society, as well as to those earnest gatherings of young idealists who wanted to change the world and argued passionately on gin and rum because whiskey was more expensive. This society Kermit did not, in fact, enjoy. The young men were too earnest and too broke. Their wives either held government jobs too, to swell the family exchequer, and were unattractively competitive and ambitious; or else they were fighting a losing battle against dowdiness and insipidity in order to raise small children, send them to private schools and provide them with piano and dancing lessons.

Time passed. By 1938, the year of Munich, Kermit was assistant to the head of a bureau. In 1939 he held the same job, but the power of the Treasury Department had suddenly increased, and Kermit found happily that luck had chosen his position well for him. The world was playing into his hands, for Roosevelt was suspicious of his Secretary of State, who had been a senator, who had a following of his own and who wanted to run for President in 1940. On the other hand, Roosevelt despised his Secretary of War, who was an isolationist and therefore could not be fired unless the President wished to be denounced as a warmonger; and was busily knocking the props out from under him by working directly with the Assistant Secretary of War, whom he also did not trust. Into the Treasury Department, headed by the President's good and loyal friend (who was a Jew and could not run for President), there therefore came numerous new functions which, by logic less realistic than Roosevelt's, should have gone to State or War.

For Europe was uneasy, there was a smell of smoke on the wind, the impossible trembled on the edge of becoming the inevitable. And when the French, having taken another look at the Maginot Line, decided they needed American airplanes, they ended up negotiating for them through Kermit's department. Not that there were really any American airplanes for them to buy, but the Treasury Department rather thought there ought to be and brought its influence to bear on the plane manufacturers. Kermit's world and the great world moved closer together and suddenly coincided. He stood for a moment in one of those narrow defiles through which history must pass. All that hot summer he held the power that justified him in his hands.

In three years he had changed very little. He was less showy, because he did not have to be showy now. He had authority and did not need to prove anything to himself. As for proving his power to other people, he very seldom wanted to. If they were to be important to him, they would find out by themselves soon enough who he was and what he was. His precious money, his passport to freedom, he had put into utility companies reorganized under the New Deal, where it had already nearly doubled.

In August of '39 he was going to New York for a week end when he saw Mr. Morrison. This was in the lounge car of the Congressional Limited on a Friday afternoon. The car was crowded and Kermit had to pass Mr. Morrison to find a seat. As he did so Morrison, who was talking to a heavy-set dark man with an astonishingly mobile face, looked up. Kermit bowed and sat down across the aisle a few places further along. He took out a report on some rather unfortunate testimony that a general had been giving a Senate Committee. Earlier in the year an Army light bomber had crashed, during a test, with a representative of the French government aboard—and aboard incognito. The Senate, having unearthed this remarkable fact, had been informed by the uneasy general that M. Chemidlin had been in the bomber through arrangements made by the Treasury. But what had the Treasury to do with giving agents of foreign powers access to American Army planes? the Senators wanted to know. The Secretary was going to have to appear, and Kermit's chief had been charged with discovering how little the Secretary need say. In practice, this meant that Kermit was given the job.

He read the verbatim report of the Senate hearing with absorption. It was obvious which Senators would be dangerous. It was not obvious how much they might know already. Kermit looked up thoughtfully, listening to the Senators' questions in his mind.

Mr. Morrison was staring at him. The man he'd been talking to had gone. He beckoned to Kermit suddenly and Kermit took his papers and went over to sit next to him.

"I know you," said Mr. Morrison.

"I'm Kermit Bishop," Kermit told him. "I went to Europe with you four years ago. How is Chuck? And the little girls?" he went on as it became evident from Mr. Morrison's face that he had remembered and was regretting his invitation to Kermit to join him.

"They're very well. Chuck's at Yale." This Kermit found completely incredible, but Mr. Morrison was too embarrassed to notice Kermit's astonishment. "Er—have a drink?" he said halfheartedly.

"Thanks. Scotch and soda, please," Kermit said to the steward. He was beginning to enjoy himself.

"You been in Washington?" Mr. Morrison asked.

"I'm with the Treasury," said Kermit gently. He imagined he could see the Treasury sink lower in Mr. Morrison's estimation and added, "I'm deputy to Baker."

"Baker!" said Mr. Morrison. "I know Baker." He took another look at Kermit. "How long have you been there?"

"Three years."

It was obvious that Mr. Morrison was impressed. The government might be an ass, but he knew Baker, and Kermit had in three years become his deputy. "Like government work?" he asked.

"Very much."

"Like to work for me instead?"

Kermit stared at him. Had Baker's name done this? Or was Morrison sorry for having fired him four years ago? Or was he planning a subtle form of revenge on his wife? "No, thank you," said Kermit politely, since none of these motives pleased him, and the steward brought his drink.

"Didn't think so," Mr. Morrison said, proving himself to be motivated by nothing but irritation. "You bright young bureaucrats all like to be safe, don't you? It's fun to push businessmen around too, isn't it? Well, wait till next year, my boy. You won't be so safe then. Roosevelt'll be out and we'll have a businessman in."

"Will you, sir?" asked Kermit mildly. "Who'll that be?"

"Notice that chap sitting next to me? That's him. Name of Will-kie. Know about him?"

"Commonwealth and Southern," said Kermit. "He's deviling the SEC."

"You do know about him! Well, you'll know more. What did you think of him, now?"

"He looked like a cross between Elmer Gantry and Bryan," said Kermit, and offered Mr. Morrison a cigarette.

But Mr. Morrison had choked on his drink. "Bryan was a Democrat!" he gasped indignantly when he could talk.

"So was Willkie," said Kermit.

"My God," said Mr. Morrison, "would you defame a man for a youthful mistake?" He mopped his face and said more cheerfully, "Anyway, it's about time we capitalists had a rabble-rouser."

"The last time you had one, you had to get a Roosevelt too," Kermit reminded him, and Mr. Morrison, who was interested in politics only when they got in his way, laughed heartily. Kermit felt the atmosphere grow warmer. Mr. Morrison's business training, Kermit surmised, had led him to the knowledge that everything, including people, must be revalued from time to time. No matter what Kermit had done to him in the past, he was prepared to find Kermit useful and interesting now, and to like him as much as he liked anyone.

The train pounded along through the hot afternoon. Morrison told Kermit what he thought about Washington: it wasn't much. He had been talking to the Assistant Secretary of War about electric power. The Assistant Secretary thought, and Morrison agreed with him, that in the event of a war emergency America would need to expand its power facilities. The Assistant Secretary also thought, and again Morrison agreed with him, that the emergency would be upon them very soon. Where they disagreed was over the financing of new installations. The Assistant Secretary, who believed firmly in free enterprise while working for the New Deal, thought the utility companies ought to build them. Morrison, who despised the New Deal, was indignant and baffled. If the government wanted them, why didn't the government finance them? Why should the power companies expand now only to be saddled with interest on debt to be paid off in lean years ahead? Paid off, incidentally, while they were being policed by the government, their rates regulated, their securities subject to investigation? "You lend us the money," Morrison told the Assistant Secretary, "and we'll be glad to build them."

The Assistant Secretary then informed him that money given out by the government had to come from funds appropriated by Congress. While this was a new idea to Morrison, it was not a particularly impressive one. He listened and grunted and left finally in disgust. His opinion of a government that knew what it ought to do and didn't do it was expressed loudly to Kermit. No business, he pointed out, could possibly be run on such lines. Hitler managed to get the money for what he wanted, didn't he? Well then, why couldn't we?

Kermit sighed. It distressed him to see Mr. Morrison being a Fascist. He disbelieved thoroughly in the contention of some of his colleagues in Washington that all businessmen were, and he disliked finding himself wrong. "You think Hitler's right, sir?" he asked.

"Right?" said Mr. Morrison. "What do you mean—right? I think he's efficient. We aren't going to lick him unless we get a little more efficient ourselves."

"Oh," said Kermit, feeling better. "Are we going to lick him?"

Morrison looked at him scornfully. "Sure we are. What's the matter with you? You one of these wave-of-the-future boys?"

"No," said Kermit. "I just thought maybe you were."

"Me!" Morrison was stunned. "I've been there! I've seen it! Do you know how many bombers he's got? Over three thousand. Do you know how many we have? Three hundred. Do you know how many Britain has? Seven hundred. Do you know how many synthetic-rubber plants he has? And they talk about blockade! My God! That's no wave of the future. That's war."

"When?" asked Kermit.

"This summer," said Mr. Morrison. "He's managed to keep the Russians from getting together with England and France. Why do you suppose they threw Litvinov out last spring? What's the matter with you in Washington? You all crazy? Have another drink." Having silenced Kermit, he now felt quite cordial toward him.

"Thanks," said Kermit. For the rest of the way to New York, Mr. Morrison discussed the iniquities of the New Deal, with particular reference to Harry Hopkins, who was, he told Kermit, going to run for Vice-President with Roosevelt in 1940. Kermit found it a tiring trip.

New York was almost as hot as Washington and not so well air-conditioned. Mr. Morrison, who had a large black limousine waiting for him, gave Kermit a lift to his hotel. "I'm on my way to South-ampton," he said abruptly as they stopped. "Why don't you come out with me?"

Arrested as he started to get out of the car, sweating in the steamy air, Kermit almost asked "Why?" He stared at Mr. Morrison.

Mr. Morrison looked at him blandly. "It's hot in town," he said, "even for a bureaucrat." He laughed then and patted Kermit's leg. "I like you," he added.

The first reason was obvious and irrelevant. The second, Kermit did not believe. "Thank you a lot," he said, "but I have a date." There was, in fact, a very attractive lady, the wife of a lawyer who was out of town, waiting for him to phone.

"Well," said Mr. Morrison, "if it gets too hot for you, you can call me tomorrow and come out by train. My office will put you through to me. Good night."

"Good night," said Kermit, "and thanks." He went into the hotel, still puzzling over Mr. Morrison. He felt hot and dirty and tired and old and as he rode up in the elevator he kept thinking of the surf on the beach at Southampton. Nonsense, he told himself. Morrison is up to something. He stripped and showered and called his lady friend.

But she, alas, turned out to be a bore. She insisted on dining in an obscure and not very good restaurant "so we won't be seen," and afterward she would not let Kermit come to her apartment ("The doorman would see you"), nor did she want to come to the hotel with him. He finally got her there, after three brandies, but it was hardly worth it, for she ended by weeping over her sins and telling Kermit that she really loved her husband, only he neglected her. "I've never done anything like this before!" she kept saying indignantly. As far as I'm concerned, you never will again, thought Kermit as he put her in a cab and went back upstairs.

He got into bed and lay thinking about himself and life and the future. He had been working so hard that he hadn't thought much lately. What did he want? Power—he had a great deal for a man of his age. Was it satisfying? It had been, but he was not satisfied tonight. What was power in the abstract worth if you could not see its result firsthand, or discuss those results with anyone but yourself? Kermit, who had always been secretive, tonight felt desperately lonely. There will be war this summer, Morrison said. Kermit believed him. If he had not been so close to where history was making itself he would have said the same thing himself. But he was too close—where it is impossible to tell the obvious from the unlikely. War. That would mean more power in Washington. It occurred to Kermit that he didn't want it, he wasn't interested.

What did he want then? Into his mind came a picture. He was in a plane. He was shooting. Bombs fell. Tracer bullets spattered about him. He was a hero, on the edge of danger and glory. Every moment was exciting. People died. Rocketing through the sky with an enemy plane in his sights, Kermit flew into dreams of destruction and triumph.

The telephone wakened him in the morning at half-past nine. He was muzzy-headed from having slept so long and when he realized who was calling him he had a moment of panic. It was the husband of last night's lady.

"Hello, Lou," said Kermit, cursing his luck. Of all the women to get caught with! Strictly a bad-luck dame, he thought bitterly.

But Lou was invincibly cheerful. "Mighty nice of you to take Dotty out," he said. "She told me you had dinner." (She would, Kermit thought.) "I was trying to get her to tell her I'd be in this morning. Say, if I'd known you'd be in town I'd have flown back last night."

"I came up unexpectedly," muttered Kermit. "Just happened to run into Dotty."

"What? I can't hear you. Say, did I wake you? I'm sorry! Listen, now you're here, how about lunch? There's a little matter—I've got to send a wire to Baker at the Treasury and I thought maybe you could tell me what approach would be effective. Or would you like to run out to our place in Jersey with us? I know Dotty'd love to have you come."

Oh brother! thought Kermit, and said, "Gosh, Lou, I'm sorry, but I've got to be in Southampton."

"Gee, that's too bad. When are you leaving?"

"Next train," said Kermit tersely. "About Baker—just lay the facts on the line. He'll listen. I'll make you a date to see him next week if you want to come down."

"Will you? That'll be swell. I'd like to have a chance to go over it with you, though. Our position is——"

"Next week," said Kermit. "I want to be able to give it time. When will you come down?" He thought about Baker's schedule and his own while Lou continued to explain his client's position. "Thursday? Make it Thursday, Lou, and we'll have a good session. Give my best to Dotty." He hung up and groaned. Damn Dotty! Now he and Baker would both have to pay for a very dull evening. Well, at any rate the story would make Baker laugh. But what was he going to do with his week end? Really go to Southampton? Well, why not? He laughed. Maybe he could find out what Morrison wanted.

He got off the train, after what seemed an interminable ride, into clean salt-smelling Atlantic air. Other week-enders, bearing tennis rackets and golf clubs, clattered down with him and began to be absorbed into station wagons. Kermit stood still, looking about him. He had talked to the butler, not to Mr. Morrison. Had that gentleman regretted his invitation and sent no one to meet him?

Then out of nowhere a small cyclone in a white dress flew toward him, crying, "Kermit!"

"Lucia!" said Kermit. "No—it's Anne!"

"Kermit, Kermit, how lovely to see you! Do I look like Lucia now? She's over in the car. She said I'd better come because she's grown so no one knows her and she'd only confuse you. Oh Kermit, before anything else I must thank you for the coach-and-four. That you sent me when I was sick," she added, as Kermit looked blank.

"Oh—did you like it?"

"It was heaven," said Anne. "Here's Thomas for your bags. Bag. I wish you had more, it would mean you were staying longer. This is us. Here he is, Lucia."

Lucia got out of the station wagon. She had been right. Kermit would not have known her. Beautiful Lucia was beautiful no longer. Adolescence had taken her badly, destroying her poise, confusing her precocious maturity. She had grown too fast, she was awkward, her features were too big for her face. Anne, who had been so silent four years ago, now sparkled and bubbled while Lucia was shy. She smiled painfully and said, "Hello, Kermit."

"Hello, Lucia dear," said Kermit, and took her in his arms and kissed her. She was terrified, his kiss lighted on her ear, and then suddenly he felt her fingers cling to his shoulders, she gave a gasp that was half a sob.

"Kermit, you stinker!" cried Anne. "You didn't kiss me!"

"That's because your beautiful sister is older and comes first," said Kermit. Lucia released herself and climbed into the back of the station wagon, and Kermit bent down and gave Anne a solemn smack on the cheek. Then he got in next to Lucia and put a box of candy in her lap.

"Oh thank you!" said Lucia. "But I can't eat it now, I come out in spots. Oh it's hell to be fifteen!"

"It's soon over," said Kermit comfortingly. "Give it to Anne."

"I will, but I'll be jealous. I think I mind food worst of all sometimes. Do you remember how I used to wallow in whipped cream? They've taken the braces off my teeth at last, but I have to wear glasses for reading. Oh dear, I don't *want* to grow up. And I keep growing. Nothing ever fits!"

"Now, now," said Kermit, and took her hand. "You haven't said you're glad to see me."

Anne had got in and knelt on the seat in front of them, leaning over the back of it, facing them. "As if we had to!" she said reprovingly. Lucia squeezed his hand and relaxed. Apparently she let Anne do the talking for them now. Anne went on, "However did you get asked out?"

"I met your father in the train yesterday. He talked, I listened. I don't know why he asked me out. He can't be in any great need of people to listen to him."

Anne looked blank and Lucia, evidently feeling that there were still things Anne couldn't cope with, said, "I know why he asked you."

"Why?"

"But it's obvious. You beat him, somehow, four years ago. When you left. Isn't that it? He didn't just fire you."

"No," said Kermit, looking at Lucia in amazement. "I really could have stayed. I did quit. But how did you know?"

Lucia blushed and shook her head uneasily. "I heard them talking. A little. Enough. Moth—Mother didn't like the man Mr. Meredith sent from Paris to take your place."

"How is your mother?" asked Kermit abruptly.

"As usual," said Lucia.

"She's learning Spanish," said Anne. "From a young man who used to be a bullfighter. But with the war in Spain, there's been no security in bullfighting. He was in Mexico for a while. Now he's here. And our apartment is being redecorated. We have decorators all over the place, with swatches of amusing material. There are three of them spending the week end. Perhaps Daddy really does just need someone to listen to him."

"Dr. Tempest listens."

"Who is Dr. Tempest?" asked Kermit.

"He's how Chuck stays at Yale," Anne explained. "You were a summer tutor. Well, Dr. Tempest is a kind of perpetual tutor. He goes to Yale with Chuck."

"Poor Chuck!"

"Oh I don't know. He's on the crew. He likes that. And he'll be a senior this year."

"Or Dr. Tempest will," said Lucia softly, and Kermit squeezed her hand. "Ask Kermit what *he's* doing," Lucia directed Anne.

Kermit told them as clearly as he could and Anne nodded and looked a little puzzled and Lucia smiled and smiled until Kermit could see by the end of the drive that her beauty was not gone for good but only in abeyance. Like a bad fairy, adolescence had enchanted her. But her loveliness lay waiting underneath.

Then they drew up before the Morrisons' enormous house and Lucia, getting out, became plain and vulnerable again. "People will be at the beach, I think," she said, looking at Kermit nearsightedly in the glare of the sun. "Do you want to go down?"

"If you and Anne do."

Lucia sighed. "I have to rest. They don't let me stay in the sun too much. But Anne will take you." With great and pathetic dignity she walked into the house, stumbling a little on the threshold.

Suddenly terrified, Kermit turned to Anne. "Is she all right?" he demanded fiercely.

"They think she will be," said Anne. "It was rheumatic fever. She was in bed all winter."

"Why didn't you let me know?"

"We didn't know—where you were."

"I'll give you my address. You must write me. Will you?"

"Of course." She took his hand and offered the reassurance that had been given her. "She has the best care. I was frightened too, Kermit. But she has the best care. There's Daddy now, looking for you." She sounded faintly relieved. "He *must* need someone to talk to."

"Okay," said Kermit. "Let him rip." They went up to the house together.

But Mr. Morrison, having ascertained that Kermit had come, permitted himself to be detoured back to his study by a male secretary who announced, "The London call, sir."

"Tell Mr. Norman I'll be there directly," said Mr. Morrison, shook Kermit's hand heartily and absent-mindedly and departed; and Kermit, having changed, found himself being escorted to the beach by Anne.

'The very rich,' he thought later, 'are different from us.' 'Yes,' the familiar repartee continued, 'they have more money.' But surely, Kermit decided, Fitzgerald had been right. Lying stretched out on the sand on the edge of the Morrison party, he listened incredulously to its conversation. Surely only the very rich would live in a menagerie like this! Or perhaps the very poor? But then at least the denizens would be related—cousins, brothers-in-law—the bond of clan would give some meaning, some reason, to the group. What possible reason could there be for the assembly of Mrs. Morrison's bullfighter, Mrs. Morrison's decorators, Chuck's Dr. Tempest? Or for him, Kermit? Lucia had been too intelligent, he thought, in producing a reason for his presence. Surely he was here on the same kind of whim which had provided the bullfighter!

Mrs. Morrison had deteriorated. Four years ago she had been charming at first meeting, and for as long afterward as she chose. Now she was waspish. Was it just, Kermit wondered, because she hated him? No, she was waspish to everyone, ordering the bull-fighter about, interrupting the decorators, being rude to Dr. Tempest. Besides, she had given no evidence of hating him. She had seemed, on the contrary, quite pleased to see him. Looking at her smiling at him, he had felt his own hate turn into acid contempt. To hate her was too much of a compliment. It put them too close to being on a level, and this was an advantage she did not deserve. Helena Morrison had lost—if she had ever had it—the ability to distinguish between one emotion and another. Hate or lust would awaken within her the same dulled numb buzzing response of which alone she was capable. Pain and pleasure had come to approximate each other in her world. As long as someone felt *something* about her, it did not matter what he felt. But someone must; otherwise she had no definition in her own mind, no assurance that she existed. Hate, lust, fury, fear—it was her constant concern to awaken some emotion that centered upon herself and thus defined her. The witch, bent on destruction, had destroyed herself. Kermit, lying face down on the sand, wanted only to vomit out the memory of her.

The voices went on over his head. Someone was going to brave the water. It was the decorator who was legitimately female. Kermit felt a little shower of sand blow across him as she stood up to pull on her cap, answering the protests and disparagements of the rest of the party with a tough ease of manner that told clearly how long she had been doing it.

"Such a *healthy* girl," said one of the other decorators.

"I know, I'm vulgar that way," she answered.

"So am I," said Kermit, and got up to go in with her.

This combination caused a sudden silence to fall upon the party as each member quickly placed Kermit on his mental battle plan and moved him into juxtaposition with Jean McDonald. Kermit and Jean went down the beach together. She was well built, with a kind of luxuriously matter-of-fact maturity. Perfectly content to weigh one hundred and forty when another woman would have starved herself, Jean had style, and it was a style of her own.

"I can't imagine what you're doing here," she said to him as they stood together where the waves swirled around their ankles.

"I was an earlier version of Dr. Tempest," he explained.

"When it wasn't yet clear that the full Prospero treatment was necessary?"

"Exactly. I was an effort at making do with the sorcerer's apprentice."

"Boil, little pot, boil."

"He never did, of course."

"It reminds me of those people in the Civil War who paid other people to be drafted for them. By the way, what's your name?"

"Kermit Bishop. I know yours."'

"How nice of you. Bishop. It seems to me I met—— Oh!"

"What?"

"I stepped on a clam. Or something. Can you swim well?"

"Not violently."

"Well, I'll meet you at the float later, then. I want to swim hard for a while." She went through a wave and straight out toward Spain in a murderous crawl that could probably have taken her halfway there. Kermit followed thoughtfully in her wake wondering whether he should take her on or not. She was in her thirties and this she would use as a weapon in her natural attempt to dominate such a relationship—"I'm older than you and should know better." On the other hand, the very fact that she had noticed him proved that a curiously sensitive spot must exist under her bravado. Amid the alien corn of the Morrisons' house party, she was looking for a companion. She needed to be approved of by someone she could admire. It is always rather touching to be set up as a judge of someone else's opinions and experiences—— And she was amusing, healthy, capable; she would not make trouble for him—at least not for a long time. He pulled himself up on the float and began to dive. With tennis and dancing, this was what he did well.

Jean obliterated Mrs. Morrison entirely. It was amazing. She simply rubbed her out, as health rubs out disease. Mrs. Morrison became a leather-skinned harridan whose sole relationship to Kermit was to provide him with food, drink and a bed for the night. All this was accomplished in the twinkling of an eye. When Jean came back from her ocean tour and found Kermit diving for her, she grinned at him delightedly, climbed on the float and lay panting while he performed. In half an hour they swam slowly into the beach and threw themselves onto the sand next to each other on the far outer edge of the Morrison group. And there they lay, drugged silent with sea and sun, muttering only once in a while some half-finished phrase that would make them both shake with silent laughter.

Of course, Jean obliterated Lucia too, and so completely that Kermit didn't even realize it. When, back at the house, he came downstairs for cocktails, Lucia was on the terrace, lying on a chaise longue, and Jean was perched near her on the balustrade. Kermit saw them together and his heart was wrung for Lucia again—but impersonally. Next to her Jean was all health, all adult successful vital process, all the absorbing wonderful inevitability of life and action and event. Lucia's fair skin was hardly touched with color, her white dress emphasized her pallor. She wore no lipstick, of course, and her heavy dark hair was bunched unbecomingly at her neck. Kermit picked up a drink and watched Lucia watching him come toward them—the princess who had been allowed to descend from her tower only under the witch's enchantment of ugliness. Poor princess! thought Kermit, and smiled at her warmly, and Jean began to talk to him. Kermit sat down by Lucia's feet, grinning up at Jean; and trapped behind their laughter, Lucia lay still while the party grew as neighbors with house guests drifted in. Finally, when it began to be dusk, she sat up abruptly and said, "Excuse me. I've got to get a sweater, I'm afraid."

Kermit turned to her at once. "Can I get it?"

"It's upstairs. Thanks, but I'll have to go myself." She went quietly to the french doors, threading her way through the party, which was now both large and noisy, and disappeared. She didn't come back.

When dinner was finally announced, it was a buffet. Many of the cocktail guests were still there and a number of them were rather drunk. Kermit suspected that Saturday-night supper at the Morrisons' was a public institution to which people came more or less regularly, with or without invitations, accompanied by as many of their own guests as they chose to bring along.

He established Jean in Lucia's chair to hold the corner against all comers and went in for food. Hams, turkeys, salmons and salads were laid out in enormous bowls and platters. Someone had already spilled salad on the floor. The girl ahead of Kermit stepped in it and stopped and groaned with disgust, looking at her smeared sandal.

"Here, let me help," said Kermit, offering a linen napkin.

The girl turned to him. It was his sister Marion.

"Good heavens," she said.

"Yes," Kermit agreed. "Positively stuffy." He bent down to wipe her shoe and the carpet.

"All the time I've wasted pitying you *sweltering* in Washington," said Marion amiably.

"And I," said Kermit, scrubbing away, "imagining you at a camp in Maine, eating fudge and braiding pigtails, surrounded by little girls with crushes on you."

"Honestly, Kermit! You know perfectly well I haven't been a counselor for years!"

"But I'm sure you made such a good one. I picture you——"

"Well, get up and look at me again."

He did so. "Yes, I see. You're much thinner."

"Thank you—just a little. Is that all?"

"Fishing, dear? Yes, you're pretty. But you were, anyway, and you still went bounding about leading cheers and playing basketball and co-operating. How do you come to be here?"

"I'm staying with the Durhams. How about you?"

"I am an authentic guest of the Morrisons, a *rara avis,* I judge."

"How lovely for you. Do you want a roll?"

"No, thank you. Turkey?"

"Yes, please. That's enough. Where shall we sit?"

"Come on outside, unless you're attached to someone."

"I'm not." Marion sounded very definite.

"Then come along."

They went out into the dark and Kermit led Marion to Jean. "Jean McDonald," he said. "My sister Marion."

Jean leaned forward in the dark. "Hello. How nice to see you again."

"Oh, you've met?"

"Last month, wasn't it?"

"Yes," said Marion. She looked about her for a place to sit, poised to move away.

Jean moved her feet off the end of the chaise longue. "Sit here. How are the Durhams?"

"Very well. They're here somewhere." There was a slightly awkward pause.

Kermit appropriated a chair that someone had vacated, pulled it over and sat down. He was intrigued to find that Marion had moved so early, while still at college, out of a totally middle-class environment into the closest thing America offered to the world of fashion. It was an odd thing for Marion to have done—Marion with her contented disposition and eager willingness to participate in the accepted pleasures of the middle class. He was full of a devious curiosity about how his little sister had got to Southampton which some hesitancy, some false note in Jean's tone, increased.

"What's this all about?" he asked. "Or shall we talk about the weather?"

"I'd prefer the weather," said Marion, "but since I'm sure you wouldn't, I'll tell you that I'm regarded as a dangerous troublemaker in the Morrison home. Chuck seems to be pursuing me."

"With honorable intentions?"

"That's the trouble. Yes."

"Well, well, well! You know, feeble-mindedness often skips a generation. Your children would probably be perfectly——"

"My children will be no relation to the Morrisons, thank you. I didn't say I was encouraging him."

"Oh. Are you sure you shouldn't? Have you thought it over? He'll have millions, and he has a kind heart. Very fond of animals and——"

"If I wanted millions and a kind heart, I could have taken Mercer Davies. At least he got through college by himself."

"Don't be too sure," said Kermit, and looked modestly at his plate.

"Oh, I know you helped. But he didn't have to have any Dr. Tem——"

"Who is sitting just over there," whispered Kermit loudly.

Marion stopped talking and began to eat. Kermit considered her thoughtfully—all he could see of her in the dusk. She had certainly changed. Mind as well as body had refined and sharpened. But there was none of what had been typical of Marion—her happiness—in her tone at all. Something was wrong, Kermit felt, and a real, if still small, concern for his sister sprang up within him. Jean, of course, was what he intended to devote himself to this evening, and Marion's affairs must not be allowed to distract him from Jean. But Marion's affairs could not be ignored—if only out of pride. He did *not* want his sister behaving foolishly in Southampton. And knew, as he thought this, that he cared about her in a much deeper and more connected way than this of vanity. Damn it, Jean would have to be a little patient. Marion—dear, funny, plump, unsophisticated Marion who had turned into someone else—Marion was his *sister!* He could not imagine that she would find Chuck Morrison attractive in any way, but perhaps she had been a little careless with him. Something had happened to her, at any rate.

"Well," Jean was saying cheerfully, as if to change the subject, "the weather has been wonderful. Hot, of course, but then it cools off at night. And several fine thunderstorms. I do enjoy a good storm, don't you? Of course it's pleasanter here than in town, but——"

"For God's sake," said Kermit, "you've made your point. Don't belabor it." Then, suddenly suspicious, he added, "Or is there more?"

"More what?" Jean asked. Marion was stubbornly silent.

"More to the situation."

"My dear, I'm an innocent bystander. How should I know?"

"I think you're both horrid," said Marion, and got up and walked away. Kermit stared after her, and his heart sank.

"I'm sorry," said Jean somberly. "I don't think I meant to do that."

"I don't know what you did," said Kermit.

Jean ate in silence for a minute or two. Then she said, "All right. Here goes, I'll be a real stinker and tell all. Except that I like your sister, and I think I'm telling you for her good. It's Hank Durham. She's been staying with them on and off all summer. The Chuck business is nothing—except I suppose you wouldn't have been asked here if it weren't for that, and I'd be sorry if you hadn't been. But she could handle that simply by staying away. After all, there are lots of other places to visit in the summer—the North Shore, Connecticut, the Cape—— Only she doesn't stay away."

Kermit literally couldn't think of anything to say. Whatever his uneasy suspicion had been, it was impossible to erase in a moment his old conception of Marion. And in his mind Marion was still, as he had said, leading cheers and braiding pigtails. It took him several minutes, during which Jean finished her meal and put her plate down on the floor, to manage to formulate the sentence, "Who in hell is Hank Durham?"

"A man. An attractive one if you like them sensitive and useless. He has some kind of small brokerage house and a crew haircut and a rich wife and baritone voice and a lot of charm and I keep wanting to step on him and then scrape him off my shoe very carefully with something I'd throw away afterwards." She thought for a minute and added, "I suppose it's because he's so close to being my type. I was almost fooled there, for a while. Actually, he's rather like you except that he hasn't——"

"Thanks."

"Let me finish, dear. Except that he hasn't any of what we might euphemistically call virility, if you follow me."

"Thanks again."

"You're welcome, I'm sure."

Kermit said, "What the devil shall I do about it?" He felt as if he were going rapidly down in an elevator, and the thought that he himself must have raised this same confused fury of emotions—rage, humiliation, disgust—in the breasts of several other young men who had sisters did nothing to comfort him.

"I can't imagine what you can do about it," said Jean.

"She was always so—so normal. Average. Healthy." Kermit sounded stunned, even to himself. I'm talking nonsense, he thought.

"My dear," Jean told him gently, "there's nothing abnormal or unhealthy about falling for Hank Durham. Marion's only about twenty, isn't she?"

"I guess so. Yes."

"I'd shudder to tell you the kind of thing I fell for at twenty. I don't see how you can stop it. She'll quit when she gets a certain amount of punishment from him. She's probably begun to get it already, or she wouldn't be so touchy. Can she—— How much punishment is she likely to take?"

"I don't know. Probably too much." The elevator was going down faster now. For a moment he hated Jean's matter-of-factness. This was his sister, *his sister,* who had been carrying on with a no-good stockbroking baritone. If Marion had been within reach, he would have shaken her until her teeth rattled in her head. How could she be such a fool! And at the same time, he knew he felt sick about the idea of Marion suffering. She wasn't built for it! She wasn't used to it! "Jesus, Jean," he went on, "I don't want her to——"

"Look, dear, you can't do anything. By this time she knows I've told you about it. She thinks I want him and I'm jealous. I've been hanging around out here most of the summer, you know, waving floor plans and color schemes at Mrs. M. I like your sister, I think she's a fine girl. But she doesn't like any part of me, let's face it. If you try to do anything—— First place, you couldn't. Second place, she'd think it came from me and she'd react the other way. You'd make it worse. Look, she's just a kid. Hanky-Panky doesn't know she's got guts and a lot of emotion, and furthermore he doesn't care. He'd *rather* his girls were superficial. He'll get tired of her and throw her over pretty fast now. The best thing you can do is wait, and help pick up the pieces afterwards."

"I doubt if I'm very good at that," said Kermit.

Jean looked at him shrewdly. "I doubt it myself. But you'll have to begin learning sometime. Listen, I have a car. Let's forget about this and go someplace and dance."

Maybe it was this proposal—for Kermit didn't like his women suggesting what they were going to do next—or maybe it was merely the fact that his guardian angel was named Arrogance; but Kermit said, "I'd like to take Marion too." He looked through his eyelashes at Jean, to see how she took this.

His tone was light, and Jean heard danger in it. She, who had been looking at him earnestly, now dropped her eyes to her hands and said, deferring decision, "Honey, she wouldn't come."

"Maybe she would," said Kermit, "if I get the Durhams too." Opposing Jean gave him a pleasant sensation of power, and mentally he transferred all these troublesome people from reality to a chessboard and moved them about there. He smiled at Jean's bent head, waiting for her to speak and give in. It was almost enjoyable to feel her stubbornness, it made his victory worth something, it made her more of a person.

She looked up now, smiling, and said, "You really are a glutton for punishment."

Kermit almost laughed. She had given in. She would put up with an evening spent, not in courting her, but in arranging Marion's affairs. It took them a long step ahead in their relationship—for Jean was admitting that she did not need to be courted. That they were already a couple. "I'm a veritable Spartan," he said. He stood up and held out his hand. "Come along and show me the Durhams."

"And then run off to powder my nose while you turn on the charm? Good old Jean, the friend of humanity." Having capitulated, she bore him no grudge and began at once to devote herself to helping him. "*She'll* be near the bar. *He's* probably out in the dark somewhere. Or no, I'm wrong. Someone's playing the piano. He'll be showing off his voice."

"I too," said Kermit, squeezing her arm, making his defection a new bond between them, "I too enjoy showing off my voice. How right you were about our being alike."

Jean sighed. "I suppose I'll never live that down. Remember my qualification."

Kermit looked at her and grinned. "I'm not likely to forget it. You've put me, if I may say so, on my mettle."

"That's right where I want you to be." She met his look. "Am I blushing? I feel as if I were."

"You've got such a lovely sunburn no one can tell. Ah—not a bad voice. Is that Durham?"

"Who else?" They paused in the door of the big room with a piano in it. A dark-haired youngish-looking man with his arm around a blonde girl leaned on the piano and sang "Molly Malone" with a considerable and not too happy brogue.

Kermit said, "Go powder your nose." Jean left, and he went over to the table where the drinks were being served, got a scotch and soda and wandered toward the piano, thinking of things to say, because he did not want to think of how he felt. If he did that he would lose his temper, and if he lost his temper he would want to fight. Even now, the thought of breaking Durham's handsome nose

—bones crunching, blood spurting—was attractive. Quit it! Kermit said to himself. What's the use of that? On top of everything else, I'd probably get licked. He had fought often enough to know that he usually did. He controlled himself therefore and wondered whether he could scare Durham by some opening remark: "My name is Bishop and I understand that you've been seducing my sister." Would it be subtle to be that unsubtle? Was subtlety called for? In the end, he simply leaned against the piano too and hummed a tenor to Durham's singing. By the time Marion came in half an hour later, Kermit and Durham were singing close harmony and presenting an appearance of inseparable friendship.

Marion saw them together and paused. Before she could turn away Kermit said loudly, "Hi there, kid. Where did you get to? Come and sing."

The girl who was playing the piano stopped, and from down the hall came a blast as someone put records on a victrola. Marion came over, her face shut and self-possessed, and said, "You can't sing against that. Hank, I have a headache. I think I'll go home."

Durham's eyes were slightly glazed with alcohol, and he looked puzzledly from Kermit to Marion, and asked, "You two know each other?"

"Yes," said Marion, and repeated, "I think I'll go home."

"What do you want to do that for?" asked Durham. He straightened himself and stretched, and put one arm casually around Marion's shoulders. Kermit felt the hair bristle on the back of his neck. Marion stood up a little straighter within the circle of Durham's arm and looked at no one. "Come on," said Durham, "have a drink and you'll feel better."

"I don't want a drink," said Marion.

"All right, all right, don't bite my head off! Come inside and dance."

"It's noisy and crowded and——"

"Let's all go someplace else and dance," said Kermit. "I feel like a good dive. Is there any such around?"

"There's Joe's," said Durham, and belched. "Excuse me. Hey, let's do that. This place is too goddamn genteel. Go on, baby, get your coat or whatever, and we'll go to Joe's."

They did go, eventually. By that time they had acquired Sally Durham, who swayed silently on her feet as she waited for Hank to find their car, Chuck Morrison, who made a goal-line tackle at Marion and could not be pried loose, a couple named Smith and Jean McDonald. Outside in the Morrisons' courtyard a floodlight competed with the moon and the air smelled of salt and new-cut grass. The Durhams had a fantastic car, an old Duesenberg as big as a yacht. Hank brought it up in a swirl of gravel and shouted for everyone to pile in, but Jean had gone for her Ford and Kermit waited. By dint of hanging back strategically, Marion did too.

When Jean drove up, Marion said, "Drop me off at the Durhams' first, will you?" as she got in.

"Why?" Kermit asked. No one, least of all Marion, was going to deprive him of some kind of climax, some emotional outlet for what he was still astounded to find himself suffering.

Marion didn't answer. Jean put the car into gear and they rolled down the drive. After a few minutes Jean said, "Why don't you come along for a while? I don't want to stay late either."

"For heaven's sake!" said Marion. "Why can't you take me home? I—*don't*—want—to go to Joe's!" Her voice was rough with emotion. It invaded the comfort and happy surprise at finding each other that surrounded Jean and Kermit with an embarrassing and helpless vehemence. "It's such a simple thing!" she cried suddenly. Her shoulders began to shake. It was impossible to tell whether she was laughing or crying. "Just take me home! It's so—easy! Just drop me off—there——" She reached for the door handle and started to open it.

Jean slammed on the brakes and Kermit grabbed Marion's hand, but the door was half open and as the car slowed down Marion wrenched herself loose and jumped out. She fell heavily to her knees. Kermit was out after her before Jean stopped the car. Marion was kneeling by the side of the road where she had fallen, staring at her cut and bleeding hands. She looked up at Kermit with horror and shock masking, aging, her face.

"You fool," said Kermit. "You goddamned idiot! How could you do that?" He put his arm around her and lifted her to her feet. "Are you all right? Can you stand? Look at your hands!"

Marion leaned against him and cried.

"You must have lost your mind," Kermit said, his fury growing as it met no resistance. "I always thought you had some sense. Did you do this for that—that—that—jerk? You must be crazy!"

Marion pulled herself away from him and began to run down the road.

"My God!" said Kermit, and followed. She almost fell as he caught her. Jean brought the car up to them.

"Do you know where to find a doctor?" Kermit asked Jean.

Marion jerked, trying to break away. "I won't go——"

"I suppose there must be someone at the hospital," Jean said. "It's all I can think of at this hour."

"Get in," said Kermit grimly. Marion got in and Kermit sat on the outside and locked the door. They drove silently through the sweet summer night, into the town where the hospital stood. Jean pulled up to the emergency entrance and Kermit took Marion's arm and walked her inside.

It took twenty minutes and a few lies before Marion's hands were cleaned and bandaged. She had bruised one knee badly, but nothing was broken or even sprained. The doctor insisted on giving her an anti-tetanus shot. She bore it all silently, saying only when the doctor was through, "Is there somewhere I could wash my face?" Kermit waited for her outside the door. He wasn't going to let her slip out and away.

She came out with her lipstick renewed and her face pale and composed. She didn't speak to Kermit, but when she got out to the car she said, "Thank you very much, Jean. You were kind."

"Get in," Kermit said.

"You can get in the middle," Marion replied with a painful bravado. "I'm through with the Perils of Pauline for the evening."

"Even if my mind believed you," said Kermit, "my stomach wouldn't. Get in the middle. I can't take any more." Marion got in docilely.

After ten minutes and several miles, Marion said, "Please take me home now, will you?" No one answered and they drove on through the moon-flooded night until Jean turned into the drive at the Durhams'.

It was a small white house and all the lights were on. The Durhams' car was in the garage. "Oh God——" said Marion. "They're all here." She sat motionless, staring at the house.

"Shall we go somewhere else?" asked Jean.

But at that moment Chuck Morrison ran down the lawn from the terrace, crying, "Marion? Is that Marion? Where've you been?" He leaned across the car door, peering in. "We were waiting for you. I made them come here to look. Where've you been?"

"She had an accident," said Kermit wearily. "Cut her hand. We had to find a doctor."

"An accident! What the hell happened? Marion, are you all right? What happened?"

"I'm all right," said Marion. "Nothing happened. I just cut my hand."

"How could you cut your hand driving around in a car?"

Nobody told him. Kermit pushed Chuck off the door, opened it and got out. "Good night," said Marion. "Thank you, Jean." Kermit helped her out. She winced as her bruised knee took her weight.

"You're hurt!" said Chuck loudly. He turned to Kermit. "What the devil have you done to her?"

Hank Durham and Mrs. Smith came out on the terrace and called down, "Hello! Is that Marion? Where've you been?"

"We've been mountain climbing and she fell off the Matterhorn," said Kermit. "Chuck, take her other arm, will you? You can clip me later if you want to. Let's help her up to the house so she doesn't need to put her weight on that leg. Come on, Jean," he added over his shoulder. "This will be a production."

"I need a drink," said Jean, getting out of the car.

"Who doesn't?" asked Kermit.

They got Marion to the house and into the living room. She said she wanted to go up to bed, but no one paid any attention. She was sat down in a big chair and Chuck, hands trembling, made her a stiff highball and knelt beside her. "It's both your hands," he cried accusingly. "And your leg too! God damn it!" He jumped up and went over to Kermit, who was leaning against the doorjamb beside Jean. "What's all this funny business about?" he shouted. "What have you been up to? She might have been killed!"

"If she'd been strangled in her cradle," said Kermit, "it would have saved me a lot of trouble."

For some reason Marion thought this was very funny and began to laugh. "Sib—sibling rivalry!" she gasped.

Chuck looked back and forth from Marion to Kermit, puzzled. The fact that they were brother and sister, though assuredly known to him, did not seem to have penetrated his consciousness. Then he shook his head angrily and balled up his hand into a fist. "You think you're funny, don't you, smart guy?" he said, and swung.

Kermit ducked, Chuck hit his hand on the wall and howled, Sally Durham and Mrs. Smith screamed. Hank Durham came over and caught Chuck's arm and said, "Wait a minute, feller——"

Chuck turned and swung on him with his right, and Hank went down on the floor like a log. Marion screamed.

There was a short pause and then everyone began talking at once. Sally Durham was on her knees beside Hank, Chuck was saying, "I'm sorry, I'm sorry, but Jesus——"

Jean said pleasantly, "It's like a nightmare. The same kind of logic."

Kermit said, "Thank you for not saying 'I told you to leave it alone.'"

"Will everybody please be quiet?" asked Marion loudly. "I had an accident. It was my fault. I sl-slipped getting out of the car. I've been to the doctor. He gave me a horrible shot of something and I feel awful. I want to go to bed and I want everybody to shut up!" She put down her drink, which she had been nursing uncomfortably in her bandaged hands, got up and limped toward the door. Chuck tried to help her and she brushed him aside.

Sally Durham shrilled, "You're not going to bed in my house! I know you've been playing around with Hank! Now look at what happens to him! And you don't even care! Get out of here, you and your friends! Get out! I won't have you around! Making trouble, hitting people, getting Hank mixed up in fights! Get out of here!"

Durham groaned and then, thinking better of it, lay still.

Marion paused in the doorway, trembling, her eyes enormous in a suddenly colorless face. She turned around and looked at Sally, who glared back at her in a frenzy; at Hank, who lay with his eyes shut on the floor; at Chuck, whose jaw had dropped in consternation and horror.

Kermit put his hand on her arm and said, "Come out to the car. I'll take you back to New York tonight."

All Marion said was, "My clothes and things——"

"Jean will get them."

"Sure," said Jean. "Where's the guest room?"

"I'll show you," said Mrs. Smith, her eyes rolling in her head with delighted curiosity. She took Jean upstairs.

"Come on," said Kermit, and put his arm around Marion.

"Hey," said Chuck dazedly. "Hey—— Wait——"

Marion turned her back and she and Kermit went to the door. Behind them Chuck began clumsily to ask Sally Durham whether she had really meant that Hank and Marion had been—had been—— He made very heavy weather of it. Kermit got Marion out of earshot as quickly as possible and settled her in the car, got in himself and turned it around ready to fly as soon as Jean appeared. He kept glancing at Marion while they waited but, though she wet her lips once as if to speak, she didn't say anything at all. It seemed as if Jean took forever, but it was actually not much more than five minutes before she came out with Marion's bag.

"That's not the best job of packing I ever did," she said, "but it's the fastest." Kermit drove off. "Now," said Jean, "let's for God's sake go and have that drink I needed a good hour ago—at least it seems like an hour—and then we'll get our stuff at the Morrisons' and I'll drive you to town."

"Oh, but I can take a train," said Marion.

"Not at this time of night you can't," said Jean. "There isn't one. It's all right. I want to be in town tomorrow, anyway."

Marion began to cry.

"Oh God," said Kermit, "don't do that."

"Let her alone," Jean told him fiercely. "It'll make her feel better." She put her arm around Marion's shoulders and stroked her hair. Marion moved unresistingly, as if she were a rag doll.

"Sure," said Kermit, and suddenly his rage was like a physical force in the car. "Let's all be sentimental. Go ahead and cry, Marion, so you can feel better and fall for another bum. Why don't you cry too, Jean? Then you'll both feel better!"

"Kermit!" gasped Jean. "Don't—— Stop!" She clutched Marion closer.

"Shut up, Jean. She's my sister. I'm going to tell her a few things. If she's been acting like a little whore all summer she can stand being told the truth·about what she's been doing. She's a mess, that's what she is, and I won't have it. Do you think you're going to help her by telling her she's a poor unfortunate misunderstood little lamb? You aren't. Marion, you wanted to make that bum, didn't you? You went after him, didn't you?"

"Kermit, Kermit!" cried Jean. "Have a little pity!"

"I don't believe in pity," said Kermit. "You did, didn't you?"

"Yes," said Marion in a whisper.

"You thought you were very grown-up and smart, didn't you, and all the lies you told were a thrill. Weren't they?"

"Yes."

"So you got yourself into a stinking mess and two other people had to help you run away from it. Didn't you?"

But this time Marion didn't answer. Kermit pulled the car over to the side of the road and stopped it. He turned to her. Jean had shrunk back in her corner. "Didn't you?" Kermit repeated through his teeth.

"Why didn't you let me alone?" asked Marion. "I asked you to let me alone and let me go home."

In the moonlight they stared at each other. They look alike, Jean thought, watching them, and was stung by a spasm of jealousy. They were both beautiful and young. And Kermit was so intent on her! Jean waited for Marion's eyes to waver.

But it was Kermit who said suddenly, "Yes, you did." He turned away, crossed his arms on the steering wheel and put his head down on them. After a while he said, "I'm sorry."

"But it was all true," said Marion. "What you said. I did all those things and felt all those things."

"So would anyone else have," said Kermit. "I'm sorry." The moonlight washed over the car. Marion stared at Kermit's bent head and Jean watched them both. At last Kermit lifted his head and said, "How do we get to the Morrisons'? Do you mind not stopping for a drink, Jean? I'd like to get out of here."

"I guess I can bear it," said Jean. "Go left at the next corner to the water and then right."

When they got to the Morrisons' the party was still going on. "I'll wait in the car," Marion said.

"Okay," said Kermit. "I—— We'll be as quick as we can." Jean and he went into the house. There were still people singing, still people playing the victrola.

In the hall at the foot of the stairs Kermit stopped and said to Jean, "I owe you an apology too, I guess. I'm sorry. I don't often lose my temper."

"It's all right," said Jean. She put her hand on the stair rail and said quickly, looking at her fingers, "Do you want me to come? Wouldn't you rather just take the car and drive her in by yourself?"

"Oh Christ," said Kermit, "don't you be difficult too." He put his hands on her shoulders and turned her to him. "I want you to come more than anything in the world," he said, and kissed her. Someone crossed the hall behind them, but neither moved from their embrace. Then Kermit let her go and said, "I'll meet you here in fifteen minutes." Jean went upstairs and Kermit prowled around looking for Mr. Morrison.

He found him in the study, listening to the radio. Out of the machine came a disembodied voice announcing that the Nazi Foreign Minister was flying to Moscow to sign a non-aggression pact with the Russians. Mr. Morrison chewed at his lip as he listened and once he leaned forward and made a note on a sheet of paper. Then he sat back and closed his eyes. Kermit stood just inside the door and tried to believe this news.

When the broadcast was over, Mr. Morrison snapped the radio off and said, "Well?"

"It's not possible," said Kermit.

"Don't be a fool," said Mr. Morrison. "They've been negotiating for months. Why else was Litvinov fired?"

"My God," said Kermit.

"Did you want to see me?" asked Mr. Morrison. "I have some phoning to do."

"I have to get back to town," said Kermit. "Would you—thank Mrs. Morrison for me, and say good-by?"

"Do you want a car?"

"No, thanks. I have—— I can arrange a ride."

"You can phone yourself if you want."

"Thanks, I—I guess not, right now. This is—— My God, the British thought *they* were negotiating with the Russians."

"They ought to get some better negotiators, then. By the way, your sister was here tonight. She's a nice girl. Can you keep her away from Durham?"

"I'm driving her in with me," said Kermit, and thought, then Jean was right, not Lucia. *That* was why he asked me. It had nothing to do with me at all. He just didn't want a mess. He passed his hand over his face and said, "Well—thanks and good-by."

"Look me up when you're in New York again," said Mr. Morrison, and pushed a buzzer. Kermit went out.

Upstairs he put back into his suitcase the little he had taken out and snapped it shut. He stood still for a moment looking around the pleasant chintzy room, wondering if Jean had decorated it. The bed that he would not sleep in was turned down to receive him. He thought, War. How many beds will I not sleep in? That was absurd, he promptly told himself, and melodramatic. The room thought so too. Whether Jean had arranged it or not, it said: Everything here will always be comfortable and in good taste. And downstairs Jean herself was waiting, and Marion, sick from her first brush with sin. Kermit picked up his bag and went out.

The moon was still high and bright. Jean walked beside him to the car. There Marion had fallen asleep. Kermit put the bags in back carefully so as not to wake her.

"Shall I drive?" he asked.

"If you want," said Jean docilely. "But I know the roads."

"You do, then."

He got in next to Marion, who stirred and said, "Don't. I don't——"

"It's all right," Kermit told her, putting an arm around her. They drove off.

It wasn't until they were twenty miles from the Morrisons' that

Kermit remembered he had not said good-by to Lucia or Anne. He felt strangely guilty about it, as if he had left them behind forever without a backward wave of his hand. But that must happen to children all the time, he told himself. They must be used to people coming and going incomprehensibly. I'll write them, he promised himself. I'll write, Lucia. A funny letter that will make you laugh, as soon as I have time.

But that was wrong, to think of time. For how much time did any of them have left? They had the present, that was all: this night that bloomed around him under the moon, through which Jean drove silently and Marion slept, as the miles whirled off their wheels. Over their heads time swung the night sky toward dawn, toward war. And if Jean and Kermit should lie in each other's arms, briefly secure, before that dawn—what defense did that give them? For the time that had passed to bring them together was passing still, carrying them to their parting. Kermit felt an immense and not unpleasant grief: for Jean, for Marion, for himself, all of them caught in the river of time, all of them condemned to feel and to lose what they felt. Poised now in the present, he felt the wind of the future from beyond the stars blow cold around him and, drowsy himself, thought: Perhaps they create time out there: imagining a huge old man with a white beard turning the crank of some celestial wind machine which blew time across the universe from the space behind the galaxies. What would happen, he wondered, dropping deeper toward sleep, if the old man caught his beard in the machine and it clanked and stopped and the wind stopped blowing? He saw the statesmen of Europe poised with pens in their hands ready to sign the peace pact that meant war, coolies halted before their rickshaws in Shanghai, elephants in Malaya arrested with one foot raised and teak trees slanted in their trunks, a troop train pulling out of a station, men leaning from its windows with cries of good-by silenced in their throats as the smoke from the engine froze against a blue sky and time stopped. Stopped; and he slept; and Jean drove on all alone in the night.

III. MARION

WHEN WE WAKE IN A STRANGE PLACE WE ARE apt not to know where we are. Marion, waking in the back bedroom of Jean's apartment, kept her eyes closed. She did not want to know where she was. How lovely to wake up to everything new, to be three years old on a sunny morning and, if you were to drink the cup of life, to have to pick it up carefully, awkwardly, with both hands, and drink in dips and gulps and have it taste like milk. A little girl in a blue dress sat at a low table, in Marion's mind, and drank like that, and Marion loved her. The sun came in the window and blessed everything.

Somewhere near a telephone rang. Marion became aware that she lay in a bed, that she was hot, that one arm was crumpled under her. The child in the blue dress vanished. She opened her eyes and saw a rectangular window with the shade halfway down and the bars of a fire escape drawing an austere pattern across it. Marion's gaze moved around the room to a bureau with a mirror over it, a chair, a wastepaper basket, a door. I have never been here before, she thought. There is nothing to be frightened of.

The door opened and Jean, in a blue dressing gown, with a cup of coffee in her hand, stood there. Marion felt her presence like a blow. Her thoughts said, But then, everything has to go on. I am here. It will all go on the same.

"Hello," said Jean. "Are you awake?" She came in and sat down on the chair by the bed. "I brought you some coffee." She put it on a table near Marion's head and smoothed her dressing gown over her knees. "Hank Durham is on the phone," she said. "Do you want to talk to him?"

Marion asked in a whisper, "Do I have to?"

"Of course not." Jean's voice was brisk. "I'll brush him off with great pleasure." She waited a minute to see whether Marion would change her mind and then went out, saying over her shoulder, "Drink your coffee."

But Marion lay still and shut her eyes. From under the lids tears forced their way out and ran down into the pillow. I have never done anything so awful in my life, she thought. It was like a talisman for tears, like a rain-charm opening the skies. How could I have done anything so awful? Waves of shame went hotly up her back. "Like a little whore," Kermit had said. "She behaved like a little whore." Worse than the words was the cold fury of his remembered voice which wiped out one Marion and set up another in her place—a Marion to be talked to with abhorrence and incredulous disgust. A little whore. I have never done anything so awful——

Hank was on the telephone. Jean was talking to him. It was real, it had happened and was happening. Marion shot up in bed in sheer terror.

Jean came back. When she saw Marion's face she shut the door and leaned against it.

"What did he say?" asked Marion.

"He said I forgot your jacket when I packed. He wanted to know where to send it."

"My jacket!" said Marion. "Did you?"

"I haven't the faintest idea."

"Does he know I'm here?"

"I don't know. I told him I had to go turn off the coffee when I came in before. I didn't say you were here. He may have guessed I wanted to tell you he was calling."

"Suppose—he comes here?"

"Suppose he does?"

"I'll go," said Marion, and started to get out of bed.

"My dear child!" said Jean, and came over to her. "Get back in there and drink your coffee. You needn't——"

But at this evidence of kindness Marion began sobbing again. She covered her face with her hands and gasped and gulped uncontrollably behind them. Jean let her cry until she began to run down and then gave her a box of Kleenex.

"I've never," Marion told her—this was very important and she got it out between sobs, before she could really talk plainly—"I've never—done anything—so awful—in my—life before." Over the Kleenex she peered up at Jean to make sure she knew this was true.

But Jean said, "You didn't do anything so awful."

"Yes I did!" said Marion in surprise, shaking her head.

"Damn that Kermit!" said Jean. She picked up Marion's untouched coffee. "This is cold. I'm going to get you some fresh." Her robe swept behind her angrily as she went out.

When she came back with coffee for them both Marion had mopped her eyes and blown her nose and was sitting back against her pillows, regarding the room incuriously. Jean gave her a cup and Marion said, "Thank you," and stirred it and sipped. Silence fell and embarrassment spread through the room.

"Where is Kermit?" asked Marion at last.

"He went out to get a paper." Jean darted a look at Marion to see what she made of Kermit's having spent the night, but Marion's face was as incurious as ever. Her own feelings made a shell around her in which she was as alone and untouchable as the yolk of an egg. She didn't care, at the moment, that Jean and Kermit had slept together, because she couldn't get past the fact that she and Hank had. Jean could see this, but she still felt a little touchy about it (she had not forgotten, either, what Kermit had called Marion in that moment of passionate anger). So she introduced a general subject for conversation. "Kermit says that Hitler and Stalin have signed an agreement to be friends, and that it means there'll be war."

"Why is that," asked Marion, momentarily distracted, "if they say they'll be friends?"

"Not war between them. War between Hitler and England and France."

"Oh." Marion drank some coffee and dismissed this rigmarole from her mind. "It's funny he should have said a jacket, because I know I didn't have a jacket with me. Except the one I was wearing, of course."

"He just wanted to know where you were."

"I know." She smiled painfully at Jean and said, "I'm not really so stupid as I sound. I just—don't seem to be functioning too well this morning. I wonder what time it is."

Jean looked at her watch and said, "A quarter to eleven."

"This is one of those times when I wish I were Catholic and could really get some good out of going to church. Wouldn't it be nice to get up and take a bath and put on fresh make-up and go out all clean and ready to come back feeling all right?"

Jean said, "Try to feel all right anyway."

"Oh yes," said Marion. "I will. I do." She blinked hard and drank some more coffee.

The outer door slammed and they could hear Kermit whistling softly as he came in. Jean tried to send Marion a sustaining look, but Marion wouldn't meet her eyes. The whistling went on for a little while, softer and then louder again, until Kermit said, not too loudly, "Jean?"

"In here," Jean called.

Kermit appeared in the doorway. His hair was brushed, he was shaved, his shirt was clean, and the fact that he was not wearing a tie was so immediately apparent that it was merely a comment on his otherwise fastidious neatness.

"How clean you look," said Marion in greeting. I don't, she might have added with justice, for she was sticky with sleep and tears. She felt messy and muddled before Kermit's unconscious statement that lucidity, neatness and positiveness were virtues, and tried to straighten her hair by running her fingers through it.

"Hello there, Helen of Troy," said Kermit. "Ready to start another fracas this morning?"

He obviously intended her to smile at his, and she did. It was probably as close as he could get to smoothing over what had happened last night. In her guilt and unease, she was eager to accept any kind of gesture from him, even this treating of horror and heartbreak as a joke. But she couldn't, of course, reply in the same vein, though she moistened her lips to try. Nothing came. She smiled again.

"Well," said Jean into the silence, "breakfast?"

At the same time Kermit said, "I'll have to phone, I'm afraid."
They went out together to deal with the events of the day and left
Marion behind.

She lay looking after them, thinking, I must get up. I should
help Jean. But no desire to be anywhere or to do anything provided
an impetus. She had done something terrible and life went on just
as it had before. She was, it seemed, to be allowed to do no penance,
to be granted no opportunity to make things right. Surely, then,
things must always be wrong! In a world that would not admit that
something terrible had happened to her she felt alien and lost.
Defiantly she thought, Hank! Hank! curling herself up in a ball,
her arms around her knees, trying to re-create the sweet pang of
love. He is a coward and a boor and a fool, he never loved you!
her mind told her coldly. Still she said, Hank, Hank! searching for
a refuge in the joyful intoxication he had given her, in the wonderful richness of those days when all life, all experience, had seemed
twice as deep, twice as thick and new, as ever before. Hank! Hank!
Hadn't he called her up? Wasn't he looking for her? She could
call him back. They could begin again—circumspectly, cautiously;
she could be careful to feel less than she had, to show him even less
of her feeling than that. And then there would still be something——

Horrible, horrible! she thought, springing out of bed in disgust.
Like a little whore! The pattern of a planned affair was so awful,
such a commitment to lies—and seemed so easy to achieve—that
she felt as if she were possessed. She might do that. She might
telephone to Hank. She might be that filthy! Trembling, she went
into the bathroom and took a shower, rubbing her body again and
again with soap as if she could never get clean. Then she dressed
in clean clothes, and applied lipstick meticulously, as if in the
physical neatness and fastidiousness that she had seen that morning
in Kermit some charm might exist to insulate her mind from longing for lies and chaos and passion.

When she came into the living room, Kermit was talking on the
telephone and drinking coffee. He was trying to get a seat on a
plane to Washington. So, apparently, were many other people.

Jean, who was now the most untidy of the party, was curled up
on the sofa, smoking and reading the Sunday paper. Her feet were

bare, her lipstick was uneven, and hair fell forward around her face. The curves of her breasts, her hips, her belly, showed through the thin stuff of her dressing gown and made Marion feel afraid. Jean seemed like a great powerful female machine designed for easy love and promiscuous kindness to those weaker than she.

She smiled at Marion and said, "Hi there," and then got up, pulling her robe about her, and went and got Marion a glass of orange juice. "How do you want your eggs?" she asked.

"I don't. Really, just toast."

"Nonsense. I'll make you an omelet."

"No, really——"

Kermit said, "Shut up, will you?" and then to the phone, "Yes, I understand that. And I'm sure everyone else has been telling you it's of the utmost importance, but as far as I'm concerned, it happens to be true. I have to—— All right, I'll wait." He put the phone in his lap and drank some coffee and said to the girls, "There are times when I find myself dwelling on the disadvantages of democracy as opposed to fascism. In Germany, if your department wanted you to be at a four o'clock meeting they'd send a bomber for you. Of course, they have more bombers to send." He picked up the phone again.

"Goodness," said Marion. "What's going on?"

"Didn't Jean tell you? Poland is about to be partitioned again."

"It is?"

"Yes it is. Hitler and Stalin have signed a treaty of eternal friendship and Poland will be the first sacrifice on the—— Yes, I'm here," he went on to the telephone. "Yes, I'll be glad to. Do your best for me, won't you? Thanks a lot. I know you will. Thanks." He hung up. "I have to go out to the airport and they'll try to stick me on something." He rubbed his eyes and yawned. "Marion, what are you going to do?"

"Do?"

"Yes. Where are you going now?"

Marion's lips opened, but she remained silent.

"She's not going anywhere until she's had some breakfast," said Jean indignantly. "Really, Kermit, do you have to be so abrupt?"

"In the present instance, I do. I have to get out to the airport right away. I want to know what Marion means to do when she leaves here today."

"She doesn't have to leave here today. I'd love to have her stay." But neither Marion nor Kermit listened to Jean or looked at her; and she was left feeling that they must have detected that part of her motive which was not to succor Marion but merely to defy Kermit and, by showing her independent of him, make her more attractive.

Marion said, "I had better go to Nina's. Mother's there. There's no one at the apartment." She looked at Kermit hopelessly while she said this, trying to transfer to his brain, like a decalcomania, the picture of what life at Nina's was like. Bridge, babies, knitting and neighbors—— Nina lived in Scarsdale now and was expecting her third child in October. Servants came and went, small children howled, Nina served on committees for community affairs, the radio played, there were buffet dinners given on Fridays, on Saturdays everyone danced at the club. Marion sometimes felt that if you were to take Nina's life and press it flat between two sheets of glass you would have to preserve nothing else to have a complete sociological record of middle-class suburbia in the 1930s; or indeed of Nina as Any-woman plunging into matriarchy and becoming a pillar of the community. That was unfair, of course, because it would squeeze out all the emotion and the fact that Nina seemed to like what she was doing.

"Will you be all right there? With the kids and the noise and everything? Nina's our older sister, Jean. She's married to a Wall Street lawyer who commutes to Scarsdale, and she has two kids and another on the way, and used to be quite bright. Last time I was there I thought I'd go mad."

"Well," said Marion, "right now, you see, I don't much *want* to hear myself think."

Kermit continued to look at her. "I can't take you to Washington," he told her. "I'm never home. I work."

"I never imagined——" Marion began.

"But listen," Kermit went on. "You mustn't take this too hard, you know. I'm—I know I blew up last night. I guess I got myself involved in it—— You were my sister and I—was acting like Big

Brother in a Victorian novel, all set to horsewhip someone. So—just forget what I said. Forget the whole thing. It was a mess, and you're just a kid and—and just try not to get into any more messes. Okay?"

"How can I forget it?" asked Marion. "Or suppose I *do* forget it? Something will still have happened to me."

"Well—yes," said Kermit. "I see that, but—— But is it important? It was a mess."

"But I was in love," said Marion.

Kermit turned to Jean, who was framed in the doorway of the kitchenette. "Jeanie, will you drive me to the airport? Can you get dressed in five minutes, because I've got to go? I'll get a cab if you——"

"Of course I can," said Jean, and vanished, calling over her shoulder, "Marion, help yourself to breakfast."

Kermit got up and wandered over to the window. Looking down into Bank Street, he said, "Don't talk about love. That's nonsense."

Marion bent her head and did not answer. Kermit turned around and looked at her sitting there meek and stubborn and wrong-headed, like the epitome of all femininity since the world began. A pang of rage against women struck him like a thunderbolt. "You weren't in love with him," he said through clenched teeth. "He's a jerk."

Marion raised her eyes. "What has that got to do with it?" she asked.

"Oh for God's sake—— Because it couldn't last. It couldn't mean anything."

"But it did to me." Unconsciously she laid her hand on her breast.

"Don't sit there looking like a madonna," said Kermit viciously. "What has love got to do with it? In love with that ape! You wanted to get made, and you did get made. You're twenty, it's natural, it's time. Love! Don't kid me. Don't kid yourself."

"But I felt it——" said Marion in a whisper. "Suppose he is—a jerk. I felt it. What difference can it make to what I *feel,* what he is?"

"How can it not? Don't you care what's real and what isn't, what's true and what isn't? Do you want to kid yourself all your life about feelings?" He waved his right arm at the real world in which he felt himself to stand. "Of course it makes a difference."

"But isn't what I feel real?" asked Marion.

"No," said Kermit. "At least—maybe it is to you. Not to anyone else. And since it won't last long, it's not very real even to you."

"But then there isn't any me. I might as well be dead. There's nothing here, if what there is—can't feel. Can't know. Can't be real——"

"Oh for God's sake. Let's not get into philosophy." He came over and looked down at her. "You had a roll in the hay with a guy who turned out to be a bum. You've been cooped up in those goddamn female schools and goddamn female camps, and you didn't know any better. That's what happened to you and it's all that happened to you. The sooner you stop feeling romantic and tragic, the better. So please forget about it. Don't sit around and brood. Go on up to Nina's and play bridge and try to teach her brats some manners."

"They're too little for manners," said Marion.

"Then they ought to be kept out back somewhere in a kennel until they get bigger. With a groom, or a nurse, or whatever. Marion —be all right. Will you?" But he did not wait for her answer and repeated, "Be all right."

Jean came back, dressed and capable. "Okay?" she said.

"Sure. I'll go close my bag." Kermit went out.

Marion took one swift look around Jean's living room—modern prints, Swedish furniture, the telephone that Hank's voice had come over—and said, "I'll get mine too, and maybe you'd drop me at Grand Central."

"But you didn't eat any breakfast!" Jean said accusingly.

"I'm only going to Scarsdale. If I've just missed a train, I'll eat something at the station." She ran out, trembling, desperate not to be left alone.

Driving uptown, no one spoke much. But when Marion got out at Grand Central, Kermit kissed her and said, "Good kid," and Jean leaned across on the seat to look out the open door and say, "I wish you weren't going. Call me soon and we'll have lunch. I'm in the book, home and office both. Call me *any time.*"

"I will. Thanks so much." They drove off and Marion stood on the pavement by her suitcase in the bright hot sun of an August noon. She had to go somewhere—— Oh yes. Inside the terminal and buy a ticket and get on a train—— She lifted her eyes to the buildings around Forty-second Street as David must have lifted his to the hills. Granite and brick, they hung above her.

And rocked. Like an earthquake. The world was splitting under her feet. Marion threw out an arm for support. A middle-aged redcap caught it and held her upright while she swayed. It took a little while for her to be able to hear his words. He was saying, "Are you all right, lady?"

"In a minute," said Marion with her eyes shut.

"That's all right, that's all right." He continued to hold her arm firmly but without getting close to her, as if he were reaching across a waist-high wall of race prejudice to help her. Finally she opened her eyes.

"Is this your bag here?"

"Yes."

"Then we'll go right along in here and sit you down in the waiting room." Taking the bag in his other hand, he led her out of the sun, through the heavy doors to the cool high-ceilinged marble room and deposited her on an oak bench. Marion leaned back and closed her eyes again, and everything went round slowly inside her head—but outside too, she was sure; if she looked the waiting room would be revolving slowly about her. And then it got faster, and faster——

And then someone was saying, "Smell this now, miss, smell it now," and she took a long sniff and it was spirits of ammonia and she choked and nearly strangled, and opened her eyes.

One of the attendants from the ladies' room was leaning over her, and the porter hovered in the background. She took their presence in but it didn't mean much—how could anything mean much if Kermit was right?—and then the ladies' room attendant put the bottle back under her nose and she sniffed it again and coughed, and everything came back into focus.

"Oh dear!" she said. "Oh I'm so sorry! Thank you so much! I'm terribly sorry."

"That's all right," said the porter again.

"You feel better now, miss?" the attendant asked.

"Oh much! Much better. I'm afraid I didn't eat any breakfast. Wasn't that silly!"

The porter leaned forward. "What train are you intending to take, ma'am?"

"Why—I'm just going to Scarsdale. The next train for Scarsdale."

He swung around to look at a clock. "You have exactly thirty-five minutes before that train departs," he told her.

"And there are lots of restaurants around," Marion said, smiling at him. "Yes, I'll go get some breakfast." She stood up. But everything was still a little unsteady, and she had to stop for a minute. "Oh—my bag," she said.

"I can keep it inside for you," said the ladies' room attendant.

"Oh would you? Thank you so much. Look—wait a minute." She fumbled in her purse and produced change for both of them.

"Would you like me to see you on the train?" the porter asked. "Please."

"Then I'll meet you here at"—he looked at the clock again—"at eleven fifty-five. Standard time, that is, ma'am. Twelve fifty-five your time."

"Fine, I'll be here," she told him, and went off into the echoing central concourse.

She chose the first little coffee shop she came to for her meal, and sat down and ordered scrambled eggs, toast and coffee. She still felt very queer when they came but as she ate, the hot food began to revive her and in ten minutes or so she was able to think: Goodness, that was a funny thing for me to do. I've never fainted in my life.

Something inside her echoed hollowly at the word "faint" and then she felt as if a slab in the floor of her mind was being lifted (like a sarcophagus lid, she thought) and something—awful—was coming out——

I'm pregnant, she thought. I must be pregnant.

And at once her hand shook so that she spilled coffee all over the table.

People always fainted when they were pregnant. It was in all the books. And then, when the doctor told them why, they were stunned. Absolutely stunned, the idiots. I wonder, Marion thought, why people in books have never read any books.

What am I going to do? She looked around the little restaurant. It offered nothing, not even a telephone.

What do I want with a telephone? she thought. She imagined herself calling up Hank to announce her sad condition. She knew exactly what he would say. He would say, "Oh my God. But you *can't* be. We were careful."

No, she couldn't call Hank.

At once the decision made her sweatingly anxious to break it. To call him once. To hear his voice. "Hi, baby. How's my honey?" That's what he said when he was alone. Of course he was out on the Island. He wouldn't be alone. Sally would probably answer. If a woman answers, hang up. *That* would certainly fool Sally, wouldn't it! Or be a wrong number. Or say I'm calling about the jacket I left behind——

Oh God, oh God, I mustn't call him. He won't help. He's no good at all!

"You want anything else?" asked the waitress, appearing beside her.

"Nothing, thanks. Just the check." Unless you know a good abortionist, Marion added in her mind.

Hank would, probably.

At that Marion shuddered all over. Hank. He must have been through this before. He must have had enough experience to wonder, first of all, whether Marion's story was true or whether it was another attempt at blackmail. Another shakedown. Hank. That's what he was. It was part of him that she was carrying, microscopically, in her belly. Hank.

How could I have done such a thing? Marion thought, standing up because she couldn't sit still under the thought.

Hank—horrible, horrible, horrible! She had thought it was bad before. But now—now she was caught. Everything existed in the real world as well as in her mind. I guess this would satisfy Kermit, she thought with grim humor. *But what am I going to do?*

Now the chatter and clatter of Nina's house and Nina's life would not be a refuge but a systematic scheme of self-torture. She could not cut off everything that had happened and run to Nina's suburban Utopia to rest. Everything was coming right along with her, thank you.

Nor could she call Hank. Again the blood seemed to drain from her heart to the pit of her stomach with desire to hear his voice, to be comforted and soothed and kissed into relaxation and irresponsibility. Again her brain told her emotions bitterly that she would get no such help from Hank if she told him what she feared.

Standing by the cash register, she opened her purse to pay for her breakfast. When she got her change, she had six dollars and fifty-seven cents. Where was she going on that? It would get her to Scarsdale and Nina and her mother and Stuart——

Or it would buy enough food for her to live for a few days at the apartment. Yes, that was the thing to do. Go to Brooklyn, to the empty apartment she shared with her mother. If she were alone she could rest, and when she was rested she might be able to think. To plan.

She went and got her bag from the ladies' room attendant and took the subway.

Hurtling along through the dark tunnel with a crowd of the strange people who come out only on Sundays in New York, she thought: Life is like this, underneath. Underneath the pattern you think you see. I must remember that. You think you are young and quite pretty and the pattern is that you will grow up and fall in love and be married and have children and love them, and a house and keep it. But that isn't what happens. If it happened to Nina perhaps it's because she didn't expect it to. And I daresay it doesn't feel on the inside the way it looks on the outside.

But the real trouble is that no one tells you about the grotesques. Things put their heads up through the pattern and look around and grin at you and kill you—kill you with fright—and then go down again underneath. And it's only then you realize that you've fallen in love, all right, but it's with Hank. And you're going to have a baby, all right, only it'll end up in a grubby back room of a doctor's office with no anesthetic and a nurse holding you down. And you begin to think that Something's shaking all over, laughing at you. Not the devil. Nothing that coherent or personal. Just Something big and slow and wrong, like an undertow in the universe, and you're caught in it. I am, anyway.

She came up out of the subway into the asphalt-melting heat and, Brooklyn Heights being what it is, was blocks from the apartment. But of course, she remembered, she could charge food at the grocer's tomorrow, all she had to pay for really was supper tonight, so her six dollars and fifty cents would easily cover a cab as well. She got into one and rode with her eyes shut through the maze of one-way streets until they stopped in front of the new apartment building. The elevator was self-service. She rode to the eighth floor and got out and unlocked the apartment door, feeling a kind of dull relief at reaching this sanctuary.

The living-room furniture was piled in a heap in the middle of the room, covered with a stained canvas. There were strips of paper across the varnished floor. The painters had gutted the apartment.

Marion stood in the doorway and didn't believe it. It *couldn't* be! It couldn't be, when she needed it so badly.

Perhaps the bedrooms are all right, she thought, and dashed into her own. It was worse. The bed was dismantled, the headboard and mattress out in the hall, and the chaise longue covered with pillows, lamps, books and toilet articles. Her mother's room was in the same condition. Obviously Mrs. Bishop had neatly planned her stay at Nina's and Marion's visit to Long Island to coincide with the re-decoration of the apartment. It was the kind of plan she loved to work out.

Marion went back to the living room. One of the straight chairs they used for dining was on the edge of the midden of possessions in the center of the floor. Marion pulled it out and sat down on it. She felt that she had come to a dead end. At quarter to two on a Sunday afternoon she had somehow got stuck, and now whatever was going to happen to her would just have to happen, because she couldn't do anything about it one way or the other. Sitting up in that chair in the paint-smelling room, she shut her eyes and went sound asleep.

She woke up to find herself lying sideways in an awful cramped position on a stack of books that were hidden under the canvas. Her head was splitting. Groggily she sat up, rubbed her eyes, went over and opened a window, and got herself a drink of water from the kitchen. The afternoon was as glassily bright as it had been, but her watch said four o'clock. Obviously she would have to do something, go somewhere. She couldn't spend the night sleeping on a straight chair in the apartment, and even if she were to improvise a better bed she did not want to be awakened by the happy voices of the painters at eight of a Monday morning, and still have nowhere to go. It had to be now.

"Call me any time," Jean had said. And "I wish you'd stay here."

Marion leaned on the window sill and looked at the skyline of lower Manhattan. It seemed to her extraordinarily ugly. But all the artists in Brooklyn painted it at least twice a year.

Where could she go if she didn't go to Jean? Who else could help her?

She could go to Nina, but Nina couldn't help her.

Kermit was in Washington. And he was busy. Six dollars and fifty cents—no, it was five ninety-five now—wouldn't get her to Washington.

Hank was three hours out on Long Island with a possessive wife and, by this time on a Sunday afternoon, a good cargo of cocktails aboard. Even if she wanted to call him. That is—she did want to. But the Hank she would call had never really existed. He was her idea of what Love should be. The Hank she could get on the telephone would say (she must know this, she must remember this) "My God! But you can't be. We were careful." Hearing again those imagined words—but it seemed like more than imagination. She knew it, she knew that was what he would say—Marion began reluctantly to cry. She had cried before that day in anger, in fear. Now she cried sadly over the death of Love. The skyline blurred. The bright afternoon, admitting this moment of agony, enclosed it like a fly in amber.

Jean was asleep when the doorbell rang. When she got back from the airport she had taken the phone off the stand, pulled off her dress and plunged into sleep. She had wanted not to think about Kermit, not to remember their love-making in the night or their parting by the gateway to the plane he had wangled his way onto. "I'll be up next week end if the bottom doesn't drop out," he had said matter-of-factly, squeezed her hand, not even kissed her, and gone. And she had loved it. Because it meant that to kiss her was not necessary, that they would be together a long time and have room in their lives for everything. So obviously she must not think about this, about this great gift of happiness that had been made to her, because to think about it, to admit it, would be the most awful, awful luck—— And so, since drinking and driving and loving had tired even her magnificent healthy body, she went promptly to sleep. Now, two hours later, she was breathing as healthily, dreaming as happily, as if she were four years old instead of thirty-four.

She waked at the first ring of the bell, but the sound ended before she could identify it and she rolled over and lay blinking. Then the bell rang again and she got up and went into the hall and buzzed the connection that opened the downstairs door. Yawning, stretching, she waited a moment, then opened her door, heard footsteps on the stairs and called, "Who's that?"

"Jean?" said an uncertain voice, a girl's voice. I know who that is, Jean thought, but I can't place it.

"Yes?"

"It's Marion." And Marion came around the bend in the stairs and stood looking up at Jean with her suitcase—that Jean had packed for her last night—still in her hand.

Jean's face changed.

Marion swayed and thought of turning and running away. Why had she thought she would be welcome? What an idiotic over-estimation of herself! Jean had been nice, she saw now, only because of Kermit! "I'm sorry——" she said, and started to turn.

But she was quite wrong. Her luck had at last changed. Jean's face had grown not angry, but merely alert and intent. And that was because she was waking up still and, having expected one of the casual Greenwich Village crowd of her friends, realized instead that trouble was here. But she didn't mind trouble.

"Marion, what is it?" she asked.

Marion looked up humbly. "I don't—I won't bother you."

"Don't be an idiot! Come up. Come in. Give me that bag. You poor child, have you been lugging that around with you all day? Where have you been? What happened? Couldn't you stand Scarsdale? *That's* no wonder! Sit down. Tell me what's the matter and then I'll brush my teeth—I was sleeping—and make us a drink. Or maybe I won't brush my teeth. Whiskey and Pepsodent, what do you think? Sounds kind of dreadful. Here, honey, hold everything. You could do with a slug right now, from your face." She bustled out into the pantry, came back with whiskey and a glass with ice in it, splashed the whiskey in and gave it to Marion, saying, "Drink that up, that's a nice child."

Marion took a sip and, looking at Jean, said, still apologetically, "I tried to phone, but you must have been talking to someone for quite a while."

"No, sweetie, I just take the phone off the hook when I want to sleep. Otherwise all the people who are due to get wrong numbers seem to get mine. Come on now, tell me why you're not at your sister's. Spit it right out and get it over with, it's easier to do it fast, like taking off adhesive tape."

Marion shut her eyes and said, "I think I'm pregnant." When she opened them Jean was still looking at her with just the same expression of curious kindness that she had worn before.

"Why do you think that?" she asked.

"I—nearly fainted this morning. In the station. I thought it was just because I was hungry and upset. And then——"

"Maybe it was."

"No. I know."

"How do you know?"

"I—just know."

"Magic? Okay. Maybe you are. Maybe you aren't. I'll take you to see a doctor and let him decide, how about that?" And Jean promptly turned around, put the phone back on the hook for a minute and then dialed a number. "Hello," she said. "Is Dr. Edwards there? When will he be? Well, can I make an appointment? Who's this, the answering service? Okay, I'll call his nurse in the morning." She hung up. "He's out of town for the week end. We'll get hold of him tomorrow. Don't worry, honey, it's probably nothing at all."

But Marion had begun to sob into her whiskey. She had cried for fear and anger and grief—now she cried in sheer selfish relief. The fact that someone was doing something to help her let loose all her self-pity by justifying it. The tension within her that had kept her going relaxed, and she rolled over on the sofa where she sat and at last had her cry out.

She went to sleep again that night in Jean's back bedroom, very, very tired and a little drunk. Some of Jean's friends had dropped in and Marion, in reaction from twenty-four hours of intermittent weeping, had got a bit high. Jean's friends seemed strange and amusing to her. They were reasonably amusing as a matter of fact, but not particularly strange, being mostly unsuccessful artists who needed Jean's vitality as much as they did the meals she served them. Jean did not get along too well with successful people unless she fell in love with them. It was not jealousy—it was just that a relationship which depended on her generosity was more comfortable to her than one that did not. Marion could have found few people better equipped to help her.

In the morning, though, she wasn't so sure of this. Her body was so taken up with having a hangover that she didn't feel pregnant any more. She felt only uncomfortable and out of place. For two nights and a day, she felt, she had been indulging in indecent exposure. Now she wanted only to go away somewhere by herself and forget everything that had happened. It seemed quite reasonable to her in this mood that all she had to do to deal with any unfortunate physical condition was to decide that it was not so, to rise above it. That would take care of it, she thought haughtily, disdaining her body, her queasy stomach, her aching head; and disdaining with them the camaraderie of last night's party, Jean's ungrudging help and, in the last analysis, Jean herself. To be someone that Jean was generous to seemed very galling that morning, hardly to be borne.

She was in consequence very polite to Jean and insisted on getting breakfast though she could drink nothing but coffee herself. Jean had an early appointment with the vice-president of a small advertising agency to talk about decorating his offices, and didn't seem to have time to pay much attention to Marion's emotional state. She dashed out the door at quarter to nine, pulling on her gloves and calling over her shoulder, "I'll tend to the doctor and call you later." When she had left, Marion sat down and experienced despair.

There is no better time to do this than at nine o'clock in the morning. The weight of the day ahead is a constant pressure, demanding that something be accomplished. All over the world—or at least all over the Eastern Time Zone—everyone is beginning the day's work, children in school, girls in offices, men in factories, women with beds to make. To want nothing, to have nothing to accomplish, is to be frighteningly alienated from humanity. Marion sat in a kind of lumpish sullen resentful terror, looking at the dirty dishes—Jean had eaten a hearty breakfast—watching the butter slowly melt and the remains of Jean's bacon and eggs congeal on her plate. Of course she intended to wash them, but to have introduced a small area of squalor into Jean's neat and pleasant apartment gave her a mean satisfaction. She knew it was mean, but she felt mean—mean and lazy and sluttish. She was an object of charity. The common reaction of objects of charity—to be unworthy rather than grateful—possessed her.

It came into her head finally that she would call Hank as soon as he could be expected to be in his office. She did not want to accept Jean's kindness. If Hank helped her she would not have to be grateful. It would be owed to her. She would be collecting a debt, not taking charity. This resolve hardened her sufficiently for her to stand up, collect the dishes, wash them, make her bed neatly and tidy the apartment. Then she phoned Hank's office.

The switchboard put her through to his secretary, who wanted to know who was calling.

"Miss Bishop," said Marion, who had thought of giving another name but had not wanted to use any of the pseudonyms she had been used to adopt when calling Hank's office in the affectionate past. Immediately that she had spoken she thought that she might have said she was Jean, but it was too late now.

"One moment please," said the secretary.

Marion waited. She was frightened now, frightened stiff. What in God's name was she going to say to Hank? She was not built to collect debts, she realized now, but only to incur them. She was acting as if Hank were an enemy, and the idea of having an enemy terrified her.

Hank's voice said, "Hello?"

Marion couldn't speak for a moment.

"Hello?" he repeated with irritation. "Marion? What is it?"

"It's nothing," said Marion. "I'm sorry."

"Oh for God's sake!" said Hank. "No, I'm sorry. Look, I have to go to Boston and I've got a mess of stuff to clean up. What is it, baby? I'm sorry about Saturday night."

"Don't be sorry," said Marion. "It's all right. I shouldn't have called. You're busy."

"Yeah, I am. But look, I'll be back Wednesday. Where are you? I can probably make dinner Wednesday."

Marion took the phone away from her ear and put it down in her lap. Out of it Hank's voice crackled, asking if she were there. What was the trouble? He was sorry he had to go away but he couldn't help it. Wasn't Wednesday all right? And then, again, was she there?

Am I? thought Marion. Will I be here Wednesday? Shouldn't she be? Couldn't she collect her debt on Wednesday?

She couldn't, she found. She put the phone back to her ear and said, "I'm here, but what I called to say is that I never want to see you again. It's all over." At the melodrama of this statement she almost laughed aloud.

Hank's voice jumped an octave and he began to swear. This too seemed funny to Marion. Seldom, she felt, had anyone bitten off her nose to spite her face with such thoroughness. It was a pity that she couldn't tell him that she was throwing him over at the exact moment when she needed him most, but her engorged pride would not let her admit that need. What a delightful revenge, to throw Hank over! What a pleasure to hate him! Hank's temper tantrum released all her own anger.

"Oh for heaven's sake," she said cheerfully, "don't carry on so! It isn't as if you cared beans about me. Go get another girl. There are lots of them around. Get a Boston girl. I'm sure you'll be a lovely change for her and she'll be terribly grateful."

He called her a slut then, and she really did laugh.

"This is a fine time to call me names," she said, "when I've just stopped being a slut. Why didn't you call me that two months ago? I don't think you know the meaning of logic."

"What in Christ's name are you talking about?" he shouted. "Are you drunk? Are you crazy? What's the matter with you? You're behaving like an idiot just because Sally lost her temper for a minute. My God, I can't argue with you now! Will you meet me Wednesday or not?"

"Never, never, never again," said Marion. In fact, she almost sang it.

"That's all right with me, then! And you can go straight to hell!" He banged the receiver in her ear.

But Marion felt quite triumphant. She was right back where she had been, it was true, dependent on Jean to be got out of this scrape; yet somehow quarreling with Hank made everything different. For one thing, there was no choice left to her now, she had to go to Jean's doctor, so she was not plagued with the necessity for decision. For another, she had indulged in the luxury of irresponsibility and, like all luxuries, it had given a return in swelling of personality and swaggering of ego. But most of her relief came from pleasure in destruction. She had destroyed her image of Hank, which had been her image of love, and so part of herself. She had purged herself of love and kindness and generosity and felt much, much better without them.

But when she met Jean to go to the doctor's office she was frightened again. They ate a quick lunch in a handy Schrafft's, but Marion couldn't taste the food and afterward, riding to the doctor's in a cab, she felt dreadfully sick to her stomach. In the taxi Jean produced a wedding ring for her to put on. "I said you were Mrs. Brown," she told Marion.

"Thank you," said Marion, and her heart sank further. It seemed that no dedication to irresponsibility could remove one from the need for contrivance. She put the wedding ring on. It was a little big. "I hope I don't lose it. Is it yours?"

"It was," said Jean. "Don't worry. No matter how awful you feel right now, you don't feel as awful as I did when I was wearing it all the time and trying to be Mrs. Richard C. Davis. Mr. Richard C. Davis should never have got married at all because he really didn't like women much, but it took nearly two years before I believed it.

Whenever I feel low I remember that whatever may have happened to the best years of my life, at least the worst two years are over."

"I'm sorry," said Marion.

"It's all right. I have a fine time now."

They had to wait at the doctor's while a couple of nondescript women had their ailments investigated. When the last one had gone in Marion said suddenly, "Do I have to pay him now? I haven't any money."

"Of course not. Tell him to send a bill to Mrs. Brown, care of my address."

Marion passed a hand over her face. It was wet with perspiration. She took out a handkerchief and wiped her forehead, saying, "It's so hot." Then the nurse appeared in the door and beckoned, and she and Jean were going inside. Marion wondered what had happened to the women who had preceded her and not come out. Perhaps the Moloch of Medicine had eaten them.

The doctor was as nice as he could be. He and Jean were old friends and they laughed together over some old friendly jokes. But nothing stopped the moment when Marion walked stiff-legged into an inside room with the nurse and was arranged on the examination table. She kept her eyes tight-shut so that she wouldn't know what was going on and all the doctor said was, "Could you just relax a little more, please?" He said this from time to time and then he went out and the nurse helped her up and told her she could get dressed.

Again everyone was very nice and after another joke or two Jean took her arm and walked her out of the office.

Outside Marion halted, realizing suddenly that no one had told her anything. "What did he say?" she gasped, clutching Jean's arm.

Jean gently led her on. "He'll phone, foolish. He has to run a rabbit test, or whatever it is. He'll phone in a couple of days."

"Oh no!" said Marion.

"Why, what's the matter?"

"It's so long!"

Jean had her out in the sunlight now, hailed a cab and pushed her in. "You need a good stiff drink," she said. "And then I'll tell you what you can do for a couple of days while you wait. Hell, I'll tell you now. You can come and work for me. I got a wire this morning from my dear, dear assistant who went to Mexico for a vacation. She's got married to a Mexican and she isn't coming back. So here I am with my busiest season coming up and nobody but an idiot typist in the office. No, don't say anything now. Wait until you have a drink and see how the idea of being my assistant sets."

Marion leaned back and shut her eyes and confused memories of *Alice in Wonderland* revolved through her head. Curiouser and curiouser, she said to herself, for she certainly felt as if she were changing her size from moment to moment. And then it occurred to her that Jean was very like the Red Queen, though kinder in manner than that bustling and dictatorial lady who had run Alice breathless to stay in the same place and then presented her with dried biscuits as a refreshment. Still and all, Alice would never have become a queen without her aid.

So Marion started to learn how to be a decorator. Jean's office was a couple of barren cubbyholes in a rabbit warren of a loft building in the Thirties. Like the children of the shoemaker who proverbially go barefoot, her office was the opposite of decorated. Samples of wallpaper, swatches of upholstery material, odds and ends of brass and bits of lamps lay about here and there, and papers covered a pair of battered golden-oak desks. The filing cabinets bulged with obsolete correspondence. Marion fell on the mess with avidity and cleaned and tidied and filed and dusted as if it were her own life she was setting in order. Jean at work was impressive to watch and to listen to. She dealt on the telephone with ladies who changed their minds about colors and periods with the deft and cheerful patience of a nursery-school teacher. Marion admired her more and more.

Every now and then of course she would remember that there was a telephone call coming from the doctor and then her busyness would be cleft by a pang of fear that was physical in its violence. Her heart would thud, her hands would begin to perspire. It was impossible that this should have happened to her, that, being just the same, she should be absolutely different. No, no, she would cry to herself, don't think about it! And she would plunge back into her work, snatch up a bundle of papers, ask Jean an unnecessary question, to get rid of the ghost.

When the doctor did call at last she was alone in the office and she thought at first that he had the wrong number because he asked how to get in touch with Mrs. Brown. She remembered just in the nick of time that she was Mrs. Brown and, collapsing into the chair at Jean's desk, said, "Speaking."

He told her she wasn't pregnant.

"Oh," said Marion.

He took her reaction for disappointment and began to tell her how sorry he was, but that there was certainly no organic reason why she should not become pregnant in the future. Her hemoglobin was a little low, her thyroid might possibly be a bit underactive, he advised plenty of rest and a diet high in protein, but there was nothing that the simplest care couldn't correct.

"Are you sure?" Marion asked him.

"Yes indeed. No reason on earth why you shouldn't have ten children if you want them."

"No, I mean about—about now. That I'm not going to now."

"I'm afraid so. Quite sure."

"How funny. I was so certain."

"Well, it happens that way sometimes. Never mind, perhaps you'll be back in a couple of months and I can give you better news."

"Thank you."

"Give my best regards to Jean, will you?"

"I certainly will."

"Good-by." He rang off. Marion sat and looked at the telephone receiver and felt empty and queer and yes, hideously disappointed. Disappointed? Was she merely reflecting the emotion the doctor had attributed to her? No. For everything was over. She had broken with Hank, thrown love, sinful foolish misguided generous love out of her life and put hate in its place to live by. And now, with her pregnancy a myth, hate had lost its point. She was Marion Bishop, entirely Marion Bishop, without a trace of Mrs. Brown or of Hank's girl friend who had been introduced into various hotel rooms under one or another of those affectionate pseudonyms of the past. And to be just Marion Bishop, not quite twenty-one, and, in another avatar, student at Vassar, seemed like having no identity whatsoever. She was absolutely no one at all.

She went out to the bathroom to wash up and discovered that she had begun to menstruate. This reduced the whole fantasy with the doctor to utter foolishness and life to the level of a bad joke. How perfectly disgusting! Marion thought, but of course it wasn't disgusting at all, it was just the way things were. No adjectives could describe life, they slid off it. Certainly in the last week life had been mean and tricky and malicious; it had thoroughly flummoxed her. But that was not the impression it left her feeling now. She felt foolish, abysmally foolish, but most of all she felt the enormous commonplaceness of life—repetitious, thorough, powerful, almost impersonal but not quite—a huge, thumping piece of machinery with little pigs' eyes that never missed a trick. Three o'clock of an August afternoon and she had been shown to herself as an idiot and left to go on with her life just the same without a moment's pause. There wasn't anything else to do.

Kermit came up from Washington Friday evening and Marion moved out of Jean's apartment for the week end. She thought she did this casually and with sophistication, but to arrange to leave her brother alone with her benefactor, who was also his mistress, was not really that easy. On top of all the shocks and changes she had been through already, it exhausted her so that she didn't feel like seeing anyone and adapting to any other social circumstances. She told Jean, therefore, that she was going to Scarsdale, and called Nina and told her in a brief and impersonal conversation that she was back from Long Island and going to New Jersey to visit a friend from college, and then she fled to the still empty but now painted apartment in Brooklyn.

Here, where she could have done as much tidying and cleaning as in Jean's office, all impulse to such activity left her. She moped. It had never occurred to her before to mind being alone; indeed, she could not remember when she had been absolutely alone for two days and three nights. She had always swum happily in a stream of social activity, taking friendship, popularity, and the constant presence and pressure of a group for granted. Now she felt as if she had fallen through some unsuspected hole in the firm floor of her world into emptiness and a foggy place. She did not know how to get out.

She was unsure of everything. She had deceived herself over Hank, she had panicked neurotically into believing herself pregnant. There was no one she could trust, least of all herself. Indeed, she felt very strange to herself. The newly painted apartment gave her no help in finding a personality for the anonymous creature who wandered about it. Her childhood's roots were all out in the big house in Bay Ridge, sold now to a Norwegian sea captain with six children. The apartment could have been lived in by anybody, and that was whom Marion felt like—anybody.

She was so numb, so without purpose, that she might never have gone back to Jean's office if it hadn't been for the woman her mother had engaged to clean up after the painters, who arrived bright and early Monday morning. Mrs. Bailey was an old friend who had done laundry and odd jobs for the Bishops on and off for years. She was a talkative soul and fond of Marion, and she told her at once that she looked poorly, fixed her an enormous breakfast and had a clean dress pressed for her before she was through eating. Marion fled to Jean's office under a barrage of questions she couldn't answer—Mrs. Bailey followed her to the elevator with a pair of gloves to ask what hospital Nina was going to for the new baby.

Jean greeted her with a handful of drapery materials, gave her directions about finding upholstery fabrics to go with them and started her off on a round of the wholesalers. This was fun, and Marion soon began feeling better. The afternoon, during which she hunted up and down Third Avenue for an inlaid Regency card table and a pair of small crystal chandeliers, was also restorative. She got back to the office tired and dirty but feeling quite human because of having exercised her taste.

"Well," said Jean, "let's go home and clean up and have a drink and you can tell me all about Scarsdale. Where's your bag?"

"Oh Lord," said Marion, and sat down limply. "I didn't go to Scarsdale," she confessed.

"Oh?" asked Jean, and waited. Marion could see her thinking, Hank?

"I didn't go anywhere," Marion told her hastily. "I mean—neatest trick of the week—I mean I just went to our apartment in Brooklyn, Mother's and mine. I didn't much want to see anyone. Things can get so complicated. I guess I forgot all about clothes and things. I don't seem to be co-ordinating too well."

"But your mother's in Scarsdale. You mean you went and sat in Brooklyn by yourself all week end? What did you do? Go to the movies?"

"Nothing. I didn't do anything." Marion laughed shakily.

"I'd never have let you go," said Jean angrily, "if I'd had any idea—— I thought you *wanted* to go to Scarsdale. You don't have to be tactful about Kermit and me. You mustn't do things like that! No one prefers your room to your company! Well, I'll get the car out this evening and we'll go get your stuff from Brooklyn—unless you'd rather stay there?"

"Jean," said Marion, "aren't you afraid of being too good to me?"

"Of course I'm not! I love having you! When your mother comes back, that's different." And Marion thankfully found herself taken in hand again, though she vowed to herself that she would move out next week end, just the same, if Kermit came up.

But Kermit didn't come up because Hitler invaded Poland on Friday morning. It was a lovely hot clear day, the prelude to the Labor Day week end. Marion started to pack a small suitcase, announcing that she really had to go to Scarsdale this week end, and turned the radio on to get a weather report. Over it came booming the information that the Luftwaffe was bombing Warsaw. She was on her knees by her bag, holding two slips and a nightgown, and she always remembered how hard the floor felt on her knees as the news babbled out of the loud-speaker. She called Jean and they listened together until the announcer stopped talking about war and began talking about cereal, and just then the phone rang and it was Kermit saying he couldn't come up.

"Are England and France going to declare war?" Jean asked.

"Wouldn't you like to know?" said Kermit. "So would I. I'm sorry about the week end. I'd say come down here, but I expect I'll be stuck in meetings and various unproductive bull sessions right through."

"That's all right," said Jean. "I feel sort of numb, anyway. Marion and I will sit and hold hands and listen to the radio until we get used to this."

Kermit asked about Marion, was told she was fine, and spoke to her briefly. While Jean talked to him again, Marion went out to the kitchen and got herself another cup of coffee. She felt excited and upset and inadequate. It made the news seem more frightening to have it change anything so minor and personal as Jean's plans for a week end. Marion had been at college when the Munich crisis burst the year before. That had been nothing but radio-listening and general observations from professors who had been in Europe in the summer. One had felt a helpless horror over the fate of the Czechs as one had felt it for so long over the Jews. But the event had been abstract and far away. The effect of world events on personal life Marion's mind was educated enough to take for granted, but her conscious emotion had never experienced it before.

Jean came into the kitchen and said abruptly, pouring more coffee for herself, "I can remember the last war."

Marion looked at her wonderingly. She had never seen Jean really upset about anything before. "Was it awful?" she asked.

"We thought it was wonderful. We knitted like mad and saved peach pits—I can't remember what for. Gas masks, I think—and silver paper and were horrid to the German kids at school. There were a lot of Lutherans in my town. We Presbyterians—not only the kids—decided they were spies. When my brothers went we hung a flag in the window with two stars on it and I nearly burst with pride. My older sister got engaged to three boys at once and had a terrible time when two of them got leave at the same time. Mother made me a Red Cross uniform and I used to put it on and walk up and down in front of the house where Judy Henkel lived. She'd been my best friend, but her father came from Hamburg. We talked about the Huns. I had a picture of Eddie Rickenbacker that I took to bed with me. I loved every minute of it. Yes, it was awful. Judy Henkel died in the flu epidemic. So did my mother."

"Oh Jean!"

"I'm a whole generation older than you are, and I feel as if it were three. Kermit's afraid the English *won't* declare war."

"Oh Jean—but Jean—— They have to! They can't let Hitler take everything he wants! We've—they've got to fight!"

"You see," said Jean. "You don't know what you're talking about.

232

You and Kermit—it isn't your fault, but you talk like idiots. You don't know what it's like. We've got to fight! We must stop Hitler! How? You're not going to stop Hitler with a concrete wall or a Maginot Line or a threat. It will take piles and piles and piles of corpses and years and years and years of blood to stop Hitler. I'd like to stop Hitler too, but I'd rather live—and have everyone live!" And Marion saw, to her astonishment, that tears were running down Jean's cheeks.

Marion threw her arms around Jean and begged her to stop. "Perhaps it won't happen!" she cried.

"It will happen," said Jean. "The corpses will happen, and the good people who get excited and enjoy themselves will happen, and the intolerance and the blood and the Red Cross shenanigans, and all I'm wishing is just selfish, selfish. I wish I didn't have to see it again. That's what I wish. I feel a million years old."

"Oh Jean, don't, don't! It mayn't—— Perhaps——"

"It mayn't! Perhaps! But it will. Well, go pack your bag and go up to Scarsdale. Everyone will be excited there."

"I'm not going. I'll stay with you."

Jean pushed Marion away and went over to the sink and washed her face. "Do as you please," she said.

Marion stood hesitant, wanting to justify herself. I can't help when I was born, she thought. But watching Jean, she slowly perceived that it was not her youth but Kermit's that was agonizing her friend. Between Jean and Kermit too there spread the gulf of a generation across which affection could throw only the most precarious of bridges—a bridge that must sway with every gust of bitter knowledge that Jean possessed and that Kermit had yet to learn. Jean is in love with him, she thought, and for the first time saw this cheerful sensible efficient creature as vulnerable to common mortal pain. Jean was in love in a world where a war was beginning to consume the bodies of young men. She loved a young man, and like all of his fellows, he was threatened and she was helpless.

"Jean," Marion said suddenly, searching for a distraction, "I didn't tell you, but last week—when I still thought I was pregnant—I called up Hank and told him to go to hell. Wasn't that funny?"

Jean straightened up at once. Nothing could have cheered her so immediately as this chance to return from her own problems to Marion's. "You didn't! What did he say?"

Marion giggled. "Well, first he swore and then he called me names and asked me if I were drunk and then he told *me* to go to hell. Isn't that just what you'd figure he'd do?"

"Yes it is! I must say I *wouldn't* have figured you'd think it was funny. I'm delighted."

"It's odd, isn't it? Of course I don't only think it's funny, I think it's awful too. But maybe I've grown up some. I do hope so. My Lord, look at the time. Don't you have a nine-thirty appointment?"

"Oh God, yes," cried Jean, and flew to get dressed.

It was that week end that Marion met Tom Hofstra. She thought during the day of asking Jean to come out to Scarsdale with her and then realized that to Jean it would not be Marion's family she was visiting, but Kermit's. She resigned herself therefore to a long hot New York week end. Jean, however, suggested Saturday morning— turning away from the radio that was reporting a speech of Chamberlain's to Commons, war not yet declared, everything still agonizingly in the balance—Jean suggested that they go and see some people she knew near Nyack with whom she'd had a long-standing date for Labor Day week end. When Marion later remembered this week end she managed to forgive herself for Hank because if it hadn't been for Hank she wouldn't have been staying with Jean and if she hadn't gone out to Nyack with Jean she wouldn't have known Tom. Sometimes the casual almost-missed chances of the past are more frightening than the future.

Not that the trip to Nyack seemed anything but disastrous at the time. Marion rode out with Jean along the crowded roads, feeling a fine confidence in her own maturity for succoring her friend who had been upset and who needed her. But Jean's acquaintances made her uneasy. It was not just one family they were visiting, but a group of people who—probably living quite decently in town during the cold months—flung themselves during the summer into a state of bohemian squalor approaching primitive communism. Two tennis courts and a muddy swimming pool were owned in common and almost everything else seemed to be, including most of the wives. Some of them had got divorces from one member of the colony and

234

married another. Some had not—or not yet—bothered to do this. There were a large number of small children whose relationships Marion never got straight. They moved about in groups from bungalow to bungalow and were fed in sixes or eights wherever they happened to be when they got noisily hungry enough for an adult to decide they needed a meal. Even quite small babies were left with neighbors when their mothers wanted to go to town for the day, were given their bottles by anyone handy and deposited on the life-giving earth to eat cookies and dirt. One of them all but ate a caterpillar under Marion's eyes. When she removed it the baby howled furiously. The half dozen cars of the community were used indiscriminately by every member. Liquor, food, phonograph records and clothes were not so much borrowed as pre-empted by those who felt a need for them. Marion zigzagged between feeling like an anthropologist in deepest Melanesia and like a provincial idiot.

She watched Jean for hints as to proper demeanor but could not use the clues. Jean was calmly, neutrally, herself—talking, laughing, playing tennis, but giving off the solid impression that nothing odd that happened need affect her. Even the dirt, which made Marion squeamish, didn't bother Jean. When presented with a glass that had leftover lipstick around the rim she simply went out to the kitchen and washed it, came back and poured her own drink. Marion was at once too curious, too surprised and too entangled in politeness to achieve such behavior. When a man named Alan decided she should go out on the river with him at twilight she couldn't think of any way not to, though she was sure his intentions were not good; and when she proved to be right, she lost her head and tipped over the canoe, though he had done nothing but talk—and couldn't after all, *in* a canoe if she didn't want him to. He wasn't particularly angry; he thought it was funny and rather complimentary that his words had roused her to such action. But *she* was angry—angry and ashamed of herself; and the moment when she had to walk, dripping and squelching, through the party drinking on the porch with Alan behind her rolling his eyes and expatiating on her virtue in the style of the news magazine which employed him—this was one of the worst in her life. Rubbing her hair dry, she cried into the towel in humiliation and exasperation.

When she came out, reasonably dry, she was presented with a drink and addressed as "Prudence." Everyone laughed and Alan, still soaking, roared for her to sit down next to him and let him try his technique on dry land. All Marion could think was that she wanted to go home, but Jean had driven to Nyack with their host to get some more gin before the stores closed, and there was no way for Marion to flee. She sat down between two quiet young men who were polite and gentle with her and began to recover herself. But then a man named Pete, who was growing a beard, hauled her up to dance with him (the phonograph was playing incessantly through all this), and told her that her new friends were homosexuals. This did not shock her, she assured herself, but it did make her cease to regard them as a haven, for she could not help feeling that she was an intruder in their lives, some large crass vulgar creature who might be interesting as a specimen but could never be liked as a friend. She felt so miserable that she had another drink and then another. By the time Jean came back she had stopped feeling miserable—or feeling anything else, really—and was dancing in a state of excited numbness with one man after another.

Late in the evening she was dancing with a large square black-haired man when the room began going up and down and she stopped, clutching him, and said, "I'm drunk!"

He led her at once out of doors to the road past the tennis courts. She clung to him, walking blindly over ruts, until they reached another cottage, where he sat her down on the stoop and said, "Wait a minute till I get a flashlight. You'll be all right if you walk a bit." She sat groggily waiting for him, wondering whether he was going to make a pass at her and deciding she felt much too awful to care. But when he came back his arm around her waist was strong as iron and just as impersonal. With the flashlight in his left hand he led her up and down the road until the ground steadied under her feet and she said, "Oh I feel much better. Thank you so much."

"You're sure?"

"Yes, really. You know, I can't remember eating any dinner."

"Perhaps you didn't. Do you want to go into Nyack and get something?"

"That would be wonderful if you don't mind."

"My car's over there."

They got in and Marion at once felt embarrassed. "I don't know your name."

"Tom Hofstra. I'm an architect. I work with Bill Ford."

"Oh. Which is he?"

"The blond one with glasses who was playing the accordion."

"Oh—yes. And his wife is Laura?"

"No, his wife is Marge."

"Oh dear. It's—it's hard to get a lot of people straight at once."

"What's your name? Prudence What?"

"*Not* Prudence. Marion Bishop. Alan called me Prudence because I tipped over a canoe when he—when he—— It was an awful silly thing to do. Weren't you here earlier?"

"No, I came out about an hour ago. I stopped to look at a house on the way and had dinner with the people who're building it."

"Oh, a house you designed?"

"No, one I wish I had. Do you know much about design?"

"About architecture?" Marion giggled. "You should see the house I grew up in, in Brooklyn."

"Gingerbread?"

"*And* whipped cream."

"I'll come see it sometime."

"Well, I don't live there any more. When my uncle died—my mother's a widow, we all lived with Uncle Van——" And Marion embarked on the story of her life. This lasted them into Nyack, where they found a diner. Over sandwiches and milk Marion learned that Tom's father was a professor of chemistry at Ohio State, that his mother was French, that he was twenty-eight, had two younger brothers, liked baseball, and was being torn by the discovery that he admired Frank Lloyd Wright less than he had, though still more than anyone else. Marion began to feel solid ground under her feet. Tom was like someone she might have gone to high school with. At first distrustfully (but she could never be distrustful for long), she began to recover her personality. The anonymous creature, who had for two weeks been spun through experiences which had one and all dealt her glancing blows, slowly found familiarity in Tom. With a return to the appetite of adolescence she ate three sandwiches and a dish of ice cream; and reluctantly became aware that they had to go back.

After they turned off the main road but before they reached the first bungalow Tom stopped the car. Marion's heart jumped.

"I'd like to kiss you once," he said.

"Oh—I don't know——" Marion quavered.

But he said, "Yes," and pulled her toward him and in his arms, after a moment of panic, she found it was all right. Nothing reminded her of Hank at all.

He let her go and said, "You're lovely," and pushed her hair gently back from her face, smiling at her through the dark. She lay back against his arm, looking at him solemnly, wondering whether this meant anything, if it could possibly be the beginning of something important. He bent his head to kiss her again.

Through the dark a siren went off like a banshee and a searchlight caught them in a devilish radiance. Marion drew in her breath to scream, but bit off the sound before it left her lips. A truck of some kind stopped with a squeal of brakes, facing them, and a dark figure leaned out behind the headlights and shouted, "Back up, there, back up and let us by!"

Tom started the car—through her trembling Marion saw that he did it quickly and steadily, she was sure she would have stalled the engine herself—and backed his car out onto the road. The truck followed him cautiously. As they pulled out of the way the siren let loose again and Marion saw that the truck, passing them with a slamming of gears, gathering speed on the main road, was an ambulance. They stared after it.

"We'd better go see what's happened," said Tom. Marion, who would have preferred ignobly to drive fast in another direction, agreed. But they saw more headlights coming and had to wait while a car dashed past them, swaying as it turned, and made off after the ambulance.

"Could you see who was in it?" Tom asked.

"No."

They drove up the rutted track to the colony. All the lights were on and a police car was pulled up to the stoop of the cottage where Marion and Jean were staying. Marion jumped out, prepared to rush up the steps, but Tom caught her arm and said, "Wait. Take it easy." He made her walk slowly across the porch to the door.

Inside, a state trooper was talking to the man with the beard, Pete. Pete sat with his hands hanging between his knees. The state trooper turned as Marion and Tom stopped in the door and looked them up and down. "Yeah?" he said.

"What's happened?" Tom asked.

"You live here?" the trooper asked back.

"We're visiting."

"Names?"

"Hofstra. This is Miss Bishop."

"Who're you visiting?"

"I'm with the Fords. Miss Bishop came with a friend. Miss McDonald."

"She's over at the Fords' with the rest of them. You can go over there for now." He turned away.

"But what happened?" Marion cried.

The trooper turned back with a kind of resigned impatience. "Lady was shot. Name of Latimer. Where've you been for the last hour?"

Marion stared at him unbelievingly. Tom said, "We were in Nyack at a diner. I guess it's called Jimmy's."

The trooper turned away from them with finality this time and looked down at the pad he was holding. As Tom drew her away Marion heard him say, "Then from eleven o'clock on you were——" The rest of the question was lost as they stepped off the porch.

Halfway to the Fords' Marion said, "I don't even know who—which—she is."

Tom took three steps in silence. "You weren't here. You don't need to know about it."

"Do you suppose she's—— Do you suppose somebody——"

"I don't suppose anything. Listen. Just as soon as that cop lets us I'm getting you out of here."

"But Jean——"

"I don't give a damn about Jean. She should have had more sense than to bring you to a—a place like this."

"You came."

239

"Yeah." His tone added, And I never will again.

They reached the Fords' cottage and went in. There was a pathetic fire of orange crates and green branches in the fireplace. A dozen or more people sat about on furniture and the floor. As Marion and Tom appeared in the doorway Jean turned and jumped up. She came across to them in a rush, saying, "Where have you been?"

"Just in Nyack," said Marion. "We wanted something to eat."

"Oh my God. I didn't know where you were or what happened——" She put her hand to her forehead for a moment. "You're sure you're all right?"

"Yes of course! We've been sitting in a diner eating hamburgers. Jean—what happened?"

"Nothing good. Dotty Latimer shot herself with an old gun Pete has to shoot rabbits. Of course he doesn't have a license for it, that's another lovely bit. At least she shot herself in the chest, looking for her heart, not in the head—I suppose she didn't want to hurt her face—so maybe she'll live."

"We saw the ambulance."

"Did you? She did it in the bathroom over at Jim's and Betty's. There's blood——" Jean stopped and looked down at her hands. Marion saw with horror that her skirt, all down the front, had been scrubbed at with water but still showed a stain. "My clothes are all over there," said Jean. "That damn trooper wouldn't even let me get at them. She screamed and screamed and screamed—— Until the doctor got here and gave her a shot. You wouldn't believe a person could—could go on so long."

"Why did she do it?"

"Who knows?" With this Jean went to the doorway and leaned against it, looking out.

Marion turned to Tom Hofstra a face of bewildered shock. Right there in the room with everyone looking at them he took her in his arms and held her against his chest while she cried. Jean turned around and looked at them after a minute. Her weary face did not change, but in a second she walked past them to the fire and stood holding her hands out, warming them.

They sat up all night in the Fords' living room. One by one people were called over to the other cottage by the state troopers. Jean was sent for fairly early, but Marion and Tom, having been absent, were left till the end, and then asked almost nothing except their names and addresses. The sun was so high that the birds had stopped singing when they were told they could go and came out together into the new day.

"I'm going to take you home," Tom said. "Get your things."

Marion wound her fingers together, looking at him. "I have to see about Jean."

"No," he told her. "You have to get home."

She shook her head wordlessly, remembering how Jean had rushed to her when she came in, how worried she had been.

"I'll meet you at the car in ten minutes," Tom said. He left her and walked toward the Fords'.

With an effort Marion turned away and went back to the cottage where the detective she had talked to was wearily leafing through notes. She thought that she could not stand to see Tom Hofstra drive away without her; and she thought also that she could not stand either to wake Jean up and tell her that she was deserting her.

But in the room she and Jean had been supposed to share there was no one. Neither bed had been slept in. Marion sat down on the edge of one blankly. It took her a minute or more to see the note on the pillow.

"Marion," it said in Jean's firm handwriting. "I'm going to the hospital. Dotty needs transfusions and my blood matches. Why don't you get your young man to drive you home as soon as they let you go? I'll phone or be in later. Jean."

Marion stood up in a surge of relief so strong that it was almost like panic. She was being let off! Then she felt that she couldn't waste a minute. She crammed things into her suitcase, grabbed her coat and ran out to the car. Tom had it turned around, the engine running. "Good girl," he said. "Now where is it your sister lives?"

"Oh Tom, I'd better go in to New York, to Jean's."

"No ma'am. You're going to your family's where you belong."

"It's in Scarsdale," she said weakly. "I'll show you when we get there. If you think——"

"Sure I think."

They drove out slowly to the main road and started down the macadam to respectability. Marion leaned back in the seat and shut her eyes. She was out of it, she was safe. Nina and her mother—she would think of some kind of story to tell them to explain her arrival—and Tom—— She found herself getting sleepier and sleepier and reached over to turn the radio on. It was thus that she learned that England and France had declared war on Germany.

It was half-past ten when Tom turned into the driveway by Nina's house. It was an old house, painted gray, with roses trained over the porch. No one was in sight except Ivan, the Persian cat, who was lying on the stoop in the sun. Marion got out and Tom followed, carrying her suitcase. Ivan rolled over and purred as she reached him and she stopped to scratch his head. The front door was open and they went into the hall, still seeing no one. The living room was empty, a toy train that Johnny had abandoned lying in the middle of the floor, but the house felt full of life. Received into it, Marion walked back to the kitchen and peered in.

Nina, very pregnant, in a cotton print dress, was sitting on a high stool by the kitchen table, crumbling bread into a big brown bowl. Across from her Hulda, the cook, was slicing onions. They were discussing recipes for stuffing.

As Marion swung open the door from the pantry Nina looked up, stared for a second and said, "Sweetie!" With a piece of bread still in one hand, she opened her arms.

Marion went over and hugged her hard. Here was home.

"My goodness," Nina said, "I'm glad you came. Where the dickens have you been? Such a social life you lead! Hulda, I told you we'd need a twenty-pound turkey."

"Hello, Hulda, how are you?" asked Marion.

"I'm fine, Miss Marion," said Hulda lugubriously. "You go along, Mrs. Fanning, I'll finish the stuffing."

Nina slid off her stool, saying, "All right, I'll waddle into the living room. Where've you come from, honey? Have you had breakfast? Do you want some coffee? Will you bring some in,

Hulda?" She opened the door and discovered Tom, large and silent, in the pantry. "Oh," she said.

"This is Tom Hofstra," said Marion behind her. "He drove me out. Tom, this is Nina Fanning, my sister."

They both said "How do you do," and Tom added, "Well—I guess I'd better run along." He was looking at Marion.

"Nonsense," said Nina. "Have some coffee. Come and sit down. You both look dead."

"We've been up all night," said Marion, "being questioned by the police!" Here, safe, remote, the horror of the night had diminished to a point where Marion's story could be the truth because the truth was, in Scarsdale, incredible.

"My God!" said Nina. "Were you in an accident?" She led the way to the living room as she spoke; and the terrible things that could happen to people were reduced to the casual violence of a car crash on a highway.

"We were staying at a place where a woman shot herself." No, even in Scarsdale its horror could touch her. Saying it, Marion found herself shocked anew.

"Oh no!" cried Nina. She looked back and forth from Marion to Tom. Their faces must have told her that they were outside it, for she sat down and said, "How perfectly frightful! How did it happen? Why?"

"I don't know. We weren't even there when it happened. It was a great big messy party and Tom and I drove into town late in the evening to a diner for sandwiches and when we came back—there were the police. I don't think I even know who she was—by sight, I mean. Do you, Tom?"

"No."

"And you mean they questioned you all night and you weren't even *there?*"

"No, of course not. They questioned everybody else first because we were so unimportant. And then they looked at Tom's honest face and turned us loose. End of the story."

"But darling, who *were* these people?"

"Oh Nina, I don't know. I went with someone—— Tom was visiting someone else, you know how it is. There were a lot of different cottages, everybody was having a Saturday night out, and some woman just picked it to—to do it. It was an awful place."

"I should think it was."

"She isn't dead, incidentally. The girl I went with stayed to give her a transfusion. So Tom brought me here."

"Very nice of Tom. Thank you."

"Don't mention it," said Tom with a grin. "I'd have driven her a lot further than Scarsdale to get her away from there."

"Just the same, I appreciate it."

"Honestly," said Marion, "you sound like a Victorian mama. Where is Mother, by the way?"

"Out back with Johnny and Toddy. Stuart's making them a sandbox which will be divine when it's done, but right now they both want to help him hammer. So Mother kind of polices them."

"What will you do when you have three?"

"Get gray hair. No, Johnny's going to nursery school this year, and the new baby will stay put in one place, thank God, for a while, anyway, and I've got a nursemaid coming. Be calm, I'll cope."

"I'm sure you will. What are you going to name it?"

"I haven't the remotest idea. Mother thinks I'm awful because I haven't bought more new things; she knits indignantly at me, booties and caps and so on. If it's a girl, shall I name it for you?"

"Oh my goodness, don't do that! Name it Elizabeth, for Mother."

"All right. Well, you poor children. I imagine you'd both like to go to sleep. Tom, you'll stay, won't you? I don't think we have any guns around, and we do have loads of room, and Hulda was so mean about that turkey! She said we'd never get it eaten. You'll do me a real kindness if you help consume it."

"Well that's awfully nice of you——" He looked at Marion again.

"Do stay," she told him. She could hardly say anything else, but she blushed and the blush made her speech more than manners. She knew it, and blushed more.

"Fine," said Nina cheerfully, and everything was arranged.

Marion found it easy enough to slip back into the proper routine of life. When she wakened in the afternoon she knew where she was at once. She lay luxuriously listening to the sounds of the house. The radio was playing below her, but it brought not news of the war, but a baseball game. In the next room Toddy was talking to himself, waking up from his nap. His door opened and her mother went in and crowed over him, and Toddy laughed. Stuart's footsteps came upstairs and he called "Nina!" softly, and Toddy shouted for him and Mrs. Bishop said "Shush!" and began to sing an old, old song Marion remembered from her own babyhood. "How many miles to Babylon?" sang Mrs. Bishop. "Threescore and ten——" And Marion called, "Mummy! Bring Toddy in and let me see him."

"How are you, dear?" said Mrs. Bishop, peering round the door with Toddy in her arms. "Are you rested? Nina told me what a *horrid* thing happened. I'm so sorry. We won't talk about it. That seems like a nice young man, Mr. Humphrey."

"Hofstra."

"Hofstra." She put Toddy down on the bed. "And what do you think of *this* young man? You haven't seen him for a month. He says Grandma now, just as plain. Say Grandma, Toddy. Say Gamma——"

But Toddy only gurgled and began to crawl up to Marion's face. He loved to explore people's faces with little wet paws.

"Oh Toddy," said Marion, "you're a lamb. Mummy, you look fine. The apartment's all done and looks very nice. Toddy, angel, take your fist out of my mouth. Mum, he's got lipstick on it."

"We'll wash that old lipstick off, won't we? Nasty old stuff. Come play with Grandma, she doesn't have any lipstick to come off on Baby's hands. Marion dear, you heard the news? About the— about the war?"

"Yes, darling."

"Oh dear. That awful Hitler! Your uncle never trusted him."

"Well, they're going to do something about him at last."

"Yes. I suppose so. But Marion—I hope—— No, I won't say it. Oh I *do* hope—— Last time, you know, I didn't worry, your father's profession was too important to the country for there to be any question of his going. And Van was over-age. But now—— Of course I suppose Stuart, with the children and all—— But Kermit——"

She stopped. And Marion, remembering Jean thinking—Kermit,

found herself thinking—Tom. How silly! She hadn't known him twenty-four hours.

"Goodness' sakes, Mummy," she said. "America's not going in! Kermit's important in Washington too, you know! You mustn't —have nightmares."

"I know. Oh I do know, Marion, really. I'm not worried. Now Baby, come with Grandma and let's wash the little hands and the little face. Say Bye-bye, Aunt Marion, bye-bye!"

"Bah-bah," said Toddy, smiling from her shoulder, and was borne off.

I have to phone Jean, thought Marion from her pillow, and wished guiltily that she didn't have to. But of course she did. She got up in a spirit of cold determination and made her call to Jean's apartment from the extension in Nina's room before she went downstairs. But there was no answer. She hung up the phone and stood for a moment debating whether to try the Fords' cottage or the hospital. But Tom had left word where she would be, she told herself half guiltily. Jean could find her if she wanted to. And that was the last she thought of Jean, for Tom drove her out of Marion's head. She went downstairs, hoping that he and Stuart had made friends. When she found them both in the living room listening to the ball game and drinking beer, she felt they were on the way to doing so. If anything was needed to cement the relationship it was provided when Tom drew a series of pictures for Johnny of fancier and fancier automobiles, climaxing in a fire engine. After that Johnny followed Tom around like a shadow and gave him a piece of paper and a pencil whenever he sat down.

That evening, Sunday, they all played bridge, with the odd man cutting in and out. The radio, turned low, provided a background to which no one listened except at the beginning of every news broadcast, when they all stopped playing for a moment until someone said, "Nothing new," and they returned to the cards. Marion played badly. She was tired, and Tom's presence was upsetting. He must be horribly bored with a family card game, she thought, but she had been too tired to think of any excuse to get out of it. She could, she supposed, have come right out and asked him whether he wouldn't rather go to the movies—but she didn't want to be rude to her mother and Nina, she didn't in the least want to go to the movies herself and, besides, it would have meant asking Tom whether he didn't want to be alone with her. She certainly wasn't going to ask him that! Let him endure a family evening, she had decided, if he likes me. But now it was making her nervous.

The eleven o'clock news and a rubber were over together and Nina yawned and said, "Well, that's all for this child. You go on playing if you want."

"That's all for me too," said Marion. "I'm exhausted. I couldn't even count that last hand."

"Was that what it was?" asked Stuart unkindly. "I thought maybe you believed there were fourteen trumps out."

"Don't speak to me harshly, Brother dear," said Marion. "I'm very young still. Perhaps I'll get better."

"It had better not be perhaps, Little Sister," replied Stuart, stretching. "Want a beer, Tom?"

"Don't mind if I do. Can I get them?"

"Come with me," said Marion. "I'll show you. Mother, Nina, you want anything?"

"Milk, darn it," said Nina. "There's some good cheese in the left-hand top corner of the icebox. You know where the crackers are."

Marion and Tom went out to the kitchen, Marion knowing perfectly well she had been too obvious about this maneuver. "I hope you haven't been bored stiff," she said, reaching into the icebox for beer.

He grinned. "I know about families. I have one myself. Yours is nice."

She put the beer on the kitchen table and pulled out a drawer. "There should be an opener in here——"

"Let me look." He came around behind her. Their shoulders touched. "Oh honey," he said, and was kissing her awkwardly while one of her hands still groped in the drawer.

Tom, she thought. Yes. Yes, Tom.

Then he was pushing her away and saying, "Hell, I'm sorry. I hate necking in corners. I couldn't help it. You're wonderful. Go 'way from me, gal, and get that cheese out."

I don't mind necking in corners, she thought, turning away, not with the right person. She felt triumphant. She wanted to giggle; but only hummed to herself while she bustled about finding the cheese, milk, plates, glasses; putting on a show of domesticity and femininity for him. He didn't intend to kiss me but he did, her mind sang happily. It was funny, funny, funny and nice.

Monday, Labor Day, they all went to the Beach Club. It was a small and not particularly grand one but a day there provided a welcome relief to distracted housewives at the end of a three-day week end, and it was quite crowded. Finals of the tennis tournament were being played off, and there was a race of sailing dinghies for children under fourteen. Nina and Mrs. Bishop sat on the terrace under an umbrella in the midst of this festival of the American middle class, chatting with a stream of friends. Mrs. Bishop was crocheting, but Nina just fanned herself. Stuart was theoretically in charge of the two little boys, but since there was an almost infinite number of children aged four and two on the beach, all clad in bright scraps of bathing suits, Johnny and Toddy soon merged into the crowd. Stuart took this very calmly. "I just keep an eye on the water," he explained. "As long as they're not where they shouldn't be, they must be where they should be." With that he stretched out on the sand and closed his eyes. Appalled, Marion searched the child-fringe along the water for her nephews. She couldn't see them at all. Just then Johnny pushed at her leg, thrust her aside and emptied a pail of water over his father. Toddy staggered up behind with a bucket of sand. Apparently it was harder to lose them than Marion had feared. Relieved, she pulled on her bathing cap and she and Tom went into the tepid water.

It was very different from the surf at Southampton, hardly the same ocean. Just as well, perhaps, she thought, watching Tom's determined progress beside her. He swam with the grim resolution of a Middle Westerner who has learned in a pool and finds the ocean very large. Before they reached the end of the breakwater where they were heading, he had to turn over and float. Marion felt amused and protective.

The rocks were weed-grown, coated with barnacles. But at least they were empty. Tom and Marion attempted to make themselves comfortable on slanting slabs of granite under the enormous presence of the sun. The beach seemed very far away. Across the harbor the red and blue sails of the dinghies swung and seemed to change shape and color as the little boats came about on another leg of their course. Sea and sun and rock. This was all there was in the beginning, thought Marion, all those geology lectures ago. Sea and sun and rock had apparently been enough, for now there were Tom and Marion uncomfortable on the rock. What an odd progression for the three to produce the two! Of course if you could believe that God had reached down and stirred the three with His finger, it was much simpler.

"Do you believe in God?" asked Marion.

Tom thought. "I guess not," he said regretfully, after a bit.

"I always think I'm just going to," said Marion. "I think perhaps when I'm old—— It seems to be one of the things I put off."

"My mother does," said Tom, "but she's very quiet about it. Of course, she's Catholic. In fact she has an aunt who's Mother Superior of a convent in France, near Limoges, I think. She must be quite a frightening old lady. Mother has a picture of her. Her face is all bone structure and will. Mother looks like her sometimes when she's tired."

"Your mother must mind this—the war."

"She said all along it was coming. Her only brother was killed last time, quite late, in the summer of 1918. He was a chemist, like my father. That's how they met, Mother and Dad. There was a big international conference or convention or something in Paris in 1908 and Dad went and got to know Uncle Charles. There was a terrific shindig before Mother could marry him—a foreigner and a Protestant. But they brought it off."

"Are they happy?"

"Oh yes, I think so. She has that good French reasonableness, she can be serious about things that must seem silly to her but are important to Dad's career, or to us boys. Teas, for instance—for faculty, for students—they go on all the time. Always wonderful food and sensible conversation, and the house shining but not looking as if it had just been scrubbed for the occasion. She plays the piano, plays well, not just sloppily, she works at it. And makes her own clothes. She's—well, she has standards about doing things well. Nothing is just patched up, you know?"

"I know," said Marion sadly. Mrs. Hofstra sounded absolutely terrifying.

"And my father—I guess anyone who works in an exact science likes that kind of—of precision and adequacy. Yes, I think they're very happy."

"What's her name? Your mother's first name?"

"Lucie. She doesn't look like it at all."

"Is she pretty?"

"No, not pretty. I guess she never was. But you notice her right away. She's—distinguished. You know right away there's a person there."

Marion sighed. "How wonderful that must be," she said wistfully.

"Your sister's rather like that," said Tom unexpectedly. "She and my mother would get on. They do things differently, but they produce the same kind of results. Things work, sort of."

Oh dear, oh dear, oh dear, thought Marion, squirming on the rock. He likes adequate people and I'm not. I'm not at all. Things don't work for me.

Of course this was much too personal to say, so she said nothing; and Tom, who felt that he had perhaps pursued the subject of his family past the limits of interest, fell silent too. Slightly embarrassed, they sat and toasted while the stone grew harder and harder. At last Marion turned over on her stomach and said, "Families. I've been trying to think what they're like. They're sort of like fungi, and sort of like icebergs, and sort of like honeycomb——"

"I can see the honeycomb," said Tom, amused and relieved because it had not been boredom that had made her quiet. "And the icebergs—because of all that's under water? Yes. But why like fungi?"

"No preparation. No roots. Just two people—and they get married, and all of a sudden, out of nowhere, there's a family—family jokes and celebrations and traditions—whether the children help trim the tree on Christmas Eve or are surprised on Christmas morning; where they go summers; what they eat for birthday dinners; are they brought up on Peter Rabbit and Jemima Puddleduck

250

and the Just So Stories, or on Uncle Don reading the Sunday comics over the radio, or what? A whole private mythology somehow gets invented. I can never imagine how anyone has the energy and the patience to do all that—and everything else—and yet everyone does it. Or lots of people do it. When I look at Nina sometimes I'm stunned. To make a whole family—I just don't know how you do it!"

"Well—it's instinct——" said Tom doubtfully.

"But imagine how awful to have to be instinctive and conscious of being instinctive at the same time! Like a bee with a mind, or that awful Kafka story about the boy who turns into a cockroach, that scares me half to death. Do we all have to be instinctive, Tom? I used to think anything was possible."

"What do you mean?" asked Tom promptly.

"Well——" Marion raised her head and looked off at the horizon. "As if I could do anything, as if everything were open. When I was little, I used to think I could go and discover a new Pole."

"A new what?"

"A new Pole—an East Pole, or a West Pole. Even after I knew there weren't any, I still used to *feel* that way. An East Pole surrounded by Mongols and leftover dinosaurs somewhere out in the Gobi Desert, and a West Pole all alone with some palm trees on an island in the Pacific, an island that came up to a point, you know, and that was the Pole. They were striped like barber poles, and because they were so old and so forgotten and no one had cared, they leaned over like the Tower of Pisa——"

By this time Tom was shaking with laughter. "What nice nonsense you talk!" he said.

Marion stared at him for a moment. But I mean it—she started to say, and then stopped, for of course she didn't mean it, and it was nonsense. She hid her face in her arm; and desolately bade good-by to her lonesome, leaning, undiscovered Poles. I never told anyone else that, she thought sadly, because I knew they'd laugh.

"Go on," said Tom affectionately, "tell me some more."

"There isn't any more," said Marion into her arm. It was true. The Poles—her Poles—were gone.

"Hey! Did I hurt your feelings, you funny little thing?"

"No of course not!" she said indignantly. "It *was* funny." But she sat up now energetically and went on, "Do you know, I'm quietly starving? Why do people get so hungry so early on a picnic or at the beach? I had an enormous breakfast, and it's probably not half-past eleven yet, but I think if I don't have at least a hot dog, I won't survive!" With this she pulled on her bathing cap again and headed for shore, feeling faintly, uneasily, indignant at Tom. Of course it was nonsense but she had still meant something by it, and he hadn't understood. Somehow a fraction of him had laughed at a fraction of her that had not expected to be laughed at. She felt hurt, and she felt embarrassed. She had thought he would understand, and when he had not, it was like assuming an intimacy that you found the other person did not want. She fled through the water with her strong camp counselor's crawl, enjoying the surge of her body, the acerb iodine-tasting greenness slipping over and past her, and for the moment pleased at the small revenge of leaving Tom far behind.

She managed for the rest of the day not to be alone with him. She had gone too fast, she felt, and all her instinct was now to withdraw from him. His laugh, and the way he had called her a funny little thing—that had implied another kind of intimacy. It had sounded almost proprietary. She was not going to let him feel that way! So after lunch she stretched out next to Nina on the terrace, shut her eyes and prepared to look as if she were dozing. Stuart drove Mrs. Bishop and the two children home for afternoon naps. Returning, he carried Tom off to watch the tennis.

Nina said, "He's very nice, Marion."

"Do you think so?"

"Don't you?"

"I don't know. Yes, of course I think he's *nice*——"

A friend of Nina's swooped upon her at this moment, exclaiming over her as if she were doing the most amazing and wonderful thing in the world by appearing in a public place when seven months pregnant; or perhaps it was simply having a baby at all.

Marion thought, Nice. Silly word. What does it mean? I wish Nina wouldn't sound so stuffy. So approvingly stuffy. Because—oh God!—I haven't been nice. If we're going to be judged by niceness,

I'll have to go home. Nice, she wanted to say, there's a great big aching world all around Scarsdale and I've been out there and it isn't nice at all. Were you ever out there? Can you remember? But Nina's friend was still exclaiming.

I was there, thought Marion. It's easy to get to. She shut her eyes. I was there, the same me that was so happy when Tom kissed me last night. Wasn't I just as happy—oh *wasn't* I!—when Hank kissed me? Hank. Remember him. Say his name. Say what you did— remember what you did! Remember that just two weeks ago you called Hank and told him you never wanted to see him again. Four weeks ago—or just a little more—you were with him in New York. She shuddered at the memory.

"Cold?" asked Nina, next to her; but the friend would not stop talking.

Hank. Tom, Marion thought. She *was* cold, cold with fear at what she had done, what she had been. They're different people, she argued with herself. There's no connection between them!

There's you, said the implacable voice inside her head.

I don't know what you mean! Do I have to feel guilty with Tom over Hank, when I didn't even know Tom then?

You don't have to feel guilty. Can you manage not to? You *do* feel guilty and you know it. Kermit belittled the whole thing at the end. But was it just what he called it, just "a roll in the hay"? And is that nothing, anyway? You didn't think it was nothing. You thought you were in love with Hank. Have you forgotten it all already, forgotten it so that you can feel about Tom as if Hank had never been? What does that make you?

You know what it makes you. What Kermit said. A promiscuous little slut. Hank—and then Tom!

Oh, but Tom—Tom is different! I feel different.

Do you really! I think you've just forgotten. And look at it this way. How long have you known him? Saturday night to Monday afternoon. He's kissed you twice, and you're worrying about his mother! What's that charming masculine phrase about "a girl with round heels"? Aren't you being a little quick with your intimacies? Aren't you being a fool again?

Yes, yes, yes! thought Marion, biting her lip. I want to stop, I want to stop! Nina, tell me how not to be a fool, how to be "nice"! Show me the way back.

But across the backdrop of beach and sea and sky Stuart and Tom came walking, and Tom smiled at her; and Marion clenched her fists and thought again, Nice is a silly word! Nina wants me to be safe and comfortable and content, because that's what she chose. But Nina, I have no talent for that! What is it I want? she asked herself, looking at Tom as he came up, said "Hello," sat down by her feet. I want to feel and experience. I want to know by being. I can't take things at second hand. Everyone wants to help me, she thought, all in their own way. Jean, and Kermit, and Nina—and even Tom thinks I'm "a funny little thing." But I'm not. I'm me. Unless I am what I am and feel what I feel—as hard as I can and as honestly and truly as I can—then I'm nothing. Let me feel guilty, Kermit. What I did was foolish, and wrong. Don't try to educate me, Jean. It won't do any good. Don't protect me, Nina. "Nice" isn't enough. And Tom—oh Tom!—don't see me as what I'm not. Please, Tom, want me the way I am!

So when Tom said that he ought to get into New York, Marion asked him to stay over till the morning, and drive her down. She had a pang of fear as she said it, that he would think her too eager. But his face lit up at the suggestion, and she drew a deep breath, determined still to be right and honest in her own way.

It wasn't easy to do. Next morning had a leftover, uncertain feeling, and Marion had to keep reminding herself that she had come to a decision and would not, could not, go back on it. She was going to manage her own life!

They started to drive in early, to avoid the post-Labor Day traffic, but so did many other people. The dewy freshness of the day vanished while they sat in traffic jams on the highway, and a heat haze hung over the city as they came into it. Marion felt tense and tired. She had explained to her family that she was helping a friend out by working for a week or two, but no one had seen the point of this and Marion, at this moment, really didn't either. Two days in Nina's house put all the family imperatives to work on her, and she remembered for how short a time she had known Jean, and how odd the whole arrangement really was. There was the whole mess in Nyack that she would have to hear about, and much, much worse—there was Tom. Jean would certainly ask her questions about him. Yesterday's decision concerned only herself. It could not solve her nervous vibration between daring and fearing to feel Tom important to her. Marion just did not know what she could say to Jean about him.

For if here beside her was Tom, there behind her was Hank. She could despise him now. But if she despised him now, she had to despise herself then. And if she despised herself, how could she trust for one moment what she felt about Tom? Had she not known a sweet excitement with Hank, too? Had she not flung herself into his arms? And been so wrong, so horribly wrong, to do it?

Tom reached over and took her hand. But Marion was too miserable at the moment to take any pleasure in this. She was suddenly frightened of Tom—of Tom, and his formidable mother. A new grotesque had risen beside her to mock her and freeze her blood. For was she not what one of her roommates last year had been inspired to call "damaged goods"? She remembered how they had roared with laughter over this fantastic Victorian label. Both virgins, they had been hotly ashamed of their state, and had looked forward to its loss as a healthy, a therapeutic step, a passport to maturity.

Marion wasn't at all certain that it was so funny now. She did feel damaged—damaged and rather dirty, as if Hank's embraces had smeared her with something that wouldn't quite wash off. Because of course no affair ever approximated the purely physical meeting between nubile maiden and male deflowering pagan priest that Marion and her roommate had unconsciously believed to be their fate. When you went to bed with a man you went to bed with a person and not a symbol. Facing this truism, Marion wondered why it hadn't occurred to them before that if the person was someone you turned out not to like you might feel unpleasant afterward. Only of course she hadn't known she didn't like Hank. Suppose she didn't really like Tom? Her hand in his trembled. It was one thing to know that you would be honest about your emotions. Suppose you didn't honestly know what your emotions were?

"What's the matter?" he asked.

"Nothing," she said.

The traffic jam began to move and he took his hand off hers to drive. She felt its removal as a loss. Even at this moment, she noted, when she was consumed with doubt, she wanted to throw herself at him. I mustn't do that! she told herself. I mustn't be greedy.

Tom turned the car away from the river. They were well down into the center of town now, only blocks from Jean's office. The streets were full of trucks, of children playing stick ball. From the windows of tenements women leaned out, their elbows on pillows, observing life. Tom said suddenly, "I hate taking you there."

"To Jean's?" asked Marion, sitting up and trying to straighten out her mind. "Oh stuff, I work there."

"I wish you didn't."

"My goodness, you sound as if it was a you-know-what and Jean was the madam. She's a decorator. You build houses, we decorate them."

"Not my houses," said Tom. "Not if I can help it. Decorators!" For several blocks he told Marion what he thought about interior decorating as practiced in America; which was basically, that it was a gratuitous insult to architecture, that it debauched the taste of the nation, that its practitioners were blood-sucking homosexuals and that if this description did not apply to Jean it only proved that she should stop being a "decorator" at once (Tom's voice put quotation marks around the word) and get an honest job. Marion listened despondently at first: she didn't herself want to go to Jean's much, and now Tom as well as her family was telling her not to. But after a bit, Marion began to feel Tom's attack on Jean as an attack on herself. Of course she had been scolding herself on and off for days, but this did not make a lecture from Tom any less irritating.

"So I wish you wouldn't go there," he ended finally.

"Thank you for your interesting analysis of my problem," said Marion acidly. "What profession do you suggest I take up instead? Or do you want to give me a vocational-guidance test?"

Tom drove a block in silence before he said in a neutral voice, "Aren't you going back to college? Your mother talked as if you were."

"I don't know," said Marion, and began nervously pulling on the white gloves she had borrowed from Nina. College was one of the decisions she hadn't faced up to yet. In Scarsdale it seemed impossible not to go back. With Jean, it seemed like the promise of a year spent in a vacuum.

"How did you get started doing this job with Jean, anyway?" Tom was asking.

"It's a long story," Marion said almost at random. "I was—kind of at loose ends and Jean needed somebody badly. I'm all right at it, I guess. At least Jean seems to think so."

After a moment of silence Tom said, "Do you do whatever Jean says?"

Marion, even as she cried hotly, "No of course I don't!" felt a quiver of fear deep within her. This—this was what it was about. This was why Tom had made that speech about decorators. Only what *was* it about? Startled and indignant, she stared at Tom, trying to understand what he meant. "Of course I don't!" she repeated.

"You're awful damn tied up with her," said Tom stubbornly, unhappily.

"But that's fantastic!" Marion cried. All the nervous tension she had been feeling, and was not used to feeling, boiled up in her. "I don't—— I'm not—— She was good to me and I'm grateful to her—but really, really! I'm *quite* independent, thank you!"

Tom said, "You're a funny girl."

"I don't know what you mean!"

But they had reached Jean's office. Tom drew the car in to the curb and turned to look at Marion. Time slowed down, the moment grew heavy. Marion, indignant, badgered, bewildered, stared at Tom, who moistened his lips and said, "Marion, I—I like you a lot."

"Thank you," said Marion coldly.

He shook his head impatiently. "More than that I guess. Hell, I'm saying this badly. But you—something's got you all mixed up. I suppose it was this business, this damn woman up in Nyack. People who've been in a mess together get close." He stopped and reached for her hand. She let him take it, let it lie slack in his.

He went on, "Well, I don't want it just like that. I don't want that background of messiness and nastiness. I want you to like me slowly over a long time. And—maybe I haven't any business to say it, but I want to have the right to say it—I think you ought to have a life of your own and something more than Jean this, and Jean that."

"You don't understand," said Marion, for though this seemed to parallel her own determination it sounded, as Tom said it, both cold and selfish. She shut her eyes and saw Hank stretched on the floor and Sally kneeling beside him and screaming at her. Tom was staring at her across this unpleasant tableau, shocked and horrified. Jean was standing beside her. She took her hand out of Tom's and said abruptly, "Jean helped me when *I* was in a mess."

"I see," said Tom. They looked at each other. Marion felt him moving away. She wanted to put out her hand and draw him back. She was conscious of an astonishing ache as Tom receded from her.

But what she said came from anger and hurt and her fantastic over-gallant decision to be honest. "I suppose that disgusts you, that I was in a mess. Well, go ahead. Be disgusted. It was a *rotten* mess."

"I'm sorry," said Tom.

"It was just as bad as you can think!" said Marion.

Tom said, "Why don't you control yourself?"

Marion stared at him, as surprised as if he'd hit her.

"You don't have to throw it in my teeth. I believe you," he told her. He was very white.

Marion opened the car door. "Good-by," she said.

He got out and took her bag and carried it toward the door.

"I'll take that," she said. "You don't have to help me."

But he went in with her and rang the bell for the old slow creaking elevator. She stood beside him, thinking, This isn't happening. What have I done? Why can't I stop it? What have I *done?* Then the elevator came and he put the bag inside for her and stepped out.

"Tom!" she said in terror.

"You can't have it both ways," he said. "Have your messes if you like them. I don't." He walked off.

She wanted to run after him, but she was frozen where she stood.

"You going up, lady?" asked the elevator man. She got in and was carried slowly and with a clanking of chains to the fifth floor.

And Jean wasn't there, and there was a strange woman sitting at Marion's desk, and it turned out that it was Jean's ex-assistant, who hadn't got married to a Mexican after all, his mother and his confessor having conspired to frighten her off. Understandably enough, Miss Barry (that was her name), was in a snappish state which Marion's arrival relieved only by giving her fury an object. She spent the morning groaning over Marion's new filing system and discarding materials that Marion had chosen. Marion kept saying to herself, I can't stand this, but she was so numb with pain and shock and confusion that she couldn't think what to do about it. Jean arrived at noon, looking very tired, and Miss Barry promptly had hysterics. All Marion could feel by this time was a kind of dull wonder at Miss Barry's capacity for being outrageous. Jean took her in hand and finally calmed her down enough to be sent home. Then she collapsed at her desk and said, "My God."

Have your messes, Marion thought to herself, but any echo of Tom would make her cry. She clenched her fists and her mind against a repetition of Miss Barry's behavior and asked, "How is Mrs. Latimer?" At least there were enough messes around to change the subject.

"She'll live. They're patching her up. The bullet hit a rib."

"Why did she do it?"

"The usual reason. She thought there was another woman in her husband's life."

"Was there?"

"There were six or eight. Sunday *he* tried to shoot himself."

"Oh no!"

"Oh yes. Over what a heel he had been. We had to talk him out of it, and since everyone agreed he had been a heel, it wasn't too easy. He seemed to feel we didn't have our hearts in it. But I guess he didn't have *his* heart in shooting himself, because we succeeded. Now I think he's feeling kind of proud. Flattered, you know. That she did it over him. He's sitting in the hospital and holding her hand and emoting."

"Oh honestly!" said Marion.

"That's people for you," said Jean. "That's the wonderful human race. What am I going to do about that bitch, Barry?"

"I'll quit," Marion heard herself saying.

"Oh don't be noble," said Jean. "She can learn——"

"No, it's not that. But I'd have to soon, anyway, if I'm going back to school."

Jean said nothing for a little while. Then she asked, "Are you?"

"Yes," said Marion. "I need some kind of routine. Some kind of—of life of my own." But these were Tom's words again, another echo. She hurried on, "I'd better go back and finish and get myself straightened out. It's only another year."

"I suppose you're right," said Jean. "It would be silly to quit with just a year to go. A degree does mean something." Then, as if she had heard, belatedly, some undertone in Marion's voice, she asked worriedly, "Are you sure you're all right?"

"I'm all right," said Marion steadily, and bit hard on the bullet of stoicism. She *would not* imitate Miss Barry's performance. One case of hysterics a morning is enough, she thought.

"Okay, dear," said Jean. "You've really saved my reason, if not my life, more ways than one. But don't think I don't want to strangle the Barry bitch, because I would enjoy every minute of it. Will she get it from me! But you're right, it'll be easier if you aren't around. Now you'd better show me everything you've been doing. Where's the Felton account?"

When Marion went back to Scarsdale that night, things stopped happening to her. She thought afterward, during the long dull autumn months at college, that a couple of years' worth of events must have been poured down upon her that summer; particularly in the two weeks that took her from Hank, through Jean, to Tom—and lost him for her. One day in a creative writing course the professor criticized one of Marion's friends who had produced an improbable piece of melodrama. "Do you really believe, Miss Dakers," the professor asked, "that a woman would give birth to an illegitimate child the same night her father-in-law cut his throat and a tornado came by and flattened the town?" Miss Dakers, blushing, agreed that she did not. But Marion felt she knew better. On the contrary, that was just the way things did happen. Dakers' only mistake was in leaving out the slow, awful, crawling days and days and days that surrounded and washed upon and, at the same time, isolated these improbabilities until *any* event would come to seem not just unlikely, but impossible. That the phone would ring and it would be Tom. That the mail would bring a letter from him. As each day succeeded each yesterday it grew clear at last that these things would never happen. So despair can become a habit and be given a new name, resignation.

Marion got up in the morning and ate breakfast and went to classes in French literature, creative writing, economics and two kinds of history, which was her major. She had lunch, she played hockey, she worked in the library, she went for walks and had coffee in the drugstore, she ate dinner, she studied and went to bed. Nothing happened. On week ends young men frequently turned up from nearby colleges, she went to the movies and danced, kissed the young men or did not quite capriciously, because none of them mattered at all, they were quite unreal. Twice she went to New York and stayed with her mother and was taken to the theater and danced with some of the young men who were most persistent, but still unreal. One of her friends at college was struggling with the problem of whether or not to get married and leave, and another was undergoing a painful psychological crisis that carried her to church and to an analyst and left her dependent on and doubtful of both. Any other year Marion would have suffered and struggled along with them. Now when either came in and sat in Marion's chairs or lay on Marion's bed and clutched her forehead and begged Marion to advise her, to listen, to tell her really, really, what was right, Marion stopped her work and did listen, but that was all. All that agony was so remote. She was walled off from it, she did not dare respond. When she remembered herself in agony—— But she did not dare do that either. She forgot Hank, she forgot Jean, she did not think about Tom. About the only thing she could really enjoy was physical exercise—walking, hockey, and dancing with her ectoplasmic young men. Then once in a while the thing in her mind that had tourniqueted her memory forgot itself, and she could relax.

Two months of grayness and then, one Sunday early in November, she had a visit from Kermit. His telephone call from New York cheered her unreasonably. For if Kermit, the last person she had expected, could find her, perhaps Tom—— But she would not finish that thought.

Kermit looked tired and pale and Marion felt jolted on seeing him and rather nervous. He kissed her and said, "Jean sends her love."

"Oh good," said Marion. "How is she?"

"Fine," he told her. "You're thin, and I'm my usual imperfect self. Shall we now dispense with personalities? How ugly Poughkeepsie is."

"You must see the campus," said Marion. "It's very pretty."

"Must I? I thought we might hire a car, if it's possible on Sunday, and drive around a bit."

"I've done better than that. I've got a car borrowed."

"Intelligent girl. Where is it? Do you mind if I drive?"

"Go right ahead."

He drove out of the city up into the hills behind it, taking every turn that promised to bring them higher, until at last they came round a shoulder and saw the river lying below them to the west. There he stopped the car and switched off the motor and leaned back with a sigh.

"I'm lost, you know," Marion told him. "I don't know where we are."

"That's what being lost usually means," Kermit answered. "It's rather pleasant, I think."

The countryside lay out before them in the drabs of late autumn. Inside the car the sun was warm where it fell through the glass on their laps, but the wind was cold. It was a no-season day, alienated from the named, familiar parts of the year. How odd for me to be here, Marion thought, and felt that the oddness wanted to tell her something: That rules did not always bind the future, perhaps? That there was always more room in one's life than one reckoned on? That truth was always stranger and more varied than the personal fictions one lived by? Some such combination of banality and revelation. With Kermit beside her the tension of pain that had tortured and paralyzed her all autumn relaxed. She was able, by the help of his presence, to draw back a little from her agony; to feel it no longer as something physical, but at one remove, as grief. She found suddenly that she could think about Tom. She thought about him with great sadness but not, any longer, with unbearable and humiliating pain.

"Kermit," she said, "does being in love always make a person unhappy?"

262

"Yes," said Kermit.

"Why?"

"Because it doesn't change anything."

"Look at Nina," said Marion. "Think how she's changed."

"Oh, Nina. She's always had a certain element of American Gothic in her. Anyway, was she ever in love with Stuart?"

"Oh yes. She really was."

"Maybe so. But did the changing have anything to do with the love? Nina's always wanted to change things. She's an activist. She'll grapple with anything. She believes she's equal to life."

"Don't you? Believe *you* are, I mean?"

"Not exactly. I used to think I was better than that. I don't know what I think now."

"You've done so well."

"Dust and ashes," said Kermit, and turned to grin at her. "Do you want to know why I came up here to see you?"

"Was it for something? I thought maybe you just wanted to see me."

"Marion darling, I think maybe I did. Even unhappy, you're very restful. That's probably my subconscious ulterior motive. But I had a conscious one too. I want to ask you to do something for me. Will you?"

"Of course. If I can."

"I want you to look out for someone for me. I think I may be away for a while."

"Oh Kermit, where?"

"That's a secret. At least until I'm sure I'm not making a fool of myself."

"Oh. Who is it you want me to look out for? I shouldn't choose myself, you know. I doubt that I'm very good at things like that. Is it——" She hesitated.

"It's not Jean. She's all right." He paused, and Marion, looking at him in some little surprise, saw that he did not know Jean was in love with him. She saw too that he was embarrassed. He took out a pack of cigarettes and offered them to her, took one himself and make a ritual of lighting them.

"It must be perfectly obvious I don't know how to begin. Everything I want to say not only sounds wrong, it sounds crazy. I'm not an altruist, am I?" When Marion did not answer, he repeated, "Am I?"

"I guess not," said Marion acquiescently.

"Department of understatement," said Kermit. "Nina, for instance, is convinced that I'm a totally selfish person. Well, she happens to be quite right. I am. I always have been. I believe in being selfish. In a pinch, I walk out. I walk away from trouble and look after myself. This is a law of nature. It's what we begin with."

Marion said in a low voice, "You were very kind to me. You got me out of a mess."

"Nonsense," said Kermit. "Pure selfishness. I didn't like to see you in a mess. It was embarrassing and unpleasant. To me, to me personally. It had nothing to do with you."

"Oh," said Marion.

"I can't help being fond of you," said Kermit. *"My* emotions were involved. I was thinking of them, not of your emotions."

"I see," said Marion.

"I doubt it," said Kermit. "However, I want, right now, to be free to do something that I'm not going to tell you about. I don't know if I will do it, but if I decide to, I want to be free. I don't want to have to worry about anyone here while I'm away. This is selfishness, do you see that? It would annoy me to worry."

Marion, looking at Kermit, who was carefully not looking at her, saw that it was very important to him for her to pretend to believe this. "I'm sure," she said soothingly, "that most people really do think about their own emotions, not other people's."

"What difference does that make?" Kermit asked with irritation. "Most people are idiots. I'm not talking about most people! I'm talking about us. Well, enough of this build-up. It's only misleading. If I go away, will you please keep an eye on a girl for me? A young girl, just a kid. She hasn't been well and there's not one soul around her who knows what she's about at all, except maybe her little sister, who worships her. I'd like her to have a friend, a nice emotional generous type like you."

"Goodness!" said Marion, staring at him.

"Yes, I know," said Kermit. "It sounds as if I'd either lost my mind or gone in for one of those unpleasant perversions indulged in by elderly sadists. Well, it's the price we all pay for having read Krafft-Ebing. It's impossible to have an innocent attachment any more. But that's what I am—attached to her. And I've never felt anything except extraordinarily innocent about it. I think she's a remarkable person. And she lives in a rat's nest, with a witch for a mother. So—I'd just like there to be someone on the outside who could help her to get out if she has to. Or"—Kermit looked at his half-smoked cigarette, grimaced again, and stumped it out in the ash tray—"or she may die. It's not at all impossible. She was very sick and isn't over it. I hate to think of her having to do it all alone. She has a great deal of courage, but it seems a shame for her to have to do it all on courage." He turned to Marion. "Well, there it is. It's all very Henry James, isn't it? Quite literally, I think she's as valuable as he ever thought Milly Theale was, and there's at least as much insensitivity around her. It would distress me—selfishly, *selfishly*—to think of her being—wasted. Oh, I forgot to say that as far as you're concerned there's another complication. It's Chuck Morrison's sister I'm talking about, Lucia. I don't know how much of a nuisance Chuck would be to you, but there's that for you to worry about too. That's a nice easy job I'm giving you, isn't it?"

"But why me?" asked Marion. "Wouldn't Nina——"

"Nina's as swaddled in family life as if she were a mummy. Which of course she is. Mummy, Mummy, Mummy, disgusting word. No, Nina hasn't any room for anybody else, and besides, she'd think I was crazy in a particularly sinister way. There's only you. I'm sorry." He took out another cigarette and lit it before he looked at her. "Why, honey," he said, "why are you crying?"

"I can't remember her!" said Marion miserably. "What a bitch I was all summer! I know she exists and that's all! I can't remember her!"

"Honey, don't blame yourself, she was sick, I told you. They wouldn't let her do anything. You couldn't have seen her more than a couple of times." He put his arm around Marion and patted her shoulder. Having now established his selfish motives, he could be pleasanter. "You're a good sentimental girl and I love you. Will you do it?"

"I'll do the best I can. I don't know how good that will be. Do you want me to call her when I go in to New York? Or write?"

"Don't do anything till I tell you." He kissed the top of her head. "Thank you, dear. Now I propose to buy you the largest, best and most expensive lunch within fifty miles of here. Where do we go?"

"Well, I told you I was lost," said Marion, drying her eyes.

"Then in the words of Thomas Wolfe, we shall have to be found. I kept coming uphill, so we'll just try to go down and hope that hunger will sharpen your wits. Think about roast duck with cherries. Think about pâté. Think about a very dry cold double martini."

"Don't!" said Marion. "Or I'll swoon. You haven't eaten college food for years. Just tell me to think about mashed potatoes without any lumps in them and I'll get us there."

She did finally make a landfall at an excellent French restaurant and they ate a large lunch. Kermit, having accomplished his conscious ulterior mission, was more relaxed. He retailed to Marion a great deal of gossip from what he called the Nation's Capital, which she found rather difficult to follow but quite funny. Afterward, driving back to Poughkeepsie through the darkening afternoon, full of food and exhausted with conversation, they were happily silent together. Kermit had penetrated the wall of shock and shame that had surrounded Marion. He had bolstered her sense of adequacy by asking her to look after Lucia.

His insistence on the selfishness of his motives she found sympathetic because pitiable. She had never imagined that anyone could pity Kermit. His need to deceive himself, his inability to admit that he might be generous, made him seem more human than he had before. After her first astonishment over his concern for Lucia she did not find it odd, but accepted it humbly as a new bit of knowledge about Kermit. Being humble, she was always willing to learn new things; no vanity prevented her from changing her concepts. Kermit, instead of being totally self-sufficient, had become someone who needed her help. Nina would have wondered darkly what he was up to. Marion was only happy that he thought her capable of helping him. And besides, today, for the first time in a long while, she had not been entirely alone.

He did not ask with whom she was unhappily in love and she did not tell him about Tom. What was there to tell, after all? Nothing except the sketchy beginning of a love affair that had foundered in a sea of misunderstanding. A false start, Marion was at last able to think, something that not only must but could be lived past. There were so many other things to do in the world besides falling in love, she found herself remembering. She would not do *that* again for a long, long time, she was sure: her young men still seemed ectoplasmic and uninteresting. But there were her friends at college and all the bustle and involvement of such friendships. There was her work and the life of the mind which she had been able to find satisfying in the past. And here was Kermit, for once a thoroughly satisfactory brother. How pleasant to love someone warmly as she loved him, with no possible prospect of having one's love become food for passion and betrayal!

They came into Poughkeepsie with time to spare before Kermit's train, but he refused firmly to be shown about the campus and introduced to Marion's friends.

"I've never known you to be scared of girls before," she said indignantly.

"Not one by one. But femininity in the mass can be terrifying. All the little human traits that distinguish one girl from another vanish and you get an appalling impression of symbolic woman and nothing else. Good God, that would scare any man. Did you ever read Malinowski on the Trobriand Islanders?"

"No, should I?" asked Marion. Kermit, she saw, was about to talk nonsense, just as she had done when Tom had delightedly found her "a funny little thing." It pleased her immensely to find Kermit on her side.

"I strongly advise it," he told her, heading straight for the railroad station. "It seems that in the southern section of the archipelago there is a season of the year when the women have the right—you might almost say the duty—of raping every man they can. Sort of a primeval Sadie Hawkins day. They travel about in gangs and any poor male who's caught out is very lucky if he lives to tell the tale. This isn't just a rumor, either. Some scientifically minded anthropologist went down there in the right season to observe this interesting primitive custom. What do you think happened to him?"

"He was caught," said Marion, fascinated.

"Right the first time. It was a deeply traumatic experience for him. Here he was, looking for nothing more than another string to his Ph.D. and engaged, besides, to a charming cultural anthropologist from Boston who was at that moment investigating potlatch among the Kwakiutl. But could he explain his position to the League of Women Voters of South Trobriand? He could not. He was male, he was there, he was caught, and his hypothesis, you might say, was verified for him willy-nilly. I've always regarded that story as a particular warning. So buy the girls a drink for me, but I don't think I'll go upstairs."

"Kermit," said Marion, "in about forty years you're going to be a nasty, filthy old man."

"And I'm looking forward to it. What could be jollier than going around with spots on your clothes and buttons off and scratching where it itches? Do you really think I'll have to wait forty years? I was always precocious. Perhaps I'll become precociously senile."

"It occurs to me to wonder," said Marion darkly, "if you will live to enjoy your dotage. An enraged Undersecretary of Something may strangle you."

"True, true. Or I may get the yaws or be attacked by thrips or undermined by termites. An overly earnest Comintern agent may mistake me for a Trotskyite. I may get public hysterics in the House gallery listening to Representative Tinkham. You have no idea how perilous Washington can be. Well, before I start back there I'll buy you a drink."

"Thank you," said Marion, and led him to a restaurant near the station where she could count upon finding at least half a dozen of her friends. Tonight there were eight. Marion introduced Kermit all around and asked her colleagues to join them. Kermit gave her one long level look of menace, and then ordered drinks for everyone and started to recite improper limericks. Marion's friends thought him very funny and one of them, a sociology major, taught him a double-barreled verse that he claimed never to have heard before.

"I think I must have learned it in the Philippines," she told him. "I grew up in Manila."

"Is that anywhere near the Trobriand Islands?" Kermit asked.

"I don't know. But it's near the U. S. Army."

In the end Kermit had to run for his train and confided to Marion, panting behind him, that her friends made him feel very old.

"Precocious—senility——" Marion gasped.

He stopped by the steps to the train. "Good-by, dear. Thank you for everything."

"Thank *you*. Come see me soon again."

"Surely." He kissed her and swung aboard as the train started to move. She was left out of breath but more cheerful than she had felt for months, enlivened by frivolity. Of course she was alone, of course she was uncertain of the future, of course she would not see Tom again. But her terrible sense of alienation from life was, at least momentarily, gone. She drove the borrowed car slowly back to the college, found her room more pleasant and rather dirtier than she had remembered, found conversation at dinner more coherent than it had seemed lately, even found the social life of the Merovingians slightly more reasonable than she had believed. The days and days and days began to crawl by again, but they were slightly more supportable. At the end of three weeks, Marion found that she had done well in her mid-term examinations, and gained five pounds. Going down to Scarsdale for Thanksgiving, she dared to wonder if perhaps she were getting over Tom. She decided that she had not yet started, but was about to.

The family, all except Kermit, gathered at Nina's for the holiday. Nina had just produced a third little boy, which delighted her, although she pretended to Stuart and her mother that she had wanted a daughter since Stuart did and Mrs. Bishop was hungry for a girl baby to spoil. Nina named him Charles after her father and this made Judge Fanning, who had grown old suddenly, very sulky— although he had one namesake already, Stuart's sister's boy. The Judge almost refused to come and after he had arrived, making clear that this was a favor, he sat about looking martyred and asking people please not to take any trouble. He was as nasty as possible about the fact that Kermit did not come up from Washington and kept inquiring just what it was that Kermit really did down there. This, of course, no one could tell him, for none of the women had any idea and Stuart was congenitally unable to give Kermit his due.

He did not say the word "bureaucrat," but one could feel him thinking it. Mrs. Bishop was too pleased at having the baby named for her
husband to be as patient as usual with the Judge, so there was a
stimulating amount of acrimony circulating through the family party.

On Saturday an expedition had been arranged to Stuart's sister's,
Janey Cushman. Marion decided she needed a vacation from the
travails of life with her sister's in-laws; particularly since Janey was
one of her unfavorite people in the world (and had been, Marion
could honestly say, even before she had carried off the maid-of-
honorship at Nina's wedding). The vision of Janey being as martyred as the Judge and saying the things that Stuart suppressed sent
Marion flying into New York to a concert.

She sat through it all alone, not quite following the music and
enjoying the slow movements more than the scherzi. After the first
three minutes she was in a trance of happiness. Happiness? She was
astounded. She had believed her capacity for it quite atrophied and
the world though bearable, and even interesting at times, funda-
mentally alien to miracles such as joy. Now Beethoven constructed a
quartet about her that housed her soul as nobly as it commemorated
Count Rasoumovsky. Usually, so moved, Marion would have cried.
But she was exalted far beyond such manifestations today, transported to a meadow of serenity where promise and consummation
were one. Incredulously she listened, incredulously watched the four
little men in black suits on the foreshortened stage below her. The
miracle was sustained, the promise kept. She was effortlessly happy.

Coming out afterward into the November dusk, she thought of
Jean. She had never phoned her since September, it had been quite
impossible for her to want to. But this afternoon she could do it. She
found a phone booth and called Jean's number.

"Darling!" said Jean. "How lovely to hear from you! Where are
you? Well, hop on the subway and come right down. I'm dying to
see you."

Marion did as she was told. The subway rumbled and bumped her
down to Sheridan Square and she emerged into the streets where she
had walked distractedly in August. But now the cold dark made
everything different, she even had to think just how to get to Jean's.
It wasn't until she stood in the vestibule ringing Jean's bell that she

suffered a pang, remembering that awful afternoon when she had run here driven by demons from her no-home in Brooklyn. Then the buzzer clicked, she pushed the door open and the stairs loomed before her. She experienced an engulfing wish that she had not called Jean at all. Perhaps Kermit would be here, and though she had enjoyed her Sunday with him so much, she had no desire at all to see him with Jean. Happiness or no, she was still too hurt to wish to assist at anyone's complications, Jean's, Kermit's, or her own. But she had phoned, she had rung the doorbell, she had started the machinery going, and so she must climb the stairs.

Now Jean flung open the door at the top of the steps and cried, "Hi there, angel! I'm so glad to see you!" Then Jean was hugging her, Jean was saying, "Come on in and see who I've got here for you!" Oh Lord, thought Marion, of course Kermit's here. I wonder, has he told Jean about going away—— But it was someone else who got up out of the big chair across the room.

It was Tom Hofstra.

Marion stood perfectly still and felt the blood drain down to her heart. Her one conscious emotion was outrage at the unfairness of life. To do this to her just as she had begun to be able to be happy!

"Hello," said Tom uncertainly.

"Hello," said Marion, and then, feeling Jean's presence behind her, made the really enormous effort necessary to force herself to cross the room, to shake hands with Tom, to say, "How nice to see you again."

"Very," said Tom.

Feeling like a tightened violin string, Marion laughed gaily. "I thought you didn't like decorators! What are you doing here? Trying to salvage Jean's better self?" She did not wait for an answer, but turned to Jean and said, "How are you anyway, Jeanie? Why don't you ever write a person a line? Kermit's not the best message carrier in the world—'Jean sends her love,' period. Actually you look awfully thin!"

Jean sat down and grinned. "So I should. I'm just getting rid of influenza."

"No!"

"Yes indeed. Don't ever have it. Kermit was up Thursday, but he had to go back yesterday morning. Just as well, too. I lay down to take a nap after he left and slept for six hours. *You* look wonderful. I must tell my dear assistant, Miss Barry, that I saw you and you were simply *radiant!*"

"Dear Miss Barry! She'll love that."

"She will indeed. Tom honey, why don't you make Marion a drink? Did you know Tom lives next door?"

"No I didn't," said Marion politely. At this moment one of her horrors put its head up through the floor of Marion's mind and repeated, in her ear, He lives next door. A whirlpool of jealousy swung about her, she could not for seconds beat it down.

Through it, Jean's voice went on cheerfully, "Well he does. I didn't know it either till I dashed madly up the stoop of what I thought was my little home one night, in a horrible rush to make a phone call I'd forgotten about, broke my key off in the lock and then discovered I was trying to get into the wrong house. Who should open the door as I stood there screaming curses but Tom, and he came right to the rescue. Led me to his phone, tracked down the janitor, borrowed a key, dashed off to a locksmith. Really, knighthood was in flower in a big way. Tell me about college. You're enjoying it?"

Marion managed to say, "I suppose so. Yes, of course."

"That's good. I'll fire Barry in the spring if you'd like and you can come work for me again."

Marion, accepting a drink from Tom, was spared the necessity of replying to this suggestion. Jean chattered on, turning the garment of her life inside out, examining the seams, brushing off flecks of dust. Marion listened spasmodically, laughed when she could manage. But her nerves were going. Emotions and memories beat about inside her. She felt as if her consciousness were a little boat riding a stormy sea. After half an hour her only aim was to get away by herself before the boat should be swamped. She told herself that her jealousy was utterly ridiculous, she knew perfectly well that Jean was in love with Kermit, that Tom "hated messes." But granting that this was so, what was Tom doing here? Jean's story really explained nothing. Marion had seen Tom and Jean as at opposite poles—had it not been because Marion would not join Tom in condemning Jean that he had walked off from her and her messes that terrible morning? Marion remembered it this way, anyhow. Now to find them together threw her into a terrible confusion. If it was absurd for her to be jealous of Tom and Jean physically, still she must be jealous of the sort of ease in living that would allow them both, disagreeing about so much, to become friends in spite of everything. What had Tom meant, what had he been talking about, she asked herself indignantly, if after stalking off from Marion he went right out and became a friend of Jean's? Surely she had once again misinterpreted everything and made a fool of herself!

Mazily, through this writhing tapestry of emotions, Marion heard Jean talking about the Latimers, who were getting divorced. "After all that business about shooting herself over him and the big reconciliation she just decided she couldn't stand him——" Across this, the clock struck six.

Marion put down her glass and interrupted to say, "Darling, it's late, I've got to fly."

"Oh no! You've just come!"

"Scarsdale, you know. Dinner in Suburbia."

"Nonsense, call up and say you're having dinner in town. I'd adore to feed you here, but I'm honestly not up to cooking yet. But why don't you and Tom go get a dish of spaghetti around the corner and come back? I've done all the talking so far—I want to know about you."

"No really, I can't. My in-laws will be furious as it is because I came into town. Nina's in-laws, that is. I don't want to make it tough for her."

"Well——" said Jean. "It's very unsatisfactory. I feel as if I'd just had a glimpse of you. You'll be in town over Christmas, won't you?"

"Oh absolutely. I'll come and spend days with you."

"Good. See you do that."

"I will. And don't work too hard. Get over this properly, for goodness' sake." She kissed Jean, she was going to get out in time, it would be all right. She could have her *crise de nerfs* in the taxi going to the station or in the train. "Good-by, Tom," she said.

"I'll take you to your train," he said, holding her coat.

"Oh no, oh no, really! You mustn't bother."

"No bother."

"No, please!"

But Jean was looking startled. Marion caught back her protest, her overvehemence. Get out of here now, she thought. Then get rid of him outside. And if he went back to tell Jean how odd she had been —well, at least she wouldn't be there to hear it.

He opened the door for her and they went out and down the stairs. Her knees were shaking, the stairs seemed interminable. Out in the street, in the dark and wind, she said, "Please don't come with me."

He stood staring down at her. His face worked. He said, "I have to. I have to talk to you."

She shook her head.

"I have to," he repeated.

"Don't you see, don't you see," she cried, "I can't stand it! I can't stand any more!"

"Oh my God!" he said, and took her in his arms.

She clung to him, shaking and saying, "No, no, no! Oh please, no!"

"Yes, yes," he told her, "if you can ever forgive me. It's got to be yes." He took her shoulders and held her away from him, looking down into her face. His expression was agonized.

"Don't you see I can't think——" she said. "I don't understand——"

Two or three houses down a door opened and half a dozen people poured out, laughing and talking. They stared at Marion and Tom with interest. He pulled her to him again, hiding her face and glaring at them over her head. When they had started toward one corner, he took Marion's arm and walked her away in the other direction. She began to cry because the wind was so cold and Tom hurried so.

"Don't cry, darling," he said. "Don't cry, don't cry! God damn it, why are there never any cabs around here! Taxi! God damn it! Taxi! Taxi!"

His roar produced one, in a squeal of brakes. He opened the door and helped her in. She put her hands over her face. He pulled them away and began kissing her.

"Where to, Mac?" asked the cabdriver, who was watching absorbedly.

"Anyplace," said Tom, still in his furious voice. "Uptown. Drive around the park. Anyplace." He reached forward and pulled the glass across, cutting off the driver. "Oh my God," he said, gathering her into his arms, "I thought I'd never see you again."

This was too much for Marion. She caught her breath with a whoop and began to cry in earnest. "How can you! How can you!" she gasped. "How can you say that? How can you do this to me? How could you go off that way and never write, never call, and then say——"

"You can never forgive me!" said Tom. "You must forgive me."

"Forgive you! How can I forgive you when I don't understand anything at all? And Jean! What have you been doing with Jean?"

"Oh Jesus," said Tom. "I wanted to find out about you."

"Oh that's funny!" cried Marion. "That's beyond belief! Where did you think I was? At the South Pole, communicating with Jean by telepathy? I was in Scarsdale! I was in Poughkeepsie! I was even in New York twice! You knew where I was!"

"I didn't dare call you," said Tom. "God forgive me, I didn't dare."

"No, no!" said Marion. But she believed him. With a great sigh she put her head on his shoulder and fell quiet. She couldn't yet believe that this was happening, but she believed implicitly Tom's reason for not calling her.

He stroked her arm. He took her hat off and stroked her hair. The taxi plunged over to Fifth Avenue. As they rode uptown he stared over her head, stroking it and saying, "I'm never going to let you go again."

As they turned into the park Marion lifted her head. This dream sequence, she felt, had gone on long enough for her to risk action. If she moved and spoke perhaps Tom's arms, Tom's lips, would not vanish away. She looked up at his face as the street lamps flashed across it. He was there. This was Tom, this was the one. "What a terrible temper you have," she said huskily.

For a moment she thought he was going to cry. He grimaced and said, "I'm a bastard. I know I am. Can you stand it?"

"Yes," said Marion.

"Oh Jesus," said Tom, and then he kissed her really, kissed her until they were both shaking. "I can't stand this," he said. "We have to go someplace. We'll go to my place. All right?"

"All right," Marion said, and heard the words blow away from her on the wind of time—All right, all right, all right—a bell in her mind spoke them over and over again. Now she had said it, now she was Tom's.

He leaned forward and told the driver to go back to Bank Street.

"Okay," said the cabbie, "I guess you know what you want," and was cut off again by the glass.

"I was so angry," Tom was saying. "I thought you were so sweet. I kept wondering how in hell you got to Nyack, even when I just thought you were a nice kid. And then, that morning, when I was trying to tell you I was falling in love with you without saying it, it was too important to say—I wanted to tell you slowly and right, I wanted us to *know* each other—that morning, then, you threw that business at me. Oh Jesus. It was as if you were making the biggest damn fool of me in the world. You were running back to Jean and I figured—— God knows what I figured. I was so angry! I kept telling myself I didn't know anything about you, that you'd had me fooled, that you'd just been playing me that week end and really you belonged with that messy gang up in Nyack. I've known girls like that, you see. Nice and respectable and cute and good manners and you give them a couple of drinks and they lie down on the floor and ask to be—to be—— Oh hell, I wish I didn't have to tell you all this, but you've got to know what I thought. I want you to know now, before, so you'll know what you're getting into. That's what I told myself about you."

"You don't know any more about me now," said Marion. "How do you know it isn't true?"

"I knew it wasn't true then," said Tom. "When I stopped to think. Only I didn't stop to think for—for a couple of weeks. I was too mad. Anyway, by that time I almost didn't care. I just wanted to see you. So I called Jean's office and some dame told me you'd quit. So I said where were you, and she said back at college." He stopped.

Marion said, "And that was a million miles away, of course."

"I know. I could have written. Or called. But I didn't know what to say. And I had some screwy idea in my head I wanted to *see* you —just watch you for a while. I figured if I saw you I'd know right away how I felt, how I *really* felt. Because part of the time I was still mad. I'd argue and argue about you with myself. And how could I write you? How could I call? I thought you'd freeze on me, like you started to tonight. I thought you'd hang up on me, you wouldn't answer my letter. And then I latched onto Jean—it was just like she said—and I thought, Here's my chance. I'll wait and keep on seeing Jean and someday I'd see you again."

"And what about me waiting?" asked Marion. She pushed him away a little and shook the hair out of her face. "What about me waiting and getting over you?"

"Don't say it!" he told her. "You didn't. You're not."

"No, I'm not. But I'd started to be able to be happy again. Just a little while ago. Just today, maybe."

"Oh God," he said. "You too. All this time."

"All this time," she said.

"I had to go to Chicago last month," he said. "I almost did call you from there. I sat in that hotel room one night and wanted to call you and I kept thinking of all those little college girls, one calling you to the phone, and you coming out and taking it—I could see you in pajamas and a nice old flannel bathrobe and no lipstick on—and the little girls all saying, 'Who is it, Marion?' and you saying, 'Who is it?' because you wouldn't know it would be me in Chicago—and I lost my nerve. And then I figured it was too late anyway and I got drunk. Listen. Say it. Say you love me. I have to hear you say it."

"I love you," said Marion. But these words did not echo as the others had, for she was already committed. And it never occurred to her to ask him to say "I love you" too although he had not said it and did not say it until they were alone in the dark in his apartment and he said it several times, feverishly, when he was clumsily, hurriedly, helping her to undress. But this did not matter to her in the least because there was Tom, Tom, Tom, all around her and through her, and she knew what love was, it was not words, it was possession and being possessed.

He did not want to let her go home. He was quite stubborn about it. "You think I didn't mean it," he said, "when I said I wouldn't let you go again. Well, I meant just that. I'm not going to let you go. I want you here. Call them up and tell them we're married."

"Darling Tom, it's half-past ten on a Saturday night. We can't *get* married. You need a license and a blood test and you have to wait three days! I know all about it because a girl at college——"

"I know all about it too, and it's a lot of nonsense. We'll do it, but do you think it'll make me feel any more married to you than I do right now? We were married tonight and you know it. My God, next you'll say you want to meet my family!"

"Oh Tom, your mother! Won't she want you to be married by a priest?"

"No she won't. Don't be silly. Now call them up and tell them——"

"Darling, I told them I'd probably be home for dinner! I can't——"

"Yes you can."

"Tom, I can't!"

But she ended by doing it. Wrapped in Tom's bathrobe, she sat by the phone and shook with fright and confusion as the call went through. She had asked to talk personally to Nina—that would be bad enough, but anyone else would be impossible—but when Nina came on she didn't know what to say.

"Marion?" Nina said. "Where are you? What's the matter?"

"Nina—I'm sorry. I'm in New York. I wanted you to know—I'm not coming out tonight."

"You're not—— What's happened? Marion, what is the matter?"

"Nothing's the matter. I'm fine. I just—— I met a friend and I'm going to stay in town. I just didn't want you to worry."

"Didn't want me to worry!"

"Don't repeat everything!" cried Marion, and burst into laughter.

"Marion, where are you and who are you with? Answer me!"

"All right," said Marion, "I will. I'm with Tom Hofstra at his apartment and I'm not coming home. We're—we're going to be married."

"You're drunk," said Nina. There was a pause and Marion thought, I asked to speak to Nina and this is Nina, and I don't know her at all.

She ran a hand through her hair. Tom was out in the kitchen making a drink. She could hear him running water into the sink, swearing at the ice cubes. But he had, she supposed deliberately, shut the door and turned on the water so that he could not hear her, so

278

that she could say what had to be said in privacy. She thought, I can't do this, and then she thought, I have to. "Listen to me, Nina," she said. "I'm not drunk. I could have lied to you very easily but I didn't want to. I wanted you to know. I'm in love with Tom. All autumn I didn't see him. Then today—I met him by accident. And he's in love with me and we're going to be married. It was bad for him too. It was awful for me, all the time apart. We're in love and we're going to be married and I'm not coming home."

"And what," asked Nina, speaking very slowly, "am I going to tell Mother? What am I going to tell Stuart? Dear heaven, what am I going to tell the Judge?"

"Tell the Judge to go right to hell! Oh Nina—I should have lied to you! But I thought—— Tell Mother I met Jean McDonald, you remember, the girl I worked for—it's true, I did see her—and that she's had influenza—that's true too—and that I'm staying with her overnight. Won't that do?"

"Let me talk to Tom," said Nina suddenly.

"I won't," said Marion.

"How do I know——" Nina began, and stopped. There was another pause.

"How do you know what his intentions are?" asked Marion bitterly. "I should think you'd know because I tell you. Nina, try to understand. We're in love. You were in love with Stuart, weren't you?"

"I didn't behave like this."

"I'm sorry."

"Sorry! I should think you'd be sorry! I only hope you won't be sorry all your life!"

"Nina—don't!"

"You're a spoiled brat, that's what you are! If *Kermit* had done something like this I wouldn't be surprised, but even *Kermit* had the decency not to—not to go to bed with someone and call up in the middle and announce he wasn't coming home because he was in love! In love! You don't mean love, you mean——"

Marion put the phone down in her lap. She would have hung up but she was afraid that if she did Nina would send Stuart or the police after her. She waited until Nina's furious voice stopped. Then she put the phone to her ear again and said, "I don't know what you said because I wouldn't listen to that. I'll just tell you again that I'm in love and I'm very happy and I'm going to marry Tom and go on being in love and being very happy and you aren't going to spoil it. I told you because you're my own sister, my only sister, and I didn't want to lie to you, because I loved you. Now, now——" She stopped because she felt sick to her stomach.

There was a long pause and then Nina hung up.

Marion sat huddled in Tom's warm robe, shaking with cold. Somewhere a clock ticked. She wondered what time it was, how long it had taken her to burn behind her the bridges that had connected her with the country of her youth. Now there was nothing but the new continent of her love for Tom. There was no one but Tom.

He came in with drinks and said, "Is it all right?"

"It's all right," she lied.

"My darling girl." He sat down on the floor by her and took her bare foot in his hand and smiled at her, refraining from saying that he had known it would be all right, that she must trust him and not fuss. She smiled back at him and drank her highball. After a while he took her back to bed. Neither of them remembered they had had nothing to eat that night.

Marion fell asleep in Tom's arms and woke to his caresses. Early light, gray and dim, lay outside the window and shaped the furniture of Tom's bedroom. Marion lay and thought, Home! Home! at the room around her. It was Tom's, it was hers. She was rich, rich because he must give her everything and she could accept everything from him, having thrown away everything else. It was not so much happiness she felt; she only knew that she lay reborn on the edge of the morning with the whole world stretched out below for her to possess and struggle and live in. She felt alive and powerful as she had never done before and at the same time enormously passive, to be moved only by love, by true desire. Never again need she do what someone else told her to do, or what someone else believed to be right. She had found the place where right and wrong began. Now she was Tom's, now she was free, because Tom and she were one, and all that she wanted and all that was right chimed together, and

Beethoven's kingdom of heaven where every promise is its own fulfillment lay round about her, here and now.

"Do you love me?" he asked. "Say you love me!"

"Dear love, dear love," she said, laughing, and kissed his eyes shut and, cradling his body, felt very wise because he needed her so.

Then they were very, very hungry and remembered, both at the same time—"Telepathy!" said Marion—that they had had no dinner, and got up to get breakfast. Breakfast with Tom, forever! thought Marion rapturously, putting the coffeepot on the table. She looked like the apotheosis of all the young wives in the breakfast cereal ads and felt like them, too, beaming, scrubbed, fresh from the tub, ministering to Tom at every moment whether she lay with him in bed or put sugar on his grapefruit. They turned on the radio and WQXR played the same quartet Marion had heard at the concert, which seemed to her a coincidence so marvelous that it double-locked her happiness, and the Sunday paper came and Tom read bits of it aloud and Marion thought dreamily that she would put yellow curtains at the windows and ivy on the mantelpiece.

The doorbell rang.

"What the hell?" said Tom.

The ivy vanished, the yellow curtains dissolved, bare light streamed in the windows, Marion sat frozen to her chair. "Oh," she said. "Oh, oh, oh!"

"Darling!" said Tom. "I won't let them in!"

"It's Nina!" cried Marion.

"Nina!" He stared at her, astounded.

Now, in this moment, she had to tell him. "It must be. Tom, it wasn't—all right last night. She was furious."

"But why didn't you tell me? I don't understand! What did you tell her? Didn't she——"

"I told her I was here. I didn't—I couldn't bear to start with a lie. I was so happy. And then—I didn't tell you because I thought for one of us to have to worry was enough."

He was struck dumb. Oh my God, she thought, I've done wrong, I've done wrong! The words tolled through her head like bells. I've done wrong. I should have lied to Nina.

Then she always remembered that he came over and took her in his arms and kissed her. "It's all right," he said. "It's all right, my darling."

The bell rang again.

"But next time tell me," he said, and went to push the buzzer.

It was Stuart, looking tired in the clear morning light. He had cut himself shaving. Tom had the door open when he came upstairs and stood back to let him in. Everyone looked at each other for a moment. Then Tom said, "Sit down, won't you?"

Marion said, "Do you want a cup of coffee? There's still——"

"No," said Stuart. "Marion, do you want to come home with me?"

"No," said Marion.

"We're going to be married, you know," Tom said. "This isn't—an escapade."

"All right," said Stuart. "I daresay you are. But I think Marion had better come home now."

"I won't go," said Marion.

"What do you want me to tell your mother?" asked Stuart.

Marion sat down on the sofa amidst all the Sunday paper and covered her face with her hands.

"Nina told her what you said to—about this friend of yours, what's-her-name, Jean, being sick. I don't know whether she believed it or not. She's upset."

There was a long silence. Then Marion said with utter despairing truth in her voice, "I don't know what to do."

"Jesus," said Stuart, "you can get a license tomorrow and be married on Thursday. Can't you wait that long?"

"Tom, what shall I do?"

"Whatever you want. Whatever is best for you. Your brother-in-law mayn't believe it, but I'd wait for you till a year from next Thursday if that's what you want."

"It isn't the waiting. It's the lying," said Marion. "I'm married to you now. I feel it. I can't lie about it."

"Who's asking you to lie?" said Stuart wearily. "Just think about other people's feelings once in a while instead of your own. I'm not arguing about your marrying Hofstra—go ahead. The sooner the better. But as it is, it's a lousy mess. Let's clean it up the best we can."

"Tom hates messes," said Marion, and began to cry. "And I al-ways—always—make them! Oh Tom, I'm so sorry!"

"Shut up," said Tom, sitting down beside her, and took her in his arms. "There isn't any mess that can't be cleaned up in half an hour. Don't let him get you down! We'll do whatever you want, and the hell with the rest of it."

"I don't—I can't see Nina!" Marion sobbed. "The things she said——"

"What about the things you do?" said Stuart angrily. "What do you expect people to say?"

"I expect—people I love—to believe me! To—to love me enough to—to *believe* me!"

"I don't know what that means," said Stuart. "Nina had a baby less than a month ago, you know. She's not feeling top of the world. Your mother's not as young as she was. I'm not going to drag you back by your hair. If you want to say the hell with them, go ahead. But don't be surprised and hurt if I say the hell with you!"

Tom said, "Shut up, will you?"

"Not for you," said Stuart. "Not for her, either. If I think she's a selfish little bitch, she can damn well hear me say so."

Tom stood up. "Get out of here, will you please?"

Stuart grinned. "You going to make me?"

"I guess so," said Tom. But Marion caught his arm.

"No, no, no!" she cried. "Stop it, don't!" After a minute Tom looked away from Stuart's grin, down into her tear-stained face.

"All right," he said. "All right."

"Tom," she said, "he's right. I have to do something about Mother." She looked at him imploringly, but Tom had already told her to do whatever she wanted. Stuart walked over to the window and stood staring out into the street. There was no one to tell her what she wanted to do but herself. Her heart contracted in fear. No one but Marion to face the decision and help Marion! She was frightened to death.

"I'll have to go to Scarsdale," she said at last, through stiff lips. "But Tom—oh Tom, could you take me out? I can't be brought back by Stuart like a—like a fugitive from justice."

"I'm not trying——" Stuart began, swinging around.

"Yes you are," said Marion. "I won't go that way anyway, whatever you want to call it. Oh Tom, I know it's a lot to ask, but if you don't mind too much——"

"Of course I'll take you out," said Tom. "And see no one bullies you, either. Listen to me, darling. Relax. I *want* to take you out."

Marion smiled at him painfully. "You won't when you get there. It's a mess, Tom, and I wish I didn't have to get you into it."

"I don't give a damn," said Tom. "I can stand it."

"I wish I thought I could," said Marion.

"Of course you can," said Tom.

Stuart left then. Marion began collecting the dishes from the table by the window where she had served their rapturous breakfast. "Honey," said Tom behind her, "cheer up."

Marion stacked the dishes. "I will," she said. "Just give me a few minutes."

"The important thing," he told her, "is that we're always going to be together. You aren't on your own. I'm here."

"Yes," said Marion, and blinked so as not to cry again; she didn't know why. Why should being told that she was not alone overwhelm her with self-pity? she wondered. She concentrated on keeping her voice steady and said, "Go shave, darling, and I promise I'll be all right by the time you're through."

"That's my girl," said Tom.

I've always liked to wash dishes, thought Marion, running hot water over them. I suppose that makes me a ducky little domestic type. Well, here I am in the middle of the real world, Kermit's real world, and it's hell. I love Tom and Tom loves me—or do we? She watched her hands carefully rinsing coffee cups. We both believe we do. I'll never be alone again. But——

I never have been alone, thought Marion.

Suddenly Tom, shaving, turned back into the stranger he was. Marion clutched the edge of the sink. I must be crazy! she thought. What am I doing here? Alone with a strange man!

She stood perfectly still, staring in front of her. Alone—and to be alone. Good-by, Stuart. Good-by, Nina. Good-by, Mother. You will not have me any more. This time I've gone and I can't get back.

Tom, she thought. This morning it felt like a new world. Someone else said that about being in love with a person. Was it Donne? "Oh my America, my New Found Land." Doesn't that show it is love? He must have known.

But how does love make you stop being strangers? I don't think I know. The funny thing is that all the people who are closest to me are strangest. I trusted Nina beyond anyone. I thought Stuart was fond of me—"a selfish little bitch" is what he said. And Tom—no other man has ever been so close or seemed so strange. I will never be alone again. Is that freedom or prison? Tom, don't I need to be alone—just a bit—just to be sure I can be? Tom, don't devour me!

He came in then, tucking his shirt into his belt, and took a dish towel off the rack. I'm a fool, thought Marion at once. This is Tom, and I love him.

"Tom," she said, "what kind of a razor do you use?"

"A Gillette," he said. "What in heaven's name——"

"I have to learn all about you."

"Dear heart," said Tom, "you will. Dear idiot! You'll have fifty years to learn me by heart."

"But you'll have to let me ask questions. You see, I'm not bright."

"Angel——"

"And I make messes."

"I'll clean them up for you."

"But I'd like to learn how not to make messes."

He took her hands out of the dishwater and held them. "Dearest, you *must not* worry about this. Look. What we have is worth a mess a lot bigger than this one. Last night was worth everything your goddamn brother-in-law and your sister are trying to do to spoil it. And a lot more. Wasn't it?"

"Yes."

"All right. We've got the best of the bargain. Will you please remember that? And stop acting as if I were Wally Simpson and you had to abdicate to marry me? Now go powder your nose or whatever the hell you have to do and we'll go out there and get it over with."

"Yes Tom."

"Now say, Tom uses a Gillette razor and likes his coffee strong and loves me, and that's what I've learned today."

Marion giggled. "And likes people to say yes to him."

Tom slapped her on the rump. "Exactly. Who said you weren't bright? Go on, get moving."

It started to snow as they were driving out to Scarsdale, a fine powdery snow that blew across the road and collected in the dead grass. The windshield wipers sighed and sighed, saying "Po-o-or simp! Po-o-or simp!" I will ignore them, thought Marion. Nobody is a poor simp. I have an unpleasant duty to do, that's all. But when Tom turned the car into the drive at Nina's she wished desperately that the duty had been done. "I feel as if I were going to the dentist," she said sadly to Tom.

"Pusscat," he said, "nobody's going to eat you. Be a brave little girl."

"I don't think I know how," said Marion.

"Then you must learn." He got out and opened the door for her, took her arm and ran her across the crust of snow on the lawn. He wouldn't let her stop for an instant, he rang the bell and tried the door at once. It was unlocked and he walked her in, right through the hall and into the living room. There was no one there; but in the dining room a chair scraped back and Stuart came out with a napkin in his hand.

"Oh hello," he said. "We're eating lunch——"

Mrs. Bishop was right behind him.

"Mum," said Marion, and ran to her mother.

Mrs. Bishop put her arms around her daughter and said, "Marion dear—I was worried."

"It's my fault, Mrs. Bishop," said Tom loudly.

"You remember Tom Hofstra," said Marion.

Mrs. Bishop's hand trembled in Marion's as she looked from her daughter to Tom, and her expression was puzzled. In a frightening flash Marion thought, She's getting old!

"Tom?" said Mrs. Bishop. She really was puzzled, everyone saw. She couldn't place him.

He came over and took her hand from Marion. "I was here last summer."

"Labor Day week end," Marion supplied.

"Oh yes, yes," said Mrs. Bishop. But she still looked puzzled.

Why did this young man wish to hold her hand? She withdrew it gently.

"Marion and I met by accident last night," Tom said. "At Jean McDonald's. I kept her so late—talking—that we thought she'd better stay at Jean's."

"I see," said Mrs. Bishop.

"I live next door, you see. Next door to Jean's. We're neighbors."

Mrs. Bishop took a firm grip on herself and rallied her powers. Marion had telephoned Nina, and Nina had been devastatingly angry, and something was going on. Nonetheless, Mrs. Bishop knew, one did not stop being polite just because there was a crisis. "Neighbors!" she said. "That is unusual in New York, isn't it?"

"Yes—yes, I guess it is." Tom took a deep breath and went at his hurdle. "We're going to be married."

"How nice," said Mrs. Bishop. "I hope you'll be very happy."

Tom stared at her as if she were mad.

Marion said, "Not Tom and Jean, Mother. Tom—Tom and me."

"Tom—and you?" Mrs. Bishop put her hand out. Stuart caught her arm and steadied her. There was quite a long pause. Then Mrs. Bishop laughed a social little laugh and said, "But Marion dear, you don't know him."

"Oh Mum, I do, I do," cried Marion. "Oh please—I'm so awfully sorry to have been so sudden. Come and sit down, Mummy. Don't be shocked! Tom and I—Tom and I are in love. Awfully in love."

Tom pulled up a chair and Mrs. Bishop sat down heavily. Marion knelt at her feet and repeated that she and Tom were in love.

"But I don't understand," said Mrs. Bishop. "How long have you known each other?"

"Just since Labor Day," said Marion, "but what does that matter?"

"But you never—spoke of him, dear."

"I couldn't. We had a silly quarrel."

"Oh dear!" said Mrs. Bishop.

"All fall—at college—I was so unhappy I thought I'd die. And Tom—Tom was too. And then, last night—— Oh dear, I can't explain! Tom——"

"Take it easy," said Stuart suddenly. "Mother Bishop, do you want some sherry?"

287

"Why, thank you, Stuart. I'm all right. But yes—a little sherry, please."

Stuart got the decanter and a glass while everyone waited and the seconds crawled. Marion could *feel* them crawling up and down her spine. Mrs. Bishop took a sip of sherry. Stuart put the decanter down on a table and took a firm position behind her chair.

Tom said, "Mrs. Bishop. I know this must be a shock to you. But we want you to understand how it is. I fell in love with Marion right away. I was a fool ever to let her get away from me. We were both—desperately unhappy. At least Marion says so, and I know I was. When I found her last night I couldn't let her go until she said she'd marry me. I know this isn't the conventional way to do things, but we both feel we can't be happy apart. We've been apart and we know what it's like. We want to be married right away. I hope—I hope you'll get to like me. I'll do everything in the world to make Marion happy."

"Why, Tom," said Mrs. Bishop, "I'm sure you would. I hope I'm not too conventional myself to understand two young people in love. But my dear, I don't know anything about you. I can't even remember your name."

"Hofstra," said Tom, and spelled it. "I'm an architect. I work in New York for a firm called Belden and Ford. I'm twenty-eight. I make a living and think I can make more. I was born in Ithaca when my father was teaching at Cornell, but I grew up in Columbus. He teaches chemistry at Ohio State. My mother's French. I have two younger brothers. One's an engineer working for GM in Detroit. The other's still in college. I graduated from Ohio State and took architecture at Yale. I——"

"Oh my goodness," said Mrs. Bishop. "Tom, stop for a minute! I didn't mean I wanted an autobiography, though of course I'm glad to know your background. I meant I would like to have a chance to know you."

"Well," said Tom, "you will. Because I expect to be your son-in-law for the rest of my natural life." He grinned at her.

Mrs. Bishop smiled back, but she had no trouble at all resisting him. "It's very nice of you to want so much to be," she said. "Good gracious, I hope we haven't ruined Nina's nice lunch. You haven't had lunch, have you, Marion? Tom? Come along, then." She stood up, still holding her almost-full glass of sherry, and led them into the dining room. Tom caught Marion's hand and squeezed it.

Thus hand in hand they faced Nina, who said, "So there you are." Nina, don't be so hateful! Marion wanted to cry. But Mrs. Bishop was introducing Tom to the Judge, who grunted and said, "Hey? Hofstra? How d'ye do," and went on eating.

Nina filled plates of salad and cold turkey for them in what Marion felt was a Borgia manner, and Mrs. Bishop proceeded to construct a conversation about the weather. Stuart answered when spoken to and Tom did his best, while Marion played with her food and Nina did not speak at all. Having exhausted the prospects for a cold winter, Mrs. Bishop moved on to Tom's profession, and asked him what kind of houses he built. This let them in for a disquisition from the Judge, who had finished and pushed his plate away, on the sins of modern architecture first, and then modernity in general. Mrs. Bishop made little distraught noises of conciliation, but no one could stop the Judge until lunch was over and he stumped away upstairs to take a nap.

By this time the conversation had been finally thrashed to death and could not revive. A long uneasy pause filled the room, full of family tugs and tensions. The remains of lunch, the soiled plates and crumpled napkins, so horribly appropriate to the general mood, held them hypnotized. No one moved.

We were all so happy together when we were little, Marion thought, and raised her eyes to study her sister. Nina looked tired and pale and thin and indefinably sharpened. Marion thought, Have I, all this time, been loving and trusting someone who isn't there any more? Where has Nina gone? Have Stuart and the children eaten up, worn away, the Nina who was generous and had time to love me? Is that what happens to people who get married? When you tell them you're in love do they ask you, all of them, what will people say? What shall I tell the Judge?

But I have Tom, and Tom loves me. Only they were trying to reduce her love to nonexistence by ignoring it. She could feel the weight of the pressure from all of them sitting about the table, squeezing and squeezing her love into a smaller and smaller space, until they could make it merely the foolish impulse of a wayward child. She sat fiddling with her watch, twisting it about her wrist, resisting them. And suddenly, on a wave of panic, remembered that she had thirty pages of economic history to read before a class the next day. Her books, her clothes, sat snugly in her room at college. Was that real? Or was Tom real?

"Mummy," she said desperately into the silence, "Tom and I are really and truly going to get married as soon as we can. As soon as we get a license. Nobody seems to realize that. But it's true! We are! You must realize it!"

"Marion," said her mother, "I only want you to be happy. Will this make you happy? I want you to be sure. Don't think about the rest of us, but be sure yourself."

Nina snorted.

Marion cried, "But I can't help thinking about you! I want it to make you happy too, that I'm happy."

"If you're happy, I will be," said Mrs. Bishop.

"But you're not happy now. You don't think this is right. Really it is, it is! Please believe me, Mum."

"Marion—dearest child—I can't say more than I've said. I can't say it's right. I don't think it's right. How can I say it's right for you to plunge into marriage with a young man I know nothing about? I don't want to hurt your feelings—or Tom's—but it's true. If you want to know what I think would be right, I think you should finish college and marry Tom in June if you both still want to. I would enjoy very much getting acquainted with Tom this winter. That's what I think is right. But if it isn't what would make you happy, Marion, you must do what would make you happy."

"Tom and I—don't want to be apart. Compared with that, college —and everything—seems so silly! Why should we be apart, and suffer?"

Mrs. Bishop said, "You must do what you want."

Marion said, "I want to marry Tom!" and burst into tears.

Nina said, "Oh my God!"

"Oh dear!" said Mrs. Bishop. "Oh Marion dear!" Stuart pushed back his chair and went to her.

Tom jumped up and half lifted Marion out of her chair. "Stop it, now, just stop it!" he said in a fierce whisper and walked her into the living room. There he put his arms around her and held her close while she caught her breath.

"I'm so incompetent!" she gasped. "I can't see why you want to marry me! I didn't mean to cry, I wanted to be brave!"

"Darling, listen to me. Forget about being brave. Look, I understand how your mother feels. If she's right, if it would make it easier for you, we'll wait. I can wait. Just tell me."

Marion said, "No! No. No. Don't *you* think that!"

"I don't. I won't. I just want you to be sure."

"I'm very, very sure."

"Then that's all we need. Darling." Marion felt the cloak of their love come round her again and heal her panic.

She sighed and relaxed against him. "What had we better do now?"

"Do you want to go back to town? Is this more than you can stand?"

Marion stood straighter in his arms. "No. I'll manage now, I promise. I had to try, Tom, I did. But now I see they'll never be on my side, and I won't try any more. We won't talk about it, because talking doesn't do any good. I'll just remember that tomorrow we'll get a license and then it will be just three days."

"Now you're being my brave girl."

She took Tom's handkerchief out of his breast pocket and wiped her eyes and blew her nose. Then, with her chin high, she went back to the dining room and said, "I've recovered. I'm sorry I bawled. Let me help you clear the table, Nina. Mummy, why don't you go inside and begin"—she swallowed and smiled—"getting acquainted with Tom?" Then she picked up a plate and a glass and marched through the swinging door to the kitchen. Her hands were shaking, but the need to clean up, to keep the world rolling along so that supper could succeed lunch and life not end in a welter of dirty dishes, geared her into reality.

Life did go on. Mrs. Bishop chatted with Tom for an hour before she said that she thought she would take a little rest. The children had come down from their naps by this time, been bundled into snow suits and sent out to roll in the snow. Having no other elevation at hand, they dragged a sled onto the front porch and coasted down the stoop. This woke the Judge, who could be heard harrumphing upstairs.

Marion went with her mother out into the hall. "Mummy dear," she said, and kissed her.

Mrs. Bishop did not cling, but she took Marion's face between her hands and looked into her eyes. Marion smiled at her with all her heart, but she did not know whether her mother found what she was looking for. After a minute Mrs. Bishop said, "My dear child," and kissed her, and let her go. "Will you be here when I wake up?" she asked, turning to the stairs.

"Yes, of course."

Mrs. Bishop paused. "You're not going back to college tonight?" She did not look at her daughter.

"No, Mum," said Marion steadily. "After Tom and I have arranged about a marriage license tomorrow I'll go up and get my things and tell them I'm not coming back."

Mrs. Bishop stood perfectly still but she seemed to shrink within herself. Then, slowly, she began to climb the stairs. Marion stood and watched her and felt her heart grieve within her. Please be happy for me, Mum, she wanted to cry, please be happy! But it wouldn't do any good. Nothing would do any good. She couldn't satisfy both Tom and her family. She loved them both and her loves were irreconcilable. No one had ever told her this about love before—that it was not enough.

While she stood in the hall, static in this place of passage, of entrances and exits, Nina came out of the living room and went to the door to look at the children. She opened it a crack and called, "Johnny, try to be a little more quiet. Why don't you make a snowman?"

Johnny, who was panting up the steps with the sled bumping behind him, said, "We're coasting."

"Yes I know, but you've coasted enough now. Make a fine big snowman for me." She shut the door without having had any visible effect on Johnny and said, "It's no good telling them. Stuart will have to go out and start a snowman for them." She turned to Marion and added abruptly, "How long is he going to stay?"

"Tom?" asked Marion.

"It's difficult enough without having to make conversation," said Nina. "Mother's tired. Couldn't he go before she comes down again?"

"Once you said you liked him," said Marion in a whisper.

"What? It's nothing to do with liking him. I just don't want any more sensations. Any scenes."

"You don't even—like me, I think."

"Marion," said Nina, "I don't know what you want more than you're getting. You're *getting* what you want! You're doing this your way. Do you expect everybody to jump up and down and cheer? People fall in love and get married every day without having to—to disrupt everything! To——" At this point a howl from Toddy interrupted her and she opened the door and flew out into the cold to pick him up, crying "Johnny, I told you to stop doing that! Now Toddy's hurt! Stuart, Stuart! Marion, call him, please!"

In the fuss over Toddy, who had fallen off the sled and got snow down his back, Marion went to Tom. "Darling, do you want to go?"

"I'll stay as long as you want me."

Marion made a gesture of despair. "It's not doing any good. You go along and I'll go upstairs and keep out of it."

"I don't care about it's doing good. Except for you."

"I'll be all right. I promised, didn't I?"

"Sure?"

"Sure. When will I—see you?"

"Call me at the office as soon as you get into town tomorrow."

"I don't know the number," said Marion, blushing and remembering, out of a clear sky, Hank Durham's office number.

"Circle 8-6933." He stood holding her hands and looking down into her face. "You're not sorry about any of this? About it's being fast? You don't worry?"

"Only that I'll be—all you want. All you think I am."

"You're all I want," said Tom. They did not kiss because Toddy and Johnny were now both howling and Johnny, who had been slapped for getting Toddy in trouble, erupted in upon them. Tom went; and Marion knelt down to comfort Johnny and remove his boots.

As much as Nina had hurt her, she found that the tension did ease with Tom's departure. When Johnny was quiet she went up to the room she always used at Nina's and lay down on the bed. Outside the bare branches of the trees lay across the gray winter sky. "Not winter, spring," said Marion to herself. She was very tired and, drifting through memories of Tom's love-making, she fell asleep. But the little boat of her spirit did not stop there. On and on it went, back through the light and shade of the years, until it rocked safe at last in the peace of a sunny childhood, so long ago that there was nothing to remember.

In the end, it wasn't until Saturday that Marion and Tom got married. Marion had found the gloomy bureaucracy of City Hall singularly depressing and after half a day of struggling with this mood asked Tom tensely if he minded very much being married in church.

"Darling," said Tom, "I'll jump over a broomstick with you if you want."

Marion looked at him worshipfully. Though she knew she had failed with her family, a church wedding was a timid peace offering to them, and it made her feel better. Now there could be a ceremonial shell of custom and tradition around the incredible secret of love: was not that what they wanted? Kermit should give her away, she decided, and her mother and Nina and Stuart should be present. She succeeded in her plan, but to get everyone there, combined with the schedule of the rector of Grace Church, meant putting the wedding off till Saturday morning. Marion spent the week half at Tom's, half at Jean's, in a mildly manic-depressive frenzy. Jean got her through it by a combination of bullying and sympathy which left her more exhausted than Marion.

"Marion darling," she said once—they were in Best's looking at suits for Marion to be married in—"how can you be so excited *all* the time?"

"Shouldn't I be?" asked Marion, astonished. "But Jean, this is the most important thing that has ever happened to me!"

"I know, I know," said Jean hastily. "I just don't see how you can keep it up, every minute, for days."

Marion sat down on a chair in the fitting room. "All right," she said. "I shall be enormously calm. *Nothing* shall raise my temperature one notch. Marriage—poof, poof! Some people do it every other year. I shall contemplate Tommy Manville and the Hollywood divorce rate. Is that better?"

"It's a little extreme. Why don't you contemplate—oh—ten years from now when you're settled and suburban and have three children and six more inches on your waistline?"

"Like Nina," said Marion at once, and shivered. Immediately she looked like a wet puppy. "Jean, she's so mad at me. I wish I knew why."

"Jealous," said Jean.

"Of *me?* Nina would never be jealous of *me!* Why, she's so efficient! She manages everything so well! I'm a scatterbrained idiot compared with Nina. It can't be jealousy, Jean. That's not fair. It's more that her life has worked out one way and she can't see— or won't trust—any other way. I wish I could talk to her, though. I can't any more. I don't mind, or I try not to mind, that she's so busy she doesn't have any generosity left over for me. I can see that that may happen to people. But she makes me feel as if she were *condemning* me, somehow, and I don't know why."

"You're young and in love."

"But she was in love when she married Stuart. Kermit doesn't think so, but she was. I can remember."

"Perhaps that makes it harder to see you now. Anyway——" Jean hesitated.

"Anyway what?"

"You commit yourself to things so. You feel everything so hard, so much. Maybe she's jealous of that."

Marion looked at herself warily in the mirror. "I suppose I do feel things too much. There are plenty of times I wish I didn't. But I can't help it. I think it must be my way of understanding things. I can't seem to do it in my head, beforehand. I have to go ahead and—and jump into things before I know where I am. Jean. Have you ever seen—or heard—anything from—from——"

"Hank Durham?" asked Jean. Marion nodded her bent head. "No." This was a lie. Jean had seen him one night in a restaurant with a little brunette who looked seventeen. They were both drunk.

Marion sighed. "I wish I could think of him as something more than an awful, awful mistake. It's so upsetting to think there was *nothing* there, that I was absolutely, totally, wrong. No redeeming features whatsoever."

Jean said, "Darling, everybody has some absolutely irredeemable blunder to live down. It just makes you human. And think how short a time it lasted and how easily you got yourself unstuck."

"I suppose so."

The saleswoman came in with some more suits, and Marion got up to try them on. "I can't get married in purple," she said. "Or green. As as a matter of fact, I can't think of *any* appropriate color. Jean, am I *really* going to get married?"

"Yes darling," said Jean. "You are. If I were you I'd take that grayish-pink job. If the fitter pins the hem, I'll turn it up for you tonight, and then we can take it right along and get a hat to match. White blouse, white gloves, gray shoes, gray bag. You'll look like an angel."

"I *feel* absolutely terrified," said Marion.

"If you start that again, I swear I'll take a hairbrush to you. Stop it! Here, have a cigarette."

"I don't think I can," said Marion, but she took one and smoked it while the fitter crawled around her feet, and so Jean got her and the suit out.

Kermit flew up Friday evening, arriving at Jean's in a mild fury —this frantic performance was, he supposed, exactly what he should have expected from Marion. Jean was lying flat on her back on the sofa, achingly tired and thinking with longing of the quiet that would descend once the wedding was over. She was all alone. Tom's youngest brother had arrived from Harvard, where he was taking his M.A., and Tom and Marion were dining and night-clubbing him. Jean had just decided that she had reached her absolute limit of making arrangements with the problem of who was going to spend the night where. If Tom's brother Richie stayed with Tom, Marion could hardly stay there. And if Marion stayed here, what about Kermit? Jean was having scruples over the night-before-the-wedding. Except, she thought, that I'm so tired I could share my couch in perfect chastity with Don Juan, Lord Byron and Casánova. I don't know. I don't care. Let someone else fix it up, I'm through. When Kermit rang the bell she literally could not get up, for a moment, to let him in.

He put his bag down and kissed her and said, "Hello, love. You look like the wrath of God. Where's this mad genius you've got my sister mixed up with?"

This was the last straw, and Jean exploded. "Kermit, doesn't it ever occur to you that sometimes the best defense is simply not needed? I had nothing to do with it *at all*. For one solid week I have done nothing but pick up small pieces of other people's egos and try to put them together. Don't pick on me! I'm tired!"

Kermit looked at her in amazement. "You must be," he said. "I'm sorry. Only don't tell me you had nothing to do with it, because obviously you——"

"Kermit," said Jean, "shut up!" She dropped on the sofa again and leaned her head back, her eyes shut. Kermit stood rigid in the center of the room. He was too angry to speak. People! he thought. The human race! Their *idiot* messes! He was sick to death of them. Well, he would leave Jean to it, he decided, and go to a hotel. Cut his losses here, clear out—— Show up at the church, of course, he had to acknowledge that obligation. But as for other obligations—— He looked at Jean. She looked forty, she looked no-age, she was simply a human mask. Poor woman, he thought. Well, she had asked for it. No doubt she had gotten from him as much as she had given. She must expect——

"Mix me a drink, will you please?" said Jean without opening her eyes. "Scotch and soda."

Kermit opened his mouth to say he was leaving, and then closed it again. No matter how cruel he might be, he was never rude. He took off his topcoat, went to the bar and mixed highballs for both of them; thinking wryly that Jean had said the one thing guaranteed to keep him there. If she had offered *him* a drink, or asked if he had had dinner, he would have gone straight out through her door and never come back. He gave her her glass and sat down with his own where he could look at her. His rage died down.

Having felt himself completely able to depart, having reaffirmed his freedom, he now was cheerfully tolerant of his weary mistress.

"I forgot you'd had a bug," he said. "It took it out of you."

"I feel about ninety," said Jean. "If I can finish one job next week, I'll go South for a while." I don't suppose you could come with me, she did not add.

Kermit experienced a small shock. So she was talking about going away from him! "Do you good," he said kindly. Evidence of independence on Jean's part always attracted him, and he was always careful to hide his emotion: he didn't want anyone to have clues to his emotions, any of them. "You're an idiot, you know," he added, "to get yourself into such a state over Marion."

"We all have our vices," said Jean temperately. "Mine is generosity."

"The gift without the giver is bare."

"Exactly. That line must have impressed me deeply at some vulnerable point in my youth. I think she'll be very happy with Tom. He's a wonderful guy. You'll like him."

"When have you ever caught me liking wonderful guys? Exhausted you may be, but don't let it sap your brain entirely. Who could like his brother-in-law? Nina once tried to tell me Stuart Fanning was wonderful. The only result was he called me a bad name and I tried to kill him."

"All right," said Jean. "I don't care if you detest him. What a wonderful thing whiskey is. This isn't a drink, it's a transfusion. I believe I'll live."

"Welcome back," said Kermit.

"Thank you." She opened her eyes and smiled at him.

Kermit at once felt uneasy. For something important was happening to him, and he couldn't control it. He was in transition, he was uncertain. He was afraid to smile back at Jean, afraid to let her close. He needed a space about him to hide and protect the weakness that had invaded him.

He was through with Washington. He'd had it. There was nothing left there for him except the repetition of things he'd had. He could accept this intellectually, in fact he had a good deal of contempt for the people who had come to Washington at the beginning of the Roosevelt administration and were now afraid to leave, the power-hungry young men who moved carefully from department to department but were so concerned over their own status that they never managed to enjoy the power they wielded. No, it was not the idea of leaving Washington that upset him: to be really powerful in Washington it might be best to leave, and build up an independent barony. The trouble was what he seemed to want to do instead.

There was a war, and something wanted him to go to it; something within him that was autonomous and immune to argument. It's sheer insanity, Kermit told himself. But the thing, whatever it was—some neurotic compulsion from his subliminal mind? some directive from Fate?—had sapped all his pleasure and interest in the career he had been making for himself. Think what you're missing, the thing whispered to him at the most inappropriate times: in meetings, when all his attention should have been concentrated on the manipulation of the gathering toward the decision he wanted it to reach. Think what you're missing! And before his eyes, gun sights swung reluctantly onto the silhouette of a German plane, tracer fire probed suddenly toward it, reached it, it turned slowly, clumsily (but slowly, clumsily, because time had slowed down), smoke poured out and it went screaming down the sky. And Kermit would come back to himself to discover that the representative of the War Department was carrying a point that he had resolved never to concede.

Now, looking at Jean smiling at him, he felt the walls of her affection about him like a trap. Uncertainty, self-distrust, could so easily make him dependent—on her, on anyone. The idiocy of telling her about it, of asking her opinion, was absurdly tempting. Jean's opinion! "I think you're nuts," she would say probably; but possibly she would say, "Kermit, how wonderful!" Kermit, how wonderful—he wanted to laugh, he was utterly disgusted. Suppose he opened his mouth and said——.

Jean spoke just in time. "Do you know if your sister's coming to the wedding?"

He had to come back about a million miles to blink at this question. "I hope so, since she's the bride. It would be a pretty one-sided wedding if she didn't."

"Honestly! I don't mean Marion. Your other sister. Nina."

You hate to say her name, don't you? thought Kermit. I wonder why? Does respectability mean that much to you? "I haven't the faintest idea," he said.

"Marion's worrying about it. She thinks Nina's mad at her."

"She might very well be. Nina suffers from the notion that she has managed her own life so magnificently that she ought to be allowed to manage everyone else's. This performance of Marion's must rile her no end."

Jean giggled.

"What's that for?"

"Well—I was just wondering if managing people wasn't a family failing."

"You mean I do too?" Kermit stretched out his legs comfortably and looked at his highball glass, amber with whiskey, as if it could show him truth and the future and the truth about the past. A profound sadness grew slowly within him, circulated with his blood. What a depressing truth, if this were truth: that all he wanted was to manage other people's lives!

He weighed it honestly, and found it unpersuasive. It wasn't true. Yes, people irritated him—as they did Nina—for being fools, for not seeing, not being able to learn the rules of living. But there was more to it than that. For him, it was not merely personal, there was a principle involved. "You're wrong," he told Jean. "I believe very, very deeply in the right of everyone to make a fool of himself. The only one I try to stop is myself. And I'm always aware that to stop myself may be the most abysmal folly of all. You think I don't believe in emotions, don't you?"

"Do I?" asked Jean.

"Sure you do. You're wrong. Maybe five years ago I'd have agreed with you. Now I know you can't stop having emotions. All you can do is find out who's in control, you or it. If it's you, fine. If it isn't, well—hell! Lean back and enjoy yourself. What I really don't like about emotions is throwing them around, because that gets to be faking. If you get used to having a lot of emotions, pretty soon you need a lot of emotions, and when you don't have them you fake."

"Do you think I fake?" asked Jean, and then could not meet his eyes. She loved him, and she worked so hard to hide it! And now he was calling it faking!

"Oh, you! You're a great big bundle of love. Sure you fake. With you it doesn't matter."

"I don't know what you mean," said Jean, nonplussed. "If you don't like faking, why do you——"

"Why do you talk so much?" asked Kermit, and got up and went over to her. "Don't you know that if you're not careful, living here in the Village, you'll turn into an intellectual?"

Jean felt suddenly happy. It was this kind of teasing that took Kermit as deep into intimacy as he ever got. "But suppose I really am an intellectual," she argued, "and it's faking not to——"

"An easy solution," said Kermit. "Join the Church. If you ever really find yourself thinking such a thing, call up the archbishopric and ask for an appointment with Monsignor Sheen. Before you know it, everything will be *all right*. And you know what else I think?"

"What?" asked Jean faintly.

"I think you're a very tired girl, and you'd better come to bed."

She got up obediently and went into the bedroom. Kermit took his suitcase and followed.

But he couldn't sleep. Making love to Jean, familiar now, was still thoroughly delightful and satisfying, and there was no reason why he did not drop off into a dreamless slumber. But he lay beside her—she was fathoms deep in sleep—and his past life slid through his head; and was, he felt, extremely dull. It was like looking at ancient, jerky movies, knowing that they had produced floods of tears in their day, or shaken theaters to the foundations with laughter, and finding all this quite unbelievable and uneasily embarrassing. What could our parents have been thinking of, to swoon over *The Birth of a Nation,* and *Broken Blossoms?* It was really better not to know. Kermit in school in knickerbockers, clapping erasers; Kermit dragging home a puppy who died of distemper;

Kermit being kissed by a girl (who was taller than he) at a high school dance—when he had not expected it; Kermit at Yale the year he blew his scholarship, getting drunk on beer and feeling absolutely certain that the world was his oyster; Kermit in London, trapped and forfeit to Mrs. Morrison; Kermit waving good-by to Lucia and Anne in the milky morning air of the Loire Valley and then not writing—*I must call Lucia up tomorrow*——

This was too much. The past wouldn't stay past, it had started to nag him about the future. Kermit got up, went into the bathroom and took a shower. Emerging, he stood for a second listening to Jean's breathing; then found pajamas and bathrobe and went into the living room.

He was still there, reading, when Marion's key turned in the lock, and he looked up to see her in the doorway with a black-haired man behind her. The wonderful guy, he thought. My future brother-in-law.

"Kermit!" cried Marion. "Oh darling, how simply wonderful of you to come up!"

"Don't make too much of it," said Kermit, receiving her embrace. "I've never given anyone away at a wedding before. I couldn't resist the opportunity."

"Where's Jean?"

"Fast asleep."

Marion said, looking like Beatrice in Paradise, "This is Tom. Tom, this is Kermit."

"Hello," said Tom. "I'm awfully glad to know you, and that you could get here."

"I'm glad, too." We sound, Kermit thought, as if we were competing to see who could make the most fatuous remark. "Can I give you a drink?"

"No, thanks. I left my brother next door—my apartment's next door——"

"Isn't that a coincidence?" said Marion, meaning, Isn't it a miracle?

"Certainly is," said Kermit, wedded now to fatuity.

"So I think I'll get back," Tom finished.

"He got a little high," Marion explained. "Not Tom, I mean.

Richie. He's *awfully* nice, though, Tom. I do like him so much. Be sure he knows that, won't you?" She went out into the hall with Tom, and Kermit could hear their murmurings as they said good night.

It made him nervous. His sister—— This stranger—— Should he not have insisted on a long talk with Tom? About his prospects? About his character? About his conception of marriage: did he want Marion to stay home and keep house for him, or was she to be allowed to find herself some occupation of an undemanding nature until the first baby arrived? Marion was marrying Mister X tomorrow—and shouldn't Kermit do something about it?

That's a real horse's arse of an idea, said Kermit to himself. How did I manage to come up with that one? Why is the natural instinctive reflex provoked by the word "brother-in-law" to act like a pompous fool? Let me rather sit here quietly, suffer the indignity of hearing those whispers outside the door, and keep my mouth closed.

Marion came back and shut the door behind her. She was in a trance of happiness. "You liked him, didn't you?" she said. A negative answer was unthinkable and she waited for none. She came and sat down beside her brother and said, "Dear Kermit. You're so good to me. I love you."

"Darling girl," said Kermit, and put his arm around her. Was ever anyone as vulnerable as Marion? "Who could not be good to you?"

"I'm so happy," said Marion.

"Yes, dear."

"It's incredible. He loves me. Just as much as I love him. And that's as much as there is."

"I'm glad."

"Like a miracle. Overnight. We hadn't seen each other since Labor Day. And oh, Kermit! I was so miserable. I can't tell you. Nothing—just nothing. Nothing made any sense. And then—and then—I dropped in here one night to see Jean and he was here and I was *terrified,* just terrified, I don't know how I got through it. Every time the clock ticked I thought I'd fall through the space between the ticks. Do you know?"

"I guess so."

"And then—— I can't tell you. Then it was all right." She relapsed into silence, leaning against his shoulder. Kermit tried to comfort himself with the thought that this bonfire of emotion was what Marion was made for. Nothing could have stopped its happening sooner or later, so why not sooner instead of later? Jean said What's-his-name was a decent fellow, and Jean would at least know that he wasn't a drunk or a sadist or a queer or a bum. If Marion was doomed to go through anguish discovering that her hero was just a normal human being, at least there would be no extra-awful twists to the anguish caused by his being an abnormal human being. Marion was born to be in love. In Kermit's view it was too bad that she had to *marry* her first love: marriage was something quite different, to be undertaken when one had developed a certain amount of judgment. But judgment and Marion were mutually contradictory concepts. She would have to do it this way. She would go out like an army with banners to lay herself down under the wheels of life, to become—as if it were to be the heroine of an epic—a wife and a mother and a housekeeper, diverting all this passion of joy to day-to-day commonplaceness. How absurd, how fantastically wasteful, how human.

Marion sighed happily. "Go to bed," said Kermit. "You need your beauty sleep."

"Yes. I want to look so pretty that being old and fat won't make any difference, he'll always remember me the way I was tomorrow." She stood up and stretched—tired, her hair disheveled, her body all a promise—and Kermit found himself suffering an amazing pain. You are here to *give her away,* he said to himself; and thought wryly of all the young girls through all millennia of history who had done this, and all the pain their male relatives had experienced in handing them over to the Messieurs X. When Nina married her fool, Kermit had been betrayed and furious, but that was personal. *This* agony was immemorial, a part of the human condition. He tried to be amused at his inability to escape it, his unexpected bondage to normality. But the amusement did not touch the pain. The irony of irony, thought Kermit, is that irony doesn't help.

"Good night," said Marion. "Oh Kermit, why don't you get married too and be terribly, terribly happy? If you had someone like Tom——"

"It's too bad I didn't see him first," said Kermit.

Marion stared at him for a minute before she perceived, through the haze of happiness around her, that this was a joke. "Someone as *wonderful,* I mean, you idiot," she said.

"But could there be another?" said Kermit, and got up and kissed her.

"I'm sure there will be," said Marion dimly. "Oh *darling* Kermit!" She hugged him and went out. And Kermit stood in profound indecision in the middle of the room and wondered whether he wished life would take hold of him and trick him and compel him as it did Marion. To cease to be the autonomous disposer of his future; to give up choice and decision. Or was this belief in choice and decision an illusion too? Was he moved too, like Marion, as a puppet on strings, doomed never to feel or find the strings because they ran through his own nerves and will? Was there pragmatically no return for the energy and effort of controlling his life because it was not he who controlled? All philosophic speculation came down in the end to the possibility of this bad joke. Kermit moved abruptly. If it was a bad joke, at least he need not waste time thinking about it. He went in and lay down next to Jean and waited for sleep.

The sun shone for Marion's wedding and Nina did not come. Stuart brought Mrs. Bishop. When Marion saw that they were alone she went quite white. "Nina," said Mrs. Bishop steadily, "was *terribly* sorry, but Johnny's temperature has flown up to 104. Nina's waiting for the doctor. It seems there are measles around. Of course now that he's at nursery school we've got to expect that he'll pick things up. She sent you her love," Mrs. Bishop added firmly.

"I'm awfully sorry," said Marion faintly.

Her mother kissed her. "What a pretty suit, darling. You look lovely."

"Mrs. Bishop," said Tom, "I'd like you to meet my brother Richie. Stuart Fanning, Richard Hofstra."

"How do you do, Richard," said Mrs. Bishop thankfully. "Well—

you Hofstras certainly look alike. Are you the one who's—let me see——"

"I'm doing graduate work at Harvard in biochemistry," said Richie.

"Goodness! You must tell me all about it," said Mrs. Bishop, and laughed. "Beginning with what it is. What an erudite family you are! Tom, your mother and father can't be here?"

"No, Mrs. Bishop, but we talked to them last night, and we're going there for a day or two when we get back from Bermuda. My father hasn't been too well."

"He and poor Johnny," said Mrs. Bishop. "I hope it's nothing serious?"

"I don't think so. They call it intestinal flu." And here for a moment the conversation died completely. They were meeting in Jean's living room and Mrs. Bishop looked around it carefully, as if she must make an effort to take in this odd stopping place in her daughter's life. How, she seemed to be saying to herself, did we all get here? With these people? Quite nice, of course, but so—unexpected! Jean's bamboo screen, Jean's printed curtains might have some message for her about what was happening to Marion.

Then Kermit came in with a tray of cocktails, Jean behind him with crackers and cheese, and at the sight of her son Mrs. Bishop's calm wavered for a moment. "Oh Kermit!" she said.

"Hello, Mum. Hi, Stuart. Where's Nina?"

"Johnny's got the measles," said Marion quickly.

"How inopportune. I hope it's not a portent of his life plan. *We* never had measles at vital moments. Have a drink, Mum. This is one of the times it's indicated."

"Oh didn't you just have measles!" said Mrs. Bishop with spirit. "You came down with the mumps just after you were confirmed, and for days I dreaded to pick up the Brooklyn *Eagle* and read that you'd given them to the bishop. You look very well, dear. Is there any sherry there?"

"There must be someplace. Jean—Jean, have you met my mother? Mother, this is——"

"This is the dear girl who's been so kind to Marion," said Mrs. Bishop. "I know all about her. It's been so sweet of you to have

Marion here this week and put up with all this fuss. I think you must be a very good Samaritan indeed."

Jean found herself helplessly caught between laughing and crying. "Not at all!" she said through the lump in her throat. Seeing Mrs. Bishop—gallant, confused and indomitably giving credit where she felt credit was due—somehow explained many things about Marion. And about Kermit? But this was not so clear, and Jean did not feel she had time to think about it now. "I'll get some sherry," she said. "It's right inside."

"Come and sit down, Mummy," said Marion. "We have half an hour before we have to go to the church."

"Do we?" Mrs. Bishop settled herself in a chair. "You know, this is really very pleasant. Now at a conventional wedding, we'd all be flying about, not seeing each other—Tom in a stew, Marion threatening hysterics, myself looking for a glove (I seem to have a terrible habit of losing one glove, usually the left one), Richard over there would have misplaced the ring and be searching high and low for it, Kermit——"

Kermit handed her a glass of sherry. "Kermit would be taking secret nips from a private bottle."

Mrs. Bishop rose even to this. "Yes, I declare you might be! And instead, here we all are, unconventional and *so* comfortable, having a cocktail together and—Jean, that looks like delicious cheese, but I don't believe I will, right now—and having a pleasant social time. I think it's the sensible way to get married. I've always thought a big wedding was like a human sacrifice. I'm sure most brides look much more like victims than like—well—brides!" And Mrs. Bishop took a deep breath and sipped her sherry and thought, There! she had done her best. If they were not now all at their ease (and she could not really feel that Stuart, for instance, was a relaxed participant of a pleasant social gathering), well, she would just ignore the uneasiness. Jean came and sat down beside her, and Mrs. Bishop, who of course would much rather have had Kermit there, put to her many questions about interior decoration.

Then it was time to go to the church. Tom and Richie went off in the first cab. Jean, Stuart and Mrs. Bishop followed a few minutes later, and Kermit and Marion came last.

In the cab Marion clutched Kermit's hand. "Do you think it would have been better if I'd had those hysterics?" she asked.

"There's nothing particularly therapeutic about a fit of hysterics," said Kermit morosely, wishing his mother hadn't put ideas into Marion's head. "You'd be feeling just as awful now if you'd had them, or even worse. The trouble with you is——"

"Why do you suppose his mother didn't come?"

"Because his father has intestinal flu."

"Do you believe that?"

"Certainly."

"As much as you believe anything," said Marion with unusual perception. At the last possible, worst possible, moment the haze of happiness had dissolved. Her hand clutched Kermit's like a talon. "What about Tom?" she asked. "Do you like him?"

Kermit gathered every ounce of himself together for this task and said, "Very much indeed."

Marion sat back on the seat and let his hand go. Kermit glanced at her out of the corner of his eye. Marion's profile was pinched, she was breathing too fast. "You don't know a thing about him," she said.

Jesus Christ! thought Kermit. What in hell do you want? *You* wanted to get married this fast, I had nothing to do with it! He did not say this but, controlling his irritation, offered her her own judgment instead. "But *you* know him."

"I don't think so," said Marion, whose opinion of her judgment was now coinciding with Kermit's opinion last night. "I don't think I know a thing. I think I must be crazy."

Kermit shut his eyes.

"*You* must think so too," said Marion. "Don't you?"

"Marion," said Kermit, "if you don't be quiet till we get to the church, I will wring your neck."

For a block she was quiet. Then she said timidly, "But Kermit, this is all the time I've got, right now. I've *got* to decide now. Won't you—couldn't you help me?"

"Decide what?" said Kermit grimly.

"Whether to marry him. Tom."

Kermit leaned forward and said to the driver, "Pull over to the curb a minute, please." The cab stopped. He turned to Marion. "Now," he said, "let's not rush. Let's just go over this together. I can tell the driver to go to Penn Station. I can take you to Washington with me. We can send a wire to the church. Stuart is there, and he can probably get Mother home more or less in one piece. Jean will do her best to cope with Tom, which won't be sufficient. What he'll do I don't know, and I suppose you think you don't know either. In Washington I can presumably get you some kind of a government job, and I'll certainly get you an introduction to a good psychiatrist. As for physical accommodations, I have room for you as long as I'm around, though that mayn't be too long. Now. Where shall I tell the driver to go?"

Marion looked at him out of an ashen face. "To the church," she said in a whisper.

"Please go on," said Kermit to the driver. Marion covered her face with her hands.

"Who in hell do you think is going to live your life?" Kermit said to her.

Marion said, "I have a right to want to be happy."

Kermit did not reply. The streets went by. It was a bright cold windy uninviting day, right out of the middle of reality, a day for irretrievable action, no nonsense about it. The cab stopped at the church. Kermit paid the driver and helped Marion out.

And she married Tom.

After it was all over and the bride had been kissed and the register signed she said, "Mummy dear, you're wrong about a nice social gathering. I *should* have had hysterics. I gave Kermit *fits* coming over—I wanted to run. Tom, I nearly never showed up."

Tom gathered her in with one arm in a semi-bearhug and laughed heartily. "Oh dear," said Mrs. Bishop, not quite able to take this entirely as a joke. Have you—— Has she—done the right thing? her eyes asked face after face.

"Well, it's too late now," said Tom, "I've got you now." Marion looked perfectly happy.

That wasn't the end of the social gathering. Bill Ford, who was Tom's boss, and his wife, Marge, were giving a wedding luncheon and everyone adjourned—or was adjourned—to the Fords' house, a redone brownstone in Turtle Bay. Here there were more cocktails, this time with caviar and pâté de foie and champagne and a massive buffet meal. Richie Hofstra began to show signs of getting high again and Marion went straight up into the air like a kite. Kermit sat in a corner with his hands in his pockets. Getting Marion to the church had exhausted both his capacity for affection and his interest in other people. Fortunately, before the party could fall apart, it came to an end because Marion and Tom had to make the afternoon sailing of the *Queen of Bermuda*. There was another mass movement to the street, another searching for cabs.

On the street Mrs. Bishop kissed Marion good-by. "I won't come to the boat, dear."

"Oh Mummy!"

"Nina and Johnny, you know. I'm anxious to get back and see how things are and do what I can to help."

"Oh Mum! Well—of course. Give—give Nina my love, and I hope everything—I hope Johnny'll be all right. Mummy—I'll write. You'll be at Nina's?"

"For a while, as long as she needs me. Marion—dear child—you know I wish you all happiness——"

"Oh Mum!" Marion trembled on the verge of tears.

"And Tom——"

"Mrs. Bishop, I'll—I mean all those corny things. I'll look after her."

"I know you will."

"Marion! Come on! Here's a cab. You've got to get your bags."

Marion kissed her mother again and ran to the cab, Tom after her. Another taxi drew up, there was a flurry. "Take it," said Mrs. Bishop, "we're in no hurry and you must get to the boat." People dived into one cab or another, and they drove off.

Mrs. Bishop stood in the street in the cold sunlight, pulling on her gloves. Stuart looked about for another taxi. One started down the street and he waved and whistled at it. It drew up and Kermit opened the door and got out. "Here you are," he said.

"Why, Kermit," said his mother, "they've all gone."

"It's all right, dear. Come and get in. Did you drive in or take the train?"

"Drove," said Stuart. "The car's downtown, though. I didn't know we were coming up here."

"Nobody knew anything," said Kermit, and Stuart, for the first time in his life, felt a momentary warmth toward his brother-in-law.

Mrs. Bishop got in the cab and sat back, suddenly too tired to hold herself straight any more. Kermit got in beside her and took her hand. She pressed his, but said nothing, and after Stuart had told the driver where to go they rode for several blocks in silence.

"How're things in Washington?" asked Stuart abruptly.

"What aspect of the subject would you like me to cover first?" said Kermit.

Stuart flushed and then laughed. "I guess that question was a little broad. Well—is Roosevelt going to run again?"

"Sure."

"Will he make it?"

"You know as much as I do."

"Who do you think the Republicans'll put up? Dewey?"

"A big shot told me Willkie."

"Oh really? Willkie." Stuart thought this over. "He's smart," he said doubtfully.

"That's dangerous for Republicans, I agree," said Kermit.

"Kermit," said his mother, "that's a *cynical* thing to say."

"No it isn't. The Republicans aren't supposed to be smart. It isn't their style. If they change their style they can go awfully wrong."

"Can't go much worse wrong than in '36," said Stuart sadly. "I don't think Willkie's such a bad idea. What'll you do if he gets in?"

"I'll get out first."

Stuart turned this over in his mind. "You know," he said, for he still felt kindly toward Kermit for the suffering they had both shared over Marion's marriage, "you're still only a kid. Did it ever occur to you to take a law degree? You could do a lot worse with your—your——"

"With my brass?"

"No, I meant——"

"It's nice of you to think that, Stu. I appreciate it."

And again there were some blocks of silence.

"Kermit," said his mother, "I don't suppose you—you would want to come to Nina's, would you? With us?"

Kermit squeezed her hand again. "I don't think I'd better, dear, if she's got a sick kid on her hands."

Mrs. Bishop was silent. How sick had Johnny really been? How much had Nina made an excuse of it? She didn't know, and she couldn't tell Kermit that it might have been—a ruse.

"I tell you what," said Kermit. "Suppose I come up at Christmas?"

"Would you really?"

"Sure thing. Ask Nina if she'll have room for me."

"Of course she'll have room! Kermit, how nice that would be."

"Will be," said Kermit, and smiled at her. "Look, Mum, I think I'll hop out here. I have a phone call I have to make."

"Oh! Oh—aren't you going to the boat?"

"There's plenty of time," said Kermit vaguely. He kissed her. "Take care of yourself. Let Nina have Johnny's measles by herself. Stuart'll get a nurse in if she needs one. Don't you get worn out."

"Of course we'll get a nurse," said Stuart, his dislike of Kermit burgeoning anew. "We'll look after Mother."

"Everyone," said Mrs. Bishop, "is much too good to me. Kermit, will you write and let me know just when you'll be up?"

"I'll phone you, sweetie, and then I'll phone you again."

But Mrs. Bishop still clutched his hand. "You think Marion—— You think this is a good thing?"

"The only thing."

"What she said—about wanting to run away—that was just a joke, wasn't it?"

"Just a joke. Good-by, dear." He kissed her and got out of the cab. "So long, Stuart. Be seeing you."

The cab drove off with Stuart indignantly realizing that Kermit had invited himself to spend a Christmas, which would also include Judge Fanning, at Stuart's home. Peace on earth! thought Stuart, good God! And with Mrs. Bishop thinking mistily, Now they are gone. All gone. When will I start to feel the pain? Or am I really aching now, instead of numb? And too tired to know it? She thought of her own wedding day, her husband's thin strong dark face as she walked toward him through the church; and a bell chimed somewhere within her to tell her that happiness was the truth. She clenched her hand to hold onto it.

Kermit went into a bar and ordered a drink. Across the back of his mind flitted the phrase, "I must call up Lucia," and he smiled pityingly at it. He wasn't going to call up Lucia. I'm sorry, Lucia, he said to the part of himself which had always recognized in Lucia a creature as extreme as himself (only she was good and he was—what? Not good, at any rate), I'm sorry Lucia, you'll have to get along without me. I tried to get you Marion instead, but it wasn't any good. And Lucia said, Kermit, how could you imagine that I don't know that? Can you manage, asked Kermit, just you and Anne against the world? Can you manage to grow up the way you are? Can you manage—the other thing that might happen? I don't know, said Lucia, but I can try. When there isn't anything else to do, you do what you can. Don't waste time wanting what you can't have, Kermit, or trying to do what you can't do. I'm what you can't do, I guess. I know it, said Kermit, but I'm sorry. He ordered another drink.

Marion said, "But where *is* Kermit? I thought he was with you."
"I don't know," Jean told her. "We thought he'd gone with you."
"Oh he'll show up," said Tom. "Steward! Steward! Let's have some ice and some glasses in here."

Nina shut the door of Johnny's room behind her and went downstairs. Well, it was measles. The spots had started to come out, and she'd better call the doctor again. Mother hadn't believed her. Well, she could believe her now.

She went into the living room and dropped on the sofa and lit a cigarette. In a minute she would call the doctor. In a minute she would get up and go tell Hulda in the kitchen and Trudi, the Austrian nursemaid, who had been with Toddy and the baby all day. Trudi mustn't go near Johnny, Nina mustn't go near the others, the trays and the dishwashing would have to be organized——

All that work, all that worry, for Nina, and they hadn't believed her. Probably not even Stuart had believed her. But Johnny had the measles, and it just served them right.

She drew deeply on her cigarette and the world revolved and suddenly came right side up again. Good God! she thought. I can't be *glad* because Johnny has the measles! Poor little mouse, poor sick little mouse, who hadn't let go her hand until he fell asleep! The misery had been so much too big for his poor hot little body, her hand had been a lightning conductor drawing it off.

Did I wish it on him? thought Nina, Vassar graduate, twentieth-century rationalist. Did I? Because I didn't want to go to the wedding and I thought, Well, if one of the children were sick I couldn't go? Did I make Johnny sick?

Oh nonsense! Don't be a fool!

But as she put out her cigarette and got up to walk out to the kitchen and break the news and organize the trays, what went with her was: Damn Marion, anyway, for doing this this way! And putting me on the spot! And making me think such things, and feel guilty! But Marion'll find out!

Find out what? What Nina knew—about marriage and children and measles and women and what happened to love and organizing trays. Not that I wish her any bad luck, thought Nina. But she needn't think it's a picnic. She needn't think she's any different from all of us, just because she's in love.

Once I was in love, and now I'm not. I'm in life. I was unkind to Marion and I know it and I'm not ashamed. Because life isn't kind and Marion had better start learning it.

But did you have to teach her? asked a little voice, deep inside. Life will teach her, won't it—if what you believe is true? You *are* ashamed, you know. You really are. And Nina, at the kitchen door, stopped, and wished suddenly, painfully, that Marion might be happy. Then she swung the door open and said, "Oh Trudi, it *is* measles, the doctor says."

"Oh, the poor little Johnny!" cried Trudi, her face crinkling up. *People* are kind, thought Nina, remember that! She started her organizing.

Kermit paid for his drinks and said, "Is there a phone around?" The barkeeper pointed.

Kermit went over and pulled out the classified directory. He looked in the wrong place first, but when he found the right heading there were several listings, most of them the hell-and-gone out in Jersey or on the Island. He checked through them and picked the nearest one. Inside the booth the buzz of the ringing sounded, sounded again and again. Of course it's Saturday, thought Kermit, but you'd think week ends would be their biggest time.

Then the receiver was picked up. "Hello?" said a voice, and then, remembering that it was supposed to be businesslike, began to reel off a name, "Seabrook Aviation Instruct——"

"Never mind that," said Kermit. "Listen, I want to learn to fly. Can I come out and begin now?"

"Why not?" said the voice of anonymity and the future.

AFTERWORD

IN 1953 *LEAVING HOME* WAS PRAISED AS AN AC-
curate novel of American middle-class life, but to readers today
Elizabeth Janeway's Bishops may seem exotic or even mythical,
the likes of them having all but disappeared from both Brooklyn and fiction. They are shabby-genteel white Anglo-Saxon
Protestants, not wealthy but comfortable even in 1933, a widowed mother and three nearly grown children living cosily with
a bachelor uncle whose business has by luck survived the Great
Depression. Among people of their sort it is expected that one
will be pleasant and amusing and polite, that both the boys and
the girls will go to college, and that afterwards the girls will
marry suitable young men and devote themselves to their families while their husbands and brothers pursue lucrative and
respectable careers. The healthy, intelligent Bishops enjoy being
clever together: the family pride is in taste and wit, with education and culture as a matter of course superadded.

Their story, which begins when Nina Bishop is twenty-one,
her brother Kermit eighteen, and their sister Marion fifteen,
tells how the Bishop family naturally dissolves as the children
make the definitive choices that initiate their separate adult
lives. Fascinating today as social history, it is more valuable as
a fiction that sets one to wondering at the mystery of that tem-
porary, arbitrary, tightly and vitally connected set of characters,
rituals, and habits most of us set out from, the family. Whims-
ical Marion, wondering too, compares families to fungi:

> "No preparation. No roots. Just two people—and they get mar-
> ried, and all of a sudden, out of nowhere, there's a family—

317

family jokes and celebrations and traditions—whether the children help trim the tree on Christmas Eve or are surprised on Christmas morning; where they go summers; what they eat for birthday dinners; are they brought up on Peter Rabbit and Jemima Puddleduck and Just So Stories, or on Uncle Don reading the Sunday comics over the radio, or what? A whole private mythology somehow gets invented. I can never imagine how anyone has the energy and the patience to do all that—and everything else—and yet everyone does it. Or lots of people do it. . . . To make a whole family—I just don't know how you do it!" (250–51).

A sense of the awesome density and fragility of family life permeates this novel.

The house that Nina and Kermit and Marion Bishop put behind them—Nina by rerooting herself in the suburbs, Kermit by fleeing roots and houses, Marion by marrying an admirer of Frank Lloyd Wright—is more telling about their kind of family than facts about income and ethnicity and education and habits. A big old Victorian "monstrosity" with gables and ornamental ironwork and gingerbread, sitting on a cultivated half-acre hedged round with privet, the house represents the old-fashioned spaciousness and comfort of domestic life for people like the Bishops, its historical continuity, and the insulation, the protected shelter of their class. The sweet pale resignation of the mother and the remote shadowy correctness of the uncle sharpen the focus on the children's relationships with one another, and on the house itself as the heart of the family: Janeway's wise insight is that childhood habits of shelter, rather than a specific parental tie, are hardest to leave. *Leaving Home* tells about how Nina and Marion Bishop come to marry entirely appropriate young men whom they love, and about the equally successful coming to adulthood of their brother Kermit. The stories are briskly and wittily told. Yet the novel is suffused with a tender, rueful melancholy, a wondering resignation to the inevitability of ties breaking and strong feelings fading. Elizabeth Janeway is a celebrated writer of nonfiction that details ways we might set about to make things better; the theme of her fourth novel is normal and inevitable loss.

The nostalgic mood derives partly from the sense that life as it was when Nina and Marion and Kermit were young is past and gone: this novel about young people of the thirties and forties was written in the early fifties by a woman approaching middle age. The pre-World War II period, usually documented in American fiction as hard times, is portrayed here as above all a simpler and gentler and more innocent era. Doors are commonly left unlocked in Brooklyn. There was one communist, silly girl, in Nina's class at Vassar. War is only beginning to brew in distant Europe, and at home the truth is not yet in about Huey Long. Although there is talk of frozen food, most peas are still shelled by hand, and blouses need ironing, and some families can depend on a servant to do the work.

Even in their time, the Bishops of Bay Ridge are "an anachronism," as the first paragraph acknowledges. Nina, for one, is aware of that. Her story begins as she walks home from the subway, irritated by the long, hot ride after a day's work as a secretary-editorial assistant at a magazine, reflecting that she's lucky to be safe in a familiar, well-hedged bit of a world she knows (she's been to Vassar, after all) has been "flattened under a storm." But this does not lessen her irritation, or her spoiled child's demand that life provide her with more excitement. Self-centered, arrogant Nina, who struck at least one reviewer as an unusually unattractive young woman, is a heroine on the order of Emma Woodhouse, about whom Jane Austen wrote that "no one but myself will much like" her. In this case even her creator had second thoughts; Janeway at one time planned to write a sequel in which Nina would be "nicer." Whether one likes her or not, Nina is quite clearly correct in thinking that her way of life is genuinely threatened, and, as clearly, she is feeling imperiled mostly because she is twenty-one and a virgin. Vassar to the contrary, her consciousness is limited to her personal (she would not call them sexual) expectations. Brimming with emotions she cannot define, she feels poised on the brink of radical change, fearful but ready for something more exciting than the eminently suitable Stuart Fanning to change her life. Or someone. That sex with Stuart in fact does the trick makes us laugh at Nina, but her intelligence keeps us on her side. In 1953, some readers were shocked by Nina's antics, and even more distressed by her more radically experimental sister Marion's; Janeway was recalling a freer time. For Nina, consummation makes marriage seem natural and logical. Janeway's unsurprised view of the easy slide from youthful sexual self-expression and self-absorption to narrow-minded bourgeois respectability is still instructive.

The fumblings and tiny power shifts by which Nina and Stuart manage to get one another into bed are described with a care for detail and the kind of regard for what makes lives meaningful that distinguishes fine fiction from records of manners. The young people are both absurd and moving. Their progression toward lovemaking, engagement, then marriage is finely plotted, emotional and social life convincingly woven together. Janeway knows how boys and girls talk so as to manage to let their meanings leak through all the wrong words, how a well-timed suggestion to buy sandwiches can alter a life, how secondary characters fade in and out of a young woman's world depending on whether she imagines herself as loved for life or lonely. *Leaving Home* coolly anatomizes its self-involved and often silly characters: Janeway keeps us at a little distance from Nina and her brother and sister, with the irony of a benign, indulgent aunt and reminders that we are looking back at the time when these people were young: "All his life [Kermit] was to admire anyone who did a job well" (134); "[Marion] was on her knees by her bag, holding two slips and a nightgown, and she always remembered how hard the floor felt on her knees as the news [that the Luftwaffe was bombing Warsaw] babbled out of the loud-speaker" (230). At the same time, Janeway's loving attention to habits and moments of the sort that only retrospect makes meaningful gives *Leaving Home* the feel of autobiography: the novel is a poignant evocation of a lost time and place, in the pastoral rather than the Proustian mode. George Sand's country novels, George Eliot's *Adam Bede,* are the monuments in this tradition of fiction. No more a woman's tradition than a strictly Georgian one, it nevertheless has the "strong local flavor" characteristic of women's fiction, to use the phrase of T.S. Eliot's that Janeway herself borrowed in her important essay on women's writing, "Women's Literature" (*Harvard Guide to Contemporary American Writing,* 1979). It charts with special interest women's destinies.

The ironies with which *Leaving Home* interrogates the marriage plot add piquancy to the flavor. Verbal irony—irony of tone—is the most important; in addition there are structural, thematic, and narrative ironies. By placing the story of Kermit Bishop between his sisters' stories, to begin with, Janeway contrasts men's expectations and destinies with women's. For Kermit, the subway, and sex, and money, and marriage, are very different from what they are to Nina and Marion. His sexual hijinks and petty crimes are seen in his set as the sort of thing boys do; from the vantage point of 1987, his creator seems rather more tolerant of him than one might like. Channeling youthful rage and brutality into a successful business and political career, Kermit remains emotionally stunted and shallow but clearly capable of continuing to get away with everything. In contrast to his sisters' stories, Kermit's ends with a promise of adventure and escape—from all his womenfolk, including the generous Jean who loves him. It does not occur to him to worry as Marion and Nina do about the relationship of his identity to his past, or to an ideal of manhood: his inner life is minimal, and his story the conventional one of a young man destined to make his mark on the world. In contrast, the youthful adventurousness, impatience, lust, and curiosity of his sisters are clouded by self-consciousness, and constrained by fear of time passing and the haunting question of whether they will or will not fit the sole conceivable pattern of women's lives and good women's characters.

Like any heroine of fiction, Nina is eager to escape the ordinary, but she is too comfortably situated, and too scared of the unfamiliar, to try; flakey Marion, impelled to "make messes," worries that she's a freak and finally falls in love with a man who attracts her as someone she might have gone to high school with. The alternatives to marriage terrify the sisters: bohemian disorder and insecurity, glimpsed in Jean's life, seem to them nearly as bad as having no life at all, like Aunts Flora and Dora. Marion makes an obviously foolish choice when she insists on dropping out of college to marry her man fast, but Nina's lurid view of the alternative to Stuart is by no means stupid:

> What is the other choice, if I don't marry him? But this was really frightening. Everything grew fluid and wavered. Years of listening to [her boss] Mr. Daniels. Of riding the subway.

Of going to parties as if she were going on a border foray, always an eye open for the right young man, the bright young man, the man who would laugh at her jokes and know what she was talking about, the wary, neurotic young man who would take her to bed but not to church and leave her to clench her fists and cry at torch songs. One of the denizens of the desert, the natural fauna of Kermit's jungle—except that he would be stupider and less successful than Kermit because he would not realize it was a jungle. He would expect laws and would be puzzled when there were none. He would want terribly to be understood and approved of, he would expect to be comforted by Nina. Send the tigers away, he would ask her. Then, when she could not, he would hate her and hurt her, calling her ungrateful, striking out at her for being woman, more than man, less than mother— (57).

Implicit in the insights of this passage are the sources of the feminist movement Elizabeth Janeway would become a spokeswoman for. The "jungle" of European travel and work and politics and sex and eventually war is a place Kermit can exploit, but it represents, and presents, only danger to his sisters; and Uncle Van's money, which goes to him and not to them, helps him to be successful in it. The unfairness of such a state of things is not remarked on in this novel, but the lines of force and causality are so clearly drawn that no comment is necessary.

By telling the story of Kermit's coming to manhood alongside his sisters' stories, Janeway emphasizes the point that the traditional "romantic" plot that hangs on a young woman's marrying is really a story about growing up. Nina Bishop, when we meet her, doesn't quite know what to do with herself because she's through with college and can imagine no other story for her life than the standard one of love and marriage. She's gratified by how good she is at her editorial job, but rightly believes she has been born and educated for better things than dazzling Mr. Daniels, who expects her to wait on him. Her own boredom strengthens the current on which she drifts toward marriage. In 1987, the feminist message is clear: when capable intelligent young women like Nina or the interior decorator Jean do trivial, trivializing work, men inevitably become the focus of their lives: their restless energies can fuel nothing but the plot of romantic fiction.

Showing that nice young women don't quite manage to leave home, that the only respectable way to leave, for them, is to make another home and family, Janeway suggests that marriage is less than the transformation conventional romantic fiction says it is: here, getting married is sensibly portrayed as an inevitable continuation of domestic life, a reasonable result of sexual desire, and the alternative to tedium and confusion. The myth of the transformative power of marriage is undercut by the fact that neither Nina's marriage nor Marion's is climactic; that sexual consummation precedes marriage in both Nina's case and Marion's is another undoing irony. What is most affecting in the love stories of both sisters is the solitary questioning that they deliver themselves from by getting married. The most memorable pages of this novel are the ones portraying young women—Jean as well as the two sisters—in the mental and emotional act of wondering who they might be on their own.

Janeway has often said her fiction aims to explore the social context of change that has produced the women's movement; her novel of bourgeois Brooklyn life constitutes such an exploration. The Scarsdale where we leave Nina Fanning is the suburban cage of *The Feminine Mystique* (Betty Friedan's book came out ten years after *Leaving Home*). Although Nina does not chafe at the bonds of her married life, the novel, which ends as she comforts herself ruefully for having missed her sister's wedding ("Once I was in love and now I'm not. I'm in life."), is clearly critical of her complacency. We are led to look with some amusement at the happy ending of her story, which strands her, smug and fruitful, in a Scarsdale that appalls her more adventurous brother and sister. Her dull and limited lot as a wife and mother seems fit punishment for the stuffiness it breeds in her; alongside Kermit and Marion, we watch her become "placid and resolute," as she once feared Stuart was, and we are pleased to shift our allegiance as Janeway changes protagonists.

From her first novel, *The Walsh Girls*, Elizabeth Janeway demonstrated a gift for portraying the complex, contradictory feelings siblings have for one another. Here it serves her well, providing form as well as content for a novel: watching the Bishops grow up one by one, we can assess them in turn, and in terms of the ways they reflect and relate to one another. Kermit is lucid as only a brother can be about the fatuousness that afflicts his sister when she discovers her sexual passion for Stuart; but Kermit is also self-deluding in his own way, and fatuous too. He aspires to save first Nina, then Marion—and in between, another, younger pair of sisters, Lucia and Anne, whose parents' disorderly home he uses to his own advantage— from the dangerous real world he thrives in by manipulating the people there. Janeway observes him with considerable sang-froid. That Kermit has a pathological involvement with his older sister, and therefore hates Stuart Fanning and feels betrayed by her marrying him, is given neither prurient nor clinical emphasis; that both Kermit and Marion live their lives in reaction to their older sister's is calmly observed; that sisters and brother love and choose to lose one another is what *Leaving Home* is about. To be adults they must grow apart, find substitutes for one another. As some psychologists have begun to notice, birth order is of enormous importance in development; and it only takes growing up in a family to know that brothers and sisters influence character as surely as mothers and fathers do. In *Leaving Home,* these home truths are evident. About in-laws, too, Janeway is shrewd: Nina and Janey, Mrs. Bishop and the Judge, as well as Kermit and Stuart. The feel of family dinners and sailing parties is convincingly familiar, even if one has not been precisely there.

II

Elizabeth Hall Janeway, born October 7, 1913, grew up in Brooklyn. She was just about Nina Bishop's age in 1933. Her father, a naval architect, unlike Nina's Uncle Van was less than comfortable in the depression years, when a wealthy client schemed to sustain him by demanding plan after plan for ever grander yachts that remained unbuilt; his younger daughter, who attended Swarthmore College in 1930–31, was obliged to drop out of college and work for a year before graduating from Barnard College in 1935. (Barnard's Janeway Prize in writing, given yearly to a student with literary talent, is only one indication of her enthusiastic fidelity as an alumna.) She married the economist and author Eliot Janeway in 1938, and they had two sons. At college she studied history, which along with anthropology continues to be her interest; this literary woman's grounding in the social sciences gives the lie to talk of two cultures, or perhaps proves that feminism connects them. Keen interest in how place and time and social conventions help construct character and fate is apparent in all her work. Her first novel, *The Walsh Girls* (1943), is about New England sisters whose politics emphasize the contrast in their personal lives; *Daisy Kenyon* (1945), which was made into a film in 1947, is about a single woman working and living on her own in New York who is obliged to choose, as war threatens, between the married politician who has been her lover and marriage to a troubled young man. In *The Question of Gregory* (1949) Janeway centered the story on a male protagonist, an official in the Roosevelt government whose marriage and life are wrecked in the emotional aftermath of his son's death in the war. All three of the novels written in the forties are haunted by the war; all but the first are strongly marked by the knowledge of Washington power politics Janeway acquired at the side of her husband, whose journalistic career took them often to Washington during the war years. In *The Third Choice* (1959) and *Accident* (1964), Janeway continued to develop the technique of shifting point of view that characterizes *Leaving Home*. Family ties, the parallel destinies of women, the opposing attractions of freedom and responsibility, and the struggle against the deadly forces of convention and time, are dominant themes of the later novels. Throughout her career Janeway's interest has been in the psychological play between assessing the shape of one's life and responding to the living moment. That every individual is to some extent engaged in such a private colloquy, while meanwhile uncontrollable events and other individuals alter destinies, is the phenomenon all her novels explore.

The Pineapple Street of Elizabeth Janeway's childhood was not exactly in the neighborhood of *Leaving Home,* but the kind of genteel, educated Brooklyn family she writes about here resembled her own. The girls' schools Kermit rails at for keeping his sister Marion ignorant of men and sex were in her experience, but on the other hand so were summers on a farm in

Vermont, and two fondly remembered aunts she has written of, one who studied art with Degas and another who went off to nurse the wounded, in World War I, in France. Brooklyn provinciality and genteel ladylikeness did not define the limits of her childhood horizon; how could they, when she had not only the independent aunts to look to but the kind of mind that recalls school in Bay Ridge as a place overlooking the dock where great ships lay in quarantine, near a house where a woman kept monkeys? On the other hand, as she insists, at the time when she was contemplating adulthood the standard opportunities for women were not what they are now.

She started writing, says Janeway, because it was something she could do (she has written that her father's family had a natural facility with words), and because it is a pleasure to do something you can do well; and she wrote—advertising copy— for money, too. She scoffs at the very idea of harboring a muscular ambition to better the writers who came before her; her work makes it clear that neither was she competing to record the most recondite or refined or archly registered perceptions. Character first of all, and the effects of social mores and groups and events on people's lives, have been her main interest as a novelist and, later, as a writer of social commentary. Clarity, humor, and a reliable and broadly ranging intelligence mark the whole range of her work: the fiction, the nonfiction, and the children's books. She has the confident voice of an old-fashioned storyteller urgent to get on with things but curious, too, about everything that turns up on the way. Her view of human nature as complex is hampered neither by preciousness nor self-indulgence; about what happens to people's lives she is neither sentimental nor sensational.

III

Reflecting on women's writing in her 1982 collection of essays, *Cross Sections: From a Decade of Change,* Elizabeth Janeway wrote that, traditionally, "Large-scale social matters had to be translated into their secondary effects in personal relationships if they were to be discussed by women writers; I should know, that's what I did myself—though at least the social and political context was always present and influential." While the force of social conventions and the life-governing assumptions about men's and women's different expectations are clear and palpable in *Leaving Home,* the Great Depression and World War II (and irregular family lives in bohemian circles) are peripheral to the stories of Nina and Kermit and Marion. Reviewing the novel when it appeared, James Michener praised Janeway for "wisely" and "meticulously" avoiding "these ready-made high lights of her era." As he recognized, she made a deliberate choice to do so, the better to convey the atmosphere of the innocent pleasant place most of us Americans still believe we started out from.

Nevertheless, *Leaving Home* firmly places the story it tells (about time) in time, as it follows the young Bishops in their ventures forth from Brooklyn. Jean's Greenwich Village apartment and her free-living friends in the country, Kermit's dubious business ventures with sex and alcohol at Columbia, his girlfriend Tony's hundred-dollar abortion, his different kinds of idle rich friends, define a period. Nina's relationship with Mr. Daniels at the magazine, as she works successfully to impress him with a sense of her overwhelming superiority to him and his job, will remind many a bright young woman of office life, but also recalls a time when men, women, and magazines were different. Janeway's wit and irony and her sophisticated, matter-of-fact attitude toward family psychodynamics that are usually not mentioned, in nice families, and toward extramarital sex, remind one of the smart New York novels of the thirties and forties, and the films of those decades. The mixture of indulgence and skepticism with which she regards her bright young people suggests she read F. Scott Fitzgerald's and Tess Slesinger's stories with admiration. Like Mary McCarthy's *The Group,* another novel about girls just out of college in the thirties that was written in the fifties, *Leaving Home* remembers when it seemed smart to be smart-alecky. The tone, frequently, is dashing:

> "Can you swim well?"
> "Not violently."
> "Well, I'll meet you at the float later, then. I want to swim

327

hard for a while." She went through a wave and straight out toward Spain in a murderous crawl that could probably have taken her halfway there. Kermit followed thoughtfully in her wake wondering whether he should take her on or not (187).

But like Brooklyn itself, this novel is not quite of the city. Janeway is sympathetic to large, free-loving, generous Jean (of the "murderous crawl"), but her view of unconventional domestic life in bulk, among Jean's acquaintances, is dim; acidulously, she describes the "bohemian squalor" where "quite small babies were left with neighbors when their mothers wanted to go to town for the day, were given their bottles by anyone handy and deposited on the life-giving earth to eat cookies and dirt" (235). Naive young Marion Bishop's point of view, here, is the one the narrator seems most attuned to: she "zigzagged between feeling like an anthropologist in deepest Melanesia and like a provincial idiot." The story of Marion, the former cheerleader and camp counselor who gets involved with a fast crowd because of a combination of curiosity, ineptitude, desire, and an embarrassed sense of her own inadequacy, is the familiar one of a young woman from the provinces.

Janeway's Bishops, their wonderfully fluttering, charming mother, and the people they get involved with, are nothing like the families of the ethnic and regional fiction of the fifties, and the quality of the novelist's attention to family life is considerably less sentimental than, say, William Saroyan's. On the other hand, this novelist is less clinical, satirical, and judgmental than John O'Hara or John Cheever. In a period when American fiction by men was marked by a characteristic she was to deplore in an essay in *Cross Sections*, hostility toward the family, Janeway wrote with wit and clear-eyed tolerance about the Bishops of Brooklyn, who were not all equally bright or equally honorable, and who did not always love one another.

A post-war novel written when war novels were the rage, *Leaving Home* is emphatically domestic. It is not a big novel on a big subject, nor is it on the other hand arty and precious, academic or symbolic, a work that turns away, in post-war distaste, from social reality. Jean's prophecy of the horror of the war about to come reflects the fear of doom that haunted Americans of the cold war period when the novel was written; the storms raging outside the shelter of lives like the Bishops' provide an ironic foil to their private pathos and pleasures. Catastrophe and war quite legitimately frame this novel; like time, which memory and novel-writing help defeat, they threaten to make personal life meaningless, as Janeway shows it is not. Meanwhile she suggests that identical domestic destinies prescribed for women tend to flatten the differences among them, and the liveliness of their minds. *Leaving Home* is a serious as well as a lively and absorbing work of fiction. The values it articulates are domestic love and loyal personal attachment on the one hand, and informed, spirited independence of thought on the other: the problem it explores is how to have both at once. It is a theme that has been important in the work of distinguished generations of women writers, and it is still on our minds.

Rachel M. Brownstein
Brooklyn College and The Graduate Center,
The City University of New York

The Feminist Press at The City University of New York offers alternatives in education and in literature. Founded in 1970, this nonprofit, tax-exempt educational and publishing organization works to eliminate sexual stereotypes in books and schools and to provide literature with a broad vision of human potential. The publishing program includes reprints of important works by women, feminist biographies of women, and nonsexist children's books. Curricular materials, bibliographies, directories, and a quarterly journal provide information and support for students and teachers of women's studies. In-service projects help to transform teaching methods and curricula. Through publications and projects, The Feminist Press contributes to the rediscovery of the history of women and the emergence of a more humane society.

NEW AND FORTHCOMING BOOKS

Carrie Chapman Catt: A Public Life, by Jacqueline Van Voris. $24.95 cloth.
Competition: A Feminist Taboo?, edited by Helen E. Longino and Valerie Miner. Foreword by Nell Irvin Painter. $29.95 cloth, $12.95 paper.
Daughter of Earth, a novel by Agnes Smedley. Foreword by Alice Walker. Afterword by Nancy Hoffman. $8.95 paper.
Doctor Zay, a novel by Elizabeth Stuart Phelps. Afterword by Michael Sartisky. $8.95 paper.
Get Smart: A Woman's Guide to Equality on Campus, by S. Montana Katz and Veronica Vieland. $29.95 cloth, $9.95 paper.
A Guide to Research on Women: Library and Information Sources in the Greater New York Area, compiled by the Women's Resources Group of the Greater New York Metropolitan Area Chapter of the Association of College and Research Libraries and the Center for the Study of Women and Society of the Graduate School and University Center of The City University of New York. $12.95 paper.
Harem Years: The Memoirs of an Egyptian Feminist, 1879–1924, by Huda Shaarawi. Translated and edited by Margot Badran. $29.95 cloth, $9.95 paper.
Lone Voyagers: Academic Women in Coeducational Universities, 1869–1937, edited by Geraldine J. Clifford. $29.95 cloth, $12.95 paper.
My Mother Marries, a novel by Moa Martinson. Translated and introduced by Margaret S. Lacy. $8.95 paper.
"Not So Quiet . . .": Stepdaughters of War, a novel by Helen Zenna Smith. Afterword by Jane Marcus. $8.95 paper.
Sultana's Dream and Selections from The Secluded Ones, by Rokeya Sakhawat Hossein. Edited by Roushan Jahan and Hanna Papanek. Translated by Roushan Jahan. $4.95 paper.
Turning the World Upside Down: The Anti-Slavery Convention of American Women Held in New York City, May 9–12, 1837. Introduction by Dorothy Sterling. $2.95 paper.
With Wings: An Anthology of Literature by and about Women with Disabilities, edited by Marsha Saxton and Florence Howe. $29.95 cloth, $12.95 paper.
Women Activists, by Anne Witte Garland. Introduction by Frances T. Farenthold. Foreword by Ralph Nader. $29.95 cloth, $9.95 paper.

Writing Red: An Anthology of American Women Writers, 1930–1940, edited by
Charlotte L. Nekola and Paula Rabinowitz. Foreword by Toni Morrison.
$29.95 cloth, $12.95 paper.

FICTION CLASSICS

Between Mothers and Daughters: Stories across a Generation, edited by Susan
Koppelman. $9.95 paper.

Brown Girl, Brownstones, a novel by Paule Marshall. Afterword by Mary
Helen Washington. $8.95 paper.

Call Home the Heart, a novel of the thirties, by Fielding Burke. Introduction
by Alice Kessler-Harris and Paul Lauter and afterwords by Sylvia J. Cook
and Anna W. Shannon. $9.95 paper.

Cassandra, by Florence Nightingale. Introduction by Myra Stark. Epilogue by
Cynthia MacDonald. $4.50 paper.

The Changelings, a novel by Jo Sinclair. Afterwords by Nellie McKay, and
Johnnetta B. Cole and Elizabeth H. Oakes; biographical note by Elisabeth
Sandberg. $8.95 paper.

The Convert, a novel by Elizabeth Robins. Introduction by Jane Marcus.
$8.95 paper.

Daddy Was a Number Runner, a novel by Louise Meriwether. Foreword by
James Baldwin and afterword by Nellie McKay. $8.95 paper.

Daughter of the Hills: A Woman's Part in the Coal Miners' Struggle, a novel of
the thirties, by Myra Page. Introduction by Alice Kessler-Harris and Paul
Lauter and afterword by Deborah S. Rosenfelt. $8.95 paper.

An Estate of Memory, a novel by Ilona Karmel. Afterword by Ruth K. Angress.
$11.95 paper.

Guardian Angel and Other Stories, by Margery Latimer. Afterwords by Nancy
Loughridge, Meridel Le Sueur, and Louis Kampf. $8.95 paper.

*I Love Myself when I Am Laughing . . . And Then Again when I Am Looking Mean
and Impressive: A Zora Neale Hurston Reader*, edited by Alice Walker.
Introduction by Mary Helen Washington. $9.95 paper.

Life in the Iron Mills and Other Stories, by Rebecca Harding Davis.
Biographical interpretation by Tillie Olsen. $7.95 paper.

The Living Is Easy, a novel by Dorothy West. Afterword by Adelaide M.
Cromwell. $9.95 paper.

The Other Woman: Stories of Two Women and a Man, edited by Susan
Koppelman. $9.95 paper.

The Parish and the Hill, a novel by Mary Doyle Curran. Afterword by Anne
Halley. $8.95 paper.

Reena and Other Stories, selected short stories by Paule Marshall. $8.95 paper.

Ripening: Selected Work, 1927–1980, 2nd edition, by Meridel Le Sueur. Edited
with an introduction by Elaine Hedges. $9.95 paper.

Rope of Gold, a novel of the thirties, by Josephine Herbst. Introduction by
Alice Kessler-Harris and Paul Lauter and afterword by Elinor Langer.
$9.95 paper.

The Silent Partner, a novel by Elizabeth Stuart Phelps. Afterword by Mari Jo
Buhle and Florence Howe. $8.95 paper.

Swastika Night, a novel by Katharine Burdekin. Introduction by Daphne Patai. $8.95 paper.

This Child's Gonna Live, a novel by Sarah E. Wright. Appreciation by John Oliver Killens. $9.95 paper.

The Unpossessed, a novel of the thirties, by Tess Slesinger. Introduction by Alice Kessler-Harris and Paul Lauter and afterword by Janet Sharistanian. $9.95 paper.

Weeds, a novel by Edith Summers Kelley. Afterword by Charlotte Goodman. $8.95 paper.

The Wide, Wide World, a novel by Susan Warner. Afterword by Jane Tompkins. $29.95 cloth, $11.95 paper.

A Woman of Genius, a novel by Mary Austin. Afterword by Nancy Porter. $9.95 paper.

Women and Appletrees, a novel by Moa Martinson. Translated from the Swedish and with an afterword by Margaret S. Lacy. $8.95 paper.

Women Working: An Anthology of Stories and Poems, edited and with an introduction by Nancy Hoffman and Florence Howe. $9.95 paper.

The Yellow Wallpaper, by Charlotte Perkins Gilman. Afterword by Elaine Hedges. $4.50 paper.

For a free catalog, write to The Feminist Press at The City University of New York, 311 East 94 Street, New York, NY 10128.

West Lafayette Public Librar
West Lafayette Indiana